PRIMAL

LEE HARDEN SERIES

BOOK 3

D. J. MOLLES

To Jon and Dave Carricker

ONE

NADIE Y NINGUNO

THEY'RE CALLED NADIE Y NINGUNO, and wherever they go, death follows.

Approximated as "No One and Nobody," if you *habla ingles*.

It is unknown whether the names were given to them, or if, somewhere along the line, they introduced themselves. No one can say for sure, because once you're introduced, your life expectancy falls suddenly and dramatically short.

There are some people who claim that they've survived an encounter with Mr. No One and Mr. Nobody, but they're all goddamn liars. There's not a soul in Texas that's met them and lived.

At least not if you're *Nuevas Fronteras*.

Cartel boys have always been a spooky lot. There's a whole pantheon of saints and demons and pagan deities that get prayed to for everything from a good cocaine yield to helping them get away with murder.

Nuevas Fronteras might not have been in the drug business anymore, but that didn't make them any less hardwired for superstition.

To Hermanco, the lieutenant in charge of the little cartel outpost of La Casa, *Nadie y Ninguno* might be men. Or they might be some Santeria hoodoo that the Texas desert shat out, for the sole purpose of eviscerating everyone under his command.

Hermanco doesn't want to believe that they are demons, because then he won't be able to kill them if they show up at his door.

A hundred miles east of La Casa, at the Triple Rocker Ranch, Joaquin Lozcano Leyva lays naked in the sweltering bedroom of the main ranch house because he has not slept well for the last several nights.

He keeps picturing those bodies, hanging from the mesquite, with their bottom halves all chewed to shreds from *los locos*. He stares at the ceiling and thinks to himself that *Nadie y Ninguno* can't be anything but men, because Joaquin doesn't believe in that other shit.

Joaquin once forced a police captain to watch as he killed his newborn daughter by cooking her in a hot frying pan.

It might be the worst thing he's ever done.

But for all the terrible things he's done, for some reason, stumbling upon a grove of mesquite trees where your men's rotting corpses have been hung from the branches like ornaments…for some reason that makes him feel an almost demonic presence in these killings.

So, Joaquin is almost sure that *Nadie y Ninguno* are just men.

They cannot actually be devils themselves.

But is it such a stretch to think that maybe they are *possessed* by the devil?

And all the way down by the coast of Texas, with the Gulf of Mexico behind him, and all of North

America laid out in front of him, Mateo "El Cactus" Ibarra stands atop one of his oil refineries and stares into the sweltering midday distance, as though he can peel back the temporal reality around him and see the souls of the two men who've caused so many problems for him.

He is sure that they would stand out, like two glowing hot coals on a dark night.

Unlike the men in his command, Mateo Ibarra is more selective in his religion. His beliefs can be summed up by saying, *whatever controls the universe—let's call it God—loves me more than any other being he's created, and favors me above all others.*

This is a difficult conviction to maintain when God has let something like *Nadie y Ninguno* run amok through what should be your birthright.

But Mateo knows they are just men.

He even thinks he knows which men they are.

After all, they appeared out of nowhere about five weeks ago. Right around the time that a few high-profile bodies couldn't be located and confirmed dead in the wreckage of the battle at the Comanche Creek Nuclear Power Plant.

And, of course, thinking about that battle makes Mateo think about Mr. Daniels.

That double-crossing gringo piece of shit.

And when Mateo begins to think about Mr. Daniels, he begins to think that, really, this whole *Nadie y Ninguno* business, with the firebombed fuel convoys and the rising body counts, and the transformation of his legions of hardened killers into superstitious children, afraid that *El Cuco* will come and snatch them from their beds…

Well, Mateo begins to think that, really, this is all Mr. Daniels's fault.

And when you think about it that way, it's tempting to go down and get that satphone and dial up that Mr. Daniels, and tell him to get his ass down here to Texas and solve the problem that he created.

Except for the fact that Mateo has told Mr. Daniels to fuck off, more or less.

Mateo told Mr. Daniels that Greeley, Colorado needed to get their act together before Mateo would ever consider doing business with them again.

Mateo told Mr. Daniels that *Nuevas Fronteras* didn't have problems, because they kept their house clean.

Well.

Now their house is looking a little dirty.

But Mateo Ibarra will be damned to the fires of hell—though he doesn't believe in them—if he asks Mr. Daniels for help. He'll solve this problem on his own, just like he promised he would.

He'll just need to be…more proactive.

Which leads us to the moment when Sean Bull and Pablo Castillo arrive at the rambling collection of buildings in the middle of nowhere, known as Elbert, Texas, because one of the crazy hillbilly cannibals that lives there claims he's managed to capture Mr. Nobody.

***

Sean noted that he didn't smell cooking meat.

Last time he'd been to Elbert, that scent had hung in the air, like standing outside of a barbecue shack.

Sean remembered that because of what he'd learned about that cooking meat.

His nose wrinkled with the memory. "They eat the infected, you know."

Beside him, Pablo made a soft chuffing noise and leaned back against the front driver's side fender of the pickup truck they'd driven out here from La Casa.

They were positioned on the shoulder of the road. The driver's side of the pickup truck was broadside to the little encampment of buildings that was Elbert. Beyond the coven of huddled buildings, there stretched an expanse of broad Texan nothingness, populated only by puffs of scrubby brush and whatever lurked in their shadows.

Sean realized that Pablo was watching him.

He shot his gaze over at his Mexican boss. Sean's eyes ricocheted off and zoomed back towards the quonset hut, about fifty yards from them. But not before he perceived a clear flavor of disdain in Pablo's expression.

Sean's lips flattened out.

He was a gringo.

In *Nuevas Fronteras*, that made him a bottom feeder.

He was there as Pablo's driver, and as muscle, should any shooting start. And they didn't say this, but it was implied, that if you showed back up and your cartel handler was dead…well…you were going to wish that you'd died trying to keep him alive.

Pablo sniffed and faced forward again. "You've never eaten the infected before?"

The way he said it, the implication was plain: *He* had.

Sean swallowed. Said nothing.

"Tastes like pork," Pablo quipped.

The side door of the quonset hut opened and issued a single figure. The figure slammed the door behind him, and began marching towards Sean and Pablo.

Sean watched him, and his fingers snugged into the grip of the short-barreled AR that was strapped to his chest. Beside him, Pablo's hand dropped to his side, where he wore a nickel-plated six-shooter, straight out of some spaghetti Western movie.

They were both on edge.

In this, the two very different men were united: They were aware that the denizens of Elbert were, to quote everyone who had come into contact with them, "squirelly as fuck."

The man coming towards them was long and lean.

Maybe too lean, Sean thought. You'd expect someone with meat in their diet (albeit meat from the infected) would not look so starved. But maybe they hadn't gotten much meat lately. Maybe that was why it didn't smell like a barbecue shack anymore.

Maybe that was why they were so desperate for the reward that went along with capturing Mr. No One or Mr. Nobody.

Of course, that begged the question: Were they desperate enough to try to lie to the cartel about it? Were they desperate enough to grab some random guy and try to pass him off as *Nadie y Ninguno*?

The man had a way of walking that Sean wasn't a fan of.

It was…too confident.

The arms swung wide. The steps were long and rangy. His head and shoulders moved back and forth. Almost like he was strutting. He had the body language of someone who was in the grip of a manic episode.

He stopped a few paces from Sean and Pablo and planted his hands on his hips.

Sean took a moment to look him up and down, checking for weapons, but also taking in the state of the man's general shabbiness. The pants were so dirty it was a miracle the man could bend his legs inside of them. He wore a cutoff t-shirt that might once have been white—it was difficult to tell whether the khaki color was all dried sweat and dirt, or whether it came from a factory that way.

His arms and chest were corded with enough muscle to imply that they had a scary, raw power to them, but were so skinny and fatless that it further implied that food had been hard to come by lately.

He had a scraggly beard, and shaggy, light brown hair.

But what got to Sean the most were the eyes.

The man had spider's eyes.

They didn't have an expression in them.

They just watched. And waited.

They were filled with quiet, violent potential.

He's insane, Sean decided.

Sean shifted his feet, blading his body so that the muzzle of his stubby little rifle was a little closer to putting rounds into this mad cannibal's chest. "Where's Terry? I don't recognize you."

The man's dark, blank eyes shifted from Sean, to Pablo, and then back again. "Terry's with the prisoner," he said, and his voice was terrible. It sounded exactly how Sean thought it would. "You're gonna hafta be okay with the prisoner being…a little beat up."

"Is he still alive?" Sean asked.

Those eyes widened, and in the growth of the man's beard, teeth flashed. "Oh, yes. He's still alive." A brief cackle that sounded like a crow cawing—if that crow were dying of thirst. "Not for long, though, huh? No, not for long."

Sean's eyes narrowed. "I want you to explain exactly why you believe he's Mr. Nobody or Mr. No One. Because we drove a long way out here from La Casa. And I'm not gonna be happy if this is just some vagrant you're trying to pass off to get the reward."

"Right, right, right," the stranger bobbed his head. He eyed the bed of their running pickup truck. "The reward. Did you bring it?"

Sean scoffed. "So you can try to rob us?" He tightened his grip on his weapon. "Once we confirm it's who we want, we'll deliver the reward later."

The stranger looked at Sean with a shrewd gaze. "Tell me honestly. Would you even recognize them if you saw them?" He leaned towards Sean. Seemed almost to be *looming*. His eyes sparkled in the shadows of his furrowed brow. "Do you even know what Mr. No One and Mr. Nobody look like?"

Sean swallowed. Decided to bluff. "Of course we know what they look like."

The man stared at him for another long second. "Yeah," he whispered. "That's what I thought."

The madman didn't telegraph a thing. He just moved.

Like a rattlesnake striking.

One second, Sean was peering at him suspiciously, and the next, he was stumbling backwards, both hands going instinctively to his throat where the stranger had lashed out and punched him in the larynx.

Pablo lurched off the side of the truck, yanking his six-shooter out.

The wild man was a blur of gnashing teeth and wiry limbs.

He brought the edge of his hand down on Pablo's wrist, and the silver revolver tumbled out of his grip. Then the madman reared up with one foot and struck hard with the heel of his boot, crashing it down on Pablo's knee with an audible *snap.*

Pablo screamed as he hit the ground.

Sean managed to rip his hands away from his neck, realizing he needed to get his rifle up, but the second he touched the grip, a flash of snarling madman was on him, seizing hold of the short-barreled rifle and ripping it up and out of Sean's grasp.

The sling caught it from being pulled away from his body.

The madman didn't seem to care. He had, apparently, already accounted for this.

Before Sean could even think of what to do next, the madman spun the butt of the rifle around Sean's head, so that the sling looped around his already swollen neck, and then the madman began to pull back on the rifle, tightening the nylon sling like a noose…

Movement out of the corner of Sean's darkening vision.

Pablo, on one knee, scooping that stupid silver revolver out of the dirt and bringing it up.

The madman looked over his shoulder, and saw the threat.

And for a flash, Sean thought he saw a flicker of concern somewhere in all that violence.

Then there was a sound like a giant zipper being yanked closed, terminating with a *THUD*.

The side of Pablo's head disappeared.

His brains and blood painted the blank canvas of the white pickup truck.

A rifle report rolled over them.

Pablo's body flopped to the ground.

And then, like a dog with a catcher's pole around his neck, Sean was yanked off of his feet and planted on the ground, on his back, his ears ringing, his vision sparkling, and the breath gone out of his lungs.

In the center of his vision, he saw the madman looking down at him, strangling him with his own rifle and strap.

The madman smiled down at Sean. "Now you know what I look like."

TWO

BLUE MOON

LEE WANTED TO KILL HIM.

He always wanted to kill them.

He twisted the stubby AR in his grip, tightening the choking sling, and watched the man's eyes go bloodshot, his face turning purple.

"Lee!" The voice stabbed into his brain.

It was distant, still. It would take Abe a moment to run the few hundred yards from his sniper's hide, on a small hillock amongst some brush. But even so, the lilting echo of Abe's voice made Lee stop twisting the choke tighter.

On the ground, the man's eyes bulged.

His jaw was clenched down, trying to muscle against the strain on his neck, but unconsciousness would come at any second.

"Ssh," Lee said to him, as soft and gentle as if he were soothing a spooked animal.

"Don't kill him!" came Abe's voice again, closer this time.

Lee snarled, casting a dark glance over his shoulder. Then he went back to the man in the dirt. He let up. Not enough for the man to get any blood into his brain, but enough to keep his throat from collapsing.

The man's expression slackened, the eyes going blank.

The body went limp.

Lee spun the rifle, unwinding the strap and then pulling it from around the man's neck.

The man wasn't exactly motionless during all this. His hands trembled at his sides, and his diaphragm fought to get air. His chest rose and fell, issuing long, low groans.

He was out cold. Or would be, for another few seconds.

Lee grabbed the butt of the rifle. Detached the sling.

The man stopped groaning. His eyes thrashed into focus.

Lee's hands spidered expertly across the short rifle, checking the magazine—*full*—and the chamber—*loaded.* He shouldered the weapon and aimed right between the eyes of the previous owner.

He put his boot on the man's chest, close to his throat. Pressed down with the ball of his foot.

"Hey." Lee's mouth was dry, and his throat hoarse. "Can you hear me?"

The man's eyes were crossed at first, struggling to bring Lee's face into focus, but gradually they righted themselves, and Lee watched full consciousness float back into the man's expression.

"On your stomach," Lee rasped, moving his foot off the man's chest.

The man complied.

Lee heard Abe approaching. The steady *thud-thud-thud* of his running footsteps.

"Relax," Lee barked over his shoulder. "I wasn't gonna choke him to death."

Abe jogged to a halt, huffing, a scoped .30-06 rifle in his hand. The bolt-action kind with the wooden body. The kind that was somebody's grandad's old deer rifle.

After a few moments of fuming silence, Lee raised a single eyebrow and met Abe's gaze.

Abe's eyes glared out from under his scrunched brow. His lips compressed to all but invisibility behind his bushy, black beard.

"That wasn't the plan," Abe snapped.

"I changed the plan. This was the new plan."

"He could've shot you. Hell, *I* could've shot you."

"I knew you wouldn't."

"Goddammit."

Lee turned and gestured to the man on the ground with half his head gone. "That was a great shot, Abe."

"Fuck you, Lee," Abe grumbled under his breath.

The eyes of the two men known as Mr. No One and Mr. Nobody reconvened on the man lying on his belly at their feet.

Abe began removing the lashing he had in the cargo pocket of his worse-for-wear combat pants. A length of bailing wire. The stuff was ubiquitous around here.

Lee stepped around to the side of the man on the ground. "Hands behind your back," he instructed. When the man complied, Lee knelt down, placing his knee at the top of the man's spine and leaning all his weight on it.

Abe began tying the man's wrists together with the baling wire.

The man whimpered.

It made Lee feel simultaneously satisfied and irritated.

"What are you gonna do to me?" the man gasped out, his breath stirring the dry dust against his face.

"Ssh," Lee whispered again, and then he bent down low, so that both his mouth and the muzzle of his rifle were close to the man's ear. "Don't worry about that right now. Just pray."

Something in the distance drew Abe's attention, and his eyes flicked up to the horizon. He scanned for a moment, and then seemed to fixate on something out there, something in amongst the low scrub. "Time to get inside."

***

The air inside smelled like death—hot, and fetid, and bacterial.

The man swung from the rafters of the quonset hut, making struggling noises.

Lee watched, an old, folding pocket knife in his hand.

The man—he'd given his name as Sean—was suspended by a chain that had been hooked to his baling wire bindings, and he could only take the tension off of his shoulders by shuffling around on his tiptoes.

"Sean," Lee sighed. "Stop trying to look at the dead bodies in the corner. Focus on answering my question."

Sean made a few more pathetic whimpering sounds, still trying to twist himself to get a good view of the bodies stacked up in the corner of the qounset hut, attracting flies. There was a single skylight in the top of the quonset hut, right above them. It provided enough light for them to see each other, but the rest of the building remained dim, like the vestiges of a slaughterhouse nightmare.

"I didn't have a choice!" Sean moaned. "They made me work for them! They said that I had to work for them or they would kill me!"

"Mm," Lee grunted. "Well, that's still a choice now, isn't it?"

Sean's gaze hit Lee's, and for one sad moment it looked like he expected to find some pity there.

He didn't.

Sean's eyes crinkled at the edges, his mouth twisting with anxiety. "Oh, man! Please, man! You don't gotta kill me!" His eyes strayed to the bodies in the corner again.

"Christ," Lee snapped. He seized Sean by the face and yanked him around to fully stare at the bodies. "Just look. You're so desperate to see them. Go ahead. Take a long, hard look. That's Terry, and his two sons, and two others that I don't know and don't care about. They fought back, so they died."

Lee yanked Sean around again, forcing eye contact. He brought the knife up, and put the extended blade right under Sean's eye. Out of his peripheral, Lee saw the initials in the wooden handle of the knife: TBW.

He didn't know what the B or the W stood for, but the T was for Terry.

"You work with the cartel," Lee hissed. "Then you die. That's the rule."

Sean didn't answer outside of squeezing his eyes shut and blubbering through his compressed lips.

A tiny dollop of spittle struck Lee's hand. He shoved Sean away and sneered in disgust.

"Tell me where you came from."

"La Casa," Sean said.

He seemed willing to talk, at least.

At the mention of La Casa, Abe Darabie perked up from fishing around in a can of expired green beans that they'd liberated from a nearby pantry.

Lee shot his partner a glance.

Leave it alone, Abe.

"You work for Hermanco?" Lee asked, patting Terry's old pocket knife against the side of his leg.

Sean nodded. "Yes. Well. You know. They *made* me work—"

"Alright, shut up," Lee snapped, slicing the air with the tip of the knife.

Sean clamped his mouth shut.

Abe walked over, picking green beans out of the can with his fingers. "What's the fuel situation in La Casa?"

Lee gritted his teeth.

Dammit, Abe…

"Uh…" Sean glanced between his two captors, seeming unsure who he should address. He settled on Abe. "There's two big tankers, just pulled in yesterday to replace two empties we sent back to the refinery on the coast to get refilled."

Abe chewed a suspiciously pale green bean. "Are they full?"

"Yes."

"Both of them?"

"Yes."

Abe looked significantly at Lee.

Lee stared back, trying not to let his thoughts show on his face, because he was thinking about how he wanted to smash Abe's nose into the back of his skull. Not that he was worried about Abe knowing that—Abe knew full well that he was pissing Lee off. He just didn't care.

Lee simply didn't want to show any signs of infighting to the man they had strung up. It was important to present a united front.

"Two full tankers," Abe said, with great import, and then shrugged, and backed off a step.

Lee dragged his attention back to Sean. "Joaquin Lozcano Leyva," Lee spat out. "Are you familiar?"

"No. I mean, yes, I know who he is," Sean backtracked. "I know he's Mateo Ibarra's right-hand man. I just…I've never met him."

"Where is he?"

Sean's eyes darted. "Well, I'm not real sure—"

Lee moved forward with the knife.

Sean writhed away. "*—But I'm pretty sure he's in Triprock!*"

Lee felt a heavy dose of anxiety shoot through his stomach.

Not anxiety born out of fear for his safety or anything so plebian—Lee was passed that now. Those were human concerns, and he'd let go of his human side a while ago. Five weeks ago, to be exact.

No, the anxiety was more the feeling of watching your prey walk towards your trap, and hoping desperately that they'll fall into it.

Lee already knew where Joaquin was. But it didn't hurt to confirm. Especially when they were so close to actually making a move on him. It was the closest to real-time intelligence Lee could get.

Sean breathed rapidly through his nose, and stared at the point of the knife—with which Lee had threatened to hamstring him. "That's what I heard, anyways," he said.

"How recently did you hear that?"

"Yesterday." He seemed to think that more clarity might be required to stave off the hamstringing. "Last night. There was some talk that he might come 'round to La Casa. But that was because we thought…" Sean trailed off.

Abe spoke up around a mouthful of green beans. "You thought that you'd have Mr. Nobody captured by then, and that Joaquin Leyva would want to come torture him for a good long while before taking his balls to Mateo Ibarra as a keepsake?"

A dry tongue darted out of Sean's mouth. It didn't do much to wet his peeling lips.

Lee and Abe both waited in silent expectation of an answer.

"Uh. Yes," Sean whispered.

Lee and Abe exchanged a long look.

Combative though their relationship was at times, you can't help but develop a form of telepathy with someone who's at your side every minute of every day, and upon which your life constantly depends.

The look only lasted a second. A raise of the eyebrows from Lee. A sideways nod of acceptance from Abe. A final nod of resolution from Lee.

In long form, what had been communicated was: *He's been honest so far. Might as well ask the final question. He'll probably give us a truthful answer.*

"Sean," Lee prompted. "What's this week's passcode for *Nuevas Fronteras* sentries?"

Sean must have somehow sensed that this was what it all came down to.

And as he realized that this was the final question, he simultaneously realized that these were his final moments.

"Wait. You can't kill me."

"Sean," Lee growled through clenched teeth. "We've had a good thing going. Don't screw it up now."

"But you're going to kill me after I answer that question!" Sean moaned.

"I'm not gonna kill you."

"You said everyone that works with the cartel dies!"

"Yeah, but I didn't say I'm the one that kills them."

Sean blubbered for another second or two, then looked at Abe.

Abe shook his head. "I'm not gonna kill you either."

"Unless you don't answer the question," Lee said. "In which case, yes, we will kill you."

"You're lying. You're gonna kill me."

"Do you *want* to die or something?"

"No!" Sean sobbed. "But you're not going to let me live after I answer that question! I'd answer the question, but I know that you're gonna kill me after that!"

Lee slid up to Sean and put the point of the knife against his right hamstring. With his free hand, he cupped the back of Sean's head. His words came out hot and harsh. "Alright, listen to me, you shit. You tell me the passcode, and you get one chance and one chance only to live. And that's when we cut you down and you run north, as fast as possible. But the infected are all over this place because your buddy Terry over there has been stinking it up and they're all real hungry for a piece of meat. So, no, your chances of making it on the outside aren't great. But I'll tell you what, Sean: They're a whole helluva lot better than they are in here with me. And every time you don't answer that question, I will cut one of your hamstrings. And guess how fast you're gonna run if you don't have hamstrings?"

"Blue Moon!" Sean yelped.

Lee twitched when the man expelled the words so quickly. He'd been prepared to go on about how he was going to sever his biceps so that he couldn't use his arms to crawl away from the primals either.

Some men were easier to break than others.

"It's Blue Moon! That's the passcode! I swear! Don't cut my hamstrings!"

"Blue Moon?" Lee repeated, as clearly and articulately as possible.

"Yes! Blue Moon! I swear—"

"Alright shut up," Lee cut him off, pushing away from him.

He looked once again to his partner, and once again, a wordless communication passed between them.

They would have to trust that Sean was telling them the truth. There was no way to confirm it without actually using it—at which point their necks would be on the line. It was possible that Sean might be saying anything he could think of to get Lee not to cut his hamstrings, and that if they tried to use that passcode with a cartel sentry, they'd get gunned down…

But that was the risk you took when you tortured people for information.

Unfortunately, asking politely had proven to give even poorer results.

"Alright, Sean," Lee said. "You've earned your one chance to live."

Sean tried to blubber his thanks, but was immediately told to shut up.

They lowered the chain that kept him dangling, and unhooked it from his bindings. Lee didn't cut the bindings off of him. And Sean didn't mention it. His eyes were fixated on the glow of daylight framing the back door of the qounset hut. He still didn't quite believe that they were going to let him go. He seemed to be afraid to utter a single word that might break the fragile spell of their mercy.

If only he knew what Lee knew.

Lee and Abe, *Nadie y Ninguno*, Mr. No One and Mr. Nobody, the merciless, bloodthirsty boogeymen of Texas, hauled Sean to the back door of the hut, one of them on either side of him.

They stopped, and Abe backed up, raising the short barreled rifle that he'd appropriated from Sean, and covering the captive as well as the door.

Lee gripped the back of Sean's neck, facing the door.

"It's your only chance, Sean," Lee said to him. "So make it a good one."

Sean nodded, his mouth open, sucking in air.

Lee's eyes coursed up and down the man, and for a brief moment in time, he searched himself to see if he felt anything. But he didn't.

Everything human had callused over. And Lee only kept abrading it, more and more, growing more and more callused, because that was his only defense.

The moment he felt anything, he was doomed.

"One more thing," Lee said.

Sean's eyes flickered to Lee.

"Have you seen any dogs over at La Casa?"

Sean blinked, confused by the question. "What?"

"Dogs," Lee reiterated with a note of impatience. "Canine animals. You seen a dog that looks kind of like a coyote? It's a light-colored German Shepherd mix. You seen a dog like that?"

Sean appeared bewildered. Slowly, as though fearing he might meet with some retribution if he answered in the negative, he shook his head. "No. Sorry."

Lee grunted. "Alright. You ready?"

Sean faced the door. "Yes."

Lee plunged the knife into his gut.

Sean jerked back, but Lee held him fast as he removed the knife, and held the blade up to Sean's face. "Ssh, Sean. Don't start screaming. Take deep breaths and listen to me."

Sean somehow managed to contain the scream.

It turned into a series of ragged, hitching breaths.

"You're not gonna die," Lee said. "Not yet, anyways. It's just a gut wound, you know? It maybe pierced some of your stomach or intestinal tract, and maybe you have some shit leaking into your abdominal cavity, and that'll probably make you real sick in a couple days, but until then, you're still alive right? Yeah, you're still alive. You still have a chance."

Sean's horrified eyes crawled up to Lee's cold, dead ones. "Why?" he choked out. "Why're you doing this to me?"

Lee nodded, like it was a good question. Then he put his hand on the door to the outside world, and made sure that his grip on the back of Sean's neck was good and solid. "I'm just giving you a chance, Sean," he said. "The same chance you gave Julia."

Then he pushed the door open, and threw Sean out into the world.

Sean stumbled, and looked for a moment like he might collapse. Then he regained his feet. He whirled around, trying to get his bearings.

"Run, Sean," Lee said, as he reached out and grabbed hold of the door, pulling it closed again.

The last thing that Lee saw of Sean was the man pointing himself north and staggering into a jog. And in the distant hills, Lee thought he saw shadowy shapes slipping through the low brush.

Lee pulled himself out of the doorway, then let the door close and latch. "You grabbed the keys to that pickup truck, right?"

Abe lowered his rifle. Patted his pants pocket, emitting a muted jangling. "Yeah, I got 'em."

"Good," Lee had already turned away from the door and started moving. "Let's get our shit and hit the road. It won't take long before they realize we took their boys down—Blue Moon ain't gonna work for much longer."

THREE

SCAVENGING

A MONTH HAD TURNED Benjamin Sullivan into an animal.

He knelt on all fours, with his nose touching the bottom of the door, smelling the gap between the door and the floor tiles. And he also listened.

Eyesight wasn't much use to him where he was. These buildings that had once housed Master Sergeant Gilliard and his team of operatives in their quiet little corner of Fort Bragg, were not built with the concept of natural lighting in mind.

There were a few offices that had tiny windows. Unfortunately, the one that Benjamin and his mother hid in, did not.

So they steeped in blackness.

For over a month.

His mother moreso than him, because Benjamin would go out, as he planned to do right now. He had tasted daylight. And yes, being so long in the dark, it had a taste. Like grass, and wind, and, very faintly, lemons.

Benjamin spent another few seconds at the crack under the door, smelling and listening.

The primals were difficult to detect when they wanted to be. When they hunted.

They didn't smell as terrible as the infected had when the plague first struck. But that was because those creatures—the first generation of people turned mad by the FURY bacterium—would defecate in their clothing and their brains seemed not to have held onto any instinct for cleanliness or grooming.

The primals, on the other hand, were different. They were mutants, one might say. Part human, and part…whatever it is they had become. Or were *becoming*. But they had instincts that the first generation of infected did not.

They hunted as a coordinated pack. They communicated through their guttural language of barks and hoots and snorts. And they groomed themselves.

But, as any animal did, they still smelled.

You couldn't detect them from two rooms away, like you could with the first generation. But Benjamin had found that he could still smell them if they were nearby. A faint smell, that was both human body odor and the distinctly musty-sour scent that came from the sweat of a purely carnivorous creature.

Sometimes it was harder than that, because they gave themselves dust baths. Benjamin had watched them do it a few times now. They would find a bare patch of dry dirt, and they would roll in it, and rub it over themselves. In their armpits and in their crotch.

Benjamin thought that this was instinctive, too. But smart.

They recognized that they had an odor. And the dust made that odor disappear for a while. Which made it easier to creep up on prey.

Finally, smelling neither body odor, nor carnivorous sweat, nor dirt from a dust bath, Benjamin eased back away from the door.

He thought about dust baths. Thought about bringing some dirt back with him so that his mother could bathe in it, too. They'd been in this room for a long time now. It probably stank of them, though he'd gone nose-blind to it, except for the first few seconds after coming back from his daily scavenging.

So far, the primals had not infiltrated these buildings. But it could happen at any time. They liked dark, insulated places, and that's exactly what these buildings were. And if they ever came into the building, Benjamin knew that they would scent him and his mother out within moments.

The door would hold for a while, if they locked it.

But eventually they'd ram their way in.

His mother was close to him in the blackness. He could smell her too.

He leaned over in her direction. "I'm going," he whispered, the words little more than a breeze.

Taylor Sullivan did not respond.

Benjamin felt a flash of irritation. He knew what her silence meant. She wanted them to find a different place—a safe place where they didn't have to be in the dark all the time.

Didn't she know that he was trying his best?

"I'll try to find a place," he said. And then, as a barbed afterthought: "I *have* been trying, you know."

After a moment's silence, he felt compelled to say one more thing: "Sorry."

Taylor didn't respond to her son's apology.

Benjamin imagined her face, the crease of disappointment that he might see if there were light in the room.

He was, after all, the reason why they were trapped here in Fort Bragg.

Everyone else had evacuated, and they'd been left here. Abandoned by Carl Gilliard, despite his promise of protection. And now Fort Bragg had been taken over. Not by President Briggs, as the Lincolnists had hoped, but by a colony of primals.

It's still your fault, a part of himself chided.

He turned back to the door, wishing that his mother could see the disgust on his face.

He took ahold of the latch and gently turned it.

His darkness-sharpened ears heard every little metallic *tink* as the innards of the doorknob worked, slowly disengaging the latch.

He pulled the door open. It did so silently. That was their one stroke of luck, Benjamin thought: They'd at least been sequestered in a building with well-oiled hinges.

He stepped into the room, and immediately felt terrified. As he closed the door behind him, he felt almost like an infant, exiting the safety of a womb. Everything outside was terror and violence. Everything beyond that tiny microcosm of safety was survival of the fittest.

Benjamin knew the way out of the building. He'd made the trek thirty-six times so far. Every day, around midday. It was the least likely time for the primals to be active.

They were not nocturnal. Nor were they diurnal.

They really followed no definite sleep and waking pattern.

But it did seem to Benjamin that they hunted less during midday.

They would become more active again in the afternoon and evening.

So he had a few hours to sneak around Fort Bragg. To find food and water for him and his mother, so that they could buy themselves another day of survival. And hopefully, if Benjamin was very lucky, perhaps a different place to stay that better met their needs.

What were their needs?

Well. Sunlight would be nice.

Locking doors were a must.

It had to be away from the center of Fort Bragg, where it seemed like the colony of primals gathered most.

It had to have easy access to cover and concealment, so that they could come and go without being seen.

Second story would be good, too. With a window to escape out of. Being on the second floor would mean they would have more warning than being on the ground floor, but weren't so high up that they couldn't bail out of a window if necessary.

Benjamin had a lot of requirements.

Which was why they hadn't made the move yet.

He made his way down the long hall to the stairwell door on the left. Down two flights of stairs. To the main floor. Turn left. Here, the first glimmer of sun was a corner of the door to the outside that glowed with daylight beyond. Even on rainy days, that upper right-hand corner of the door always seemed to blaze after so much absolute darkness.

It took him nearly ten minutes from the time he left the room with his mother, to the time that he reached the door to the outside world. He stopped often, listening, and smelling. His heart hammering. Terrified, as he felt his way along the walls. His imagination always playing for him a scene were his hand touched not wall, but the hard musculature of something waiting for him in the blackness.

His mind obsessed over the concept of being eaten alive.

You might think that he would have grown numb to it. But that wasn't the case. His imagination ran away from him, multiple times every day, and it never got better.

His chances of surviving another month—another week, even—were getting slimmer and slimmer. He knew this. And he knew that the end point—which could be today, or could be tomorrow, or could be a week from now—would be him, dragged to the ground with a primal's jaws latched around his throat, feeling their claw-like fingers ripping into his stomach, feeling their teeth tearing away the meat of his legs…

It's still your fault.

Yes. It was his fault.

But that didn't stop him from hating Angela Houston and Carl Gilliard for what they'd done. For locking him and his mother up. For forgetting them here. Or perhaps not even forgetting them—maybe they'd deliberately left Benjamin and Taylor. Maybe they'd thought to themselves, "Well, this solves a problem, at least."

At the door to the outside, he finally placed his hand upon the latch, and he eased it open. He paused with just an inch of daylight showing. He let one eye linger there in the crack, allowing it to adjust to the blazing daylight.

It wasn't actually blazing. As his sight began to clear, he saw that the day was thickly overcast. It had that dank, humid scent of coming rain. Outside in the gravel parking lot between buildings, he saw puddles of standing water. It must've rained during the night, and was about to rain again.

He got his other eye acclimated to the daylight, and by then, he'd listened to the outside and scanned across the tops of all the weeds that grew between the gravel in the parking lot outside, and he was relatively sure there weren't any primals in the vicinity.

Or they were hiding well.

He pulled the door open about a third of the way, then stopped. This door had a squeak in one of the hinges. Benjamin had been keeping an eye out for some sort of oil that he might use to lubricate it, but so far hadn't come across anything he could use for that purpose.

The squeak happened right about halfway. But Benjamin was a slim young man, so he squeezed out without opening the door all the way. Then, before easing the door shut behind him, he checked, and re-checked, and then triple-checked that the lock was in the *unlock* position.

Otherwise he'd be trapped outside.

Today, he decided to check the lock four times, and then, obsessively, once more, before easing the door shut.

Still, when the door latched, he always had a little spurt of panic go through him. He tested the door knob. Found that it was unlocked. And he supposed that would have to be reassurance enough. He couldn't hang out in the open all day, panicking about the lock.

He needed to find food and water, and—if he was lucky—a place for them to move.

Benjamin navigated Fort Bragg like a mouse.

He stuck to corners as much as possible. He kept low. He stayed as quiet as he possibly could. And he sprinted across open spaces, and tried to leave himself exposed as little as possible. He avoided the woods whenever possible, preferring the cover of buildings, because buildings had places that you might hide. Buildings had doors that could be locked. It was easier to lose the primals if they chased you into a building.

In the woods?

Well, in the woods, you were cooked.

There weren't enough hiding places. Your scent was too easy to smell in the midst of nothing but trees, and you could forget about running fast enough. It simply wasn't going to happen.

There were small sections of pine that Benjamin had to get through—either that, or walk along the dirt road, which was suicidal, in his opinion—but he took his time scouting these to make sure that nothing lurked, and he sprinted through them like he did in the open spaces.

Eventually, sweating and breathing hard through a wide-open mouth to mitigate the sound, Benjamin found himself looking at the edge of one of the numerous neighborhoods that had been used, once upon a time, to house troops and their families.

More recently, it had been used to house the citizens of the United Eastern States.

This was the safest place for Benjamin to scavenge. The primals seemed to congregate near the larger buildings towards the center of Fort Bragg. And here in the neighborhoods, Benjamin had a theory that his scent was difficult to pick out amongst all the old houses with so many years of human scent built up in them.

That was his theory anyways.

So far, he hadn't been found by the primals.

He knew that bigger stores of food could be found nearer the center of Fort Bragg, near the hangars where they used to do the food distributions. But it was just too dangerous. So he was relegated to picking from what scraps he could find in people's old homes.

Luckily, part of the evacuation plan had not been for people to pack out all their food, and there was still some left that had not rotted. Produce was out of the question. But there were still some dried meats that were good, and the grain allotments would be good indefinitely.

The neighborhoods didn't look much different. One could almost imagine that they were still full of people. That at any moment, people would be walking along the sidewalk, heading to work, or coming home from a shift.

Benjamin worked his way into the neighborhood to the last house that he'd scavenged. He'd been interrupted last time by a pack of primals that he'd heard calling to each other. They'd been close, but he'd never caught sight of them. And, as was common knowledge at this point, when they howled to each other, that meant they weren't pursuing prey.

The house had shown some promise, so he went back to it, picking up where he'd left off.

He slid into the back door and closed and locked it behind him.

From what he could tell, this had been one of the homes that had multiple families living in it. Which meant that they'd received multiple ration allotments. Which gave him a greater chance of finding something leftover.

He went to the fridge first. After doing this so many times, he knew to hold his breath when he opened the fridge. The smell was usually putrid. In the dark, unpowered interior of the fridge, there was a cabbage that had turned black, swimming in a soup of its own dark juices. There was a cardboard box with a collection of what had once been produce but was now fairly unrecognizable. The bottom of the box was sopping wet and fuzzy with mold.

Benjamin wrinkled his nose, despite the fact that he was still holding his breath.

On the top shelf, luckily placed far above the seeping rot of the produce, there was a package of grits. This was one of the staples that he'd found in almost all of the houses, usually in a large tin, sometimes in a mason jar. They ground the grits from the corn they'd grown in the numerous fields out beyond Fort Bragg.

This was in a tin, with an open top. Not ideal. It would have taken in some of the moisture from the rotting produce. Perhaps rotted a bit itself. He withdrew the tin and closed the fridge door, then retreated to the far side of the kitchen where he finally allowed himself to breathe again.

The stink of the fridge had permeated the entire room. It smelled like a dumpster.

Benjamin took a couple of breaths to clear himself and then smelled the grits.

They had indeed taken on the rotted scent, but they didn't look moldy. He stuck his fingers into the granules and felt that they were mostly dry. A bit of clumping at the top. But he thought they would be okay.

He could let them sit in some water for a while and he and his mother would have a nice meal. Flavorless, but it would at least fill their bellies. Flavor was for people who didn't need to worry about starving to death.

He set the open tin of grits on the kitchen table and prepared to return to the fridge for anything else that showed any promise, when he heard it.

A bark.

Not from a dog.

Benjamin knew the difference.

Everything inside him suddenly drew taut.

His adrenaline glands dumped everything they had into his body, and he stood stock still for a moment, forcing himself to take large, measured breaths of the stinking air.

Shit, shit, shit.

They were here. Again.

Maybe there was something about this house.

Fuck this house. He'd never come back here again. Maybe coming back a second time had been a mistake. Maybe the primals had a den nearby.

The bark was answered by another, and then another.

They were close. Maybe a few houses away.

Benjamin sank down onto his haunches, then scrambled his way from the kitchen into the living room. There were windows here, the shades hanging half open. He crept up to them on all fours and slowly lifted his head above the sill.

Outside, the neighborhood streets stood, still and silent.

Should he run? Or would it be wiser to sit and stay?

Last time, they hadn't been so close, and he'd had ample time to get out of the area. This time they sounded like they were right on top of him.

All they would need to do was catch a whiff of him, and they would come into this house. Locked doors or not. They would batter the doors down or come in through the windows.

Suddenly, his theory about his scent being obscured by all the old scents of humanity sounded dumb.

Across the street, between two of the identical houses, a shape seeped out of the shadows of the pine forest beyond.

Long arms. Thickly muscled shoulders and neck. Hunched, predatory posture.

Its eyes scoured the street. Its mouth hung open, tongue protruding, its sinewy chest heaving like it'd been running.

All of these details appeared to Benjamin like his vision had suddenly developed binocular capabilities.

With a quiet mewl of fear, Benjamin backed away from the window, just as the thing's eyes coursed over him.

Did it see me? Did it see me?

Benjamin stared at blank, white-painted wall. It smelled of dust. And people.

His heart slammed so hard it made his vision twitch.

From outside, there was no sound.

No barks.

No howls.

That means they've found you.

A new level of panic bloomed like a dark flower in Benjamin's brain, and it crowded out all reason and thought. He was just an animal. He was just prey. And his brain told him to run.

Run!

He scrambled away from the window, still on all fours, the sense now overpowering that the creatures outside were going to burst in the door at any moment. He found his hands and feet slapping their way up the staircase of the split-level residence. He was going high, because he didn't have the courage to leave out the back door where they would chase him down and rip him to shreds and feed on him while he was still awake and screaming.

The attic, a flash of clarity went across his mind like a bolt of lightning in a black storm.

Some little vestigial section of reason-capable brain knew that this was an all-in bet.

Because once you were in the attic, you couldn't get *out* of the attic.

And so you'd better hope that your hiding place fooled the creatures that were after you, because if they figured out where you were, if they sniffed you out, then you had no place else to go. You'd trapped yourself.

But this was a dim argument in the face of complete panic.

Benjamin at least had an *idea*, and that was about the best he could hope for in this circumstance. The other alternative was to simply go blank in the mind, curl up in a ball, and start praying.

To the top of the stairs.

Here he finally came up to his feet again, his breath coming in short, hyperventilating gasps. The only thing that he could actually see was a little dot of reality directly in front of his face, and everything else was a mélange of dark colors. Like looking through a drinking straw.

He stood in the center of a landing, around which there were several bedroom doors and a bathroom. If the attic would be anywhere, it was here.

It took his eyes five agonizing passes over the ceiling to finally fixate on the attic door.

A simple square in the ceiling.

Not a pull down.

Shit!

Down on the ground level of the house, something rattled a door.

Front door? Back door?

It didn't matter.

They knew he was in here. They were coming for him.

Benjamin found himself whimpering: "Oh-please-oh-please-oh-please…"

He jumped for the attic access but it was a stupid idea to begin with. His fingertips hit the bottom and jarred the square piece of plywood, but it didn't open.

He needed something to stand on.

Did he have time for that?

On the ground level, he heard something like the snarling of a dog. And then a loud impact. The sound of a body hitting the door, and it seemed to rattle the whole house.

"Oh-please-oh-please…"

His tunnel vision scoured around him for something—anything—that would give him just a few feet of height.

There. In one of the bedrooms.

A nightstand.

A cheap piece of pine furniture.

It might not even hold his weight, but it was all he had.

He rushed to it, his feet and hands clumsy like they'd turned to rubber. He grabbed the thing and felt his heart drop at how light it was. The chances of it holding his weight were slim. He glanced around for something else that he could use, but another reverberating impact from downstairs struck all further thought from his brain.

Dragging the nightstand, he stumbled back into the landing area, underneath the attic access. He jammed the nightstand down and clambered up. It creaked and swayed treacherously. His legs wobbled underneath him. But he was two feet higher.

Another impact, and this time it didn't shake the walls as hard, because this time it ended in a terrifying *crash*, and Benjamin knew that they'd battered the door open.

He heard the scramble of their claws on the linoleum entryway.

He couldn't even speak anymore. All that came out of his mouth was a whine.

Chuffing, barking, snarling.

They're coming they're coming they're coming

He had one chance to save himself.

He leapt.

The thrust cracked the nightstand beneath his feet, and sent it spinning away, broken.

His hands jammed the attic access up, and out of the way.

His hands slapped down on a ceiling joist, and he grabbed it.

His body swung underneath him, hanging there like a sack of meat.

The creatures tumbled to the bottom of the stairs—more than one of them.

He heard their breathing, their snarling, the tumble of their limbs as they hauled up the stairs towards him.

They're going to eat me

I'm going to die

He pulled with everything he had left in him.

Up, into the attic, but he had nothing for his flailing feet to purchase on.

He screamed.

Claws thrashing through carpet, sounding like they were just beneath him.

He managed to get one elbow up onto the ceiling joist, and then another. Every bit of strength went into a maneuver that Benjamin hadn't done since he'd been a boy climbing trees, and he pulled, and rolled, his abdominal muscles cramping with the effort of muscling himself up.

Half his body in the attic, with his legs still hanging in the opening. He reached for the next ceiling joist, a mere sixteen inches away. Grabbed it and pulled.

Just beneath his exposed feet, a growl that he swore he felt in his toes.

Something caught his right foot.

He couldn't scream. His lungs were locked down, empty of air, burning.

He thrashed and kicked. Felt his shoe fly off.

And then he rolled. Up into the attic.

His back hit a box of something left there from ages ago, and sent it clattering off of the joists where it was balanced. Benjamin crabbed backwards, thoughtless of the fact that there were only ceiling joists and no floor to support him.

His hand hit the insulation between the joists, and his weight came down on it.

The sheetrock beneath him collapsed and his hand shot through in a gout of dust.

He yanked his limb back up, but he caught a glimpse through the hole in the ceiling that he'd just created, and saw the feral eyes below him, the gnashing teeth, a horrible grin as though it knew it had him trapped.

Trapped! I'm trapped!

He caught the bare impression of at least three primals circling below him.

He started to crab backwards again, away from the hole and the attic access, because that was all he could do. He could only squirm into the far corner of this dark space. He could only extend his life by precious seconds now.

Joist by joist, he moved backward, trying not to fall through the ceiling.

A grunt of effort from below.

A pair of gnarled hands appeared in the attic access, their strangely elongated fingers latching onto the ceiling joists, the claws gripping the wood.

They pulled with the effortlessness of animal strength.

The head loomed up through the access. Wild, inhuman eyes fixed on him. The wide mouth slavering, the teeth bared.

Benjamin rammed himself against the roof, and knew he couldn't go back any farther only when he felt the roofing nails gouge his shoulder and the back of his head.

The thing squirmed further upward through the opening. Lifted one of its legs up…

A popping noise came from below.

Loud. Sharp. Rapid.

Benjamin huddled, pressing his body against nails.

Half through the attic access, the primal appeared to hesitate.

Screeching from below. Snarling. And…

Shouts.

Human shouts.

Words.

The rapid popping noise again. The clatter of projectiles smacking into flesh, and into walls. The primal hung there and seemed caught in a moment's indecision—whether or not to continue after Benjamin, or address the threat.

There was the thunder of footsteps on stairs.

More shouts, and Benjamin heard the words but he couldn't make sense of them.

The primal turned, apparently intent on whatever the hell was happening down below. It seemed about to drop back to the ground. It turned its head and bared its teeth at something and began to let out a horrendous howl.

Then the ceiling around it erupted. Tufts of insulation blew up all around it. Bits of drywall. Dust. And blood—chunks of its flesh tearing off of it, jerking it around, enraging it…

And then something must have passed through its brain, because Benjamin watched the moment when the lights went out in its face.

Most of its body went limp, and it wilted down, tumbling out of the attic access.

Except for one of its hands, clutching the ceiling joist, holding on for a second more, just the random firing of synapses upon death.

Then it slipped.

A second later, Benjamin heard the sound of its body hitting the floor.

Benjamin gasped for air. He smelled the smell of primals, but also of drywall dust, and blood. He only realized that he was weeping when the image of the attic access hole blurred into an impressionist glare of white light in darkness.

The popping sound, again. But this time more deliberate. Steady.

Then more human voices, except this time the words finally made sense to Benjamin's ears.

"Clear!"

"Clear!"

"All clear," the last voice spoke. And then it shouted up at him through the attic access. "Hey kid! Kid! You still alive up there?"

FOUR

DIPLOMACY

"I'VE LOST VISUAL."

Captain Perry Griffin frowned at the last radio transmission.

His operative on the ground in Fort Bragg was narrating a pretty odd chain of events, involving a lot of unknowns—an unknown male subject, an unidentified military vehicle, filled with unidentified military men.

His operative continued: "Unidentified vehicle turned onto a neighborhood street. Looked like they were hauling after something. Griffin, you got that drone up yet?"

A handful of miles north of where the operative reconnoitered the movements of the unknown entities—and tried to figure out who they were and where the hell they'd come from—Griffin stood safely ensconced in the Eastern Tactical Operations Command.

ETOC was nothing glamorous. It was a building in the northern wing of the Shughart Middle School in Spout Springs, North Carolina.

Their main command center was a large classroom. Chairs and desks sized for middle-schoolers had been ejected and piled up around a few of the barricaded entrances to add a little extra defensibility should they come under attack from the infected or anyone else.

The whiteboard in the room was now covered with notes and maps and satellite pictures. Folding tables had been appropriated from various places around the school and erected here in the classroom. These tables were crowded with computers and communications equipment, and soldiers from Greeley Colorado now sat at them, using adult-sized office chairs taken from teacher's desks and the staff break rooms.

Griffin stood behind one of these soldiers, looking over his shoulder as he operated their small reconnaissance drone.

Griffin keyed his radio handset. "Griffin to Rollins, hold your position. Don't put yourself in harm's way. Drone will have eyeballs in just a few." He released the PTT and addressed the drone pilot. "How long?"

The pilot eyed a map that showed the location of his drone as a dot creeping southward across the grid of streets. "One mike. Maybe less. Standby."

Griffin raised his eyes to another soldier down the table, this one with a satphone pressed to his ear. "Edwards, what's the ETA on the Predator?"

Edwards relayed the question through the satphone, speaking directly to Greeley. Then he looked to Griffin. "It's on site in three mikes."

Griffin nodded.

The drone they had over Fort Bragg was merely a glorified camera on a quad-copter base. It was battery operated, and not big enough to carry any sort of munitions payload.

Until Griffin could secure Pope Air Base, which was attached to Fort Bragg (which was currently overrun by infected), then Griffin had no direct control of the Predator drones that *did* carry munitions. Greeley had two of them, but they had to launch and be operated out of Colorado.

Griffin crossed his arms over his chest and waited in silence for his reconnaissance drone to get overhead of the unidentified Humvee and perhaps figure out who the hell they were.

These must be some of Angela and Harden's goons, he thought. *The infected kicked them out of Fort Bragg for us, but naturally, they're going to come sniffing around again.*

Griffin had no intention of letting Angela or any of her quasi-military insurgents get a foothold here again. As far as Griffin was concerned, he owned Fort Bragg now.

He just had to get the infected out of it before he could move in.

Once they moved in, they could get the power back on, secure the high voltage fences that had kept it safe, and then Greeley would have a base of operations right in the UES's backyard.

At that point in time, the UES would be finished. It was already on its deathbed since the fall of Fort Bragg. When Greeley moved troops into the vacuum they'd created, that would be the official end of Angela and Lee Harden's little mutiny.

With a local force of troops at his disposal, Griffin would easily snuff out the remaining so-called Safe Zones of the United Eastern States, and bring the Carolinas, Georgia, and Florida back into the fold.

"Alright," his drone pilot said, leaning forward in his seat. "I'm there. Have Rollins confirm that street for me again."

"Griffin to Rollins, confirm the street where that Humvee was last seen."

A pause over the airwaves.

Rollins came back: "Pretty sure it's Volturno Street."

The drone pilot nodded. "I'm on it. Standby…there we go." He kept one hand on the drone controls and with the other pointed to the screen.

Griffin leaned over the man's shoulder again and frowned at the screen.

There in the middle of Volturno Street was indeed a Humvee. It was little more than a tiny tan square in the middle of the street, lined on both sides by duplex military housing.

"Zoom in," Griffin ordered.

The pilot did as requested. The image magnified.

Griffin keyed his radio again. "Rollins, I see our mystery Humvee. It's stopped in the middle of Volturno. I'm seeing two males, military uniforms, full battle rattle. Looks like they're waiting for…Hold on…"

From the duplex they were parked in front of, a cluster of new figures emerged. They weren't running, but it was obvious they were in a hurry.

"Got three more coming out of one of the houses," Griffin continued. "Two more uniformed military. And another person, possibly a civilian. Unarmed. It looks like they're escorting the civilian. They're all piling into the Humvee now. Shit.

Standby again." Griffin released the airwaves. "What about that Predator?" he shot over his shoulder.

"Coming on site now," the soldier with the satphone called.

Griffin pointed to the screen. "There's something on that Humvee. Flag or banner or something." Griffin turned to the soldier on the satphone. "See if that Predator can come in a little lower and get a visual on that flag. I can't ID it with our drone right overhead."

The soldier began mumbling back and forth, communicating with whoever operated the Predator, all the way over in Greeley.

The pilot of the recon drone shifted in his seat. "Let me see if I can drop altitude here."

Griffin watched the screen, and narrated what he saw for Rollins. "They're moving now. Looks like they're hauling ass—yup, they have infected moving in on them. Rollins, be advised that's not too far from you, if you can shift to be downwind of that pack."

"Roger."

"They're leaving the infected behind, heading towards Normandy Drive."

The image on the screen changed its angle. The recon drone dropping in altitude, and shifting eastward, towards where Volturno Street intersected with Normandy Drive.

The bird's eye view of the Humvee became a sidelong view.

"What the hell?" Griffin mumbled over the radio. "Rollins, I'm seeing a Canadian flag." Griffin straightened up and looked at the soldier on the satphone. "That Humvee is displaying a Canadian flag."

The soldier nodded. "Predator pilot is reporting the same thing."

Griffin blinked a few times, trying to adjust to this new load of information. "Well, what does Greeley want us to do?"

"Just because they're flying the flag doesn't mean they're CAF," the recon drone pilot pointed out.

Griffin swore and reached over to where his own satphone lay on the table. Yet another shit sandwich to feast upon. But there was no way in hell he was going to eat this one all by himself. He was going to go direct with Daniels or Lineberger—whoever was available—and let them make the call.

The soldier on the satphone swiveled in his seat. "Captain, the Predator's being told to stand down."

Griffin glanced up from dialing the number to Greeley command. "On whose orders?"

"Mr. Daniels, sir. He says not to engage anyone displaying Canadian Armed Forces markings."

Griffin stared at the other soldier, his expression blank.

This didn't seem like a sudden decision. This seemed like there were things going on already, that they just hadn't told Griffin about. And while he appreciated the old adage of soldiers being like mushrooms—kept in the dark and fed shit—he considered his position to be one that required a good deal of intel.

He resented when that was withheld.

He turned back to the phone, and continued dialing Greeley.

***

The line between military contracting and actual military had become officially nonexistent.

Daniels was aware of this shift. He'd seen it coming for quite a while. He'd even nudged things in that direction, using his influence as a friend and former colleague of President Briggs to make it happen.

But that didn't make the actual practice any less complicated.

He stepped out of the Box—the dim room where the single on-duty Predator drone pilot sat in front of his glowing screens and controls—and into harsh daylight.

It would've been easier to have these control rooms inside FOB Hampton, the Hampton Inn and Suites that had become the main hub of military operations and government control in Greeley, Colorado. But the equipment would have been impossible to squeeze into the conference rooms where the rest of the command operations were hosted. They'd've had to take out a few walls to accomplish it.

So now Daniels had to sit and stew in his irritable juices, while one of his Cornerstone operatives drove him back to FOB Hampton.

He clambered up into the black Tahoe and slammed the door with a huff. "Command center," he grunted, and the driver sped off the flight line of the Greeley Airport where their single working Box was situated.

Another irritating complexity: He held no official military rank. And yet he was, for all intents and purposes, on equal footing with Colonel

Lineberger. In fact, he'd recently been given control of Project Hometown, for the simple fact that Briggs had started to lack a certain necessary trust in his military, fearing that a misplaced sense of patriotism might cause them to betray him.

Which was not paranoia.

It'd happened several times already.

Daniels held two technical titles: CEO of Cornerstone, the military contracting company that now worked alongside what remained of the American military; and Military Consultant to Command. The former being something that Daniels felt was rather made-up.

He wasn't just *consulting* or *advising*.

The fact was, he was *commanding*.

And yet, without rank, no amount of inventive titles was going to smooth out the friction between him and the military forces that were under his control. There was still the distinct sense that he was the outsider. The merc. The somewhat-seedy pitbull that Briggs had called in to straighten things out.

Another line that had been blurred: the line between soldier, and mercenary.

Because the fact of the matter was, whether you were Cornerstone, or Army, or Marines, or Air Force, you worked for the same damn thing: Food, and a safe place to sleep.

It all felt so ad-hoc sometimes, that Daniels was forced to question whether this type of arrangement could really hold the fractured United States together for as long as it would take to rebuild itself. And he wondered how it would fly if he demanded an official officer's commission.

Colonel would do nicely.

The drive to FOB Hampton was quick. The red triangle emblazoned on the side and hood of the black Tahoe got them through the checkpoints with no questions asked. They didn't even have to stop—the crossing arms were already raised by the time they got there, and they sped through.

He arrived, somewhat calmer, but no less irritable.

What was being played at here? What did the Canucks think they were doing?

And the Brits, for that matter.

Daniels stalked through the re-purposed conference rooms of the former hotel. The smell of lumber smacked him in the face, as it always did. Cubicle walls, filled with administrative positions. Plywood offices built onto the walls for higher ranking officers.

He made his way through it all, to a larger office built into the corner of the main conference room. He stopped. Took a breath. Knocked on the door.

"What." A grizzled bark, about as irritable as Daniels felt.

"It's Daniels."

A grumble, unintelligible through the door. Then: "Come on."

Daniels pushed through the door and into Colonel Lineberger's office.

Lineberger, lean and hatchet-faced and gray, lurked over his desk like a vulture over a bit of roadkill. "Close the door," he ordered.

Daniels did so, then turned to the colonel. "Where are the envoys?"

Lineberger hiked a thumb towards the ceiling. "Penthouse. With the president."

Daniels strode to the desk, his hands on his hips. “We got a Predator over North Carolina, supporting Griffin.”

“Uh-huh,” Lineberger mumbled, as though to question what this had to do with him.

“They just ID’d a Humvee in Fort Bragg, doing God-knows-what, and flying the fucking maple leaf.”

Lineberger stiffened. “Please tell me they didn’t shoot the bastards.”

Daniels felt another bolt of irritation. “No, colonel,” he ground out. “I told them to stand down. Obviously.”

Lineberger’s salt-and-pepper eyebrows cinched down over his sunken eyes. “What the hell are they doing in Fort Bragg?”

Daniels raised his palms up. “What a fantastic question. That’s what I’m asking you.”

Predictably, Lineberger bristled.

He couldn’t stand that Daniels was on equal footing with him.

And Daniels loved making it oh-so-apparent.

“Sounds like you’re about as in-the-know as I am at this juncture,” Daniels continued. “The question is, do we ask the envoys about it?”

“That sounds decidedly un-diplomatic.”

“They’re trying to play both sides,” Daniels finally asserted. Getting the suspicion off his chest felt relieving, but saying it out loud only served to make him more suspicious. “That’s what they’re doing. They’re not even sure who they want to support—us or the UES.”

“You don’t know that.”

Daniels snorted. “Please. Of course I do. That’s what any reasonable person would do. You’ve got two geopolitical entities where there used to be one. Both claim they're legitimate. Naturally, you send teams to both. Try to ascertain who's the better bet."

There was a knock at the office door.

"Christ," Lineberger snapped. "What?"

"Sir," a hesitant voice spoke on the other side. "I have Captain Griffin on the line from ETOC."

Lineberger looked skyward as though wishing for intercession from the heavens. "Come on."

The door opened and a lieutenant walked in, holding a satphone.

But he didn't bring it to Lineberger. He stepped up to Daniels. He cast an apologetic glance in the colonel's direction, and mumbled, "He asked to speak to Mr. Daniels."

Lineberger looked like he'd just smelled shit.

Daniels plucked the satphone from the lieutenant's hands. Griffin was technically a Project Hometown operator. And Daniels was technically the new head of Project Hometown.

"Daniels here," he said into the satphone.

Griffin's voice came over the line, sounding ruffled. "You got something you need to tell me?"

"Yes," Daniels replied. "Two days ago, we received a small contingent of Canadian and British troops that were sent as an envoy to Greeley. We had no prior warning of this. They just showed up. They didn't tell us that they had any other forces anywhere else in the States. But, as I just learned about ten minutes ago, it looks like they sent some down to Fort Bragg. Does that cover the bases?"

Silence on the line for a moment. "They're driving away. They captured, or possibly rescued, someone that was sneaking around Fort Bragg. Possibly a leftover civilian. Possibly a UES scout."

Daniels nodded to himself. "I understand. Thank you. Do nothing."

"Do nothing," Griffin echoed.

"For now, captain," Daniels sighed. "I'm getting my own feet underneath me. When the footing's more solid, I'll let you know. But for now, do nothing. Understood?"

"Understood. And if they engage us?"

"Then engage back. Anything else?"

"No, sir."

Daniels didn't say a goodbye. He turned the phone off and handed it back to the lieutenant, then shooed him out of the office and closed the door again. He turned back to Lineberger. "Diplomatically speaking, wouldn't it reflect poorly on us if we *didn't* notice their forces in North Carolina?"

Lineberger considered this. "If they really are testing our competence. Then yes." He leaned forward and pointed at Daniels. "But you need to get the fuel flowing again."

Daniels expression darkened. "You don't think that Canada has oil flowing? With the Yukon pipeline running right through their backyard?"

"We don't know what they have," Lineberger growled. "And whatever they do have is *theirs*, not ours. Until we make an alliance. And if they're looking to make an alliance with the stronger player, then it all comes down to the Gulf, and that asshole Ibarra."

Daniels let out a lengthy, disgruntled sigh. "He made it pretty clear that we were on the outs."

Lineberger smirked. “That was *your* doing. Your mistake. Now it’s your mess to clean up. Our limited access to oil makes us weak. If you can’t make peace with *Nuevas Fronteras* and get them shipping fuel to us again, then our alliance with Canada might be dead before it starts.”

“I’m working on it,” Daniels grumbled.

“Well, whatever you have working, work it faster. Our time table is shrinking.”

“Maybe.” Daniels folded his arms over his chest. “Are you going to talk to Briggs and our guests, or should I?”

That gave Lineberger pause, as Daniels knew it would. Here was a sticky situation. And no one wanted to get the stickiness on their hands. If Lineberger left it to Daniels then Daniels might end up screwing himself. Which would make Lineberger look good.

Then again, Daniels was pretty savvy, and Lineberger knew it. He might pull it off and come out looking clean on the other side. Which would only encourage Briggs to give him that official officer’s commission that he’d been gunning for.

Daniels knew the dilemma he was putting Lineberger in. And he enjoyed it.

“I’ll talk to them,” the colonel finally decided, erring on the side of political caution.

Daniels smiled, for no other reason than to make Lineberger feel that he’d done what Daniels wanted. “Sounds great.” He turned to the office door and shot over his shoulder, “I’ll work on soothing Ibarra’s hurt feelings. I’ll figure out how to get some oil flowing again.”

FIVE

TRIPROCK

"WHAT YOU DID WAS STUPID," Abe grumbled into the silence of the baking Texas afternoon.

Lee pulled his head up from the scoped .30-06. Propped himself up on his elbows and relaxed his neck. He sighed.

"I just want to make sure," Abe continued. "That we both understand that."

Lee kept his irritation in check by pretending that he was an unassociated third party, letting Abe vent. Because that's all this was about. Abe needed to get it off his chest. Lee's best option was to let him get it out so that they could move on with business.

"What part, exactly?" Lee asked, his voice devoid of inflection.

"The part where you decided you were going to try to kill both of them without my help."

"You helped. You shot the guy that was about to shoot me."

"I was *supposed* to shoot him first. And then you were going to kill the other guy. It should've been over in two seconds, not turn into a damned brawl."

Lee smacked his lips a few time. God, but he was thirsty right now. He settled back down onto the rifle and peered through the scope. In the distance lay their target: Triple Rocker Ranch.

"I'm sorry," Lee said.

"You don't sound very sorry."

"What do you want me to say, Abe?"

"I want you to tell me that you don't have a death wish."

Lee took a long time to answer, staring out through the shimmering mirage of the Texas plains. Should he care more about staying alive? Was he taking risks that he normally wouldn't take? Was he being reckless?

To a third party, maybe that's what it looked like.

But it wasn't recklessness. It was just…

I thought I'd be dead by now.

"Lee."

"I don't have a death wish."

"That took you a long time to answer."

"I don't have a death wish," Lee repeated. "I've got too many people to kill to want to die, Abe."

Lee's vision was focused through the scope, but he thought he could still feel Abe studying him, as though his gaze might peel back layers of deception and get to the truth. Lee let him stare. If there was another truth hiding inside of him, he wasn't aware of it himself.

Eventually Abe grumbled something under his breath, and Lee felt him settle down into the dirt beside him, refocusing on their objective.

The Triple Rocker Ranch—known locally as "Triprock"—was a smaller ranch, as far as Texas ranches went, and nowadays it housed more people than cattle.

It was too hard to keep the primals from eating the cattle anyways.

As far as Lee could estimate, it housed roughly two hundred people.

About fifty of them were cartel.

And one of those cartel was Joaquin Lozcano Leyva.

Down inside the barbed wire fences of Triprock, the people milled about in the hot sun, doing what needed to be done to survive. Taking care of what livestock they could manage to protect from the primals—smaller things like goats and chickens. A few, skinny cows that had to be guarded constantly while at pasture.

They also grew whatever they could pry out of the dry ground.

Those people not involved in the growing of food still had plenty of other tasks to get done. Survival was labor, and the labor was hard, and you had to keep long days if you hoped to see more of them.

As these peons scurried about, the cartel watched them from shady spots on the porches of the ranch houses. Or from the machine gun nest built into the hayloft of the barn. They ate their fair share, but they didn't work. Unless you considered it a legitimate vocation to keep a population tamed through the explicit threat of violence.

From twelve hundred yards away, Lee watched this through his riflescope. The dappled sunlight that reached him beneath the mesquite tree he was using as shade was still hot enough to make him sweat, but he blinked that sweat out of his eyes, and watched the reticle jitter as it hovered over the heat-shimmering image of a cartel man in a white cowboy hat with an AK-47 in his hands.

Lee placed the reticle over the man's heart and imagined easing slowly back on the trigger, feeling the gun buck, and then settling back into his sights during the three second flight time of that bullet, so that he could watch the hit. The splash. The body crumpling.

But he didn't.

Couldn't have done it, even if he'd wanted to.

Their current range was a little too much for a .30-06 projectile.

Besides, they weren't there to shoot anyone.

Not yet anyways.

"How much longer you wanna watch?" Abe mumbled, watching through a set of binoculars.

"Just wanna confirm that Joaquin is there."

"He's there," Abe asserted. "He never leaves without a dozen of his soldiers guarding him."

"You counted them, did you? They're all there?" Lee was being sarcastic. It would be hard to confirm whether a dozen out of fifty people were missing.

"No," Abe grunted. "But all their cars are here. The two technicals, the Humvee, the deuce-and-a-half, and the Mercedes. And Joaquin never goes anywhere without at least one technical. And he favors the Mercedes."

Lee panned his view over to where the cartel vehicles were all parked in what used to be a corral. "Yeah, I counted the vehicles up earlier," Lee sighed. "But I still wanna put eyes on."

"I'm surprised. Usually you're all hellfire to go and snap necks."

"Well. We only have a small chance of making this work. And all the ordnance we stole from that last cartel convoy is tied up—once we blow through it, we don't have any more left. So, you'll have to pardon me if I want to make absolutely sure Joaquin is there before we shoot our load. Figuratively speaking."

"Fine by me," Abe said. "You spotted any fuel trucks?"

Not this again.

Lee sighed through his nose, but kept his eyes in his sights, scanning Triprock for any sign of Joaquin. "If we see a fuel truck, we will commandeer it. And then you can drive it back to Georgia."

At the mention of the United Eastern States, Lee's brain did a strange little jig. It twirled through a series of images and feelings, and none of it was good, and all of it left him feeling hollow inside, like bad memories from another life.

Angela, who loved you once, and who you…what?

Marie, who doesn't even know that her sister is dead.

All those people, looking for a hero.

There's no heroes out here.

I can't go back.

I can never go back.

"Ranch house," Abe said.

For a second, Lee didn't compute. Then realized Abe had spotted something at the main ranch house. Lee panned steadily over, the image blurring as he shifted his hips and realigned his body…

There, stepping out onto the front porch of the ranch house.

Loose, light gray button up. Charcoal dress slacks. Short-cropped hair.

Joaquin Lozcano Leyva.

He stopped at the edge of the porch, one hand on the weathered railing, one hand holding a cheroot in his mouth. A puff of gray smoke from it caught in the hot breeze and carried away. His reflective sunglasses hid his eyes, but he seemed like he was looking out at the people as they scurried on their way, and Lee thought he saw the people scurrying a little faster.

Lee wanted to kill him. He wanted it bad enough to make his stomach tremble and his breath catch in his throat.

But they didn't have a rifle capable of shooting twelve hundred yards.

So this was going to get a little more personal.

"Target marked," Lee said, his voice all business now. "PID confirmed."

"Roger that," Abe replied, and his voice too had lost its conversational tone. "Let's get it done."

***

Lee faced six guards, all of them armed.

He stopped their stolen pickup truck at the main gate to Triprock, and he and Abe scanned across the cartel men that stood around it.

One had an old M60 machine gun that sat casually upon a sandbag nest. The others had a mix of rifles. A couple AKs. A couple ARs. One FAL.

Lee's heart knocked steadily on the inside of his chest. Fast, but more than anything, it knocked *hard*. But he kept his face relaxed. His body loose, though it jittered to move. To squirm under the weight of secrecy.

Behind the guards were the gates, which were just simple stamped metal—Lee could easily drive through them if he wanted to. But that would just turn the whole thing into a gunfight. And that would be counterproductive at the moment.

Beyond the gates, lay Triprock. Four houses, three barns, and a few large sheds. All lined by a cedar post and barbed wire fence. The cedar paling and deteriorating, and the barbed wire dark and rusty red.

Guards patrolled the inner perimeter, and stood watch from several key vantage points.

Lee and Abe, against fifty hostiles.

Not great odds.

Directly in front of them, the gate guards separated, and began to approach. Two hung back—the guy with the machine gun, and one other. The remaining four split into pairs, one pair going to Lee's side of the vehicle, the other going to Abe's side.

They did this without coordinating. They were practiced.

Probably decently trained.

Lee already had his window down.

The first man to reach him—the one with the FAL—was Hispanic. His partner looked white, and hung back, near the front tire.

"Who're you?" the leader with the FAL asked, blunt and aggressive.

"I'm Hank. This is Brody. We're from La Casa."

The leader remained suspicious. Lee noticed that, though the FAL was tucked under the man's armpit, the muzzle pointed right at Lee. If things went south, Lee was a dead man. He already knew what it was like to have a bullet penetrate his chest. This time it would be several bullets, and Julia wouldn't be there to bring him back to life…

The thought of her squeezed something painful in a deeply buried part of him.

Some of the fear left him. Displaced by hatred.

The leader traded a quick glance through the cab of the truck to the guards on the other side, who were eyeballing Abe. Lee and Abe remained relaxed, and focused on the leader. Just another day working for the cartel.

"Gimme the password," the leader demanded.

Lee's heart took a pause, and then started hitting harder than before. The adrenaline spiking his blood pressure. The blood pressure reshaping his cornea. Flattening it. Causing tunnel vision. He wanted to try to blink it away, but that would only make him look unsure of himself.

The relaxed expression remained fixed on his face with massive effort.

"Blue Moon," Lee said. Knowing, acknowledging, accepting, that his life hung on two words, and whether or not they were the truth or a lie.

The leader frowned, then took a step back and pointed at the front tire well. "You got a bullet hole, my man."

The bullet hole. From where Abe had shot the cartel man earlier. It had penetrated the man's head and gone through the sheet metal.

They'd cleaned the blood and brains off, but they couldn't do anything about the hole.

Lee nodded, hoping this meant that the password had worked. "Yeah, it's been there a while now."

He immediately regretted saying that.

The man could very easily inspect the bullet hole, where the paint had been ripped away and the metal exposed. If it had been there a long time, the metal would have begun to rust.

Shit. He should've kept his mouth shut.

The leader shrugged. "Alright. So what do you want at Triprock?"

Lee swallowed on a dry throat, but he tried to make it as natural as possible. "Hermanco sent me. Private message for Señor Leyva."

The leader pointed his chin towards Abe. "And what about him?"

"He's my backup. In case anything happened on the road."

The leader seemed to be weighing how many more questions he wanted to ask, but he also seemed to be getting bored. His initial suspicion now allayed, he was fast losing interest.

He took a step back. "Alright. Listen to my instructions and do exactly as you're told."

"Okay."

"Pull in through the gate—very slowly. Then turn to your left, and park it right up against those barrels. You see them?"

"Yes."

"Then you will exit the vehicle. If you have weapons, don't touch them. Leave them in the vehicle. We will escort you to Señor Leyva. Understand?"

"Yes."

The leader waved them on.

Lee tried to read him, to see if he was just getting them to relax and park the truck so that when they started pumping Lee and Abe full of lead, they didn't accidentally accelerate into one of the houses.

But the leader seemed bored. Uncaring.

Lee pulled his foot off the brake, and let the truck coast forward.

The man beside the machine gunner opened the gate for them, and they rolled through, then parked it right where they'd been instructed.

Lee took that time to breathe, trying to lower his heart rate. A high heart rate meant muddled thinking and lack of dexterity. And Lee was going to need all his faculties to pull this off.

Too bad he was half-starved and partially dehydrated.

But there wasn't much he could do about that.

He shut the engine off, and stepped out.

The leader with the FAL had remained at the gate. That was clearly his duty. But he'd dispatched the two men with AKs to escort them. Both looked like they were original cartel members—not local populace pressed into service. They had that lean, feral look to them.

One took up a position a few paces away and leveled his AK at Lee and Abe.

The other let his rifle hang on a strap and gestured at them. "Turn around. Hands up. Feet apart."

Lee and Abe exchanged a quick, worried glance, but complied.

They'd planned for this. This was a part of the procedures.

One of their "sources" had told them so. And Lee had to trust that intelligence. Because without it, they didn't have anything. That particular source Lee had been forced to hurt a lot more than the others. So there was a chance that the intelligence was born more out of desperation to get Lee to stop.

Lee stood there, facing the bed of the truck with his feet spread and his arms up. One of the two men stepped up and patted him down. He did a good job. Kept a grip on the back of Lee's collar, and a leg pinioned right behind Lee's, so that if Lee started to bow up, the guard could easily take him down.

As the pat-down continued, Lee stared straight ahead, letting that fear alchemize into hatred again. His eyes fixated on the main ranch house. On the porch where Joaquin Leyva had stood, smoking his cheroot, not so long ago. He was in that house. The man that Lee wanted.

A stepping stone.

All of these bodies were just stepping stones to Lee.

A way to get to where he was going.

And at the end of that path of bodies, there was Mateo Ibarra.

Somehow, someway, using some method that Lee didn't even have a shadow of a concept of yet, he was going to do it. If he kept going. The way would open up. If he stayed focused, the opportunity would arise.

Mateo could not hide from him forever.

The guards finished patting Abe down.

"Okay. Turn around."

Lee and Abe turned.

One of the cartel men gestured between them. "Which of you has the message?"

Lee nodded. "That's me."

"Give me the message and I'll deliver it to him."

Lee pulled a breath into his lungs, and then let it out, so that it wouldn't get trapped in his chest and he wouldn't appear tense. "I'm sorry. But Hermanco instructed me to deliver the message directly to Señor Leyva, and no one else, on my life. I swore to him. Otherwise I would give you the message."

The guard squinted at Lee like he was trying to perceive through a veil of bullshit.

Eventually he sneered, but relented. "Fine. You. Alone." He gestured to Abe. "You can wait here, or…refresh yourself." The guard motioned for Lee to follow with his head, and then began walking away, towards the ranch house.

Lee followed, separating from Abe.

***

Abe watched him go, feeling his pulse thumping in his neck, but knowing that his thick beard probably covered it. He turned to the remaining guard, who looked like he was about to dismiss Abe and go back to the front gate.

"Got any good girls around here?" Abe asked him.

The suspicious expression melted and the guard's eyes gleamed. He chuckled. "Take your pick."

Abe looked out at Triprock. With the arrival of more apparent cartel, the people of Triprock had made themselves as scarce as possible. Best not to be noticed. But there were still a few people out—no choice but to do their chores and hope to be ignored.

There was a pretty girl filling up water from a windmill powered well. Young. Dark haired.

"What about her?" Abe asked, pointing at her.

The girl glanced up at him, noticing his attention even at fifty yards. She immediately looked back down. Like she wanted to get away. But the water jugs would only fill up so fast.

The guard peered at her. "Oh. Yeah. *Muy bonita.* But scary. She'll scratch you. *Como el gato.*" A smile directed at Abe. "But maybe you like that."

Abe smiled back. "Well, I guess we'll just have to see."

Abe patted the side of the pickup truck as though to bid it farewell, and then set off across the yard towards the girl and the well. The yard that sat between a cluster of buildings—the main ranch house to the left, the main barn to the right, and a few smaller structures filling in the gaps—was mostly hard-packed dirt. But some green Bermuda grass clung to the edges of the heavily trodden paths.

The girl remained agonizingly focused on her task, like she was willing the water to fill up faster. But as Abe drew closer, her eyes glanced up at him fearfully, and then back to her slowly-filling water jugs.

Filled, the jugs must've weighed close to eighty pounds. And she was such a small thing. But Abe saw the wiry strength in her tan-skinned arms.

He stopped on the other side of the cement trough.

The girl said nothing.

"I have a gift for you," Abe said.

Her whole body stiffened. She straightened up. Looked Abe in the eyes. And gave him the tiniest of nods.

Abe moved around the water trough, heart thudding. He could tell that a few of the cartel men were watching. Curious as to how scratched up Abe was going to get.

He slid up next to the girl. Intimately close. His hand touched hers where it gripped the side of the trough. His other hand touched her shoulder.

The girl stared at the water jugs.

Out of the side of her mouth, she whispered, “Red building to your left. The room in the far back, to the right.”

Abe’s hand crept down her body to her lower back, and up her arm towards her breasts.

She spun and slapped the shit out of him.

It was a hard hit. Abe was shocked at the force behind it. He almost stumbled.

He came back at her. She let out little cry and sunk her fingernails into his face under his eyes, and kneed him hard in the thigh, but thankfully missed his crotch. By then he’d closed the gap between them and managed to get his arms around her. He spun her around and yanked her off her feet while she continued to kick and spit at him—very much like a cat.

He wrenched one of her arms behind her back, pulling the wrist up so that it was almost up between her shoulders, and with the other hand he buried his fingers into her long black hair and twisted until he had a solid grip.

“Easy now, bitch!” he growled at her.

Up in the hayloft overlooking the yard, the cartel guards in the machine gun nest hooted and made catcalls.

Abe hauled her forward, forcing her onto her tiptoes so that she couldn't get enough traction to resist him. She groaned and cried out from the pain, but she couldn't resist without dislocating her shoulder or ripping a chunk of her hair out.

Abe angled for the red building. He made it up the steps and kicked the door open. It was a shotgun house. One long hall going straight to the back. Doors on both sides of the hall. A bunkhouse.

Abe loosened his grip as he pushed her into the hallway and kicked the door closed behind him. The other doors on either side of him were all closed as he passed them. But he wasn't sure if they were occupied or not. And he wasn't sure whether the occupants were sleeping or screwing.

At the far back, the last door on the right hung open a few inches.

Abe shouldered this open.

The room was empty, save for a dirty mattress on the ground. A single window over the bed.

Abe shoved the girl, aiming for the mattress, then turned around and closed the door behind him, and locked it. He whipped around, not sure whether she would attack again, but the girl now sat on the edge of the mattress, rubbing her shoulder, and glaring up at Abe.

Abe stalked across the room, and she didn't move to get away from him.

He squatted down, about arm's length from her. "I'm Abe Darabie," he whispered.

She nodded. "I'm Sally Sigman."

"Are you okay?" Abe looked at her shoulder. "I had to make it look real."

She smiled. "Oh, I'm fine." She nodded towards his face. "Your face, though…"

Abe grinned, and felt the scratches on his face burn. "I'm not worried about my face. But thanks for not actually kneeing me in the balls." Abe glanced up at the window. "Did the Robledos get our last drop?"

Sally's head trembled up and down. "Yes. Eric and Cat are ready." She pulled a white piece of cloth from her pants pocket, and scrambled up to the window. She lifted it a few inches, put the cloth over the sill, and then slid the window closed again, all the while keeping her head down.

Abe looked around the room. Worry starting to mount on his chest. "You did stow the stuff, right?"

Sally nodded and then stepped off the mattress.

Abe nodded, understanding. He knelt down next to the mattress, then paused and looked at Sally. Oddly, as rough as their acting had been outside, his next request made his face flush. "You should…uh…probably make some noises."

Sally's face turned about as red as Abe's.

How old was she? No more than eighteen.

But she nodded.

Abe lifted the mattress, as Sally covered her own mouth and began to make muffled noises of pain and violation.

Under the mattress was a loaded M4 and three extra magazines.

SIX

JOAQUIN

LEE DIDN'T KNOW the layout of the main ranch house.

He could make educated guesses, based on information given to him by Eric and Catalina Robledo—their contacts inside Triprock. But this was the first time he'd actually stepped foot in it.

"Wait here," one of the guards grunted at him, and then left him standing in the foyer.

Lee took steady breaths.

Smelled the musty, grassy scent of faint cigar smoke.

Joaquin and his cheroot. Close by.

Lee was in the lion's den now. And he couldn't turn around and walk back out.

Get the layout.

He let his eyes scan across the interior of the ranch house, absorbing it with an almost robotic intensity of focus.

The atrium was front and center.

To his left, a dining room. To his right, a living room.

Both the dining room and living room were occupied. Two men in the dining room, playing cards at the table. Three men in the living room—two lounging on a couch, the third, looking out a window.

All were armed. Long guns and handguns.

They gave him passing, suspicious glances, but no one's gaze lingered on him. They evaluated him, and then decided he was nothing to worry about, and went back to doing whatever they were doing.

Lee had learned how to become someone else. He'd been all sorts of people, since Julia left him. He'd been an animal. He'd been a killer. He'd been a manic cannibal. Several times he'd been a member of *Nuevas Fronteras*.

Now he was a messenger bitch.

He stood with his shoulders slumped, and his eyes cast down. Hands clasped at his waist.

He was someone you didn't need to worry about.

The guards returned, coming out of a swinging doorway down the main hall that Lee suspected led into the kitchen.

"He's ready for you. Come."

Shit.

Lee had hoped they would keep him waiting longer. He hadn't given Abe enough time.

Lee hesitated until the two guards that had escorted him nudged him forward, and then he began to follow.

They escorted him down the hall and pushed through the swinging door, holding it open for Lee. It was indeed the kitchen. He saw the men in the dining room to his left. To his right, a small kitchen table.

Joaquin Leyva sat at the table, puffing on his cheroot. Tobacco smoke hung around the ceiling over their heads. It smelled heavy and dark.

Joaquin inspected him as he entered.

Lee dipped his head, properly intimidated. This wasn't entirely an act, though what Lee truly felt in his chest was a mix of hatred and the sort of tentative respect you gave to wild animals. Animals that could be unpredictable. Animals that could maul you out if you rubbed them the wrong way.

A short, dark-skinned man stood off to the side of the kitchen, eyeing him.

Joaquin's body guard, perhaps?

Lee stopped a few paces from the table. His two escorts hovered close on either side of him, and slightly behind.

Again, Lee took in as much as he could with a quick sweep of his eyes.

The short man had a pistol in his waistband.

Lee assumed that Joaquin was also armed, though he kept it covered under his shirt.

Joaquin raised his eyebrows at Lee. "Well?"

"Uh, yes sir," Lee glanced at the two guards to either side of him. "Hermanco has sent me with a message for you, sir."

Joaquin nodded. "I'm aware of why you're here. I'm asking you to give me the message now."

Stall.

"Yes, sir." Lee made another pointed glance to the guards. "I was told that it was for your ears only."

Joaquin considered this, taking a pull on the cheroot and letting the smoke leak out of his lips, all the while watching Lee with sharp, scrutinizing eyes.

Abe needed ten minutes. That was what they had agreed upon.

It had only been about five. Maybe six.

Four minutes was a long damn time to stall with someone like Joaquin.

“I’m not in the habit of doing what Hermanco says,” Joaquin quipped. “You will give me the message now.”

Lee’s heart tried to accelerate, and he needed it to slow down. His palms began to sweat. He resisted the urge to wipe them.

He had to play their ace in the hole.

Unfortunately, they only had one. And how trustworthy it was, again came down to whether or not you could trust the word of someone you tortured.

Lee took a tentative step forward. Not too close, but enough to seem like he was earnest in his desire for privacy. He lowered his voice. “Sir, he told me to tell you that it is about the…*Los Zetas.*”

Joaquin gave no reaction to this. He sat there, very still, his cigar in his left hand, trailing a thin line of smoke towards the clouds swirling over their heads. He kept his right hand below the table where Lee couldn’t see it.

Lee knew he was right-handed. Which meant he was either keeping that hand free to go for his gun, or the gun was already in his hand, pointed at Lee under the table.

Joaquin gestured to the chair across from him with his left hand. “Sit.”

Lee didn’t want to sit. Sitting would put him in a disadvantaged position. He wouldn’t be able to move and react as fast. In the space between heart beats he weighed the possibility of refusing to sit and decided that would cripple him even worse.

He took the seat.

Slowly.

Every second precious, and bought with the currency of the tenuous trust that still wavered between him and Joaquin like a rickety rope bridge over a chasm. If he did too much stalling, Joaquin was just as likely to kill him without warning. If he didn't do enough, then the entire mission would go down the shitter.

He sat. Fidgeted. Looked at the guards again. Then back at Joaquin. Then placed his hands on the table top. Clasped his fingers together, and then separated them, laying them flat on the table. Giving every indication that he was wildly uncomfortable.

Sending the signal that Joaquin was in control.

Joaquin sighed. Looked at the inch of ash on the end of his cigar. Frowned. "Hermanco didn't tell me that he was sending a messenger. Usually he tells me ahead of time if he has a private message for me. That way I can be prepared to receive it."

The statement hung in the air.

Did Joaquin want Lee to address this concern, or was he just talking?

Lee's source hadn't told him anything about advanced messages, warning of other incoming messages. He'd just told Lee about the *Los Zetas* cartel, which had made a resurgence in Mexico. The problem was, a lot of *Nuevas Fronteras* had originally been *Los Zetas*.

Now, apparently, some loyalties were in question.

How much time do I need?

Joaquin remained silent.

Lee decided to push forward. "Hermanco did not confide in me. I understood that he was concerned about...certain people's loyalties."

"Perhaps," Joaquin squinted at Lee, and Lee didn't like the expression in his eyes. Like a cat waiting to pounce. "But I would have thought he would communicate this to me when we spoke, not twenty minutes ago."

Shit.

Lee resisted the urge to swallow.

Joaquin leaned forward. "What he *did* tell me, was that he had lost contact with a small group that he'd sent out from La Casa. Two of his men that he'd sent to investigate a claim from one of our locals about having captured *Nadie y Ninguno*."

Lee's stomach plummeted.

"When I asked Hermanco about it, he told me they were in a white pickup truck." Joaquin's lips twitched. "Same make and model as the one you arrived in."

Lee had to say something. He felt the guards tensing up behind him. They were getting ready to execute him, and Lee knew he was on a razor's edge—all Joaquin had to do was nod, and Lee would be snuffed out.

Lee frowned at the man across from him. "La Casa has a half dozen of those pickups."

It wouldn't be enough, and Lee knew it.

He forced himself to relax. His demeanor shifting.

As he relaxed back into his chair, he placed the heels of his palms against the edge of the table, and he placed his foot against one of the table legs.

"Besides," Lee said, his tone changed from nervous to confident, hoping it would be enough to capture Joaquin's curiosity. He didn't need to convince Joaquin—only to keep him talking for another minute. "At this point, I have the strong suspicion that I'm the only person that knows who in

Triprock has been leaking information to your enemies."

Joaquin's eyes were half-lidded with lack of concern. "If I'm curious, I'll just have Hermanco tell me."

"Hermanco is an idiot," Lee said. "You and I both know that."

"Ahhh," Joaquin sighed. "So now you lay your cards on the table. You are an ambitious man, then."

Lee didn't respond.

Joaquin leaned forward. "And if you betray Hermanco to me, do you think that I will be impressed with you, or do you think I will believe you have a lack of loyalty?"

"I'm not betraying Hermanco," Lee said. "Hermanco is loyal to you. I'm just stating the obvious. He doesn't see the problems that are right in front of him. I'm not looking to take his position, Señor Leyva. Consider my offer one of good faith, as I can tell that you suspect me."

"Why don't I just get on the phone with Hermanco right now and confirm whether he sent you?"

"Yes," Lee nodded. "Please do."

It was a gamble.

Obviously, Hermanco wouldn't back up Lee's story. But if Joaquin decided to call him, it would take time. Precious time. Maybe just enough.

Joaquin considered Lee for a moment longer, his lips pursed.

Lee took the moment to throw even more confusion into the mix. He glanced sideways at the short, dark-skinned man, then back at Joaquin.

Quirked his eyebrow. Then repeated the very obvious gesture.

Joaquin followed Lee's look.

The short man stood to the side of the kitchen. He became abruptly aware that Joaquin was looking at him.

Joaquin tilted his head. "Arturo, you would never betray me, would you?"

Arturo came upright off the counter. "Of course not!" Then Arturo uttered something in Spanish that Lee took to be some sort of oath or swear.

Joaquin pointed the smoking stub of his cheroot at Lee. "Because this gringo is saying that you are betraying me."

"Let me kill him."

Joaquin looked at Lee. "That is what you were implying by your eyes, no?"

Come on, Abe! Lee pled. Then, aloud: "Of course not. Arturo would never betray you."

Joaquin frowned, now not sure what the gringo across from him was actually trying to say.

Arturo took a step towards Lee, issuing a rapid and vehement string of Spanish.

Lee smiled. Not because he felt any joy or confidence, but simply because he thought it might confuse Joaquin further. "Señor Leyva. You know what I'm saying."

Joaquin let out a small chuff of breath. Then shook his head. "I know that you are playing games with me. Arturo—"

Lee rocked forward and spoke over Joaquin: "Eric and Catalina Robledo! They're working against you! Surely you've noticed? They've been secretly passing intelligence to *Nadie y Ninguno.*

And they've been receiving weapons and ordnance in return. They're planning to overthrow you!"

Joaquin's lips grew thin. "You speak too much nonsense."

"Bring them in. See if they don't admit to it."

"I think you are just trying to confuse me."

"You're already confused!"

"Enough!" Joaquin snapped, and snatched his pistol from his waistband.

Outside, thunder crashed.

A detonation of high explosives.

As Joaquin brought his pistol up and over the table to point at Lee's head—and probably to plow a hole through it—Joaquin flinched at the thump of the explosion and his eyes jagged up to see the flash of light outside.

Abe had come, not a second too soon.

Lee snatched the muzzle of the pistol with both hands, pressing it away from his face as it fired, sending a round blasting off into the house. His right foot against the table leg, Lee shoved with everything he had, and twisted the pistol out of Joaquin's grip.

The table struck Joaquin in the midsection. The two of them separated. The pistol went with Lee.

At the same time, Lee flew backward in his chair.

The two guards stared in shock as Lee arced between them, and as he fell, he racked the spent shell casing from the chamber of the pistol…

He hit the ground on his back. The chair cracked. The breath exploded out of his lungs.

He punched out so fast that the guards barely even registered the motion before he put two 9mm projectiles through the face of the guard to his left, and then pivoted—

—the guard to the right had more warning, and he brought his AK up—

—Lee fired without aiming, four rounds that clattered across the AK, and then into the man's torso.

The bodies were still dropping, rifles still clattering to the kitchen floor.

Arturo, still clawing his pistol out of his waistband.

Lee pumped rounds into him, hammering him backwards into the kitchen sink, until Lee's pistol locked back on an empty magazine.

Joaquin tried to pull himself upright.

Lee hurled the empty pistol at him.

It smacked Joaquin dead in the face, causing him to yelp and stagger, and giving Lee an additional second.

Lee rolled off the broken chair. Into one of the fallen bodies. He seized the AK.

The front of the ranch house erupted in automatic fire—both incoming and outgoing.

The rounds moaned and warbled, so close over Lee's head he swore he felt them splitting his hairs.

He flattened himself to the ground.

Joaquin must have realized that this was the healthiest option. He dropped and curled into a ball, his teeth bared, hands up near his face like they might ward off bullets.

The air was filled with violence. The crashing gunfire, the smack of projectiles. Men screamed. White drywall dust floated thickly in the air.

Ten feet from him, Joaquin stared at Lee, and Lee stared back.

The only thing keeping them from going for each other's throats was the deluge of lead, inches above them.

They watched each other, their bodies like greyhounds in the slips, waiting for the cessation of gunfire. Each planning an immediate action without knowing what the other was going to do—their actions were simply going to ram into each other, and the faster one would win.

But Lee had an edge.

He knew when the gunfire would stop.

Blow up the machine gun nest, he and Abe had agreed. *Then soak the front of the ranch house with gunfire for ten seconds.*

And Lee had been counting.

Three.

Two.

One.

Lee moved on faith, even before his numb ears detected the stop in the gunfire. He lurched off the ground, and then threw himself, feet first, towards the overturned kitchen table.

Joaquin saw him coming. Tried to get to his feet.

Lee's feet hit the top of the overturned table, and he kicked as hard as he could manage. The table shot towards Joaquin, ramming the man in the face and chest with a cracking noise and a yelp of pain.

Lee hit the ground again. Rolled.

Two guards, stumbling through the kitchen doorway, coughing through air that was thick with dust and smoke.

It seemed they thought the kitchen might be a refuge.

They were wrong.

Lee fired two bursts.

The first guard spun in a little circle.

The other simply slumped where he stood.

Lee rolled again, this time pulling his feet under him.

Joaquin pushed the table away from him with a roar and then shoved it at Lee, aiming to use it as a ram just like Lee had. Lee saw it coming and raised his shin, just in time to catch the edge of the table. Pain spiked through his leg, but the table shoved off, deflected.

Joaquin dove for Arturo's dead body—and the pistol still in his waistband.

Lee took two quick steps and punted Joaquin right in the face.

Joaquin hit the ground on top of Arturo's dead body, twitching and moaning.

Gunfire burst into the kitchen, directed at Lee.

Despite the fact that Lee's body was criss-crossed and pockmarked with the scars from old bullet wounds, he'd never got over his aversion to them.

He dropped.

The rounds went over his head.

He hit the ground hard on both knees, dimly aware that his legs were going to be wrecked—if he managed not to die.

He fired a long burst at the swinging kitchen door, and heard a cry, and the tumble of a body hitting the ground.

Lee wheezed a curse, then struggled to his feet, his bruised knees and aching foot making his lower limbs feel like clumsy wooden protrusions.

Gunfire chattered back and forth outside. People screamed commands at each other. They screamed in rage at the people they tried to kill, and in fear of the ones that tried to kill them back.

Was that Sally or Eric or Catalina screaming?

Can't make an omelet without breaking a few eggs.

Lee turned on his aching legs and evaluated Joaquin.

The man was coming to, his eyes no longer rolled back, but blinking and trying to focus. Insensate hands groping for reality.

Footsteps reverberated through the floors of the ranch house.

There's still bad guys in here with me.

And their first instinct would be to rally at their boss.

Lee crossed to Joaquin and gave him a buttstock to the temple to put him under for a little longer. Could've also caused serious brain damage, but again, broken eggs and omelets and whatnot.

Joaquin went back to twitching.

Lee growled and seized a hold of the table and dragged it to the swinging kitchen door with all the bullet holes in it. He shoved it into the doorway, jamming the door in an open position so it blocked the hall.

He snagged the other guard's AK on his way back to Joaquin. Grumbling and swearing and limping, Lee seized Joaquin by the collar and heaved him over to the other side of the kitchen where they were less exposed.

Up against the counters, with the bulk of the refrigerator standing between him and the swinging kitchen door. The cased opening that led to the dining room was dead ahead, and the backdoor that led from the kitchen to the outside was directly behind him.

He considered using Joaquin as a bullet shield, but decided that Joaquin was a fighter, and would make trouble for Lee when he regained consciousness. So he put the man on his belly and then knelt on his shoulders.

Shouts in Spanish. Footsteps from the hallway he'd blocked with the table and the swinging door.

Lee leaned out and fired a burst from his AK that clattered through the walls and into the hall on the other side. Then he pulled himself back behind the fridge. He couldn't tell if he'd hit anybody.

Return fire belched back at him. He felt the impacts of the bullets striking the fridge.

Lee issued a steady stream of invectives.

From somewhere outside, another sizeable explosion rattled windows and shook walls.

That would be the crew house. They were a little late in blowing that one, and Lee wasn't sure how many cartel had been inside when they'd reduced it to splinters from the ordnance that Catalina Robledo had placed in the crawlspace beneath its floors.

But it made Lee smile.

That would be the last of their ordnance, but it was worth it.

Someone peeked into the kitchen from the dining room.

Lee fired off a three-round burst that smattered across the cased opening, but the shots were too wide.

The person ducked away and started yelling at his comrades.

Hopefully they'd seen that Lee was perched on top of their boss.

Maybe that would make them hesitate, rather than blind-firing a magazine at him.

Lee began firing his AK at a steady rate—one round every second or so. He did it with one hand, and with his support hand, he reached down and stripped the mag out of the other AK, aware that he was going to go empty very soon.

One of the cartel made a brave dive into the room, yelling and firing wildly.

Lee took a half-second to use the iron sights on the rifle and plugged four rounds into him. He collapsed, moaning and struggling for wind, but his hands clutched his chest rather than his rifle.

Lee didn't finish him.

Let him sit there. His body would serve as a small barricade, and his blood and tears might convince the others that being brave was a bad idea.

Lee fired another two rounds at the edge of the cased opening, further reducing the moulding to splinters.

The AK went empty.

Lee swiped the old mag out and rocked the new one in before the empty one had hit the floor. He slapped the bolt back and let it forward on a new round.

The brave man in the opening went ahead and died, finally.

From the front of the ranch house, someone yelled in English: "Hands up!"

Lee didn't know who had spoken it, or whether the person they'd spoken to even understood English, but it didn't matter. What followed was an explosion of gunfire.

Lee stayed where he was, keeping the doorway covered, and waiting.

Beneath him, Joaquin started to come back to consciousness.

Dammit, Abe, come on!

Lee could only split his attention in so many directions. They were so close now that it would be just typical to get distracted by Joaquin and then have one of his thugs dip into the doorway at the wrong moment while Lee was trying to subdue Joaquin, and then Lee would be dead.

Just goddamned typical.

The backdoor rattled on its hinges, causing Lee to start.

Beneath him, Joaquin began to move with more purpose, and his heavy breaths started to form words in Spanish that sounded a lot to Lee like he was being cursed out.

Lee tucked the buttstock of the AK under his armpit, and with his left hand, seized Joaquin by the back of his neck. "Don't start! I'll snap your goddamn neck!"

The backdoor was silent for a few beats of Lee's thudding pulse.

Then someone on the other side knocked.

"Condor! Condor!" A voice said. "Lee, you okay?"

Relief came over Lee like a warm blanket.

"I'm good," Lee called back. "You're clear."

The door opened, and Abe stood there, eyes wide, beard glistening with sweat. His rifle was up, and he scanned straight through the kitchen to the door into the dining room. "All clear!" he shouted through.

Lee kept his grip on the back of Joaquin's neck.

Joaquin strained to turn his head and put his eyes on Lee. "You're dead men. I'll gut you alive for this. I'm going to pull your intestines out of your asshole and hang you from them."

Lee considered ramming the muzzle of the AK repeatedly into Joaquin's skull, until the angled tip of it broke through and started mashing his brains to jelly.

He was a rabid dog that needed to be put down.

Lee *needed* to put him down…

But right when he thought he might just pummel this animal's skull in, Sally swooped in through the cased opening to the dining room, holding a scoped rifle that Lee recognized—it was one of the guns they had smuggled in to Eric and Catalina.

She looked at Lee, and her expression was one of absolute amazement, and that was the only thing that saved Joaquin's life in that moment. "Holy shit," she muttered. "I didn't actually think you were going to pull it off."

Joaquin tried to strain his head around to get a look at Sally. "You little bitch. You cunt!"

Abe nudged Lee in the arm, and Lee looked over at him. In Abe's hand was a long strip of cloth, wound tightly into a roll.

It took some doing, because Joaquin refused to cooperate, but after Abe slammed a fist into his gut, Lee was able to get the rag into his mouth, and then between the two of them they planted the man's face into the floor so that his nose crunched and cracked and blood began to pool. Lee tied the gag at the back of Joaquin's head—extra tight.

While Lee and Abe handled the gag, one of the rebellious residents of Triprock used baling twine to bind Joaquin's wrists together.

Sally stood, glaring down at Joaquin with utter loathing.

"How's the rest of Triprock?" Lee asked Abe.

Abe nodded, but glanced at Lee. "All good. It's secure."

The underlying message of Abe's look told Lee that not everything was perfect, but he didn't want to discuss it in front of Joaquin. Lee nodded and gave Abe an understanding look. They would talk about it later. In private.

Lee rolled Joaquin onto his back and looked down at him.

Abe stood over Lee's shoulder.

Joaquin's eyes flipped back and forth between the two of them.

Lee and Abe both smiled.

Like starving men might smile at a fat, cornered hen.

"Look," Abe commented. "He's putting it together."

And indeed he was. All the clues connected in Joaquin's brain.

And for the slimmest moment, through the rage and defiance that clouded Joaquin's features, Lee saw a glimmer of true, abject fear.

Because he knew who they were. And he knew what came next.

SEVEN

THE VALLEY

IT WAS SOMETIME AROUND SUNSET, when Joaquin was staring at the ceiling, repeating the same prayer in Spanish, that Lee wished he had found Joaquin's family.

Joaquin smartly kept separate from them, so they couldn't be used against him. But Lee had uncovered some whisperings of where they might be—a wife, and two daughters.

Lee had wanted to hunt them down and use them against Joaquin.

Abe had restrained him. His arguments had been in the name of humanity.

Lee had heard his arguments, but not listened to them. He didn't *feel* them. He was not convicted. He simply agreed to it, because he knew that if he displayed that level of cruelty, he would push Abe away.

So.

Lee had to do it the old fashioned way.

Which, on someone like Joaquin, took a lot of time, and a lot of effort.

But everyone breaks. Eventually.

The settlement of Triprock had taken back what was rightfully theirs. And they'd given Lee and

Abe a small slaughterhouse in the northeastern corner of the complex. It was here, out of the way, amongst rusted hooks and cement floors with drains in them, that Lee discreetly did what he needed to do.

Hopefully out of earshot of the people of Triprock.

Though Lee suspected some of the members of the community who'd had family murdered and raped by the cartel that had taken up residence amongst them, might find comfort in the sounds coming from the slaughterhouse.

After the last glimmer of sunlight died in the west, Lee determined that he was probably wearing Joaquin numb, and that wouldn't do. So he decided to give the man a respite. They unhooked him from where he hung, battered and bruised, and purple-eyed, and swollen-lipped. They threw him into a corner, and then used a chain to secure him to a support pole. They gave him a cup of water. And then they retreated.

The slaughterhouse was not large. Lee reckoned it had been used more for smaller livestock than cattle, and maybe hadn't even been used in the last few decades. It might've been a holdover from earlier times—everything in it seemed very old.

It was only a single room, so Lee and Abe went to the far side to quietly converse, and they were able to keep an eye on Joaquin while they did it.

"Some people just don't break," Abe mumbled, looking over Lee's shoulder at Joaquin.

"Everyone breaks," Lee said.

"With time. But do we have that kind of time?"

"We have the time that we have. If he doesn't break, then oh well. We move on." Even as Lee said it though, he had an uncomfortable feeling that Abe was right. They just didn't have the right buttons to push. Yes, they caused Joaquin pain. But that wasn't enough. Not for this man.

He wasn't telling Lee what he wanted to know.

He wasn't telling Lee how to get to Mateo Ibarra.

Lee changed the subject. "What happened during the takedown?"

Abe worked some saliva around in his mouth. Spat it off to the side. "First explosion went off well. Took the guys in the barn, in the machine gun nest. Eric and Catalina and their people were in proper position. Laid some good hate down on the cartel boys. But we didn't get them all."

"Shit." Lee made a face. "How many got away?"

Abe shrugged. "Dunno. They took the Mercedes and one of the Humvees. That's all I can tell you. I wasn't witness to it—got told about it later. But some amount of them—a dozen at the most—got out of here."

Lee started to rub his face, but then thought better of it: Joaquin's blood was all over his hands. "Which means we really don't have much time."

"No."

"Is Triprock aware?"

"Oh, they're aware."

"Are they mounting a defensive?"

Abe looked sad. "Yeah."

"You don't think it'll be enough."

Abe gave Lee a look that told him it was a stupid question. “Of course it won’t,” he murmured. “NF is going to roll in here and wipe this place off the map.”

Lee turned and looked back at Joaquin, chained to the post. Lee shook his head. “I don’t wanna be around when they get here.”

Abe didn’t respond.

Lee looked at him. “We got bigger fish to fry, my friend.”

“Like what?” Abe said, sounding tired. “Joaquin hasn’t told you how to get Mateo. You have no plan.”

“I do have a plan,” Lee insisted. “I want La Casa.”

“They’ll be on high alert after this,” Abe pointed out. “Might even be some of the boys that escaped from here ran over to there.”

“Maybe. But it’s been pretty shabbily protected. It’s worth taking a look at anyway. Because I’d like to pour more salt in Mateo’s wounds. We keep pissing him off, eventually he’ll do something stupid. Eventually he’ll show himself.”

Abe didn’t respond to that. He shifted his gaze out into a neutral area, and Lee knew he wasn’t looking at anything in particular. Just *not* looking at Lee.

“La Casa’s got tankers,” Lee said. “Thought you’d be happy about that.”

Abe didn’t look happy. More like he just wanted to sleep for a couple days. Lee felt the exhaustion coming up on him as well. But they had no time to rest. Not here in Triprock anyways. Not with *Nuevas Fronteras* pissed off and on the war path.

"When did you stop giving a shit about the UES?" Abe asked, beleaguered.

Lee's gaze narrowed on his partner. "When did you lose your stomach?"

Abe took in a deep breath through his nose and sighed it out. He nodded towards Joaquin. "What are you gonna do with him?"

"Kill him," Lee said, not bothering to keep his voice down. And if Joaquin heard, he didn't show it. He was a cool customer. "Or give him to the people here."

"They might be able to use him as a hostage," Abe pointed out.

Lee shrugged. "I highly doubt Mateo will give a shit."

"Probably not. But it's the best chance we can give them. We owe them that much."

Lee nodded. "You're right."

He walked back to Joaquin and squatted in front of him.

Joaquin raised his eyes. Or, more appropriately, his *eye*, as the other one was purple and swollen shut. He still managed to look defiant.

Lee smiled at him. "Salty to the last, my friend. Good for you." Lee felt the exhaustion that Abe had already hinted at. It came over him in a sudden wave that nearly demanded he lay down, right there in front of Joaquin. "These two questions will not betray *Nuevas Fronteras*. I simply ask them, fighter to fighter."

"Fuck you."

Lee smirked, as though he expected that, but pressed on anyways. "Has *Nuevas Fronteras* killed Terrance Lehy?"

Joaquin gazed at Lee for a long moment. And Lee wasn't sure what made him decide to answer the question, or even whether the answer was honest, or designed to poke at Lee somehow. But whatever it was, Joaquin gave the tiniest shake of his head. "No. We haven't killed him. Yet."

Lee bobbed his head. "Last question." He peered at Joaquin. "Have you seen a small, brown and tan dog? It almost looks like a coyote…"

***

Near the entrance to the ranch, the bodies of the dead cartel burned, and the air smelled of charred flesh and scorched hair.

The rest of the populace of Triprock—the people to which this settlement originally belonged—were gathered in front of the ranch house, like it had become a sort of village square. They watched Lee and Abe approach, with the prisoner between them, and in the people's eyes was a riotous hunger.

Lee stared at the burning bodies as he and Abe escorted Joaquin's limping form towards the people of Triprock. The tongues of fire danced, all consuming, never satisfied.

They needed to get rid of the bodies somehow, but burning them was probably not the answer.

Those residents of Triprock that had died during the gunfight would be buried, probably. Deep, where the primals couldn't dig them up again.

As Lee and Abe approached the crowd, there were a few shouts, a few curses. People overcome with emotion and rage. Ready to rip Joaquin limb from limb. But mostly it was quiet. Mostly they watched, though in the firelight their faces looked drawn and feral.

People liked to play at being better, but down in their bones, they were all the same.

They were no different than Lee.

They were no different than Joaquin.

They were no different than the primals.

Eric and Catalina were the first to step forward and meet Lee and Abe, before they reached the edges of the crowd. Because when Joaquin reached the crowd, there would be no holding them back. They would go at him like dogs after a piece of meat.

Joaquin only stood there, staring at the people that wanted to kill him, and his face was completely without expression. They might as well have been trees.

"Did you get what you needed out of him?" Eric asked, scowling at Joaquin, though Joaquin didn't look back.

Lee didn't answer the question. Instead he found himself glancing over at the pile of burning bodies. When Eric followed his gaze with a question in his eyes, Lee cleared his throat and spoke. "You shouldn't burn them."

Eric looked confused. "But if we don't get rid of them, they'll attract teepios."

He used the local term for the primals. A name Tex and his men had come up with.

Lee nodded. "Yeah. But burning them…all that fat is just gonna render down and get into the soil. You'll have a big, greasy, smelly patch underneath those ashes. It won't wash out for a long time. And it'll draw the teepios in just as much as rotting bodies will. 'Cept there won't be anything there for them to eat, so they'll just come after y'all."

Lee hesitated in the explanation, and the thought flitted across his mind, *Why are you even telling him this? These people are all going to be dead in a few days anyways.*

"In the future," Lee went on, as though these people had a future at all. "Take the bodies out into the wilderness. Let the teepios eat them."

"We don't want to feed them," Catalina put in, looking aghast.

Lee quirked an eyebrow at her. "Well, they're gonna eat whether you want them to or not. The question is, *what* are they going to eat?"

To Lee's right, Joaquin whispered the same prayer that he'd prayed when Lee broke his ribs and fingers and toes. Lee glanced in that direction, then back to Eric and Catalina. "You're aware of the problem, right?"

Eric frowned, not sure which problem Lee referred to.

At his side, Catalina shifted, nodding. "*Nuevas Fronteras*. They're going to come back."

"Yes," Lee said. "What you do with this man is up to you. But I'd hold onto him. I can't guarantee that using him as a hostage will be effective. But it's a chance."

Eric nodded.

Catalina scowled at Lee. "Where are you two going?"

Lee met her gaze. "Away."

"That's it?" Catalina looked incredulous. "You're not gonna help us fight them?"

"Cat," Eric warned.

Lee's expression was blank. He actually…didn't feel defensive. "We did help you fight them. We gave you the guns and ordnance. Now we need to get out there and figure out how we're going to replace what we gave to you."

"But you could really help us!" Catalina persisted.

A laugh bubbled up into Lee's throat. Tired and unstable. But he caught himself right as his belly started to quake and he stuffed it back down as he stared into Catalina's earnest face. Earnestly seeking help. Earnestly believing that help would make a difference.

It was all so fucking hysterical.

And he was a terrible person for thinking so.

Anyone with a sliver of a soul left in their chest would feel sorrow, perhaps. Or urgency to try to convince these people. Or maybe even anger that they would even argue the point. Or perhaps they'd feel guilty.

But Lee…

Lee'd been down this road so many times already. He'd tried to save so many people. He'd tried like hell to keep them alive, to keep them breathing, to protect them, to do their fighting for them so that they wouldn't have to be in danger.

But it never worked.

They all died in the end.

And there was a sort of cosmic hilarity when he saw himself beating his head against the wall. A humor born out of pure frustration, out of being stymied in your efforts so many times that you must truly be an idiot to continue on.

And that was what was hilarious to him.

He guessed that *he* was hilarious.

Lee cleared his throat, and shoved Joaquin into Eric's hands. "You want help?" he asked. "Then take my advice. Get lost. All of you. Leave this place. Go somewhere else. Don't stick together. Scatter. Live in the hills. Stay on the run. Fight back only when you can definitely win. Otherwise, keep your head down and survive."

"But this is our home," Catalina said, as though she was shocked at the mention of leaving it behind.

"Yeah?" Lee let out a soft chuff. "Well, that's the difference between us: We don't have a home."

Joaquin spoke, almost dreamily, his one good eye lolling over to Catalina. "You should listen to them. My brothers will come. And you don't want to be here when they arrive. Especially a pretty lady like you…"

Eric jerked Joaquin hard, but it didn't have the mean edge to it.

And that's why you're going to die, Lee thought, as though he saw the man's future so clearly from the nature of that one little move. *You're strong enough to stand up for yourself. But you're just not mean enough to win the fight.*

Lee and Abe exchanged a glance, and it seemed that Abe had seen the same thing, and in this, they both agreed.

The two of them hoisted their packs onto their shoulders—full and heavy, from the goods they'd taken from Triprock. There would be more in the pickup truck they'd arrived in, along with a gas can, to give them a little more mileage.

"Good luck," Lee said, and then he nodded to Eric, and then he nodded to Catalina, and then he and Abe walked through the center of Triprock, and the people parted out of their way. They went to the white pickup truck with the bullet hole in it. It was parked right where they'd left it, and the bed had a few satchels of food in it.

Food was good.

But food couldn't kill Lee's enemies.

They needed to find more ordnance. But until they figured out how to get access to all the bunkers of supplies that Project Hometown had stashed all around the state of Texas, then their only source of materials to fight *Nuevas Fronteras*, was *Nuevas Fronteras* itself.

They could keep themselves going a little longer if they hit another small outpost—like La Casa.

But eventually they were going to need to find Terrance "Tex" Lehy—if he was even alive.

They drove out into the hostile darkness, and the flicker of burning bodies glimmered in their rearview mirror. Ahead of them, the Texas plains were just blackness. At the horizon, the last glimmers of daylight still managed to hang on, turning a tiny portion of the sky sapphire, while the rest of it was midnight blue.

Lee saw none of that.

He sat with his head against the passenger's side window, in a sort of suspended animation. If an external threat had appeared, he would have reacted to it, like a mental sentry left on autopilot. But everything else had gone down inside of him.

His eyes only saw the past.

His ears only heard his father's voice.

He used to come to Lee in his dreams, but Lee didn't have dreams much anymore. He had darkness, and he had insubstantial nightmares. Things he could never recall upon waking, but that left him with his eyes and cheeks wet, and a deep hollow in his gut like a part of him had been stolen while he slept.

No, the only time he saw his father these days was in his memories.

In silent moments like this, when his mind wandered away from him, and whatever subconscious effort kept him bound together and operational, simply let the leash slip through its fingers.

In this memory, his father's face was indistinct. The surroundings were blurred. The memory was incomplete, or perhaps his brain chose only to remember the voice, because the voice was all that mattered.

"We'd go to the Outer Banks when you were a kid," the voice said. It creaked through its own recollections, like an old man on a rocking chair. The sound of it made Lee think that maybe his father was older in this memory. Starting to feel his age. "You were two years old. Maybe three? When we first went. And you loved the ocean, but you didn't want to go in the water, you just wanted to run. You'd take off running through the sand, like it was your job. Like you had a place to be, and you were gonna get there, and me and your mother be damned if we lagged behind. We'd just walk. You'd be running three steps on your toddler legs for every step of ours. You'd run, and run, and run. You never thought to save some energy for the return trip. You just ran until you could barely even move anymore, and then I'd have to carry you back, crying, because you'd run the skin right off the balls of your feet." A smile in the voice now. Wistful. "You'd do it every time we went to the beach. You'd run until you couldn't run anymore. And we never did find out where you were trying to get to. Hell, I don't think you ever reached it."

Lee let go of the memory. It felt almost like the theater lights coming up, breaking the spell. The memory started over on its loop, and that was Lee's cue to get up and leave it be. He'd re-discovered it, like a dusty relic, buried beneath layers of beaten and hardened self.

He put it back where he got it.

He pulled the hardness back over him.

His armor. Best to keep it on at all times. You never knew when you were going to need it. Sometimes you pull it away, just to let your skin breathe for a moment. But you never stop needing your armor. Not when you're in the middle of a war.

Lee couldn't afford to take it off.

Not yet.

Lee wasn't even sure why he'd thought up that memory of a memory.

Perhaps wondering what had put him on the long, and violent road, right to the shadowed, death-filled valley that he now found himself in.

EIGHT

TOWN HALL

THEY WATCHED HIM the way gazelles watch lions: Wary. Unsure if the lion is hunting or not.

The gazelle doesn't immediately run just because it spots a lion. But it waits, its entire body on a hair trigger, ready to start sprinting if the lion makes a move.

But this particular lion was not hungry today.

Today, the lion needed to deal with the prey it had already taken down.

Carl Gilliard moved through the Butler Safe Zone, straight-backed and steady.

The morning was overcast and humid, and already he was beginning to sweat. His icy, gray eyes slid this way and that, from crowded building to crowded building, and saw the prey-eyes of the people watching him back as they went about their daily doings.

The Butler Safe Zone now resembled nothing so much as a refugee camp. People everywhere. The adults sullen and irritable, squabbling at the drop of a hat over the tiniest things. The children running around heedless, or sitting, blank-faced, wondering when this purgatory would be over and life would go back to normal.

They were jam-packed in. And that was a problem. People were social creatures. But problems always arose when there were too many of them in one place, and Carl didn't need any more problems. Neither did Angela.

A little more than a month ago, the Butler Safe Zone had housed a little over a thousand people, and been about two-thirds full. Now it also housed the two-thousand survivors that had made it out of Fort Bragg as it had fallen.

Butler was not the closest safe zone to Fort Bragg, but it was the quickest to get to. The Charleston Safe Zone in South Carolina—which was not actually in the old city of Charleston, but west of it—had been closer. But a few bad hurricane seasons had wrecked some of the main roads and turned them into impassable swampland.

With busloads of refugees fleeing from Fort Bragg as their defenses went down and massive clusters of primals beginning to infiltrate and hunt, the Butler Safe Zone had been the easier alternative.

The Charleston Safe Zone would have had more room, but that ship had sailed, and now Carl was crammed in here in the massively over-crowded Butler Safe Zone, and all these watching eyes made his job very difficult.

Carl arrived at the only private place there was left in this Safe Zone—the jail.

Attached to the Sheriff's Office where Ed, the elected leader of Butler, shared power now with Angela Houston, the elected leader of *all* the Safe Zones, the jail provided Carl with a few things that he needed in order to do his job: A building with no windows, places to keep people that didn't want to be kept, and a way to come and go without being observed, which was fulfilled by the jail's underground sally port.

Carl didn't go through the sally port that morning though. He went straight into the front entrance, and he nodded to Ed, who sat at what had once been his secretary's desk, back in the day when he had actually been Sheriff.

Angela hadn't wanted to take Ed's office because she thought it might undermine him. She was always considerate of other people. That was the nice thing about her.

And, unfortunately, one of her greatest faults as a leader.

Carl had pushed on Ed, and Ed had insisted, and so Angela now sat in Ed's office, and Ed sat outside of it.

Ed nodded his balding head of snowy hair, and his expression was mostly unreadable beneath the white handlebar mustache that dominated his face.

"Master Sergeant," Ed acknowledged.

"Ed," Carl muttered back.

Through the glass front of the office, Carl saw Angela sitting at Ed's desk. She held a sheet of paper in each hand, like she'd been studying them, but now watched Carl approach from underneath her arched eyebrows.

She was different now.

Harder. Colder. More Machiavellian.

Regrettable, Carl felt. But necessary.

The change might not make her a better person, but it made her a better leader. From Carl's perspective, she was finally doing her job correctly, worrying less about what people thought and approved of, and more about how to keep all these assholes alive.

"This isn't the full list," Angela said, the second Carl stepped into the office.

Carl closed the door behind him. "I'm aware."

Angela slapped the papers down on her desk. "That would've been useful information to pass on."

Carl shrugged. "Ma'am, it doesn't make much difference whether you knew it was the full list or not. It changes nothing. The names on it are the names on it. Yes, there are more names. And we will eventually recover those. When we can get back inside Fort Bragg." Carl gestured towards the papers on Angela's desk. "As for right now, that is the best I can provide, working from the memories of Lieutenant Townsend and the surviving foremen."

The fall of the Fort Bragg Safe Zone had been the fault of a group of dissidents called the Lincolnists. On the day of their attempted coup, ninety-eight of them had failed to show up to their assigned jobs. The foremen had called in the absences, as was required. But, unfortunately, the list of names now languished in Fort Bragg somewhere. And Fort Bragg was overrun by primals.

The sheets of paper that Angela now had was the best that Carl could re-create based on the memories of the foremen and forewomen, and Townsend, the soldier they'd called the absences in to.

Angela eyed the papers again. "Thank you," she said, somewhat begrudgingly.

"Shouldn't you be practicing your speech?" Carl asked.

Angela shot him a look. “It’s not a speech. It’s a Town Hall. Question and answer.”

Carl studied Angela, searching for her intentions, for her emotions. Angela saw his look and leaned back in her chair. “Relax, Carl. We’re in the same boat.” She sighed and looked back at the desk. “Besides, even if I wanted to come clean, now would not be the time. Not with Charleston out of comms and Georgia and Florida wavering.”

“Agreed,” Carl nodded.

Angela’s lips pressed down to a line, and she leaned forward and placed her fingers on both sheets of paper, turning them so they now faced Carl. Then she took a pen and laid it on the desk between them.

Carl stepped up to the desk and took the pen. Then he bent over the papers. The tip of the pen went down the names. Occasionally it stopped and marked an X next to the name, and then continued on. When he was done, there were five X’s on the two papers.

Angela watched him work with an expression of distaste.

“Anyone new?” Angela asked, when he was done.

Carl nodded and reached into the sleeve pocket of his combat shirt. He drew out another piece of paper, this one folded in fourths. He placed this on the desk, between the two other papers. “Six additional. But only two confirmed. They’re highlighted.”

Angela looked at the folded piece of paper the way you looked at a shot of bitter medicine that you knew you had to take. Eventually she nodded.

When she looked up at Carl again, her eyes were almost pleading. “How many more now?”

Carl gave her a comforting smile. "Not many."

He left Angela's office, said nothing to Ed on the way out, and then proceeded down the stairs into the basement, which was where the majority of the jail structure sat.

The jail was a simple building, created for simpler times, in a small town that didn't have much crime. There was a drunk tank, two communal holding cells, and two solitary holding cells. In the main area, where sheriff's deputies used to intake prisoners and fill and file paperwork, Carl's team had now made their home.

The intake counter was a square island in the middle of the large main room. Inside the confines of the chipped Formica counter, the island overflowed with all manner of gear, equipment, and surveillance and investigative notes. The notes were written in long hand on whatever paper was available, often the unprinted backs of other documents they'd raided from various buildings and businesses.

It was crowded, but at least Carl and his team had their own space.

The equipment for Carl's team of operatives had spilled over the counter and onto the floor, like lava flows from a volcano. On the outskirts of their equipment pileup were two cots, a mattress, and two sections where the heavy, rubberized seating provided for prisoners to await their intake paperwork had been crammed together and covered with poncho liners and blankets to make beds.

It was on one of these that Carl slept each night. If he was actually sleeping.

Half the time he stared at the ceiling with his heart bumping around inside of him, like a tireless beast that wanted to get out. When sleep descended, he would often jolt awake with a full-blown adrenaline dump, and lay breathless and stiff for a time, hoping he didn't wake the others.

Not that any of the others were free of demons.

Rudy spent most of the night rolling over and over—what he called "rotisserie-ing" himself.

Logan, the youngest of their crew, had been dealing with sleep paralysis nearly every night. He would try to scream, aware that he was trapped, but unable to move his body. His screams would come out as groans and whimpers, until someone finally kicked him awake.

On the positive side, Logan had become more accustomed to these episodes, and now his groans had less of an edge of panic to them.

And then there was Mitch.

Poor Mitch.

Mitch stood at the corkboard they'd liberated from a roll call room upstairs, staring at the notes pinned there. Carl approached from the side, and he could tell from the look of Mitch's profile, that the man wasn't quite there at the moment.

"Mitch," Carl gruffed, even as he felt a stab of pity.

Mitch jerked, then looked at Carl with a stare that started out a little vacant, and then gradually honed back into reality. "Fuckin'-hey, Carl."

Mitch had died.

He'd taken a round to the neck during their last firefight in Fort Bragg before they evacuated. He'd lost a lot of blood, and by the time they got a transfusion into him—taken from Carl, who was a match—he'd been dead for a few minutes, his body kept viable only by a load of IV fluids to bump his blood pressure up, and Rudy's constant chest compressions.

Then he'd been in a coma for two days, and when he'd come out, it was obvious he'd suffered some brain damage. It'd taken him nearly a week to start speaking full sentences again, and even now, he spoke out of the corner of his mouth with a strange drawl, and started nearly every sentence with a grunt or a "fuckin'".

He'd lost a lot of weight. Carl saw it in his hollow cheeks and the way his shirts hung off of him where they used to be snug across his well-muscled chest.

Mitch knew that he wasn't quite right, and he hadn't done operations with them since then, concerned that his physical tremors and occasional mental fugues would put the team in jeopardy. Mostly he stuck to the basement, and tried to keep things organized and help with the investigations as much as he could.

Carl was a hard man, but it broke his heart to see Mitch this way. And he couldn't help comparing it to Lee, who had also died for a short time, and been saved, and spent time in a coma, but come out the other side mostly fine. Carl didn't begrudge Lee, but there was a part of him that thought it…unfair.

Carl had so few friends, and it seemed they were all being taken away from him, piece by piece.

"Are they all packed up?" Carl asked of Mitch.

Mitch nodded. "Mm-in the pickup. With the camper shell."

"Why don't you ride shotgun with me?"

Mitch looked unsure.

Carl jerked his head towards the sally port door. "Come on. Grab your stuff. That's an order."

This wasn't an operation. There was minimal chance that anything would go wrong. And Carl wanted to get Mitch working again, even if it was just to give him something to do. Maybe it would steadily rebuild his confidence.

Mitch turned and went to his cot, his gear stuffed underneath it.

Carl's armor and rifle leaned against the intake counter. He pulled his gear on, then grabbed one of the radios from the charger and tested it with a quick, "Check, check." He heard his voice echoed back to him from one of the other radios on the counter.

Logan sat on the other side of the intake counter, his feet up. He peered over at Carl. "You need anything?"

Carl shook his head. "Just keep an ear out." He looked over to where Morrow and Rudy lounged on a bed, playing a card game. "You guys stay ready as QRF. You'll have the Tacoma. We'll be back within an hour."

Morrow, Rudy, and Logan all nodded.

They knew the drill.

With armor, rifles, and pistols, Carl and Mitch exited the sally port and went to the pickup with the camper shell. Carl took a quick look into the back and saw the forms stacked in the back. He counted five.

Carl took the driver's seat, and Mitch took the passenger's seat.

The back glass was open, and Carl heard a quiet mewling noise coming from the camper shell.

Mitch whirled on it as Carl started the engine. "Fuckin'-shut up!" he growled.

And all was silent.

They drove out of the basement garage and into broad daylight, and the people of Butler and the people of Fort Bragg, all crammed in together, watched the pickup truck with the camper shell pass them by, but they didn't see what was in the back, because Carl never stopped. He slowed as he approached the gates to the Butler Safe Zone, but the guards were aware that Carl was coming, and the gates were open, and then Carl drove them out into the world beyond, as the gates slid closed behind them.

He took Highway 19, heading north into the empty Georgia countryside, surrounded on all sides by forest. After perhaps twenty minutes, he came to an overgrown dirt road on the left, and he took that heading west. The tire marks showed the red clay beneath, but the weeds that grew up between were high, and they tickled and scratched at the undercarriage.

They stopped in a place where nothing was.

Carl did a three-point turn on the narrow road so that the truck faced back the way they'd come and the tailgate faced west.

Carl left the truck idling, and stepped out.

Mitch met him around the back of the truck and opened the camper shell. His face impassive. Empty.

Five pairs of bare feet faced them.

"Out," Carl commanded, and began grabbing them by the ankles and hauling them out, dropping them on the ground like a careless baggage handler.

Mitch stood by with his rifle in his hands, covering them.

The figures groaned and whimpered when they hit the ground.

Three men. Two women. Their hands bound behind their backs with zip ties that cut into their skin, and their mouths gagged with cloths knotted at the backs of their necks.

Carl turned to look into the faces of the Lincolnists now huddling on the ground before him. Their eyes were fixed on him, terrified, knowing that death was coming for them sooner rather than later. They all wept, save for one woman who simply stared, like she was already dead.

Carl pointed to where the dirt road meandered endlessly back into the trees. "That is west. If you want to live, that's the direction you should go. You are banned from the United Eastern States. If you show up at any Safe Zone, you will be shot on sight. Nod if you understand me."

All five heads nodded, a glimmer of hope in their eyes. A possibility for survival.

How stupid of them.

"Word to the wise," Carl said, as he closed the tailgate. "You'll be tempted to scream for help, or to scream at us as we drive away. But there isn't anything in these woods that's going to give you help. So my recommendation to you would be to stay quiet, and move fast."

Maybe they expected Carl to cut them loose.

But that was their problem, not his.

Carl and Mitch got back into the truck, and sped away, leaving a cloud of dust to settle over the huddled and miserable forms of the five Lincolnists.

As they drove back towards Highway 19, Carl looked out into the dappled shade of the forest to his left, and thought he saw sinuous shapes slipping through the trees.

***

"Master Sergeant Gilliard is completely within his legal boundaries, I assure you." Angela stood on the top step of the Butler United Methodist Church.

On the large concrete patio at the front of the church, and crowding the street beyond, Angela was surrounded by several hundred of the three thousand people that were now crammed into this Safe Zone together. The day was hot, and the sun glared down on them, and there wasn't a cloud in the sky to give them shade.

It smelled like the sweat of a crowd, and hot concrete.

Beside Angela, and slightly behind her, as though to give her deference, stood Ed. His hands clasped in front of him. His steely cowboy's eyes squinting out into the bright daylight. His expression hidden behind the mask of his white mustache.

In the crowd stood a man with sweat rings showing under the armpits of his gray t-shirt, who had asked Angela some uncomfortable questions, and didn't seem to be happy with her answer.

Angela was about to try to shift to a different question—and hopefully a different topic—but the man with the sweat rings wasn't going to let her go that easy.

"Excuse me," he called over the rumble of the gathered crowd, forcing Angela's attention back onto him. "You talk about legal boundaries, but what laws are you referencing, specifically?"

Angela's gaze narrowed at the man, and she tried to play it off as a thoughtful squint, or perhaps the fact that the sun was in her eyes.

She thought she recognized him from Fort Bragg.

Maybe he was a Lincolnist himself. One of the many that had weaseled their way into the evacuation convoys, in order to escape the catastrophe that they themselves had caused, when they'd taken out the power to Fort Bragg's high voltage fencing and allowed them to be overrun by primals.

The man with the sweat rings maintained his eye contact with Angela, and in his expression she didn't see a man that was trying to trap her, as often happened with her detractors. Rather, she saw a man that was genuinely concerned with how things were shaping up.

You and me both, Angela had to admit, if only to herself.

The man pressed on, doggedly speaking over others who wanted their concerns and arguments to be heard. "I mean, if you're talking about traditional constitutional law, then I have to ask, are you familiar with the *Posse Comitatus* Act?"

Angela felt her stomach tighten at the mention of it.

Honestly, the man echoed some of Angela's own arguments.

Arguments that she'd made in private to Carl, and Lee, back when he was still around…

Lee, where are you now?

Angela nodded her head. "Yes, sir. I'm familiar with the *Posse Comitatus* Act. And while the United Eastern States may have some differences from the original United States Constitutional law—out of simple necessity—I can assure you that we are not using the military to uphold domestic laws, or using them against citizens."

The man scoffed at this. "But that's exactly what you're—"

"First of all," Angela interrupted, projecting her voice so that it could be heard over his, but so that she wouldn't appear to be yelling. "The entire concept of *Posse Comitatus* enables whoever is in charge of upholding the law—in this case, me—to organize a group of individuals that will help enforce those laws. And there is no one—and I mean no one—who is better qualified for this action than Master Sergeant Gilliard, which is why I have chosen him to act in this capacity."

There were some shouts of people trying to be heard, but Angela wasn't done.

"Secondly," she called. "We aren't dealing with simple common law breakers, such as thieves. The people we're talking about, the people styling themselves the 'Lincolnists'—" here she put up dismissive air quotes "—aren't just dissidents. These are people actively working to sabotage your safety and security. These are people who are actively working with the so-called President Briggs, who wants to come and take you back over for his own personal gain."

The crowd had quieted somewhat under the force of Angela's words.

"Those of you who've been with us since the beginning will remember that Briggs is a tyrant—a dictator—who starves his own people if they disagree with him, and who, if you'll remember, completely abandoned us four years ago to fight the massive hordes of infected coming out of the northeastern population centers. When he abandoned us, he relinquished any right to govern us, and so we govern ourselves. That's the whole reason why the United Eastern States even exists." Angela took a breath. "So I can assure you, once again, that Master Sergeant Gilliard is well within his legal boundaries to carry out his investigation."

The man with the sweat rings glowered, but seemed partially mollified.

"But what have you done with them?" Someone shouted.

A woman's voice.

Angela scanned the crowd and found the speaker. It was a woman she didn't recognize from Fort Bragg. It was someone from the Butler Safe Zone.

She stood, holding the hand of a small boy, and with a baby on her hip.

The sight of that made Angela's throat catch.

"I have friends," the woman proclaimed. "And they're gone now. Gilliard came and took them in for questioning and they never came back!"

Angela's heart pulsed uncomfortably a few times, but she never let the discomfort reach her face. "Ma'am, I can promise you that I personally oversee everything that Master Sergeant Gilliard does, and he has not harmed your friends, whoever they are. However—"

"Then what happened to them?" the woman demanded.

"However," Angela repeated, sterner. "I know for a fact that some of the people—many of the people—that have been investigated have chosen to leave the United Eastern States for their own personal reasons." The lie felt thick, like gummy mucous in her throat. "If they've chosen to do that secretly, and without telling their friends and families…well, I can't do anything about that."

The woman seemed bewildered. "But why haven't we seen any of them leave?"

Angela allowed an expression of compassion to come over her features. "I imagine that if I were sabotaging my fellow citizens—putting them in danger—then I wouldn't care to look them in the eyes either. I imagine they left discreetly. And I cannot speak to where they've gone, other than to suspect that perhaps they intend to make the trip to Colorado where they'll find out for themselves the kind of tyrant they've been idealizing this whole time, at the cost of thousands of lives."

Angela looked up, and out, and for a moment her eyes strayed to the back of the crowd that was gathered around her, seeking answers to things that couldn't be answered—at least not truthfully. Not if Angela intended to keep these people safe from the dangerous world that surrounded them.

At the back of the crowd, her eyes met a woman with sharp features and curly brown hair.

Marie stood, and in her eyes there was a look of understanding. And…absolution.

After all, it had been Marie that had told her, only a month ago, to let Carl off the leash, and simply deny it to the people.

Maybe Marie had become the devil on Angela's shoulder.

Or maybe Marie was just wiser.

Angela had rejected the idea when Marie had said it. But times change. And people have to change with them.

Across the crowd of angry, confused, and accusing faces, Marie gave Angela a small nod. A nod that told her, *You're doing the right thing.*

Angela gave the slightest nod back, then readdressed the crowd.

"Next question."

NINE

HUNTER-KILLER

SAM STILL TOOK an enormous amount of shit, mainly from Jones. But it seemed that during the fall of the Fort Bragg Safe Zone, he'd proven his mettle to his squad.

They didn't call him "half-boot" anymore, and he no longer had to be the gunner.

Though Sam was indeed a "half-boot"—one of the many soldiers from Fort Bragg that had not been "real" soldiers back before the world went to shit, and who had gone through an abbreviated form of infantry training—the subject of Jones's derision had become the new private.

The second that Sam heard that the new private's name was Pickell, he knew he was largely off the hook.

Private Pickell was also a half-boot. Tall and lean, with an angular face. His helmet looked oversized on him, and his OTV looked too small. He was a little on the older side for a half-boot, most of which were between fifteen and twenty. Pickell was probably somewhere in his early thirties, which made him the old man of the group.

Old Man Pickell was currently in the turret of the Humvee, and when Sam squinted up at him from his new position directly behind the driver—Chris—he saw Pickell's face scrunched against the wind, his upper teeth visible.

The Humvee rumbled on, heading northeast on Highway 540, towards Augusta.

Billings—recently promoted to sergeant—was taking them straight into the thick of it.

In the front passenger's seat, Sergeant Billings held an old paper map that seemed to unfurl to take up half the cab. He rustled about on it, frustration clouding his features.

"Dad, are we lost?" Jones asked from his spot behind Billings.

Billings ignored him, kept tracing their route with his index finger.

"Dad. Dad. Dad. Dad. Dad. Dad."

"Don't give in," Chris advised from behind the wheel, his shoulders gradually tightening each time Jones said "Dad."

Billings tried mightily to focus. But he was already irked by the old map, which was about twenty years old, and some of the roads were named wrong, or were just wrong altogether. Not to mention that most of the road signs had been ripped up, torn out, run over, or otherwise destroyed in the four years since there'd been anyone to maintain stuff like that.

"Dad!" Jones continued. "Dad!"

Billings shook his head.

"Pay attention to me!" Jones shrieked.

In the turret, Pickell had dissolved into fits of laughter.

Billings took a moment to breathe. "Do you need something, Jones?"

Jones didn't respond. He jammed his head against Pickell's leg, looking upwards and shouting at him as though suddenly enraged: “You shut the fuck up, Pickell!”

Pickell stopped audibly laughing, but Sam could still see him shaking.

Jones shook his head and righted himself in his seat, casting an irritated glance at Sam. “Goddamned Kosher-Dill thinks he can laugh with the rest of us. Like he’s real person or something.”

Sam smiled, but knew better than to join in at this particular point. Jones was in a mood to roast anyone who gave him an opportunity. He could not be trusted. He would lure Sam in and then turn on him.

“Alright,” Billings raised his voice, still looking at the map. “Settle down, my children. If my incredible navigational prowess is correct—”

Jones let out a bark of laughter.

“—Then we’re about five klicks from where Squad Three got into their little fracas.”

“If we’re lost, I vote we eat Pickell first,” Jones called, facing his window.

“He’s too old,” Sam pointed out, deciding to brave the treacherous tides. “The meat would be too gamey.”

“Yeah, but it’s briney,” Jones replied. “That keeps the meat tender.”

“You *would* want to eat my pickle,” Pickell hazarded.

Jones and Sam were silent. Not giving Pickell the benefit of even the slightest courtesy laugh.

“That’s hilarious, Pickell,” Jones finally deadpanned. “Good one. How about you do this: How about you cut your fucking tongue out and never speak again?”

"We're not lost," Billings announced, slapping the map closed in more or less its original condition. "See?" Billings pointed out the passenger's side, where an ancient and weather-bent sign stooped so low that it was barely visible as they passed.

The sign proclaimed that they were currently on State Highway 540/4, National Highway 1.

"Exactly where I said we were," Billings said, shoving the semi-folded map back onto the dash. "Incredible. Navigational. Prowess."

As the last bout of humor petered out, Sam felt the nerves settle into his gut. They weren't as bad as they used to be—he was growing accustomed to them. They didn't make him tremble. But he still got…jittery. And his stomach always felt sour.

It wouldn't last.

Things would clarify. Once the shooting started.

Billings leaned back to project his voice up into the turret. "Bread and Butter, we're a few klicks out from the objective! Look sharp!"

"Roger," Pickell replied.

Jones shot a look at Sam and rolled his eyes, "Listen to him. 'Roger.' What a tool."

One thing about Pickell that Sam respected—and maybe it was due to Pickell's additional years—but the man was pretty unflappable. Even with Jones constantly going at him, Pickell took everything in stride.

He's a cool cucumber, Sam thought, and almost burst out laughing.

He'd have to remember that one for later.

Laughter was the best medicine. It was how they passed the time. It was their armor. Without it, the fear got stronger. But when you made everything a joke, when you turned everything—even the horrific and the gruesome—into satire, then you took its power away.

Even now, Sam realized that this was a sort of mental loan system.

He was borrowing on his mental stability, for peace of mind today.

But eventually he would pay. Everyone paid in the end.

Billings grabbed the radio handset from the cradle between him and Chris and transmitted across the series of radio repeaters that had been erected along this route over the past month, giving them the ability to talk to Butler.

"Alfred, Alfred, this is Squad Four," he said.

Butler Command came back after a moment: "Squad Four, Alfred, go ahead."

It was a woman's voice. One of the many people that were now working the interim Tactical Operations Control, coordinating the squads that were clearing the route from Butler to Fort Bragg, and, ultimately, hoping to clear Fort Bragg itself.

Jones leaned forward in his seat, staring at the radio set. "She sounds hot. Ask her what her name is."

Billings shook his head. "Yeah, we're gonna be arriving at Checkpoint Scarecrow. Nothing further. Out."

"Roger," the woman replied. "Thank you, Squad Four."

Billings hung up the receiver and turned a focused gaze back out to their surroundings. "Slow up a bit," he mumbled to Chris.

The Humvee began to decelerate.

Another dilapidated sign to the right of the road welcomed them to the city of Augusta.

The objective of the last few days had been to punch Highway 1 straight through Augusta. Clear it, and set up radio repeaters, so that convoys wouldn't need a satellite phone to communicate with Butler.

Clearing Highway 1 all the way to North Carolina was just one aspect of their larger mission: to retake Fort Bragg. But before that ultimate goal was met, they would have to secure the route, not only so that they could set up a more reliable system of communication between Butler and Fort Bragg, but also so that larger convoys could get through unmolested.

Sam, his squad, and eleven others, were the tip of the spear.

Well…*ten* others now that Squad Three had been wrecked.

Twenty-four hours prior, Squad Three had hit resistance, right in this area.

They'd been attacked by primals.

Two of the squad made it back to Butler.

One of those two died that morning. He'd lost his arm to a primal. How his buddy even got the rest of him away from the beasts and back to Butler was a mystery at this point in time. None of the dirty details had leaked out to the rest of the squads yet.

The radio crackled: "Squad Seven to Squad Four."

Billings's mouth tensed. He pressed the PTT without taking the handset from the cradle. "Go ahead, Loudermouth."

Billings liked to use that sergeant's name whenever possible, and to say it with a faint inflection of sarcasm.

"We're probably about a klick away from that same spot," Loudermouth said. "Coming in from the west."

"Roger," Billings replied. When he'd released the PTT, he glanced in the back. "I'll be damned if Loudermouth gets more CKs than us. You hear me, Pickell?"

"Loud and clear, Sarge," Pickell replied.

Billings looked forward again. "Sam. Jones. Get on it."

Sam and Jones both dropped their windows and rested their rifles so that the muzzles pointed out into the world beyond.

On Sam's side, everything was a green and tan blur. Fields left fallow for years blew by, with six- and seven-foot-tall pine trees sprouting up all across the waist-high weeds. The forest gradually reclaiming its territory.

"Houses," Chris called as he drove.

Sam glanced up ahead and saw the beginnings of civilization—more than just a farm house here and there, but collections of houses now. Neighborhoods. Suburbs. The inevitable heralds of an approaching city.

"The five-twenty loop should be coming up here soon," Billings advised. "If you can get a clear on-ramp, take it."

"Roger."

They continued forward.

The sky above them was alternately slate and sunny. Large skeins of flat, gray clouds hung in the sky. They seemed motionless, but they must have been moving because the sun would occasionally hit an empty spot and everything would be bright for a while before turning to dull gray again.

"Squad Seven, Squad Four," Loudermouth transmitted again. "We're on an overpass. Clear line of sight down I-Five-Twenty. We got eyes on the barricade that Squad Three hit yesterday."

Billings made a small huff, then transmitted. "Alright. What do you see, Loudermouth?"

"Just a line of cars, all the way across the outer loop."

"Does it look like someone put it there on purpose, or is it a traffic jam from four years ago?"

Loudermouth took a moment to respond. "Yeah, it definitely looks like someone set it up to be a barricade. We're gonna back up and get on the interstate. See if we can't ram some cars out of the way and clear the path."

"Fuck that," Billings remarked to himself, then transmitted. "Roger. We'll meet you down there." He released the PTT. "Asshole's just trying to get more CKs."

Confirmed Kills were the new currency of the Hunter-Killer squads, of which Sam and his squad were now a part. Command had decided to start rewarding their squads, based on how many primals they took out during route clearance, the thinking being that less primals meant a safer route.

Sam wasn't entirely sure this was true.

It sounded good on paper. They weren't *forcing* the troops to go out and put themselves in dangerous situations to get a few more CKs. They were just incentivizing taking an extra step to kill them, rather than what had become the norm—a general policy of deliberate avoidance, sometimes causing them to lose entire days, routing themselves around small towns where they'd seen primal movement from a distance.

But, what command hadn't taken into account was how competitive a bunch of twenty-somethings could be. Now, the weekly incentives for being the squad with the most Confirmed Kills—usually something simple, like they all got an extra day off, or an extra ration of a more commodity-type item—had become icing on the cake to simple bragging rights.

To add to that fire, the nodding deference of their fellow survivors, the whispered usage of the phrase "Top Tier" to describe the squads with the most CK's, and, perhaps most of all, the impression that it made on the opposite sex, were like gasoline to these young men's egos.

Sam frowned, thinking of the opposite sex.

Thinking of Charlie, his…could you say girlfriend? Well, they'd slept together. But that was primarily because she was a Lincolnist and was pumping him for information. She was, as you might expect, not one of the girls who cared much for the Hunter-Killer squads.

Not that it mattered—on the off chance that Sam and Charlie bumped into each other in the Butler Safe Zone, they each shared a moment of near-panic, as though everyone around them would know their deep dark secret, and then they averted their eyes and ignored each other.

That secret being that Charlie was a Lincolnist, and that Sam knew it, and had let her get away with it.

As he did so often when his mind strayed into Charlie, he shook his head to clear it and deliberately turned away from the thought of her—of how she was a traitor, and how he had protected her, and, ultimately, how she'd played him like a cheap toy.

All of that nonsense aside, there *were* girls in the Butler Safe Zone that *did* look at Sam differently, and who Sam was pretty sure weren't trying to pump him for information. Because he wasn't just a kid anymore.

He was one of the Hunter-Killers.

Two months ago, they'd all been nobodies, walking perimeters inside of the Fort Bragg Safe Zone. Now people looked at them like they were tucking their dicks into their socks.

In just a few short weeks, the Hunter-Killer squads had become a complete subculture.

Squads were coming up with call signs and emblems and various off-shoots of esprit de corps.

Jones was a fountain of squad name suggestions—Tiger Cats, Screeching Freedom Eagles, and Pussy Kings, to name a few—but Billings hadn't found one that he liked yet. A few squads had started to use their call signs on the radio, and they hadn't been corrected by command, which was only encouraging it further.

All of this promoted two things.

Bravery...

And possibly stupidity.

Sam had to give the whole thing its due. They'd made quick progress securing hundreds of miles of route and erecting the radio repeaters along the way.

But sometimes he wondered if they'd become reckless.

Up ahead, the sign for I-520 was crumpled, laying on the concrete, with some weedy vines growing on it. But you learned to read signs like this.

"Here," Billings pointed to the right. "Take this on-ramp. Come on. Speed up."

Chris turned onto the ramp. The straightaway lay ahead of them, and Chris began accelerating down it. A few cars were clustered on the shoulders of the on-ramp, now just rusty humps emerging from a sea of weeds.

Up ahead, on the interstate, Squad Seven's Humvee was visible, just passing the merge lane of their on-ramp, and heading towards the barricade of cars.

Loudermouth hadn't been exaggerating. The line of cars was obviously deliberately placed, and they stretched from the concrete median that divided the inner and outer loops of the beltway, all the way across three lanes of traffic, and down into the woods.

"Dammit," Billings grunted. "Fine. Slow up. No need to rush. Let this asshat do his thing."

Jones made a disgusted noise. "Loudermouth? You're going to let *Loudermouth* beat us out?"

"No," Billings said, shouldering his rifle and leaning heavily into his window, as Chris slowed their Humvee to a crawl. "I'm going to let him do the work." He reached over with his support hand and keyed the radio again. "Loudermouth. We got overwatch on you. We'll let you know—"

"Shit! Contact!" Pickell belted out.

The second that Pickell said it, Sam saw it.

It would have been easy to miss, except for their elevated position on the on-ramp.

Movement, on the other side of the median barricades.

A lot of movement.

"Loudermouth!" Billings transmitted. "Pull out or punch through! You got company!"

Squad Seven's Humvee was now sitting still, three vehicle lengths from the barricade of cars. As Billings transmitted, Sam watched their gunner spin in a circle, looking for the threat, but his attention was to the woods, not the median.

"Take 'em, Pickell!" Billings ordered.

Pickell opened up with the M2. The massive .50-caliber rounds lanced out and smashed the top of the concrete barrier, tracking the movement of the shapes on the other side.

Down on the interstate, Squad Seven's gunner spun about, seeing where Pickell was shooting and deciding that might be a good direction for him to shoot as well.

And then a fifty-foot section of concrete median seemed to disappear.

A mass of shapes swarmed over it, seeming to engulf it, giving the impression that the concrete itself had simply dissolved. Sam couldn't count them. And the way their Humvee was angled, he didn't have a shot on them either. He would need to get out.

He started to push his door open, but felt Jones grab him by the shoulder. "Stay in the truck!"

Billings yelled over the radio: "Loudermouth! Ram those vehicles and get out!"

The M2 thundered over their heads.

Down on the interstate, Loudermouth's Humvee backed up with a chirp of tires, but no less than a dozen primals had now swarmed it, like wolves converging on a lumbering moose. The gunner ducked below his turret as two primals launched themselves at him.

"He's not gonna ram the barricade," Billings observed, his voice weirdly cold. "Chris, we gotta clear that barricade."

"Dammit. Okay."

"Go!"

Chris stomped on the accelerator.

On the interstate, Squad Seven's Humvee was now reversing at top speed, the engine roaring, while six or seven primals hung onto it and tried to get into the open turret, and one of the side windows that hadn't been shut in time.

Squad Seven's Humvee swerved, the driver trying to correct, then overcorrect, and then their escape terminated in a sudden crash, as the Humvee slammed its rear end into the concrete median, throwing a few primals free.

"Loudermouth!" Billings called on the radio as they hauled down the on-ramp towards the barricade and the crowd of primals. "We're gonna hit the barricade! Follow! Follow!"

Sam remembered the hordes of infected that had coalesced in the cities in the early days of the infection. This looked similar, but it was not the same. The primals on the interstate were already splitting up into several packs of five or six each, moving to flank Squad Seven's Humvee, working in concert with each other.

And just now noticing Billings's Humvee, roaring towards them.

The first generation of infected would have run right at the approaching Humvee in a deluge of rage and screaming. But the primals were different. They were smarter, and the self-preservation centers of their brains were intact.

They parted as the Humvee approached them, dodging out of the way, clearly cognizant that the ram bars on the front of the vehicle would leave them as a slick patch of red on the blacktop.

But they didn't retreat.

Chris had both hands on the wheel now as he roared onto the interstate, his shoulders pinched up, like he was cringing.

"Windows!" Billings yelled at them, then reached behind and started yanking Pickell back inside. "Get inside! Chris, ram the cars, but don't wreck us, okay?"

Which was a tall order in the moment, surrounded by primals.

Chris let off the accelerator, but they were still approaching the barricade of cars at about forty-five miles an hour.

They were almost abreast of where Squad Seven's Humvee had crashed into the median.

Sam looked out his window, and for a flash, stared directly at Loudermouth as he fought the primals that were yanking his door open, pulling his squad out.

Beyond the glare of the windshield, the shaded shapes of limbs, thrashing, and muzzle flashes strobing. But there were too many of the primals, and the primals were too quick, dodging the wild gunfire and then lunging in, latching onto necks, ripping weapons from hands…

One of the soldiers was pulled apart, and his ghastly face looked across the empty stretch of interstate, and Sam thought, in that slim second where they were adjacent Squad Seven's Humvee, that the soldier was looking right at him.

Then the moment whipped by.

A blur of fleshy shapes.

Gnashing teeth.

Predator's eyes.

Something slammed Sam's window—a passing claw, trying for purchase as the Humvee drove by.

"Everyone hold on!" Chris yelled, his voice pitching high.

Sam looked forward. Through the windshield.

The line of cars seemed to loom up in front of them. In Sam's sudden, fearful vision, it looked like a towering wall.

Chris stomped on the brakes.

They all slammed forward in their seats.

Then Chris hit the accelerator again, with surprising precision, and with the Humvee's ram bars right between the bumper of two sedan's, he *pushed* through them, with little more than a hard jostling that felt like hitting a nasty pothole.

Something hit the roof of the Humvee as the engine roared again and they began to accelerate away from the barricade of cars, a hole punched in it now. Sam looked out his window and caught the bare flash of a gnarled foot, the toes splayed almost like fingers, as it scrambled up onto the Humvee.

Sam let out a yelp of warning and rolled his body so that he pointed his rifle up at the ceiling—the best he could manage in the cramped confines of the vehicle—and he fired on automatic.

His hearing went out

The slugging of his rifle became a dim, background chatter.

His squad yelled at him.

He watched bullet holes sprout in the ceiling, punching up at whatever was scrambling towards the turret hole.

Sam tracked with it.

Two demon faces stared down at him. Teeth bared, mouths wider than was humanly possible, no longer people at all, but something else, something terrible.

Hands reached for him—fingers like claws, nails like talons.

Sam didn't let off the trigger. He pushed his muzzle towards the grasping hands, watched fingers fly off, and then the snarling faces beyond morphed, consciousness—however animalistic—fleeing from their eyes as jacketed lead pierced their brains.

Chris swerved the Humvee, and Sam watched the ruined faces of the primals slip out of sight, and perceived the distant tumble of their limbs as they rolled off the fastback of the Humvee, limp and dead.

He realized he'd gone empty.

The Humvee kept tearing onwards.

Billings had the radio in his hand and called something into it, looking over his shoulder at his troops in the back.

Sam's dazed eyes scanned his squadmates, and saw Pickell struggling up, with a smattering of blood across his face, but alive. Across from him, Jones had lowered his window and was now half out of it, firing his rifle behind them and screaming things that didn't register with Sam.

Billings held the radio with one hand, and with the other pulled at Pickell, yelling, "Get on the turret!"

Sam let his rifle fall out of his hands and he grabbed ahold of Pickell and helped the man extricate himself from where he'd managed to get wedged between Sam and Jones.

Pickell surged to his knees, and then clambered into the turret again, cursing all the way.

"Ryder!" Billings yelled at Sam. "Get him another box of fifty!"

Jones slammed back into his seat, stripping an empty mag from his rifle and reloading. "Slow it down, Sarge!" he called. "Let them chase us a bit! We got a goddamned turkey shoot!"

"Chris, stay just ahead of them," Billings ordered.

Sam felt the Humvee decelerate again. He strained, reaching into the far back for one of the extra cans of .50-caliber ammunition.

Above them, Pickell scanned, but didn't fire.

"Why aren't you shooting, Pickell?" Billings demanded.

Pickell hunched to shout back inside. "They're not coming after us!"

"Stop the truck," Billings grunted.

"You want me to stop the truck?"

"Stop the fucking truck!"

Chris slammed on the brakes, almost spitefully.

Sam was thrown onto the ground. Still couldn't quite reach the box of ammunition, but Billings had kicked his door open, and Jones was following, and Sam thought it would be a good idea to do the same.

Sam reloaded his rifle as he extricated himself from the Humvee. Pushed out of his door. His feet hit blacktop. Median barrier directly in front of him. He wondered what might lurk on the other side, but he turned to his left, looking back the way they'd come.

He was just in time to see Squad Seven's Humvee, all four doors hanging open, rolling slowly off the interstate. It was completely empty. It picked up speed as it hit the slope of the shoulder, and then trundled off the blacktop, down the shoulder, and slammed into the trees.

At the median, which was a concrete wall about six feet high, the last of the primals slipped over the top. They'd left no bodies behind. Not even their own.

Every bit of meat, they took with them.

Escaping with their kills.

On the other side of the Humvee, Sam heard Billings and Jones cursing anything and everything as they watched.

After a moment, Billings stalked back to the front passenger's seat and snatched the radio. "Squad Four to Alfred," he didn't wait for them to answer back. "We have positive contact with a colony of primals inside the Augusta beltway. Confirming, no less than a hundred primals. They just took out Squad Seven, but it looks like they're pulling back into the city. I want you to scramble all available squads and have them meet me at Checkpoint Scarecrow for a direct hunt."

He slammed the receiver back down, irritable and amped up. But a shaky smile crossed over his face. "We're gonna earn some CKs tonight, gents!"

TEN

MATEO

MATEO LOOKED AT THE SAD GATHERING before him, and wished he could be furious with them.

Mateo was not a man given to bouts of dominant anger.

His predominant pattern of thought was a serene trust in the providence of the universe—that in the end, he was destined to be victorious over everyone, and everything.

And when he looked out at the men that had tucked tail and run from Triple Rocker Ranch, he didn't feel enraged by what they'd done. Just disgusted.

There were five of them before him. Two gringos, and three original cartel. Each one had been in charge of their own "squad" of five to ten men. Mateo had let their men go—they were just riff-raff. He didn't expect them to stand their ground when their leaders ran away.

The whole lot of them stood atop Mateo's preferred place—the top of the refinery. A wonderful lookout over everything that he had conquered, and everything that he would conquer. It was like a throne room for him.

This was a different refinery than the one he had occupied a month ago. A month ago, he had been at what he considered his "front lines," in Louisiana, pushing his territory forward, and claiming his birthright.

Unfortunately, as *Nadie y Ninguno* had arisen out of the darkness, he'd been forced to return back to Texas, and reconvene his base of operations at one of the refineries that they had taken control of nearly a year ago.

One step forward, and two steps back.

And now this.

This downtrodden cast of faces standing before him, unable to meet his gaze. These men who considered themselves monsters, but who had run screaming when the real beasts showed up.

Mateo smiled without mirth. "*Tres triste tigres*," he sighed. "That's what you all remind me of. Sad tigers. You claimed that you were brave and ferocious, and yet, here you stand, like geldings freshly neutered."

"*Los demonios*," one of the men murmured, desperation in his voice. One of the Mexicans. "*Nadie y Ninguno. No puedes luchar ellos.*"

That *did* manage to make Mateo angry.

And when he was angry, he did not hide it.

He crossed to the man in a flash, and seized him by the back of his hair and bent him over backwards so that he was leaning out over the safety railing, and a three-story plummet to the sandy Texas ground lay beneath him.

"You *can* fight them, you ignorant fuck! There are no demons! The only demon here is your pathetic superstition!" Mateo reeled himself in with a sudden jerk, as though his rational self had suddenly caught his animal self red-handed. He released the man. Straightened his own *guayabera* and flashed his white teeth at the other men, like a snarl. "They are just men. Men that can be killed with bullets, just like any other man."

Mateo turned. Stepped away. He paused, thinking. Then whirled around and pointed.

Out over the edge.

His eyes locked on the one who had spoken out of turn.

The man looked shaken, but it took a moment for him to realize what was going on, that his master was looking at him. And then he raised his gaze and saw. And he followed the pointing finger out over the edge of the refinery platform, and he began to tremble.

"Go," Mateo said, his finger like an unyielding signpost.

"You want I leave?" The man attempted English.

"I want you to jump."

The man's body began to quake so hard, it almost looked like he was nodding emphatically, though his eyes showed that he was far from agreeing with Mateo.

"I die," the man squeaked. "I jump. I die."

Mateo stared at him. "Maybe. Maybe not. It's three stories. Men have survived worse falls. Maybe you will too. I promise it will be better than staying up here with me."

The man's eyes were as wide and white as full moons. He dropped to his knees.

He began to beg.

Mateo's lips curled. Nose wrinkled.

The man standing next to the beggar suddenly bent down and seized his comrade, hauling the blubbering man to his feet. For a moment, it seemed that the beggar thought his friend was simply standing him up—encouraging him to have some self-respect.

Reality crashed into this idea, and obliterated it, as his friend propelled him backwards, against the safety rail, and began to push him over.

The cries for mercy gave way to animal snarls, wordless growling between two cowardly creatures. Like rats fighting.

Mateo watched it with the interest of someone viewing a sad and somewhat revolting act of nature.

The beggar teetered on the small of his back, arms and legs flailing, clawing at his friend—at his face, at his clothes, alternately trying to harm him, and trying to grasp hold of him to keep himself from falling.

And then he went over.

He didn't scream.

Roughly two seconds later, there was a dull *thump* from down below, barely audible over the heavy breathing of the man who'd tossed his friend over the side.

Now, that man turned around, his chest heaving, but still unwilling to meet Mateo's eyes. He took his place back in line with the rest of the sad, neutered tigers.

Mateo thought about killing them all.

Maybe it's what he should've done.

But his exasperation got the better of him in that moment, and he was too tired to go through all the rigmarole. There was a part of him that wanted to cut off the infected branch from his tree—namely this pervasive superstition—but the larger, more rational part of him knew that he was already hemorrhaging men because of *Nadie y Ninguno*. He couldn't start massacring the people he had left.

One would be enough.

Enough to teach a valuable lesson.

"The only devil around here is me," Mateo said to the remaining four. "*Nadie y Ninguno* are only men. Is there anyone else that believes they cannot die? Anyone else who intends to run when they show up again?"

Predictably, the remaining four stayed silent.

"Leave me," Mateo waved them off.

They left. Quickly.

Mateo walked to the edge and braced his hands on the safety rail. He looked over. Down to the ground.

Two of his men stood beside a crumpled form whose brains had scattered across the ground like a burst melon. They looked up at Mateo with a question in their eyes.

Mateo just stared down at them.

Wordlessly, they began the work of removing the body.

Mateo raised his eyes to the north. Somewhere out there, beyond the horizon line, the body of his closest friend and most trusted advisor lay in the hands of peasants.

Joaquin.

What had they done with him? How had they killed him? Had their rage been so quick and hot that they killed him quickly? Or had they pulled him limb from limb? Or burned him alive? Or done one of the terrible things that Joaquin Lozcano Leyva had done to them?

Joaquin.

How dare they?

If Joaquin had been a mere man, then it might seem like justice for the things he'd done to other men. Like the karmic flow of the world. But Joaquin was a part of Mateo. They were god-like. And their destinies were intertwined. America had been a part of Joaquin's birthright, as much as Mateo's.

Joaquin should not have been killed.

His death shook Mateo's beliefs.

The only logical thing to do was to admit that his beliefs had been mistaken before. Joaquin was not meant to be at Mateo's side. Joaquin must have made a mistake, somehow.

Joaquin must not have been as god-like as Mateo.

That was the only logical conclusion to come to.

So, he questioned himself. *What are you going to do about it?*

What was he going to do that he hadn't already done?

Over the course of the last five weeks, he'd done everything in his power to hunt *Nadie y Ninguno* down, short of completely abandoning his original plan of conquering the southern states of America.

And he wasn't going to upend all of that for just two men.

He grimaced as he looked north.

He was not a man to swallow his pride and admit he was wrong.

But he also wasn't a man to admit defeat.

As much as it pained him, he needed to call on Greeley.

They needed to come clean up their mess.

Mateo cracked a rueful smile at the oddities of life that sometimes backed you into a corner.

I guess I'll burn in the fires of hell after all.

It's a good thing I don't believe in them.

***

Daniels snatched the satellite phone from his desk on the first ring, but then stared at the faceplate of it. Recognizing the number.

He frowned, but a little bloom of dormant anticipation woke up inside of him.

He extended the antenna, and pressed the answer button. Put it to his ear.

"Mateo Ibarra," he said, cordially. "I'm glad to hear from you again."

On the other end of the line there came a shush of static—or perhaps it was Mateo, sighing into the microphone.

A corner of Daniels's mouth twitched up.

This was going to be interesting.

"Mister Daniels," Mateo said, after a pause. His voice was begrudging. Longsuffering.

Like calling Daniels was perhaps the last thing on the face of the earth that Mateo wanted to do, right behind eating broken glass.

Daniels thought Mateo would continue, but he didn't, so Daniels simply smiled and prompted him: "Yes, sir. It's me. What can I do for you today?"

Mateo spat it out. "I cannot maintain control of my territories, continue to produce all the oil that you and I both need, *and* continue a manhunt for these *Nadie y Ninguno* characters."

Daniels raised his eyebrows. "These what-nows?"

"It is Lee Harden. Or Terrence Lehy. Maybe both of them. Maybe some other guy from your so-called…what was it? Project Home and Garden?"

Daniels leaned back in his chair. He knew that Mateo knew the name of Project Hometown. But this was a fairly low-brow jab for Mateo. He usually considered himself above such petty cock-measuring. Which meant that something was going on down in Texas that really had him nervous.

And, apparently, that something was called *Nadie y Ninguno*, whatever the hell that meant in Spanish.

So. Mateo is having problems corralling Harden and Tex. Or some other group of wannabe dissidents.

Daniels had a good nose for opportunity.

But he also knew when to reel a fish in, and when to let it run out a little line.

"I'm sorry to hear that, Mr. Ibarra. I understand from our previous conversation—I think it's been over a month since I've heard from you last—that you didn't want to do business with us. But I'd be happy to offer my services to consult with you, and give you any advice and intelligence I can on how to handle the situation you find yourself in."

"I don't want your advice."

"Oh."

"I want you and your goddamned mercenaries to come and clean up the mess they created. And make no mistake, this is *your* fault. This is *your* mess."

"Yes," Daniels said, allowing a tiny tinge of sarcasm to enter his words. "You've told me already how impeccably clean and orderly you keep your house. Naturally any disorder would probably be my fault."

"Don't play with me, mercenary."

"I wouldn't dream of it."

"You want my oil? You want to rebuild a working relationship between *Nuevas Fronteras* and Greeley?"

"Yes. Very much so."

"Then handle it, Mr. Daniels. Handle the mess you made."

Daniels stared across his desk—which had once been John Bellamy's desk—to the corkboard with the map of the United States on it and the icons on each state telling the disposition of each Project Hometown Coordinator—"In Greeley," "Non-viable," or "Unknown."

He stared, in particular, at the state of New Mexico, and the image of Captain Tully.

Question mark.

Unknown.

"Yes," Daniels said into the silence he'd left in his moment of concentration. "Actually, Mr. Ibarra, you'll be pleased to know that I'm already working on something, as we speak."

ELEVEN

SUNDANCE

ONE OF THE UPSIDES OF STARVING: You didn't need to eat much to feel full.

Lee chewed on the rind of a slice of salt pork. One of the foodstuffs they'd appropriated from Triprock. After so long with so little to eat, his mouth felt burned out from the salt, and his hunger had already left him. He would finish it because he knew he needed the calories. Though he wished he could be more liberal with his water bottle.

It was mid-morning. Already the inside of their hideaway was getting hot.

They'd slept the night before. It'd taken the edge off his exhaustion, but he could still feel it, deep in his bones.

He sat in a creaky wooden chair, at an east-facing window. His jaw moved absently, his eyes fixed on some far-off point through the window. Out beyond, there was scrub, and waist-high grass, and copses of juniper.

He thought about Julia.

He thought of everything that never would be.

Why had he even let himself think that she and him could survive all this and be together? What an idiotic thing to do. He should have never let her get close. He should never have opened himself up like that.

Hope and love.

They were caustic.

All they did was strip away your defenses.

When they were done with you, they left you raw and red and exposed.

You were a mistake, Julia, he thought. *And now everyone has to pay for it.*

Abe let out a loud snort that jerked Lee out of his thoughts.

He glanced sidelong at Abe's sleeping form.

Abe had taken watch for the first half. Lee had taken it for the second half. And then he'd decided to let Abe sleep a little longer. It wouldn't make a huge difference in the entirety of their day, and he thought that Abe needed it.

Abe had gone to sleep at two o'clock. It was now eleven. It was evidence of the man's own fatigue that, despite nine hours of sleep, he still hadn't gotten up.

But it was time.

Nine hours would have to be enough.

Lee finished the chewy rind, then wiped his fingers off on his pants. He stood up. The chair gave a loud protest.

Abe didn't even twitch. His breathing remained deep and even.

Lee walked over to him, but stopped short. They both knew full well the dangers of actually putting hands on each other to wake them up. You were liable to take a right hook to the jaw. Or worse, since they both slept with their arms curled around loaded rifles.

"Psst," Lee hissed. "Abe."

Abe finally stirred.

Lee pressed on, louder. This was standard operating procedure. "Abe. Wake up. You lazy bastard."

Abe's eyes opened, squinting against the strong sunlight coming in the east-facing window. He rocketed upright. "What time is it?"

"Eleven."

"What's wrong?"

"Nothing's wrong."

Abe rubbed his face. "Wow. I feel terrible."

"You're welcome."

"Thanks."

"Eat something. I want to be at the lookout by twelve."

***

They made it there by eleven-thirty.

The lookout was a small clearing, on a small hill, just north of the house where they'd holed up for the night, and about two thousand yards west of La Casa.

With the exception of this small hill, the rest of the land was flat as a griddle. The hill didn't seem like much, but at the very top, on this little clearing, it gave them enough altitude to see over the mesquite and scrub oak, and get eyes on the twenty cartel men that held La Casa.

They traveled light, taking only water, one scoped rifle, and an M4 apiece.

After the "liberation" of Triprock, they'd been able to get reacquainted with the weapons they'd smuggled into the settlement to arm the populace. It was nice not to have to make-do with whatever bullshit they could rob from a dead body.

They'd also appropriated a rifle with some better range than the .30-06 they'd been using. They'd taken this one from the cartel's stash. Found it in the back of one of their vehicles. It was a Barrett Model 95.

Ostensibly, the .50 caliber rounds could reach out and touch someone a mile away.

But Lee had no intention of using it today. He just liked having the capability.

The downside was that they'd only been able to find ten rounds for it, five of which were currently in the massive rifle's box magazine. Lee had fired it a single time, to confirm its zero, which brought their round count down to nine.

And with only that single data point—the test shot had impacted approximately a foot low at five hundred yards—Lee wouldn't be using it to engage at two thousand yards if he could help it.

But you never knew.

Lee and Abe used some scrub to build up a small hide on the hilltop, and then settled in.

The sun stood overhead, baking their backs. Burning the dark patch of skin on the nape of Lee's neck.

Lee took the rifle first. Abe lounged more comfortably with his M4 in his hands, keeping an eye on their surroundings, while Lee focused downrange.

La Casa meant "the house" and that was about all it was. A single—albeit large—house. Several barns and outbuildings which had been repurposed to house men instead of animals and farming supplies.

A month ago, La Casa had been OP La Casa. It had been one of the numerous small outposts that Tex owned, scattered around north and central Texas. Then one night, a convoy of technicals had shown up and pushed Tex's troops out of La Casa, then pursued them north to Caddo before finally giving up the chase.

Looking back with hindsight, Lee believed this had been orchestrated by Cornerstone, in an attempt to draw him into attacking the Comanche Creek Nuclear Power Plant. They'd then tightened the noose on Lee's assaulting force, and massacred Tex's soldiers.

That had been the night that Julia had died.

Gone.

It'd been slow, and yet it seemed like she'd just up and disappeared. Like the wind had taken her.

Gut shot. But at least she'd bled out before she could go septic.

At least she'd died with Lee holding on to her.

That was something, right?

Died in the rain, and the mud, and the blood. Died, and then he'd had to leave her behind. And he hadn't been able to go back for her, and he never would. He had nothing that was hers. There had been no funeral to attend, no last rites, no grave to dig.

No opportunity to grieve.

All he had was a memory.

And all the thorny things that might've dulled if there had been time to grieve, well they never saw the light of day, and they were never given an outlet. So they sat inside of Lee, and they curdled, and, in a way, they went septic, like Julia's wound would have if she'd lived longer.

Now the only way to kill that infection was to kill every human being that had caused it.

Sometimes, Lee thought he was stuck in one of those nightmares he could never remember. Sometimes he felt trapped by his decisions.

But he was in too deep to go back now.

Now, the only way out was through.

Lee took a sidelong glance at his partner.

Abe chewed on a stalk of grass.

He seemed pensive.

"You see something wrong?" Lee mumbled.

Abe shook his head. "Just thinking."

Lee said nothing. Waited.

"It was weird, how we met. You remember that?"

"At selection?"

"Well, yeah. But more specifically…the beach that night."

Lee nodded. "Yeah. I remember. What was weird about it?"

"That we're sitting here. Together. Over a decade later."

Lee raised his eyebrow, searching for a bit of humor, but Abe's gaze was outward, his face serious.

"We both must have left the dorms at about the same time. What was it? Midnight?"

"Something like that."

"You must have just left a minute or two ahead of me. And you ran out there on the beach. You picked the same direction I did. And you must have ran as far as you could go."

"What makes you say that?"

"Because I ran as far as I could go. And when I stopped, you were standing there." Abe squinted at Lee with a slight smile on his face. "And you were never able to beat me in the run. So that must've been as far as you could go, too."

Lee chuffed with a faint smile. Abe was right. All through selection, he and Abe were head to head on the runs. But Lee could never quite catch Abe. Abe was always a second or two faster, or had a little bit left in the tank on the final mile.

"Isn't that weird?" Abe said again. "Of all the places to be on that night, we wind up standing right next to each other. We both wind up running all-out to clear our heads, and we both gas out, right at the same spot on old Coronado Beach." He shook his head. "It's weird, man."

"And now here we are," Lee said.

"Yeah. Here we are."

His father's voice, like an echo: *You'd run until you couldn't run anymore. And we never did find out where you were trying to get to. Hell, I don't think you ever reached it.*

Abe shook himself out of his reverie. He spat a bit of the grass stalk out, then nodded in the direction of La Casa. "Anyways. What's on the menu?"

Lee readjusted his cheek weld to take the strain off of his neck. Flicked a drop of sweat quivering on his eyebrows. "Well. You'll be pleased to learn that those two tankers are still there."

Out of the corner of his eye, Lee noticed that Abe did seem to perk up.

"You think they're still full?" Abe pondered.

"They've only been there for a day, so probably." Lee sucked his teeth, and let a note of exasperation tinge his voice. "We could always just light them on fire and see how long they burn."

Abe made a disgruntled noise in the back of his throat. "Lee. You're my brother. I have your back. I'm not gonna say shit about you getting your pound of flesh. But I'd like for you to shut the fuck up about me trying to send some tankers back to the UES."

"They're a distraction," Lee replied, his voice flat.

"To you."

"You want to get them back for Julia just as much as I do."

Abe didn't respond.

Well, Lee thought. *Maybe he doesn't.*

"What we need to be doing," Lee grumbled. "Is focusing on doing damage to *Nuevas Fronteras*. The more damage we do, the more likely Mateo Ibarra is to show himself."

"Or less likely," Abe said. "You're operating on this assumption that he's some sort of hot head. What if he doesn't give a shit, Lee? What if he's cold as ice?"

Irritation caused the bottom of Lee's throat to tighten and feel hot. "He'll come out. Somehow. I'll get a shot at him. We just have to put our heads down. Focus."

"You know what would be a great way to do damage to *Nuevas Fronteras*?"

Lee propped himself up on his elbows, looking out across the distance with his naked eye. He already knew what was coming, but invited it anyways with a snap of temper. "What's that, Abe?"

"We could have the Marines come fuck their shit up," Abe shot at him. "If only we could get them enough fuel to make it here in force."

"You're like a broken record."

"And you can't see the forest through the trees."

"Fuck you."

"Yeah, fuck you too. Asshole."

Lee sighed through his nose. Clenched his teeth until the desire to start swinging ebbed. "Moving on." He smooshed his cheek back onto the rifle's buttstock and looked through the scope again. "I've got two guards at the west side of the house. What appears to be another two on the east side, though I've only caught shirtsleeves at this time. There's one roving unit. Two men. They're circling the perimeter."

There lasted several long seconds of silence.

Lee's heart thudded against his sternum.

A breeze moved a strand of grass that tickled against his forearm, but felt good as it dried his sweat, if only for a moment.

"What's their attitude like?" Abe finally said, with a more relaxed voice.

Both men let out a quiet breath of release.

They were back on track.

Back to business.

Beating the shit out of each other would have to wait for another day.

"They look bored," Lee observed, reading the faces and body language of the cartel foot soldiers milling about La Casa. "Everyone looks bored."

"Bored is complacent."

Lee nodded. "If we can hit 'em in the middle of the night, we might be able to skip the firefight part. Might be able to get a decent stock of ammunition if we don't spook them into wasting it all."

"How close are the tankers to the house?"

"About twenty yards off."

"That's far enough that we could fire the house while they're sleeping. Take them when they bunch together outside." Abe spat again, and seemed about to say something else, but then stopped.

Lee heard it, right at the moment when he watched Abe's shoulders tense up and his grip tighten on his rifle.

"That's an engine," Lee said, rolling out of his prone position behind the Barret .50 caliber and swiping up his M4.

Abe came to one knee, his rifle at a low ready. He faced west—away from La Casa—back towards the dirt road that accessed their hideout. "You think they found the truck?"

They'd hidden the truck a good distance away from their hideout. But if the cartel patrols had been ranging out a little further than normal from La Casa, they might've seen fresh tire tracks, or any number of other spoor that could've given the truck away.

And if they found the truck, they'd recognize it as the one belonging to their missing friends.

Lee stood up. "I don't know." He kicked brush over the Barret. He hated to leave it so soon after acquiring it, but he wasn't going to get into a firefight with that stupidly heavy chunk of metal. Not with only nine rounds to spare. And he had no way to carry it on his back while keeping his M4 in his hands.

He'd have to call it a loss.

They listened for a moment, but couldn't hear the engine any more. It had definitely come from the road behind them. Lee was sure about that. It'd been too clear and loud for it to have come from La Casa.

Abe stood up as well. "Should we go back to the hideout?"

It was a risk. Just because a patrol might've found the truck, didn't mean that they'd found the hideout. And the hideout did have all of their food and supplies. Without them Lee and Abe might find their chances for survival suddenly dwindling.

But recent events had made them extremely wary about traps.

"We go," Lee said, finding himself whispering. "We'll put eyes on from the tree line. If there's a goddamned speck of dust out of place, I'm calling it and we run."

Abe seemed okay with that plan.

The two of them started moving, immediately dipping into the clusters of trees that surrounded the clearing at the top of the hill. They weren't far from the hideout. Maybe five hundred yards. But they couldn't see it through the brush. They would have to get closer.

They moved at a steady clip, but they kept it slow enough to be quiet.

Stands of juniper created hedgerows that were like walls. Lee hated them. You couldn't see through them, and you had to walk around them. They turned the woods into a maze. The only upside was that their needles made a soft blanket on the ground and kept their footfalls nearly inaudible.

They worked their way down the hill.

Up ahead, Lee caught a flash of white siding through the trees.

The hideout.

He stopped there, and listened.

His ears strained. Seeking the sounds of vehicles, or men speaking, or doors opening and closing.

All he heard was the quiet countryside.

Birds sang, oblivious.

A slow breeze shuffled some leaves.

Up ahead, another dense wall of juniper. Beyond that, they would have a view of the hideout. They could use the juniper as concealment. At least it would serve them somehow.

A deer trail made an obvious path through the center of the juniper. It looked like the deer used it as a bedding area, so that it created a sort of cave amongst the green boughs.

Lee squatted down on their side of the row of junipers. Through the deer trail, he saw most of their hideout. But not all of it. He would need to slink into the junipers to get the full view of the structure.

He stooped low into a squat, then shuffled forward, duck walking as quietly as he could, into the tight confines of the hollow space. He heard the slight rustle of the evergreen brush as Abe followed him in.

Squatting on his haunches, his rifle tucked to his chest, Lee peered out from under the juniper. Their hideout was only about fifty yards away now. His angle currently put them at a diagonal, off the back-left corner of the house—what Lee referred to as the "B-C corner."

As Lee already knew from being in the house for the last twenty hours, it didn't have many windows. It was a very simple ranch house. But Lee saw the larger window that faced east. The one he'd sat at earlier.

Unfortunately, the reflection of the sky completely obscured the glass.

He could see nothing inside.

"No visual through the window," Lee whispered.

The second that he breathed the words, everything went to shit.

Men started yelling, very close.

"You in the bushes! Don't fucking move! DO—NOT—FUCKING—MOVE!"

Lee and Abe's instinctive reaction was to move.

Abe started to spin, to get out the way they'd come in.

Lee shifted his weight to plunge straight forward.

The next words stopped them.

"I got five soldiers that are gonna rip those bushes to shreds if you twitch! I can see you, motherfucker! Put down your weapons!"

Shit, shit, shit.

They were right on the other side of the junipers. The damn bushes had hid them from Lee's view.

Lee and Abe were caught, dead to rights.

They'd known this day might come, and they'd agreed that they would never let the cartel take them alive. They'd agreed on a code word that meant they were going to go out in a hail of gunfire—better to die fighting.

Abe invoked it with a growl: "Sundance."

But Lee grabbed his arm to stop him.

Something that had been said had given him pause.

It was the word "soldiers."

Lee knew it was possible that the man shouting at them was cartel, and he was simply referring to his men as soldiers. But Lee decided to take a gamble, all of this flashing through his head in a bare instant.

"The cartel is on the other side of that hill," Lee said, loud and clear. "If you start shooting, they're going to come for all of us."

A momentary silence fell.

If this didn't work, then it would indeed be *Sundance*, and all Lee had to do was release Abe's arm. Then they'd tear out of there, shooting at anything that moved, until their fingers could no longer pull their triggers.

The one that had shouted at them spoke again, but this time with more hesitation. "Come out of the bushes. Do it slow."

Lee thought that he knew what that hesitation meant.

Both parties had thought the other to be cartel. Now that was being reevaluated.

It was Lee's only hope. And a slim one at that.

Maybe he was being an idiot.

He'd made mistakes before.

It was possible this would be his last one.

"I'm coming out," Lee said, more to Abe, than to the people that had them in their sights.

He didn't release his rifle. That, he would not do. But he left it pointing at the ground, his gun hand on the grip, and his support hand raised in front of him.

He shuffled forward.

Emerged from the hollow in the junipers.

He immediately became aware of several figures that he'd missed before, expertly hidden by the thick juniper stands. One immediately to his left, about ten yards away. Two more behind that man, about twenty yards, and a final two, about ten yards to Lee's right.

Lee noted that they all wore a conglomeration of US military fatigues. A patchwork of worse-for-wear UCP, MARPAT, and even some old ACU.

Lee stood up very slowly. His support hand still raised. His eyes sought out the man that had given them commands, and thought that he spotted him, in the group off to his right.

As Lee scanned the faces, he noted a wave of recognition go over them. They blinked at him, suddenly uncertain, but they didn't lower their own weapons.

Lee locked eyes with the one that seemed like he'd been the speaker.

The man frowned, and spoke again: "Take your hand off your rifle."

Lee wasn't going to do that. Instead, he rolled the dice yet again. "You recognize me," he said, hoping this was true, and that he hadn't misjudged their expressions. "Do you still work for Tex? Or Menendez?"

A subtle stir went through them.

They were disciplined enough not to make it obvious, but Lee saw it all the same.

The speaker—a man with corporal's stripes on his battered OCP uniform—took a half step forward, his rifle still pointed at Lee. "Your man in the bushes. Have him come out."

Lee made sure not to move too much or too suddenly. He didn't want to invite a barrage of gunfire from some itchy trigger fingers. His heart thudding hard in his throat, he looked over his shoulder and saw Abe's bearded face glaring up at him from inside the juniper.

Lee gave him a small nod.

Abe's face twisted. Lee saw his teeth flash behind his beard. But then he slowly slid out. Also raising his support hand—and also not taking his gun hand off his rifle.

He stood up, about a pace away from Lee, instinctively facing the opposite direction. Covering his back. If the shooting started, they'd be able to fire in two directions at once. The better to punish their attackers before they themselves were snuffed out.

The corporal craned his neck to look over his sights, focusing on Abe. "You with the big beard. I want you to very slowly turn and look at me."

Abe glowered, but then did as he was told, glaring at the other man from under his eyebrows.

Lee watched the corporal. Watched the muzzle of his rifle dip.

"Shit," was all the corporal said.

He recognized them. Lee was sure of that.

And that meant one of two things: Either Lee was horribly mistaken, and they were soldiers from Greeley who had seen Lee and Abe's face in photographs…

Or they had been a part of Tex's crew.

"Corporal," Lee said, speaking carefully, like a man balancing on a high wire. "I need to speak to whoever is in command."

The corporal stared at Lee for a long moment of silence, and then, keeping his rifle up with his gun hand, he used his support hand to key a PTT on his chest. He mumbled something into the mic that Lee couldn't make out. He had an earpiece in, so Lee couldn't hear whatever the response was, but after a moment, the corporal gave a faint nod and transmitted back, "Roger."

The corporal shifted his feet, both hands back on his rifle. "Captain Harden. Major Darabie. You're going to have to work with us. You can keep your rifles slung, but put your hands on your heads and interlace your fingers." Without waiting for them to respond, he raised his voice. "Gents, if they don't comply, hose them down."

Lee and Abe exchanged a glance.

Abe's gaze was fierce and suspicious.

Lee gave him the tiniest of shrugs.

Then they both raised their hands over their heads, and interlaced their fingers.

TWELVE

THE MEET

LEE AND ABE STEPPED THROUGH the front door of their hideout.

The corporal that had captured them led the way, and four of his soldiers followed behind Lee and Abe, who still had their hands clasped on top of their heads. The soldiers looked wary. But also…awestruck.

Lee had encountered these expressions before. He remembered when he'd stepped into Tex's bunker, after the firefight in Caddo, and had seen the wide eyes and heard the whispers as he walked past.

It used to make him feel uncomfortable.

Now, he didn't really care.

Nowadays, his reputation served a purpose.

Around them sat the musty detritus of an abandoned house. The corporal led them through the kitchen, where dirty dishes sat clustered on the counters, too old to even have a smell anymore. Then into the living room, which had the east-facing window, and Lee and Abe's supplies.

A dark-skinned soldier knelt, hunched over the old feed sack that contained a portion of the foodstuffs from Triprock. As he poked through the items, it didn't escape Lee that the soldier looked gaunt and hungry himself.

Still, he hadn't taken anything.

When Lee and Abe entered the room, the man stood up and faced them.

"Sergeant Menendez," Lee said, doing a decent job of keeping the shock out of his voice.

Menendez looked Lee right in the face, his eyes scouring over Lee's features, as though seeking to confirm his identity. Then he looked at Abe.

It seemed that maybe he hadn't believed who his corporal had claimed to find. But then realization crashed over his face, and he faltered.

"Holy shit," Menendez muttered, not bothering to hide his own surprise. His eyes coursed back and forth between them.

Lee noted that his tone was not entirely friendly.

Menendez raised a finger and gestured at the two of them. "You two. You have some explaining to do."

Lee raised his eyebrows. "Oh? That's funny."

Menendez's expression flared. "Most of our men are dead. And you call it funny?"

Lee's eyes narrowed. "Their deaths? No. Not funny at all. What's funny is you thinking that I have shit to explain to you."

Menendez took a step forward. "Who the hell do you think you are?"

"Me?" Lee shook his head. "I'm Nobody." He nodded towards Abe. "He's No One."

The blow struck, exactly as Lee had intended.

Menendez's head pulled back, like he wanted to retreat a step. "*Nadie y Ninguno*," he muttered.

Lee didn't give him the benefit of a confirmation. "Here's what I know, sergeant. Me and my friend have spent the last month hitting *Nuevas Fronteras* in every place we can make them hurt. We've been drawing blood. We've been making them pay. And while we've done it we've starved and nearly died a hundred times." Lee leaned forward, his words becoming sharp. "So no, I don't think I have shit to explain to you. But what I'd love to hear from you, is what *you've* been doing?"

"I should kill you right now," Menendez breathed, but it lacked heat. It lacked conviction.

Lee wasn't ignorant of the fact that he was pushing his luck. He felt Abe's tension beside him, though Abe knew better than to intervene. They might not agree on everything, but Abe trusted Lee's instincts. And Lee's instincts told him not to give an inch.

So he shrugged. "Should you, then? I wonder why?"

"The assault on the power plant was your operation!"

"Bullshit," Lee spat. "It was Tex's operation and you know it."

"How did you make it out alive?" Menendez demanded.

"I stood over Julia's corpse and I decided that I didn't care if I lived or died anymore. The first Cornerstone operative that approached, I took from behind. I used his weapon to shoot his partner. Then I shot him under his chin. Then I drew the rest of them in, and I took out their comms, and I killed them, one by one, until it was just me and their commanding officer in a truck. Him I stabbed to death."

Out of the corner of Lee's eye, he saw Abe looking at him.

He'd never even told that story to Abe.

Abe had never asked.

"You want me to believe that you took out an entire squad of trained operatives by yourself?" Menendez said, trying to rally himself. But he sounded like he did believe it, despite himself.

"I don't want you to believe anything," Lee murmured, calm now. "You asked a question. I gave you an answer. How did *you* make it out alive?"

Menendez seemed on the verge of rebelling. But then the tension went out of his shoulders. He slouched. "We hid. In one of the guard shacks in the power plant." His voice was quieter. Exhausted. "We heard them killing everyone in the forest. We heard the gunships raking the woods with fire. We waited until they pulled back. Then we ran back for the beach head. We found one canoe that didn't have bullet holes in it. Four of us in the canoe. The rest hanging onto the sides when they couldn't swim for themselves anymore. And we went back across the lake."

"Did anyone else make it out?" Lee asked, gentler than before. The initial challenges now dealt with, it was time to be more diplomatic.

Menendez shook his head. "I don't know. We thought we were the only ones that made it out. Until now."

Lee considered this for a moment. Did that mean that Tex was dead? Had Joaquin simply lied to Lee for the sake of lying? One final piece of misinformation?

"Can I put my hands down?" Lee asked.

Menendez eyed him. Suspicion gave way to resignation. He nodded.

Lee and Abe both unclasped their hands and let them hang at their sides.

The soldiers surrounding them visibly relaxed.

The final barrier now removed, it felt like they were all on the same side again.

"Are you and your boys hungry?" Lee asked.

Menendez managed a grim smirk. "Is it that obvious?"

It pained Lee to do it, but an olive branch needed to be extended. Food was a good way to make friends out of starving soldiers. He nodded to the sacks of supplies at their feet. "We have enough. Help yourselves."

The soldiers around them looked at the satchels eagerly, but Menendez didn't make a move just yet. He gestured to the foodstuffs. "Where'd they come from?"

Lee took a cautious step forward, and when no one tensed or seemed ready to intercept him, he continued. He knelt down and opened the old feed sack that Menendez had been poking around in. "We got it from Triprock."

Menendez stood over Lee as he drew out the salt pork. Lee offered it to Menendez. The sergeant hesitated, but then gave in and took it.

"Triple Rocker Ranch?" Menendez asked, handing the pork off to one of his soldiers that was not so hesitant, and who immediately drew out his knife to begin carving it. "I thought that was held by the cartel."

"It was. Until last night." Lee upended the sack and spilled the rest of the contents out. There were some mason jars with home-canned vegetables. Some smoked meats. A large sack of some sort of grain meal.

Menendez's hesitation finally ceded to his responsibility to feed his men, and he began helping Lee distribute the foodstuffs to the soldiers. "Make sure the boys on watch get some."

Lee took a seat on the floor, folding his legs, as comfortable as if it were his home and the soldiers around him his guests. Abe followed suit, putting his back to the wall near the east-facing window. Lee gestured to the floor across from him, offering Menendez a seat.

The sergeant sat with a tired huff. "What happened at Triprock?"

Lee took a measured sip of water, then gave the bottle to Menendez who gulped from it eagerly. Then he relayed the basics of what had gone down the previous night. Not entirely sure how much to give away, Lee left out a few important factors, such as their capture of Joaquin Leyva and his subsequent interrogation.

Menendez listened, chewing at a slice of what Lee figured was smoked antelope.

"In any case," Lee concluded. "Triprock won't be around much longer."

"You think the cartel will come back?"

Lee nodded. "I know they will. And whoever decided to stay in Triprock…well…hopefully everyone takes our advice and gets gone."

Menendez eyed him. "Do you think they will?"

Lee avoided the eye contact.

His thoughts jumped back to Sally and Eric and Catalina. He pictured their faces, staring at him, telling him that they needed his help.

He'd turned his back on them.

I told them to leave, he railed against the small part of himself that seemed to stand in judgment of his actions. *I told them. If they didn't listen, then that's on them! They're not my responsibility! I can't save everyone!*

And that was true.

He couldn't.

But maybe what bothered him was that he hadn't even tried.

Sometimes it's not the things we do that cause the most regret.

Sometimes it's the things we don't do.

In the end, Lee shrugged in response to Menendez's question, because that was all he could do. "If they stay, that's their problem," Lee said, and he knew he was wrong, but he thought maybe if he kept telling himself that, it would eventually take.

He unclipped his rifle from its sling and laid it beside him. He regarded Menendez for a moment, and then the four soldiers that had taken up seats around the room, sharing a can of this, or a slice of that.

"You don't have access to the bunkers, do you?" Lee asked, though it was more an observation than a question.

Menendez shot him a look. "Obviously not."

Lee had suspected as much—otherwise Menendez and his surviving crew wouldn't be half-starved. He still felt disappointed. "Then I'm also assuming you've had no contact with Tex."

Menendez paused in his chewing. Then continued, slower. He stared at the bit of jerky left in his hand. Swallowed. "Tex is dead," he said with finality, then shoved the rest of the jerky in his mouth.

Lee felt his stomach dip. But he kept his expression level. "Did you see him die?"

Menendez sighed. "No."

"Have you seen his dead body?"

"No."

"How do you know that he's dead?" Lee was earnest with this. He was not trying to deny facts. He was just trying to get to the truth.

Menendez wiped his fingers off on his pants. "Suppose I don't. I just..." he hesitated with his words, and didn't pick them up again, leaving the silence hanging.

"You figured he would've reached out by now," Lee suggested.

Menendez nodded.

Lee felt marginally better now that Tex's body hadn't been confirmed dead. That didn't mean he was alive. But there was other evidence that pointed to him being out there still.

"If I were to take a guess, Tex wasn't entirely sure who was in on the trap. I think he knew enough to know that Captain Bellamy from Greeley was the one that set it up, and he may have even known enough that Cornerstone was the one that sprung it. But Tex, for all his bluster, he's a cautious guy." Lee stretched his back, feeling the tightness of hard nights and harder days. "If he is still out there, he's probably waiting for the snakes to reveal themselves before he comes out of hiding."

"There are no snakes," Menendez remarked. "Bellamy, of course. Cornerstone, as you pointed out. But none of Tex's guys were in on it. That I can guarantee you."

Lee considered telling Menendez that he couldn't "guarantee" him a damn thing, but chose to keep that tidbit to himself. He had other things on his mind.

"Have you been to the bunker north of Caddo?" Lee asked. "The one we ran the power plant operation out of?"

Menendez looked at Lee's bottle of water with a certain note of longing, so Lee passed it to him and he took another deep gulp before answering. "Yes."

Lee leaned forward. "And you didn't get access, I'm assuming. Or you wouldn't be starving."

"No. We didn't."

Lee nodded. "Correct me if I'm wrong here. Tex gave me the lowdown on his coalition when we first got here. He told me that he'd changed the bunkers' security settings to allow anyone with a passcode to access them. That way his outposts could use them for resupply and fallback points without him and his GPS unit having to be there."

Menendez nodded. "Yeah. That's right."

"So if you weren't able to access it, then he changed the settings back to default. Closed them off to anyone but himself."

Menendez shrugged. "That's possible. But I wasn't able to get access to that bunker because I was never given the passcode to it. I have the passcode to two other bunkers, but they're in northern Texas, close to the Oklahoma border."

"Did you attempt to open the bunker north of Caddo?"

Menendez smirked. "No. You don't want to enter the wrong passcode."

Lee smiled back. "The bunkers defend themselves, that's for sure."

Automated Vulcan cannons and grenade launchers made sure of that. Anyone trying to tamper with the system would be reduced to mincemeat.

"How long did you watch the bunker?" Lee asked.

"Not long. Six hours. We had to keep on the move."

"We'd left wounded there, before the power plant operation."

"Yeah. Breckenridge had control of the bunker when we left that night."

"And I'm assuming you saw no sign of him?"

"No." Menendez took a breath. "No sign of anybody. Up until now."

"So what brought you over here?" Lee asked. "I'm beginning to think you've been tracking me."

"Nothing quite so sexy," Menendez admitted. "We had our eye on this house for the same reason I'm assuming you did."

"La Casa," Lee intuited.

Menendez nodded. "Small target. Small-ish, anyways. Thought we might get ourselves some food and fuel."

Lee took a drink from his water bottle again. "How many men do you have?"

"Eight. Including myself."

Lee considered this as he recapped the bottle. "Well, sergeant, I think we can work something out."

THIRTEEN

CIVILIAN

ANGELA SAT AT HER DESK in the sheriff's office.

Directly across from her, Ed and Carl had just taken their seats.

They were waiting on a fourth.

Carl pushed the rolled sleeves of his combat shirt up past his elbows. "First Sergeant Hamrick just reported in."

Ed adjusted his seat and regarded his neighbor with hesitant curiosity. He was less concerned about military matters. More concerned with his own people. But, almost out of politeness, Ed seemed compelled to ask, "Any good news?"

"No, Ed," Carl replied. "Not good news."

Ed nodded, and looked away.

Angela tapped an irritable finger on the desktop. "Go on, then."

Carl kept a level face, but she saw a small tightening of the tension around his eyes. "Squads hit what looks like a potential colony as they were trying to secure Augusta for a comms relay and route-through. We lost another squad."

Angela blinked a few times, and Carl seemed to understand what she was thinking before she had to ask it.

“Sam’s fine,” he said. “It was a different squad.”

Angela nodded, surprised at the release she felt in her chest. Sam wasn’t her child, and she wasn’t blind to the fact that he didn’t want to be. It had simply been…unfortunate circumstance that had landed him in her care.

But he didn’t need mothering anymore.

He was, for all intents and purposes, a soldier now.

But, she still worried about him, the same as she worried about Lee. And Julia. And Marie. And all the other people that she knew were out there, putting their lives on the line.

“How long until they can clear the route?” Angela asked. “Have they given any projections?”

It wasn’t supposed to be Carl’s job to be the go-between for First Sergeant Hamrick. He wasn’t supposed to have become the oversight for the Hunter-Killer squads.

But then again, Angela wasn’t supposed to be a leader. And here she was.

Sometimes you fell into your circumstances. Like fate had left a trap for you.

Besides, Carl might’ve had ulterior motives for getting involved in pushing the Hunter-Killer squads to work faster. There was a list of Lincolnists that he needed. And he needed to get to Fort Bragg to get it.

“On the outside,” Carl answered. “Maybe a week.”

Angela drew her thumb and forefinger down across the corners of her mouth. “Week’s a long time. Maybe they should just pass it by.”

“They used a roadblock,” Carl said.

The words hung there.

"The primals?" Angela clarified. "Used a roadblock?"

Carl nodded. "That's what the squads are reporting."

"I highly doubt they created a roadblock."

Carl leaned forward. "It doesn't matter if they created it, ma'am. It matters that they used it. They knew that it would hem the squads up, and they used it as a trap."

Angela leaned back, feeling the ever-present anxiety compact her stomach even further. She felt like people kept adding small weights to her stomach. It was gradually getting harder to breathe.

Through this, Ed remained still and quiet. His wizened eyes watching Angela the whole time. And, she felt, judging her.

A figure appeared on the other side of the glass-fronted office, and the door opened.

Angela stood. "Brinly. Please come in."

Brinly's large frame filled the doorway. Gone were the sergeant's stripes from his desert-digital Marine uniform. Replaced by a major's oak leaves. A drastic and sudden change to be sure. One he'd argued against: "It's not how these things are done."

But nothing was done as it once had been.

Despite the fact that there existed other Marine officers, Brinly had been Colonel Staley's senior enlisted man for the past four years. In fact, he'd been Staley's right-hand ever since the survivors at Camp Ryder had made contact with the Marines from Camp Lejeune, nearly five years ago now.

It'd been Staley and Brinly that Lee had met the first time.

It'd been Staley and Brinly that had helped them defeat the massive hordes of infected migrating southward from the northern population centers.

Brinly had been the closest to Staley. And the one with the most command experience. Also, he was the one that Angela already knew and trusted.

Command structure being as ad hoc as it was, the existing captains and lieutenants were already accustomed to taking orders from Brinly. Angela figured they could swallow their hurt feelings at being passed over to fill Staley's spot.

"Madam President," Brinly said, then nodded to the other two. "Master sergeant. Sheriff."

Angela cringed at the title, but forced a smile. "How many times are we going to go over this?"

Brinly took a seat at the one remaining chair. He regarded her with intelligent blue-green eyes. "Old habits die hard, Ms. Houston," he said, in his faint Chicago accent.

Better.

"How are your Marines adjusting?" By which Angela meant *the officers that had been passed over.*

"They're adjusting."

Angela nodded. Brinly had always kept his words sparse. Moreso now since his commission. "Thank you for joining us," she said with off-handed politeness. She settled into her chair, leaning forward with her elbows on the desk. She considered each of them in turn. They knew what this meeting was about. But they still waited for her to fire the first volley.

She raised her hands and folded them in front of her face. It was not the commanding posture that she would have liked, but in that moment, she didn't care. “Not to put too fine a point on it,” Angela said, her mouth moving just above her hands. “But we’re up against the ropes, gentlemen. We need to figure out what we’re going to do about it.”

She flicked a finger in Brinly’s direction. “Major Brinly has been down here since Lee’s first contact with this *Nuevas Fronteras* cartel. Now he’s sitting on our entire contingent of Marines. That’s a resource that needs to be used.”

Next, she looked to Carl. “Carl’s been working hard on his investigations, and is also working with First Sergeant Hamrick to secure the route back to Bragg, and erect communications relays.”

She shifted to Ed. “And Ed’s been working on making contact with some of the other Safe Zones here in the UES, to take the temperature of the political situation, you might say.”

Ed’s moustache betrayed a slight twitch.

Angela took care not to let her breath come out of her in a great, irritable whoosh. She knew what was coming. She dipped her head in Ed’s direction. “Go ahead, Ed. Lay it out.”

Despite the preamble, Ed still managed to look put on the spot. Or maybe he was just that uncomfortable with being the bearer of bad news. “Well,” he began in his jowly growl. “Charleston is still out of contact. I’ve tried multiple times, over the course of the last week. No success. That makes five weeks, by my reckoning.” His gaze avoided Angela’s. “They’ve been out of contact since Fort Bragg fell. Our Georgia sister, the Moody Safe Zone, is still with us.” Ed’s hands drew together in his lap. The thumbs wrestled with each other. “Florida has…a lot of questions.”

Angela cleared her throat. "Ed's a very kind man. Let me cut through the crap cake here. Charleston is most likely out of contact because they want nothing to do with us anymore. And Florida is wavering. Two months ago, everything was peachy. The fall of Fort Bragg has shattered everyone's confidence." Angela's jaw worked for a second. "Despite the fact that it was primals that pushed us out, a lot of folks are speculating that it was a Greeley victory. And if we can't even hold our so-called capital, they think, then the war against Briggs must be unwinnable."

Carl rubbed a thoughtful finger on the armrest of his chair. "Is it possible that something happened to Charleston? Maybe that's why they're out of contact?"

Angela nodded. "Oh yes, that's possible." Here, she looked to Brinly with a shrewd squint. "But what did Staley do at Camp Lejeune when Briggs wanted them to abandon North Carolina? Did he get in contact with Briggs and tell him what he was doing?"

Brinly raised one graying eyebrow. "No, ma'am. We just…dropped out of contact."

"Exactly," Angela said. "If something bad was going down in Charleston, I believe they would have attempted some sort of communication with us and *then* dropped off. And then I would be concerned for them. As it stands right now, they were in contact until right after we lost Fort Bragg, and then magically, with no warning, all the sudden they're off-line. All signs point to them willfully withdrawing from the UES. And Florida is right behind them."

She pushed back from her desk. "So, as I stated, we're up against the ropes. As Lee would say, it's do or die time for the United Eastern States."

"Okay," Carl said. "Maybe Charleston is a lost cause. But if we can reestablish a foothold in Fort Bragg, that might bolster some confidence. Keep Florida from flying the coop."

Angela nodded. "I agree. Getting back into Fort Bragg would give us access to a lot of supplies we had to leave behind. As well as the crops and cattle—if the primals haven't ripped them to shreds already."

"The cattle were sequestered inside the fields, correct?" Carl asked.

"Yes. Fields Ten, Twelve, and Fifteen." She held up a finger. "Just like all the other fields, they have high voltage wires to protect them from the primals. But we evacuated our crew from the power plant. If anything has happened to the power grid in the last month, those fields might be down. Same goes for the crop fields."

"The primals never showed any interest in the crops," Carl pointed out. "Just in the workers tending them."

"So if the power is still on when we get back, then yes, we might have some food available. Getting food moving again, and getting Fort Bragg secured again, would alleviate a lot of the rationing and overcrowding here in Butler, and could bolster Florida's loyalty. But we're still weeks away from getting back to Fort Bragg, and who knows how long it will take to secure it. And how much manpower it will require."

"My Marines are ready, ma'am," Brinly put in. "They've been on standby for too long."

"And there's a reason for that," Angela replied. "What's the fuel situation?"

"We have enough to sustain a decent combat operation," Brinly answered. "Maybe a month's worth."

"And then we won't have enough to run the farming operations."

"No, we wouldn't."

Angela picked up a pen and began fiddling with it, staring at it as she did. "My point being, gentlemen, we don't know if we'll get more fuel or not. We don't even know if Lee is still alive."

She said it without much emotion. And she was glad of that. Though her chest felt like someone had gripped it in two enormous hands and was squeezing the life out of it.

She dragged her eyes up to Brinly's. "So we are now at the point where we need to decide what we are going to do with your Marines, Brinly. Originally, the plan that had been orchestrated was that Lee would continue to steal fuel from *Nuevas Fronteras*, and send it our way. With that, we would fuel a Marine incursion into *Nuevas Fronteras* territory, and hopefully stabilize operations there, and secure a more reliable source of fuel. With a reliable source of fuel, we could stand on our own. Without it, then the clock is ticking on the UES. It's just that simple. So, do we use what we have and send the Marines to assist in the retaking of Fort Bragg? Or do we stick with the original plan and go west, in the hopes that we still have some sort of allies waiting for us on the other side?"

She raised her hands, as though offering the dilemma up to the others.

Carl looked around at the others. He exchanged a quick glance with Brinly, and Brinly seemed to offer the floor to Carl.

"Re-establishing the Fort Bragg Safe Zone would be my first priority. It's not a one or the other scenario, ma'am. We can send the Marines north to Fort Bragg. They'll speed up the timeline for the retaking of Fort Bragg. In the meantime, you can use that as a carrot to keep Florida in line, and maybe even get Charleston back. Once things have stabilized, and we have the whole of the UES—or as much of it as possible—working with us, we can mount a stiffer assault on the cartel controlling the oil." He shrugged, as though to say those were his two cents, and relaxed back into his chair.

Brinly's eyebrows cinched more and more into a frown as Carl spoke. He stirred himself. "All respect to Master Sergeant Gilliard, but Hamrick's troops are already making good progress towards Fort Bragg. My Marines would certainly accelerate the timeline. But at what cost? By the time things are done, we may not have the fuel necessary to mount *any* sort of incursion. And then we're back at square one, which is where we found ourselves at the start of this whole thing: We need fuel, and the only foreseeable source of that is currently controlled by a cartel—a cartel, that, I might remind you, looks like it's in bed with Greeley. As long as *Nuevas Fronteras* maintains control of the oil, we grow weaker and our enemies grow stronger."

Angela ran a thumbnail over her eyebrow. "So, you're saying we leave Fort Bragg to Hamrick's army, and use your Marines to go west—the original plan."

"The original plan has merit," Brinly stated.

Angela found that to be something of a non-answer. She maintained eye contact until it was obvious that she wanted him to take a stance of some sort.

He smirked, knowing what was required of him. "Yes, ma'am. I think the better option would be for me and my Marines to go west. If we can't secure a constant source of fuel, we can at least steal what there is from the cartel. Marines are very good at stealing things. Plus, we might be able to reestablish contact with Lee, or any other allies we have over there." He shrugged. "If not, then that's okay. We can still rob them blind. Upset the balance of power. Grow our own capabilities, and deny resources to the enemy."

Carl and Brinly appeared to have a mutual respect for each other. However, Angela wasn't sure this extended into friendship. Carl listened to Brinly, keeping his face a mask of impassivity, and when Brinly was done, he gave the Marine a slight nod, and then refocused on Angela.

"Major Brinly raises some excellent points. However, opening up another war front when we're currently displaced out of our capitol might be a turnoff to the other Safe Zones. You could risk alienating them further."

Brinly nodded. "All due respect to the master sergeant, but I believe it might be smarter to play the long game here. Those other safe zones aren't going anywhere, even if they lose faith in you. And when you capture a means of oil production, I have a feeling their faith will be restored."

Carl didn't emote much, but Angela saw a twitch of irritation in his features. Finally, he turned and spoke directly to Brinly. "Sir. The other safe zones aren't just empty pockets of survivors. Those are potential resources. They also have crops. And they also have troops. If they switch sides, we can't just shrug that off. That means they would become threats in our own backyard, as opposed to allies."

"I'm confident we can maintain them as allies if we have access to fuel," Brinly returned.

"I'm not sure we have that kind of time. While we're trying to get our shit in order, Angela will be speaking with the other Safe Zones, essentially negotiating with them to stay together. We don't want her entering into those negotiations empty-handed."

"A promise of a reliable source of fuel won't be empty-handed."

"Half our fighting force indisposed somewhere in Texas will be a weak bargaining position. Better to have them close at hand, helping retake Fort Bragg."

Brinly frowned. "How much of this is about the overall strategy? And how much of this is about your vendetta against the Lincolnists?"

Carl met Brinly's gaze coolly. "I would think that handling saboteurs and insurgents in the middle of a war effort would be of paramount concern to everybody."

"Stop," Angela said. "Thank you Major Brinly. Thank you Master Sergeant Gilliard. Your perspectives are always valuable. And they're quite clear at this point." She turned to the only person in the room whose opinion remained a mystery. "Ed? Would you care to weigh in?"

Ed managed to look put on the spot again. Like he'd hoped to be a fly on the wall the whole time. He took a deep breath. Nodded to the two military men to his left. "All good points," he said with some obvious discomfort. "I'm sure these two gents know a helluva lot more about war fighting than an old has-been law dog—"

"I just want your opinion," Angela interrupted him. "We're all adults. Say what you mean to say."

Ed managed a small smile under his white mustache. "Yes, ma'am. Of course. My opinion is…uh…" he shuffled about in his seat. His eyes crinkled up, peering at Angela. "Are we putting the cart before the horse a bit here?"

Angela raised her hands. "I don't know. What do you mean?"

"I mean, we don't even know how hard it's gonna be to retake Fort Bragg. Things seem to be changing real quick around here. It seems to me like sending the Marines off before you know the situation right here at home…well, that seems a little…maybe a little rash."

I need a bigger council, Angela thought, looking at Ed's old eyes. *One guy says one thing, another says the opposite, and the tie breaker doesn't want to take sides.*

But more people would only lead to more opinions. And more opinions weren't going to clarify the right course of action. They'd only muddy the waters. Angela was dreaming a dream if she thought that a meeting like this would ever reach any sort of consensus.

Ultimately, the decision was up to her.

She had to keep reminding herself of that.

Time to put on your big-girl pants and make a decision.

"Brinly," Angela said, turning to him. "Do you have an officer that you trust?"

"Captain Trenton," Brinly answered without hesitation.

Angela nodded. "I want you to assign to him control of half of your Marine forces. He's going to assist in the route clearance operations to Fort Bragg, and with the efforts to retake it. He can coordinate with Master Sergeant Gilliard, and First Sergeant Hamrick."

Brinly nodded, but with a crease in his brow.

Angela answered the obvious question that Brinly was thinking about. "I want you to take the other half. Hand pick them. Use whatever resources you think you need. I want you to go west, no stops, straight to the last known position of Lee and his team. I think that would be in mid-Texas somewhere. I want you to maintain constant contact with me while you do. I want to know what the hell is going on over there. I want to know if it's practical for us to get involved, and what that entails. Priority number one will be reconnaissance. Priority number two will be getting fuel back to us." She raised her eyebrows at the Marine. "Questions? Concerns? Speak now or forever hold your peace."

"Yes, ma'am," Brinly bobbed his graying head. "One major concern: I'm not sure how wise it is to split the Marine forces. Better to have one effective fighting force than two forces at half strength."

Angela always found herself hesitating in moments like this. Commander-in-chief was one of her supposed titles, and yet she always felt woefully underprepared to make military decisions like this. She tended to defer to the military men, as she didn't want to be "that civilian" that made terrible decisions against the advice of the people who knew better.

And yet, she'd deferred and deferred and deferred for her entire time as president.

And look where that had gotten her.

It was time to change tactics.

"Your primary objective isn't as a fighting force, major," Angela replied. "It's reconnaissance."

Brinly considered this. "And the half of my forces that will be on route clearance? And retaking Fort Bragg?"

"They'll be working alongside Hamrick's Hunter-Killer squads."

A long few seconds of silence fell on the room.

"When would you like us to leave?" Brinly asked, resigning himself to his new mission.

"How soon can you?"

"Give me a day to make arrangements with Captain Trenton and the boys I'll be heading west with."

Angela nodded. "Would today be enough of a day?"

Brinly nodded. "Yes, ma'am."

"Then tomorrow," Angela said.

She eyed the three men across from her. She found it a good sign that both Ed and Carl appeared mollified. Only Brinly seemed to have reservations. And that, she thought, was about as close to consensus as she'd ever get.

She hoped she'd made the right decision.

And God help her if she turned out to be "that civilian."

FOURTEEN

AUGUSTA

FIFTEEN MEN STOOD in a tight circle.

Inside that circle was Sergeant Billings, and an impromptu sand table.

They were at Checkpoint Scarecrow, located in a small, gated industrial building, south of Augusta. It wasn't completely secure, but it was *more* secure.

Kind of like a *relatively* Safe Zone.

A collection of Humvees, pickup technicals, and MATVs created an outer perimeter around the men, like circled wagons. Just in case. Their gunners had their various mounted weaponry pointed outward, scanning for anything that looked like it might want to take a bite out of them.

Sam hung over Jones's shoulder, peering down at Billings as he drew in the dirt with a stick.

One big circle.

"This is I-Five-Twenty," Billings said. Then he drew another line that intersected it. "This is Highway One, our main route onto the loop." A squiggle in the dirt, not far from the intersection that he'd just drawn. "This is the barricade where we lost Squad Seven, and Squad Three, the day before. The primals have hit this area twice. I can't speak to what happened with Squad Three, but we were there when they took out Loudermouth, and they went north, straight into this area here." He tapped a general area of dirt inside the main loop, then looked up at the gathered soldiers. "We do not have a positive ID on wherever they're shacking up, but we know these things keep a wide hunting territory. It could be anywhere within Augusta. But we're going to start here and see what we get. They like houses and small cozy buildings, so I think this neighborhood area right here is the most likely candidate. That's what we're going to come in on."

Billings leaned back, squatted on his haunches. "I'd like to get in and out before dark. I'm gonna call that six hours." He met the various gazes of the team leaders huddled around him. "We're going to come in via Highway One, up to this road here—Richmond Hill. Squad One, you'll position here, at the intersection of Highway One and Lumpkin."

Someone guffawed and mumbled, "Lumpkins. That's a good name for Squad One."

Billings ignored the chuckles and continued: "Squad Two, you're going to be right up the road at Highway One and Wheeless Road. Squad Six, you're at Highway One and Richmond Hill. Squads Ten and Twelve, you're with us, spreading out along Richmond Hill. My squad will go deep, all the way down Richmond Hill to Overlook Road, which will get us access to the neighborhood."

One of the squad leaders shuffled his feet and frowned. "You making us all containment so your squad gets all the CKs?"

Billings smirked up at the man. "Relax. We estimated about a hundred primals. If they're in this area, we're all gonna get some CKs. There's enough to go around, so let's not get stupid about it, hua?"

A smattering of "hua" trickled back.

Billings scanned the gathering until he found the face he was looking for. "Scots, you and your Highlanders are gonna be parked right in front of an apartment complex. You know these things love an apartment complex, so keep an eye on it. While the rest of us get in position, you'll need to take a lap through the complex and see if you don't find any activity."

Scots, a tall, skeletal redhead nodded.

"Once everyone is in position and the Highlanders have cleared that complex, we're gonna start rolling into this neighborhood on our individual streets. If you ID any activity, call out the location and we'll begin to move to you. Squad leaders, there's gonna be a lot of moving parts and street names coming over the radio, so pay attention and keep your maps handy and try to avoid catching each other in crossfire."

Billings stood up, his knees cracking. He stretched his back. "This will be our rally point if shit goes sideways."

"You mean 'when,'" Scots said, with a smirk.

Billings nodded. "Right. I don't want anyone to take unnecessary risks, but let's remember that if we can clear these things out, we'll have a path to Columbia, South Cackalacky, and then the next stop is back home. Y'all ready?"

Everyone was.

Twenty minutes later, Sam was back in his seat behind Chris.

Their Humvee was at the lead of the column, heading down Highway One. They'd already passed over the I-520 loop, and now approached their target street.

Sam stayed in his open window. The warm air flowed past him. He could faintly smell the exhaust from their own vehicle, but mostly it smelled like spring. All around them, the determined Georgia vegetation took back the city. Large stands of wisteria had bloomed purple across areas that had once been manicured. Sam smelled them strongest of all, and if he closed his eyes, it might've seemed pleasant.

But he wasn't going to close his eyes.

Others might have found the blooming flowers and trees beautiful. Sam only saw ruin.

He saw shadows. He saw hiding places. He saw danger points.

Nothing beautiful there.

"Right up here," Billings said, pointing out his window.

Chris slowed their truck and took the turn onto Richmond Hill.

In the center of the truck, the ball bearings on the turret rumbled as Pickell scanned around and around, looking for anything that seemed like it could use a large caliber projectile to the face.

So far, everything was still and quiet.

Houses. Buildings. Businesses. All slumped in their various stages of dilapidation.

The squads began to sound off as they took their intersections, building a perimeter around the target neighborhood.

"Alphas, in position."

"Wardogs, at One and Wheeless."

"Lead Farmers, we're here."

"Awww," Jones moaned, sounding stricken. "Lead Farmers? Godammit. Why didn't I think of that? Sarge, all the good names are getting taken."

Billings sighed. "Don't worry, little one. We'll find a good name."

"Ultimate Destruction Squad."

"No."

"The Giant Hard Dicks."

"No."

"Briny Bastards!" Pickell shouted from up top.

"Oh, Christ! Shut up, Pickell!" Jones elbowed him in the leg. "You're ruining it!"

They passed the apartment complex on the right. The one Scots's Highlanders would be covering.

Jones took a moment of professional interest, scanning the buildings over the top of his rifle as they passed by. "No obvious movement in the complex."

They continued on. After another few moments, the last two squads checked in behind them.

"Reapers, at One and Richmond Hill."

"Highlanders, covering this apartment complex."

"Roger," Billings responded over the air. "Squad Four, we're getting in position. Scots, go ahead and roll through that complex, see if you can't stir anything up."

"Copy."

Jones shook his head. "Squad Four. So fucking lame."

"Four's not bad," Sam said, looking out his window. The Humvee was positioned diagonally in the intersection, so that Sam was able to look south, where Richmond Hill continued on out of sight. "Like a four-leaf clover. A Shamrock."

Jones blew a raspberry. "You Irish, Ryder? 'Cause you don't look very Irish to me."

"Whoa." Sam managed to sound offended. "You racist bastard. You assume because I'm dark-skinned I can't be Irish?"

"Nah, you're right," Jones replied. "You probably do have some Irish in you. The Irish screwed everyone. But, on the other hand, you don't handle your alcohol very well."

Sam shook his head. "Jones, no one wants to drink fermented grape mix from your MREs."

"Hey. It gets you drunk."

"It does something. Maybe rots your brain. Exhibit A: You."

Jones whistled. "Listen to Ryder. Gettin' all uppity now. Hey, what's your real name anyways?"

Sam turned and looked at Jones, not sure how he felt about this incursion. He hadn't mentioned his real name in years. Everyone called him Private Ryder now. He'd *become* Sam Ryder. The old version of him seemed like an uncomfortable dream.

"I got a bet with Chris," Jones continued, looking mischievous as he usually did when he stirred the pot.

"That's a lie," Chris pointed out from the front seat.

Jones continued, undaunted. "Chris bet me that your name is Mohommad-Mohommad."

"No, I didn't," Chris sighed.

Jones gave Sam a shit-eating grin. "I was thinking it was Dirka-Dirka."

"Jesus Christ, Jones," Billings mumbled, shaking his head.

Sam raised his eyebrows. "Wow. That's…shockingly offensive." And yet, he found himself smiling back at Jones, knowing that no matter what came out of Jones's mouth, he'd fight for that man's life, and Jones would fight for his.

It was a strange feeling to Sam.

"Alright, you trailer trash honky," Sam said, looking back out his window.

Jones snickered.

"What was your bet with Chris?"

Chris shook his head. "I didn't have a bet, Ryder. He's lying."

"We bet whatever we get for our next five CKs," Jones asserted.

Sam nodded, his eyes coursing over their environment out of habit—half his brain always searching for the next threat, even as he continued to mess with Jones. "Well, you're both wrong."

"Impossible," Jones stated. "What is it?"

"Sameer Balawi," Sam answered, feeling the name more like someone he knew as a child. He glanced over his shoulder at Jones, who appeared contemplative concerning this new development. "You owe me whatever you get for your next five CKs."

"Ha," Billings proclaimed from the front seat. "He got you there, Jonesey."

Jones frowned, but then shrugged. "Alright. Deal."

The radio crackled. "Scots to Billings, we've made a lap through the complex. No sign of life."

Billings reached over and keyed the handset. "Roger that. Billings to all squads, let's start rolling in, nice and slow. Don't be shy with the horns. Call 'em when you see 'em."

Chris let off the brake, and their Humvee began to crawl forward onto Lumpkin Road. On the other end of that road, Squad One would be doing the same.

Chris put his palm to the center of the steering wheel and began honking a couple of short bleats every hundred yards or so.

Sam already knew that the horn on a Humvee sounded ridiculous coming from such a storied fighting vehicle—it sounded more like a tiny imported sedan. Somehow, it never ceased to surprise Sam when he heard it.

But it was still loud. And that was all that mattered.

Through his open window, Sam heard the distant sound of the other horns. Altogether, it sounded to Sam like a flock of geese calling out to each other. Which was a somewhat silly thing to picture for a bunch of squads of fighting men styling themselves as Wardogs and Reapers and Lead Farmers and such.

To the left, a series of abandoned businesses passed by the muzzle of Sam's rifle.

A seafood shack.

An oriental market.

Then a church. In the wide parking lot, the vestiges of some sort of aid station sat in tatters. The remnants of white tents. Perhaps a gathering point for evacuees, during the collapse, when FEMA was still trying to stem the tide of the plague.

It felt odd to be reminded that the world hadn't always been the way it was now.

Then more trees.

Everything was typically overgrown.

The radio remained quiet as they made their slow, plodding progress onward. Chris never accelerated past ten or fifteen miles per hour. No reports of contact came in.

Sam shifted in his seat. Somehow, the lack of contact only made him more nervous.

He would have preferred that the primals had just come out at them. It would be terrifying, but it would be better than this sick tension, growing greasy and black in Sam's stomach.

A few houses drifted by. Some of them burned down.

Broken windows. Trees growing out of them.

Dark doorways, hanging open like raided tombs.

No movement, though.

Up ahead, a long, wide driveway. A large sign at the front of it: Augusta Technical College. Some ivy had overtaken half of the sign, but Sam could still read the bold white letters.

They drew abreast of the long drive heading down to the college. Sam's eyes strayed down it, peering through the crowding overhang of trees, to a cluster of college buildings about a quarter mile away.

A figure stood there in the distance.

Sam's heart skipped a beat, adrenaline flushing through him.

They passed by, taking the figure out of his sight.

"Wait," Sam blurted.

Chris stomped on the brakes.

"Left side," Billings called up to Pickell, then twisted in his seat. "You got contact, Ryder?"

Pickell whipped around to face left.

"Back up," Sam said, craning his neck to try to catch a glimpse of the figure again, if that's what he'd actually seen. Maybe it wasn't. Maybe his eyes had played tricks on him. The view down the drive had been so fleeting.

Chris put it into reverse and eased them backwards.

The drive down to the college came back into view.

"Stop," Sam said, clutching his rifle and pulling it tight into his chest.

The college buildings.

The brush grown up around everything.

But no figure.

"What'd you see, Ryder?" Billings pressed.

"I'm not sure," Sam answered honestly. "Possible contact. One figure, down at the end of that drive."

"Was it moving?" Billings asked.

That would be the expected thing. With all these vehicles rolling around, honking their horns, the primals would come to investigate. That's what they'd always done.

"No," Sam said. "It was just standing there."

"Primal?"

"Can't say."

"Was it wearing clothes?" Billings queried, sounding a little irritated at the lack of information.

"I can't say for sure," Sam admitted. "I don't think it was."

"Alright," Billings grumbled. "Chris, hold here. Pickell, keep coverage down that drive and scan the woods." Billings grabbed the radio again. "Billings to all squads, we have a possible contact down on Lumpkin Road, right at the college. We're holding position here. Continue your routes. We'll keep you advised."

"Sarge," Chris said.

Sam glanced forward, and saw that Chris pointed out the windshield, where Squad One's MATV rolled towards them.

The bigger combat vehicle came to a stop on their passenger's side. Squad One's team leader—Sergeant Ron Paige—had his arm and rifle out his window.

"Whatcha got, Billings?" Paige asked.

"Private Ryder got a possible contact, down at the college."

"A pack?"

"No, just one."

"Was it running?"

Billings shook his head. "Just standing there, he said."

Paige ducked his head, glancing into the Humvee at Sam, as though he could determine the veracity of Sam's sighting by inspecting him personally. Then his eyes went forward, and he nodded down the road. "Here comes Scots."

Billings took the radio again. "Scots, come up here with us. I want you to hold position here and wait for the other squads to finish their rounds." To Paige, Billings said, "You wanna come check it out?"

The team leader shrugged. "Might as well. No one else has shit." He peered down the long drive. "Not a fan of that narrow road. Woods on either side. Ambush alley."

Billings nodded. "We'll roll slow. If the map's right, there's another exit out of the college that'll take us out to Highway One. If we hit anything spicy, we'll punch through and rendezvous on the highway."

"Roger that."

"Alright Chris," Billings said, taking a deep breath. "Take us in there."

FIFTEEN

SURVIVOR

CHRIS EASED THEIR HUMVEE down the drive.

There were two lanes, bisected by a median that had grown up almost as tall as the woods to either side. Across their lane, a pine tree had fallen during some windstorm years ago, and was now half-rotted.

It crumbled under their tires and brush guard as Chris nudged the Humvee over it.

Sam tried to keep his focus out of his window—*watch your lane*—but he kept wanting to look forward, towards the buildings where he'd seen…whatever it was that he'd seen.

Definitely a primal, he thought. That was his gut reaction. But he'd learned not to put too much weight behind your gut until it was provable. Sometimes your gut would betray you and leave you looking like an ass.

Sam forced himself to look back to the woods on their left.

Pickell had the turret facing forward, plus Chris and Billings were facing that way. If anything popped up, they'd see it. He just had to trust.

"Contact," Billings announced. "Dead ahead."

Sam found himself pressing against Pickell's legs to get a view out the front of the vehicle. "Where?" he demanded, *needing* to see what it was, and if it looked like the same thing he'd already seen.

Billings leaned forward in his seat, one hand on the dashboard, his other holding his rifle in the window. "It's gone now. Just a flash. Between those two buildings." He shook his head. "Not a fan of this shit. Everybody, windows up." He keyed his radio as Sam and Jones slid their windows closed. "Hey Alphas, there's definitely movement down here. Recommend windows up."

"Ya scared, Billings?" came the reply.

Billings frowned at the radio. "What a prick." He didn't bother answering. Just closed his own window. To his own team he grumbled, "If he'd seen Loudermouth's crew get ripped out of their vehicle he wouldn't be talking shit."

Chris watched the MATV in the sideview mirrors. He snickered. "They just put their windows up, Sarge."

"Of course they did," Billings remarked.

"Fancy-ass fuckers," Jones commented under his breath. "In their fancy-ass MATV."

The road split, and they stayed to the right. Ahead, several large, square, brick buildings loomed. Their road intersected with another, and here, Chris slowed them to a crawl.

Billings gestured to the left. "Bring us up on that side of the building, towards that parking lot right there."

Chris cut them in a tight left hand turn, their driver's side tires bumping the curb, then settling back onto the street. Behind them, Alpha Squad's MATV followed.

Sam kept looking through the windshield, then back out his own window with a flush of anticipation, as though every time he looked in one direction, the threat would come from the other.

Watch your lane.

They headed toward a large parking lot, the big square building to their right.

"There!" Jones yelped with excitement. "Did you see it? It just ducked into the building!"

"I saw it," Pickell called from the turret.

"Was it a primal?" Billings demanded.

"Definitely-maybe," Jones answered.

Billings grumbled a curse, glued to his window, staring at the building. "Why aren't they coming at us?"

"Maybe it's just that one. Maybe it got separated from its pack."

"When's the last time you saw a solo primal?" Billings asked.

No one answered.

"Stop," he commanded. "Pickell, when I tell you, I want you to send a couple test rounds into the building and see if we can't scare up a response, you copy?"

"Roger 'at, Sarge," Pickell said. His voice remained light and cheerful as it always did. Consistently devoid of the tension that the rest of them felt.

Billings keyed his radio. "Hey Alpha squad, we got definite contact, but it seems to be avoiding us. My gunner's gonna hit that building with a few rounds to see what happens."

"Alright," Paige said, sounding bored. "Go ahead."

"Send it, Pickell."

CHUG-CHUG-CHUG

The M2 blasted out three rounds, smashing the side of the building.

Most of the windows were busted out, particularly along the ground floor. A few more were added to the casualty list.

Then they sat there.

The silence seemed to hum after the shocking blast of the rounds.

No response came from the building. No primals pouring out of nooks and crannies like they usually did. Everything was dead still.

Pickell fidgeted in the turret. "Hey, Sarge, you hearing that?"

"What?"

"Drop your window and listen."

Billings swore, but dropped his window.

Sam looked back out his own window, but the woods to the left were motionless.

With Billings's window open, though, Sam started to hear something.

"That sounds like screaming," Billings said.

"Yes, sir," Pickell answered. "Is it primals?"

"That don't sound like primals to me," Billings responded.

Sam looked back over his shoulder towards the driver's side. Billings pressed his head out of his window, listening to the sound.

"That's a person," Billings said, his voice ratcheting up. "Someone's in there."

Sam heard it now, too, but couldn't tell what they said. It definitely was not the hoot and howl of primals. This was human.

Billings came to a rapid decision. "Fuck this. We're gonna dismount."

"Aw, hell," Jones said.

Billings kicked his door open, grabbing the vehicle radio as he did. "All units, we have a possible human contact at this building. I want you guys to start converging down here at the Augusta Technical College. Squads Four and One are going to dismount. You'll see where we're parked. See if you can't get a perimeter around this building we're at."

Then Billings stepped out.

Jones and Sam followed.

"You want me to come with?" Pickell asked.

"No," Billings snapped. "You and Chris stay here. Chris, be ready to tear out, and Pickell be ready to give us some support fire."

"Got it," Pickell replied.

Sam ran to the other side of the vehicle, facing the structure. He heard the screaming clearer now. Hoarse and dry and desperate.

"It sounds like they're screaming for help," Sam said, his voice tight.

"Yeah, I'm hearing it," Billings nodded.

"Yo, Billings!" Paige stood outside his MATV, his leg still in the door. "What the hell is this?"

Billings glared over at him. "Ya scared?"

"I don't wanna dismount," he shot back.

"Well, then stay here," Billings said, then started moving for the building.

Sam and Jones fell in behind him, rifles up, scanning every window and door, fingers tense outside their trigger guards.

Sam heard the MATV's doors opening and closing and assumed that Alpha Squad was getting their asses in gear.

There was a wide area of what had once been a lawn, leading up a slight hill to the building. The weeds were now waist-high, a few saplings standing thin, about the height of a man.

Anything could be hiding in those weeds.

Billings snapped the fingers of his support hand and then waved, calling Sam and Jones up to him.

They hustled up to his side.

Billings moved up the hill towards the building at a controlled but determined walk. "We're gonna hit this corner of the building," he said, replacing his support hand on the foregrip of his rifle. "We're gonna peep in these busted windows. Stay back and don't let anything grab you from inside, you hear?"

"I hear that," Jones said.

"Yessir," Sam said, his breath shaky with motion and adrenaline.

For a few moments, the screaming had died out. Then, about halfway to the building, it started up again, clearer than before.

"Hey!" Someone—a man—was screaming. "Hey! Don't leave me! Don't fucking leave me! Help!"

Muted.

Coming from inside the building.

Billings's mouth clamped shut.

Jones whispered a constant blue streak.

They hit the corner of the building.

Billings turned, saw Alpha Squad jogging up.

No more snark now. Everyone heard the screaming.

"We'll clear the windows," Billings said. "Alphas, watch our backs and don't let us get eaten."

"We got you," Paige nodded, him and two other soldiers spreading out to provide three-sixty coverage for them.

"On me," Billings ordered Sam and Jones, then spun around the corner of the building. He vaulted over a short brick wall that separated the lawn from the side of the building. Sam followed, thinking that the wall was just one more hurtle they'd have to get over when the primals started chasing them.

The first window was intact.

Billings gave it a once-over, but he'd already realized that the only way they'd hear the screaming is if it was coming from one of the rooms with a busted window.

In which case, why didn't the person just jump out the window?

Were they restrained?

Or was something else going on here?

Billings moved to the next window. This one was half broken, a single corner of the glass leaving a jagged, shimmering edge. Billings went from side to side in the window, clearing the interior rapidly, and then inching closer to it, trying to see into the corners.

Sam and Jones moved to Billings, ready to pull him back if things started reaching for them through the broken window.

But then he stepped back and murmured "clear" and dashed to the next window.

Alpha Squad kept pace with them, staying outside the low brick wall, their rifles addressed out to the surrounding woods and structures.

Billings began to run as the shouting grew clearer.

They were getting close. Honing in on the source.

Then it trailed off, like the person shouting had lost hope.

"Keep yelling!" Billings shouted. "We're coming for you! Keep yelling!"

It was like Billings had supercharged whoever it was. Their screaming came back with renewed vigor, hope giving them strength.

"I'm in here!" the person screamed. "In a room with a broken window! Right here! There's a tree right outside the window!"

Billings immediately raised his eyes, and Sam tracked what he was looking at.

There, about halfway down the building, and three more windows down, stood a sapling tree that was crowding the frame of a broken window.

Billings broke into a dead sprint. "Check my back!" he called over his shoulder.

Alpha Squad ran to keep up, and Sam and Jones followed, pausing only long enough to scan across the broken windows that they streaked passed, making sure there weren't beastly shapes lurking inside.

"Right here!" the voice scraped out, raw and desperate. "Right at the tree!"

We're moving too fast! Sam thought. His heart skipped into his throat, adrenaline pumping it just as much as the running. *We're going too fast, and we're not being careful enough!*

Billings slid to a stop, about two paces off of the window next to the tree. It had a large hole in the glass, directly in the center of it, with jagged edges all around.

"I see you!" Billings called, then he shot a glance over to Sam and Jones as they hustled up. "He's here! Right here!"

On the other side of the brick wall, Paige hollered at his men, "Keep watch! I'm gonna help!" Then he vaulted over the wall and came running up the short slope to the side of the building.

Sam and Jones nearly tumbled into Billings, who was working urgently back and forth to clear the corners of the room, edging closer and closer to what was left of the glass.

Sam's gut turned circles inside of him, every instinct telling him that something bad was going to happen.

He saw a shape inside the window, and he heard the voice, but it was all a jumble of incomprehensible syllables to Sam. The remaining glass was too dirty to see details. Covered in four years of dust and pollen and mildew.

Paige pulled up next to them. "Is he in there?"

"He's in there," Billings replied. "I'm gonna break the glass, stand back."

He used the muzzle of his rifle to punch the glass clear of the frame. Then he used the barrel to rake the frame of the window, clearing as much of the pointy bits out as possible.

Sam stood back with Jones, his rifle trained on the gaping window, seeing the dark interior of the room beyond. And the shape that was sprawled on the ground, on its stomach.

Someone in uniform.

The man didn't seem to be able to move his arms or legs, but he raised his head.

"Holy shit," Sam uttered.

Billings stopped raking glass and stood, shell-shocked.

"Get me out of here!" the man cried out.

"Loudermouth!" Billings gaped.

The shock immediately dissipated into urgency.

"Ryder! Jones! Cover!" Billings snapped. "Paige, help me!"

Sam took the left side of the window and Jones took the right. Billings and Paige started to negotiate themselves over the sill of the window. A bit of broken glass could open an artery just as easily as a bullet could.

Sam jerked back from the window and brought his rifle up, checking high.

He remembered how he'd seen the primals pour over a rooftop and down the side of a building, clinging to impossible handholds.

His instincts screamed at him, telling him he would see savage faces peering down at him…

But there was nothing.

Just the wall and the roof.

Inside the room, Billings and Paige charged through a series of desks and chairs, slamming them out of the way to get to Loudermouth, who still hadn't moved.

Why wasn't he moving?

Sam checked their six, and then whipped back to the room.

Billings and Paige each took one of Loudermouth's arms and started to try to haul him up.

Loudermouth screamed in agony. "No-no-no!"

"What's wrong?" Billings demanded.

"I can't!" Loudermath gasped with the last bit of breath in his lungs, then took a big, shaky inhale. "They broke my arms and legs!"

Billings and Paige exchanged a glance.

"Okay," Billings said. "Take him by the armor."

Loudermouth still wore his plate carrier. Billings and Paige bent down in tandem and grabbed his back plate, using the plate carrier as a sort of carrying harness. They lifted him up off the ground. Loudermouth groaned through gritted teeth, but didn't scream again. His arms and legs both dangled from his torso.

Sam scanned again. Back behind him. Up top.

Still nothing.

Back to the room.

Billings and Paige hauled Loudermouth's form towards the window. "Ryder! Jones! We're gonna pass him to you and then take up coverage!"

"Roger!" Sam replied, slinging his rifle.

The two team leaders grunted with effort, lifting Loudermouth's form up onto the window sill so that his front plate rested on the jagged edge. Sam and Jones immediately grabbed the handholds under his plate carrier as Billings and Paige released them.

Loudermouth was heavy.

Sam strained, red in the face, his breath clenched in his torso, trying to lift the wounded man up over the broken glass. Inside the room, Billings and Paige grabbed his legs and pulled them upright so they wouldn't drag over the glass.

Loudermouth let out a gasp of pain, but managed not to cry out.

Then he was through.

Billings and Paige both snatched up their rifles. Paige turned and covered the door of the classroom immediately across from them, while Billings carefully straddled the sill again.

"Clear," Billings called. "Move!"

He took up coverage from the outside, and Paige climbed out.

"Get him to the Humvee!" Billings ordered, still addressed to the interior of the building.

Sam and Jones started hauling ass down the hill.

Loudermouth moaned, but in between ragged breaths he kept saying, "Thank you! Thank you!" He craned his neck around, and for some reason fixated on Sam. "Ryder. You saved me. You got me out of there…"

Ryder didn't know what to say to that.

Jones answered for him, straining the words out with effort: "You're good, brother. We got you. You're safe now."

"Ryder…Thank you…"

In the parking lot, dead ahead, Sam saw the other squads' vehicles beginning to converge.

They made it to the brick wall.

"Alphas!" Sam barked, his arms already aching from hauling Loudermouth's body even such a short distance. Christ, but full-grown men were hard to carry. "Take him! Take him!"

Two of the soldiers on the other side ran to the wall. They looked at Loudermouth in shock, but didn't stop moving. One of them said, "Holy shit, it's Loudermouth," but that was it.

Sam and Jones passed the man's body over the wall, and the two soldiers from Alpha took him, dragging his limbs over the bricks, causing

Loudermouth more pain, but he seemed too overwhelmed to scream now.

"Get him to our Humvee," Sam said, then grabbed his rifle up in arms already filling with lactic acid and held coverage for Billings and Paige, who were right behind them.

Working in pairs, they cleared the stone wall, and then started heading for their vehicles.

Paige stayed with Billings as he headed for Squad Four's Humvee. The two Alphas carrying Loudermouth posted up at the backend of the vehicle and Billings popped the fastback. They spilled Loudermouth's limp body into the back. He flopped over, now on his back, his chest heaving, his useless limbs jumbled at odd angles. His face was pale and sweaty and drawn with pain.

"Loudermouth," Billings huffed. "Can you hear me?"

"Yeah," Loudermouth managed, his eyes clamped shut.

"Are there any more survivors?"

Loudermouth's face suddenly changed from suffering to abject terror. His eyes opened wide. Found Billings's face. He shook his head. "No one else."

Billings stared at him for a moment, and Sam thought he knew what Billings was thinking.

Was Loudermouth just saying that because he was desperate to get the hell out of this place?

Paige seemed to perceive this as well, and bent close to Billings. He lowered his voice, but Sam could still hear him.

"I don't hear any other screaming. If there are others, they're not alive."

"Or they're in places where we can't hear them," Billings returned.

Paige grimaced. "I say we pull back and figure it out from a safe distance."

Billings considered it, then made a rapid decision. He keyed his comms. "All units, pull back and rendezvous at Checkpoint Scarecrow. We've got a situation."

SIXTEEN

ENVOY

BENJAMIN SULLIVAN WOULD FOREVER be grateful that he hadn't been eaten alive.

However, as time dragged by, and the soldiers that had snatched him out of that house still hadn't said much to him, he started to get worried.

He wasn't sure what to worry about—only sure that he should worry. But his concerns were as indistinct as they were numerous. Who were these people? Did they intend to hurt him? They didn't seem like it, or at least they hadn't hurt him *yet*. But they had put a bag over his head, and he was not a fan of that at all. That made him feel distinctly like a prisoner.

No restraints though. Which was odd, he thought.

Apparently they didn't want him knowing where they were taking him.

They'd piled him into their truck, and then taken off, zipping through the streets of Fort Bragg. They'd got onto one of the main drags that headed out of Fort Bragg, but then they'd put the hood over his head, and one of the guys told him it was for their safety, and not to take it off.

His actual words were: "You take this off, I'll knock you unconscious."

So, again, Benjamin felt that his footing was tenuous.

The darkness inside the hood wasn't that disorienting to Benjamin. He'd been living in darkness. It felt…normal.

They'd driven for what he guessed was about twenty minutes. Then they'd hustled him into a building. Up some stairs. They passed some commands back and forth, but didn't speak much to him except to tell him to watch his footing on the stairs.

Then they'd parked his ass in a chair and taken the hood off.

He was in what looked like an office of some sort. It had a modern-looking desk made out of glass and metal tubing. The only chair in the room was the one in which Benjamin now sat. There was a single, black bookcase that contained rows upon rows of white, three-ring binders with inscrutable numbering on the spines.

Benjamin decided this had been some sort of tech company.

It was a random guess based on the desk and the numbers on the binders. But it made him feel a little more secure telling himself he knew what type of building he was in, even if he had no clue where it was.

Twenty minutes outside Fort Bragg is where it is, Benjamin noted.

A tall soldier that looked to be in his mid-twenties gave Benjamin a large bottle of water. When Benjamin opened the cap, he marveled at the fact that it was sealed. This was a brand-new bottle of water—not something that had been refilled.

The soldier watched Benjamin as he gulped down half a liter of water at one go. Benjamin watched him back as he drank. The man's blond crew cut was matted down in little squares—from the pads on the inside of a helmet.

The man gave Benjamin a nod, and then retreated to the door. Before closing it behind him, he said, "Sit tight. Don't make me come back in here."

Benjamin thought this was the soldier that had told him he'd knock him unconscious, and Benjamin believed him. So he sat tight.

And so it was with a measure of alarm, wondering if he'd done something to earn that threatened beating, that the blond soldier came back into the room, nearly three hours later.

"I didn't do anything," Benjamin blurted. "I've been sitting here the whole time."

The soldier raised an eyebrow, then smirked, and closed the door behind him. "Relax, kid. No one's gonna hurt you."

"You said you'd knock me unconscious."

The soldier nodded and approached. He held what Benjamin recognized as an MRE, the outer packaging cut open, but otherwise brand-new. "I told you I'd knock you unconscious if you took the hood off. And you didn't. So we're good. Right?"

Benjamin nodded. Sure. They were good. His attention was on the food now.

The soldier noted his hungry gaze. He held the package out to Benjamin, and Benjamin didn't hesitate. He grabbed it, and immediately went for the entree, ripping it open with his teeth and squeezing the contents into his mouth, foregoing the packaged utensils.

"When's the last time you ate a full meal?" the soldier asked, a note of pity clouding his curiosity.

Benjamin chewed his mouthful just enough to swallow it. "Full meal? It's been a while." He squeezed more of the contents up—chicken and rice. Before devouring his next mouthful, he glanced up at the soldier. "Who are you guys? Are you from Butler? Did Angela send you?"

The soldier frowned.

Is he Greeley, then?

"I'm Captain Marlin," the soldier eventually said. He reached up and indicated a patch on his shoulder. "Canadian Armed Forces."

Benjamin stopped chewing for a moment, eyeing the man and his earth-tone Canadian flag.

Canada?

Captain Marlin appeared to be waiting for something, and when he didn't get it, he prompted, "And you are…?"

Benjamin chewed, slower now, taking time to think.

Was this a good time to be honest or a good time to lie?

But he wasn't sure what would be gained by lying.

"Benjamin Sullivan," he said, the words muffled around a mouthful of food.

"And how did you come to be in Fort Bragg alone?"

"Not alone."

"No?"

"My mother's still there." Benjamin frowned, a new slew of worries invading his mind. He stopped eating. Guilt ripped his appetite away from him.

"Captain, I have to go back and get my mother."

Marlin held up a staying hand. "Alright. Slow your roll. One thing at a time."

Benjamin felt heat rising up his neck. "But I have to. I can't leave her there." Benjamin found his voice rising into a panic. "She's my mother! I can't leave her there!"

"Stop," Marlin commanded.

Benjamin stopped, his breathing a little quicker than before. His lips trembling.

"Listen to me," the captain said. "I'll help you. But you have to help me first."

"Fine," Benjamin decided. "Whatever. What do you want?"

"I want to know what happened to Fort Bragg."

"It fell," Benjamin answered. "It got overrun."

"Yeah, I can see that," Marlin sighed. "Let's try to be a bit more specific. We had intel that Fort Bragg was the seat of government for something called the United Eastern States. I was sent down to make contact with whoever was in charge. I'd like to know if the United Eastern States even still exists at this point, where I can find whoever is in charge of it, and how the so-called capital is now abandoned."

Benjamin blinked a few times, trying to figure out how to condense months of rapid developments into something Captain Marlin would understand. Finally, in a fit of frustration, Benjamin whined, "It's a long story!"

Captain Marlin looked irritated. He brought a hand up and scratched at his forehead. "Start at the top, Benjamin. Let's start with what happened to Fort Bragg, and we'll go from there. It was supposed to be a safe zone, wasn't it? I reconned it. I saw the high voltage wires you guys had all around the perimeter. What happened? How did it fall?"

Benjamin fidgeted in his seat.

He had a sense of urgency about getting his mother. But…it wasn't like she was going anywhere, was she? And Captain Marlin seemed like the type of guy that wasn't going to give an inch until he got what he wanted.

So Benjamin took a deep breath, and started at the beginning.

"Angela fucked up."

***

Maclean Marlin stepped out of the office and closed the door behind him. His brow beetled, hazel eyes on the old industrial carpet tiles under his feet, but he wasn't seeing it. He was picturing everything he'd just been told.

The kid had been a gold mine of information.

Provided that his information was accurate.

The building they occupied used to be a call center on the far eastern edge of Fayetteville. The area was more corporate, and therefore, had suffered less from looting, because there wasn't much in a corporate building that could help people survive.

Marlin and his team had taken over the third and highest floor of the building. They'd barricaded all the entrances, and all the ways up to that level except one. Their egress, should their single entrance get compromised, was a pile of repelling ropes near a bay of windows on the opposite side of the building. Bust the window and descend. That was the plan of action.

Marlin had no idea what to expect here in what used to be the USA, so he operated out of an abundance of caution.

Most of the southeast of Canada was a shit-show, and had suffered a similar fate to that of the American northeast. But Canada's north and west had been so sparsely populated that it hadn't been too difficult to survive there and reseat the government in areas less affected by the plague.

There were even a few areas so isolated that they hadn't been affected by the plague at all.

So the Canadian government had taken its time, consolidating itself and saving what it could. Only within the past year had they begun to turn their attention outwards again.

Marlin and his small team were one of two fact-finding missions that had been deployed to recon the lay of the land here in the wreckage of the United States. And the more that Marlin learned, the more complicated he believed the situation here was.

The kid was sequestered in one of the managerial offices on the third floor.

Marlin walked over to the middle of the call center floor, where his team had set up their little base of operations in a tight grouping of desks and short cubicle walls.

There were ten men total, including Marlin.

Marlin grabbed one of the ubiquitous rolling chairs and plopped into it, still looking contemplative.

His second in command, Lieutenant Thomas Wibberley, was perched on one of the call center desks, leaning back against the cubicle wall and watching his captain with curiosity.

"What's the word, Mac?" Wibberley asked. "The kid have anything good?"

Marlin nodded, bringing his attention back to the present. "Yeah. He had a lot to say."

Wibberley gave him a knowing look. "But you're not sure it's accurate."

Marlin shrugged. "Hard to say for sure. He seemed like he was being honest. But it's also pretty obvious that he's not a fan of whoever was leading this United Eastern States thing."

"Angela Houston," Wibberley noted from the small amount of intel they'd been given before coming south. "So is it as bad as Greeley is making it sound?"

Marlin pushed his chair back and forth and waffled a hand in the air. "I dunno. Some of the shit they say smacks of propaganda, you know? Like they really want us to believe that Angela is off the rails or some shit. But…it seems like the kid agrees with that. So maybe we are dealing with some crazy warlord bitch after all."

Wibberley smirked. "Angela Houston," he said, as though testing the flavor of the name. "That doesn't sound particularly warlord-y."

"I'll tell you one thing," Marlin said. "If it's a viable ally that the prime minister is looking for, I'm not sure Angela is it. She had her shit pushed in for sure. Apparently they had a group of detractors—folks that wanted to ally with Greeley—and they sabotaged Fort Bragg. That's what brought the grid down and let the eaters in."

"So is there even a United Eastern States anymore?" Wibberley wondered.

Marlin nodded. "At least, according to the kid there is. He says there are several cities—safe zones—that are a part of the United Eastern States. The kid claims they evacuated to one of these places, further south. He called it the Butler Safe Zone. In Georgia."

"Shit," Wibberley looked crestfallen. "We gotta keep going south?"

"It would seem that way," Marlin said. He stood up from the rolling chair and seized his helmet and rifle where he'd placed it on a nearby desktop. "But first, we gotta try to find this kid's mom."

Wibberley raised his eyebrows. "You're kidding me."

"No, I'm not kidding you," Marlin said, buckling his chin strap. "That was the deal I made with the kid."

"Fuck the kid."

Marlin shrugged, slinging into his rifle. "The kid and his mom might get us through the door down in Georgia."

"I think the Canadian flag will probably get us through the door."

Marlin sighed. "What do you want me to say, Wibberley? I told the kid I'd find his mom. I'm at least gonna roll in there and give it a good faith effort. You stick around for QRF if we need you. Otherwise I'll just take Team One with me."

Wibberley grunted, but stood up. "You went in on the last recon. Let me and Team Two take this one."

But Marlin shook his head. "Nah, you sit tight. We're more familiar with the street layout now.

Makes more sense for us to do it. Besides, shouldn't be a big deal. We're gonna pop in, see if we can't find her, then pop out. If shit looks squirrelly, I'll call it and the kid's just gonna have to deal with it."

Wibberley didn't look too pleased with this, but he raised his hands in surrender, then shook his head. "All to get in good with a bunch of rebels in Georgia. Jesus. The things we do for the Queen, right?"

Marlin smiled as his Team One began to strap up again for the trip back out. He gave Wibberley a reassuring wink. "Dressed in green, livin' the dream, servin' the Queen."

SEVENTEEN

FACE TO FACE

THE TINY TOWN OF MOSQUERO, New Mexico, stood out to Daniels's eye.

He peered out of the window of the UH-60 Blackhawk as it sped southward, the desert spread out beneath them, vast and flat and atonal. And there, right smack dab in the middle of all that nothing, was a something.

Mosquero.

Perhaps a square mile—if you were being generous—of small dwellings. A school. A church. And one gigantic hangar in which to park…farm vehicles, Daniels guessed.

But what made Mosquero stand out the most were the three plumes of black smoke rising from it and mingling with the crystal clear desert air.

Daniels wasn't a cruel person. He hadn't been the type of kid to torture the neighbor's cat, or pluck wings off of flies, or even burn ants with a magnifying glass.

Daniels was simply *practical.*

He was a utilitarian to his core.

And so he smiled at the columns of smoke, because he knew that this town was his, and that owning this town put him one step closer to having his hands around Terrance Lehy's throat. Figuratively speaking, of course.

And having Tex was the key to Daniels's whole plan.

A delicate plan. A bit of a house of cards.

Complex plans always carried a large amount of risk.

But the bigger the risk, the bigger the reward. And the reward was astronomical. The reward was everything from an official position for Daniels, to oil independence for Greeley, to a strong bargaining position with their maybe-allies in Canada and the UK.

Conversely, failure would mean the annihilation of everything he'd been working for.

And probably death.

The Blackhawk slowed its steady progress across the desert and began to drop in altitude. The fuel was nearing the halfway mark, so the pilot would return to Greeley.

That was fine. Daniels anticipated that Mosquero might take him a while.

The helicopter roared in, just over some long-defunct power lines, and set itself down in the center of the Mosquero Municipal School running track. Two of Cornerstone's technicals awaited him on the other side of the brick-colored running lanes.

"I'll call for pickup," Daniels said into the headset before he took it off.

The pilot nodded and gave him a thumbs up.

The crew chief pushed the door open and Daniels slid out into the buffeting downdraft and trotted across the field. Even with the rotor wash whipping at his clothes, the midafternoon sun was hot.

Behind him, the Blackhawk dusted off again, and the buzz and clatter of its rotors dwindled as it headed back to Greeley.

Daniels's lead man on the ground met him at the front of the two technicals.

"Mr. Daniels," the man greeted him. He offered no salute, and Daniels expected none. They were all mercenaries here. All Cornerstone operatives, dispatched and directly controlled by none other than Daniels himself.

"Mr. Griesi," Daniels nodded back, pronouncing it *gree-uh-see.* He removed his sunglasses and cleaned the dust off the lenses with his shirt before replacing them. "How many?"

"Forty-five total," Griesi responded. "We have them gathered in the hangar."

Forty-five was good. Human lives were like dollar bills. The more of them you had to spend, the more you could accomplish.

Griesi opened the passenger's side door of one of the technicals and Daniels slipped into the seat. Griesi closed the door and then stood on the running boards outside the open window.

He smelled like gunsmoke and dirt and body odor.

The two technicals cut a tight U-turn in an almost synchronized formation, and then accelerated. They didn't have far to go. The giant, white hangar was the largest thing in Mosquero, both in girth and height.

The massive bay doors on one end stood open, and peering through the bright glare from the white metal siding, Daniels could make out more of his men inside. And civilians.

Forty-five of them, to be exact.

The technicals drove straight into the hangar and stopped in front of the line of people, a wash of dust following them in and then billowing over the gathered people, who squinted through it and coughed and waved their hands in front of their faces.

Griesi opened Daniels's door and he stepped out again.

Was it truly necessary that Daniels was here?

Perhaps not. And, he had to admit, it was a contradiction of his usual ethos of "delegate, delegate, delegate."

However, since *literally everything* rode on the success of a delicate plan that existed only in his head, he forgave himself for micromanaging, and his men would have to as well.

Daniels stood, between the two running engines of the technicals. The wind from the outside didn't quite make it into the massive hangar, and so the heat from the two engines simply clustered there and baked him.

His attention was outward, on the pathetic people lined up before him.

Griesi had done it right. He'd put them all in one long line.

Forty-five men, women, and children. A smattering of elderly.

They all stared at Daniels. Squinting. Glaring. Whimpering.

Daniels took off his sunglasses. Sunglasses dehumanized you. It was best to let people see your eyes. The eyes, they said, were the windows to the soul. And Daniels was unafraid of letting them see what was inside of him. Most of the time, it made people more cooperative.

They could see that to Daniels, their lives didn't mean much.

Daniels spoke loud and clear, so that all forty-five of the captured civilians from Mosquero could hear him and understand exactly what he wanted. "I know for a fact that you have had contact with Captain Tully of Project Hometown. I would also like to have contact with Captain Tully. One of you is going to tell me how to make contact with him. I only need one person, brave enough to stand up and save the lives of your friends. Otherwise, we start killing."

A shockwave of murmurs and cries rippled through the forty-five people facing him.

None of them had the balls to fight back at this point. They'd already done that, and now their homes burned, and their loved ones lay dead, killed during Cornerstone's takeover of the town.

Now they were surrounded by Cornerstone men, and their options had dwindled.

Daniels counted to twenty. Ample time for someone to make the decision.

But no one did.

Daniels turned his head towards Griesi. "Kill the elderly first," he said, loud enough for all to hear, and amid another wave of cries, he lowered his voice. "Save the children. They might be a good motivator for Tully."

Griesi stepped forward and gave a nod.

Two of the Cornerstone operatives that stood behind the line began to move. They started at opposite ends of the line of people. No one fought back. No one tried to stop them. They were sheep, trapped in a corral of wolves.

Seven shots rang out, slow and deliberate.

Seven bodies fell. Four older women, and three older men.

The remaining thirty-eight civilians devolved into hysteria.

Daniels let them sit in it for a moment. Let them think about what they were doing. Let them look at the scattered brain matter of their grandmothers and grandfathers and think about what they actually were trying to accomplish by staying silent.

"Contact with Captain Tully," Daniels reiterated, having to raise his voice to be heard over everyone's mewling.

He waited. Again, counting to twenty. A good long time.

Still, no one stepped up.

"Kill seven more," Daniels said. "Your choice."

The two Cornerstone operatives moved to opposite ends of the line again.

"Wait!" someone shouted. "Stop!"

Daniels frowned, eyes scanning the line until he came to one man who had his hands out, pleading for mercy, his eyes locked onto Daniels's.

"Yes, sir?" Daniels prompted. "You have something to tell me?"

The man took a tentative step forward. "Captain Tully. He gave us a satphone. We use that to contact him. I'll show you where it's hidden."

Daniels nodded, then beckoned the man forward.

The man hesitated, looking to either side of him, first at his fellow civilians, and then at the Cornerstone operatives. When no one moved to stop him, he shuffled forward, his steps becoming more confident as he went, until he stood there, right in front of Daniels.

Daniels dipped his head, looking at the man from under his eyebrows. "You wouldn't be lying to me, would you?"

The man shook his head. "No, sir!"

"And you realize that if you are lying to me and you don't produce this satellite phone, then I'm going to kill all the people behind you and make you watch?"

The man paled. His lips trembled. He seemed to have lost his voice, so he simply nodded.

"Good," Daniels said. He looked past the man and raised his voice again. "The rest of you are free to go back to your homes. I'm a man of my word. But listen carefully." He held up a hand to keep them from fleeing just yet. "My men are going to remain here in this town for some time. I have a flight of gunships on standby. If even one of you raises a finger against my men, I'll have your entire town wiped off the map." Then he shooed them with a flippant hand. "Go."

The gathered sheep moved, much as the man standing before Daniels had: Slowly at first, cutting a wide berth around the technicals and the Cornerstone operatives around them, and then, as they reached the bay doors of the hangar, they quickened their pace, some of them breaking into a run.

Daniels watched them go, thinking absently of how his two Apache gunships were old as hell, and hadn't even been up-armored. But what did you need armor for against a bunch of sheep?

He turned to the man standing before him. "You did the right thing, sir. Now show me where this satphone is hidden."

***

The man took them to a house that looked like it had been ground zero for a good amount of the fighting. Which made sense to Daniels. The occupants had clearly been allied with Tully, if they were the ones hiding the satphone. They would've been the ones to fight back the hardest.

It hadn't worked out for them.

The front of the structure was riddled with large caliber bullet holes. The machine guns on the backs of the Cornerstone technicals had raked it hard.

The inside still stank of spent propellant. And faintly of shit.

Five bodies lay, in various poses of death. The structure had already been cleared by Cornerstone, and the weapons that the five dead men had used to defend themselves were stacked up in a corner, away from the dead bodies.

The man that led them into the house trembled, but, to his credit, remained focused on his task. He led Daniels and Griesi and two other operatives upstairs into one of the bedrooms. Here, a dingy, gray carpet covered the floors under a collection of mattresses with tossed bedding.

The man went into the far corner of the room and began to hunch down.

"Stop," Daniels said. "That's far enough. I'm assuming it's under a floorboard?"

The man stood, raised his hands, and nodded, backing away from the corner.

Daniels gestured to Griesi. The Cornerstone man stalked to the corner and squatted down. He used a knife to peel back a corner of the carpet that was already obviously loose. Beneath it, there was a floorboard that had been cut away.

He jammed his knife into the gap and pried the floorboard up. Then peered into the cavity below. “One satphone,” he reported. “And a pistol.”

Daniels gave their prisoner a sidelong glance. “You weren’t intending to use that on me, were you?”

The man quaked, his knees looking like they might go out. “No, sir! I promise! I was just trying to show you where the satphone was!”

Daniels put his hand on the man’s shoulder. “Alright. Okay. Calm yourself down.”

Griesi spent a moment further inspecting the interior, and Daniels knew he was checking for booby-traps. When he decided there wasn’t a trap, he scooped up the pistol and the satphone and took them to Daniels.

Daniels ignored the pistol. Griesi checked the chamber—loaded—and slid it into the back of his waistband, beneath his plate carrier. Daniels took the satphone, extended the antenna, and turned it on. The little screen blinked into life.

Daniels was quite familiar with these little devices. They seemed to be all over the place nowadays. The Project Hometown bunkers each had a quantity of them. It was a good sign that Tully had given one to Mosquero. That meant the town meant something to him. Otherwise he might’ve just left them with some radios and repeaters. Or nothing at all.

Daniels scrolled down the screen. Only one number appeared, which was a common occurrence. The satphone was only used to contact Tully directly, so only one number would be present in the call log.

Daniels turned away from the others, looking out the window of the upstairs bedroom. Three bullet holes marred the glass. Beyond it, Daniels saw one of the houses that had contributed to the smoke columns he'd seen on approach. It had begun to burn down now, the flames low, the structure just a blackened skeleton.

He glanced at the man that had led them here.

Daniels's word was golden—most of the time. But it came with caveats. "You can leave us now," he said. "It's in your best interest to convince your friends not to be stupid. Keep me happy, everyone keeps their lives. Very basic, quid pro quo."

The man swallowed. Nodded.

Daniels shooed him away.

He hustled out of the bedroom door.

Daniels listened to his feet tumbling down the stairs.

He turned back to the satphone. He selected the only number in the call log, and pressed the call button. He brought it to his ear, feeling his pulse accelerate. Feeling…satisfied. Maybe even happy.

A gruff, weary voice answered. "Tully here."

It felt like taking the first long gulp of an ice cold beer after working in the hot sun all day.

"Captain Tully," Daniels said, unable to contain a smile. "This is Mr. Daniels of Cornerstone Military Applications. I'm here in Mosquero with a good amount of your folks. A lot of women and children. And I've been dying to speak to you. Do you think we could meet, face to face?"

EIGHTEEN

TANKERS

LA CASA FELL in a roar of flame and a burst of gunfire.

Lee, Abe, and Menendez's crew, hit it right at the tail end of dusk.

Usually you waited until the wee hours of the morning, but a few things had occurred that made them decide to accelerate their plans.

Obviously also under the assumption that attacks happened in the wee hours of the morning, the cartel men at La Casa had all gathered in for an evening meal, and they'd left only two men on guard, and those men weren't even on the perimeter.

They were close in with the rest.

In fact, Lee watched them receive plates of food from the fire.

And, as the sky turned a deep orange, and the land around them turned navy blue, the lonely two sentries were distracted by eating their plates of food, their rifles slung on their back.

Lee couldn't help but let out a wheeze of dark humor as he watched the sentries constantly turning back towards the blazing campfire of their companions, and trading jokes with them. They were cooking away their natural night vision.

Lee couldn't have asked for a softer target.

He'd already scrambled everyone into position along the perimeter of La Casa when he'd seen the entire cartel crew gathered in one spot. Seeing the sentries destroy their night vision decided him.

Menendez's crew had loaned him one of their radios and earpieces—the batteries kept alive by judicious and obsessive use of a solar recharger—and it was over their squad channel that he transmitted, keeping his voice to a low husk: "This is a go. Everyone open up on my first shot."

He aimed his .50 caliber Barrett right at a sentry's chest. Through the optics, the man smiled and shoveled food into his mouth.

Lee almost felt like he was standing right there with the man.

He wondered what he was smiling about.

Lee wasn't positive about the vertical adjustment he'd dialed into the scope when he eased the trigger back and let the bullet fly. But then a massive hole opened the sentry's chest and sent his body tumbling.

The western and southern perimeter of La Casa suddenly twinkled, like a cloud of lightning bugs had erupted into existence, and a second later the sound of a rolling fusillade of gunfire thundered over Lee.

Thirty seconds after that, all was quiet, and nothing inside of La Casa was moving, save for the dancing flames of the campfire.

Lee and Abe jogged across the mile of plains between them and La Casa.

Over the comms, he heard Menendez's men quip back and forth to each other, and an occasional security round blasted out into the night as they cleaned up a survivor.

Seven minutes after Lee's first shot, he arrived at the fence surrounding La Casa.

He keyed his comms. "Lee here. Me and Abe are coming over the perimeter on the west side. Check fire."

"You're clear. Come on," came Menendez's reply.

Lee climbed over the fence, his arms tiring from lugging the heavy Barrett. Abe followed him, and then the two strode casually into the wreckage that had been La Casa.

They walked into the circle of orange light made by the campfire. It crackled merrily, as though unconcerned with the carnage around it. Men lay in every state. Spread eagle. Curled up. Slouched in sitting positions. Heads scooped empty by passing rounds. Eyes staring at nothing.

Their blood was splattered across their food, and sat in patches that looked black in the pale dirt.

Lee surveyed the scene without expression, then went to a weathered old picnic table where several dead shapes were slumped.

He set his heavy rifle down in the center of the table. The two men sitting on the bench seat seemed to regard it with empty eyes. Lee shoved them so they fell backwards into the dirt.

Old habits died hard.

You never assumed anyone was dead. And you certainly didn't want them within arm's reach of a loaded weapon.

Abe poked around the plates of food, but didn't seem to find anything that wasn't contaminated with blood and brain matter.

Two of Menendez's men made the rounds, stripping weapons and piling them up off to the side. A few others had taken up positions on the outskirts of the camp, keeping watch.

Menendez approached, holding something. He shoved it into Lee's hand.

It was a satphone.

"One of the guys was holding it," Menendez said.

Lee turned it on. "Did you check the call log?"

"It wasn't on."

Lee checked anyways. "Few calls placed today. Nothing within the last hour." He turned it off. "Still. I'd prefer not to stick around. Just in case they managed some sort of distress signal."

Menendez nodded. "I've sent runners to get our vehicles."

"Good."

Menendez pointed to the satphone. "That a Project Hometown satphone?"

Lee eyed it. "Could be. We knew Greeley had given *Nuevas Fronteras* some bunkers."

Abe appeared at Lee's side. "That thing still work?"

Lee nodded, knowing what was coming next.

Abe looked at Lee with an expression of hope. "We can contact Fort Bragg."

Lee looked down at the satphone in his hand.

It felt, for one heart-stopping second, that the little brick of plastic and microchips was going to pull him off the face of the earth, into some black void from which he could never return.

He shoved the satphone into Abe's hand. "Go ahead."

Abe looked at him, a question in his eyes.

Lee knew beyond a shadow of a doubt, that the second he touched that satellite phone to his ear, and it connected him to any of the people from the United Eastern States—people that belonged to a version of him that felt buried and dead—then he would cease to be.

Not *him*, exactly.

But the version of him that he needed to be right now.

It would dissolve like a puff of smoke, and he wasn't sure what it was going to leave behind. He wasn't sure what was left anymore, underneath all the armor he'd build up, all the calluses. He wasn't sure who he was without it.

Lee cleared his throat. "You remember the number?"

A tinge of concern crossed over Abe's eyes as he regarded his friend, but he nodded. "Fort Bragg Command is the only number I have memorized."

"Same," Lee responded. "Make the call, then."

Abe hesitated for a moment longer, but then extended the antenna and dialed the number.

Lee looked away from him, a slight grimace on his lips as his stomach continued to turn circles inside of him.

Distantly, he heard the line ringing against Abe's ear.

Ringing.

Ringing.

Abe pulled the phone away after a few more moments. "No answer."

Lee shrugged, trying not to show his relief. "Try again later."

Menendez cleared his throat. "Where you wanna go after this?"

Lee considered going back to the hideaway a mile from here. But that was too close. "Well, worst-case scenario here, but if they managed to get some sort of distress signal out, I don't want to be too close when the cartel cavalry rolls in." As an aside, Lee perked up and looked at Menendez. "You wouldn't happen to have any Claymores, would you?"

Menendez smirked, but shook his head. "Unfortunately, no."

"Damn."

"Good idea though."

"Well, sergeant, here's the situation. We need to get in contact with Tex, if he's still alive. You knew him best out of all of us. Where do you think he is?"

Menendez grew uncomfortable again, as he had back at the hideaway. "Frankly, Lee, I still think he's dead. I think he would have tried to make contact with me if he were still alive. And I've been to every outpost within fifty miles of here over the course of the last month. If he's taken up residence anywhere, it's not around here."

Lee looked thoughtful. "The bunker north of Caddo. The one we ran the power plant operation out of."

"Yeah?"

"You said that you'd been there. Watched it for six hours."

Menendez nodded. "We did. No sign of anyone."

"But you said that Breckenridge and some wounded had been left there before we assaulted the power plant."

Another nod.

"Did you get close enough to the bunker for the security systems to see you?"

This time Menendez hesitated. After a moment, he shook his head. "We weren't real sure of what was happening, or who was in control of what. We didn't want to reveal ourselves."

"So it's possible that Breckenridge and twenty-some-odd number of wounded are still holed up in there."

"Yeah. I guess that's possible."

Out on the road north of La Casa, a series of headlights appeared.

Lee watched them for a moment. "Those your guys, right?"

Menendez confirmed via the squad comms.

It was them. Menendez's two trucks incoming, as well as the one that Lee and Abe had stolen. They'd given the keys over to Menendez's men to bring the vehicles around.

A moment later, the trucks pulled into La Casa.

Menendez turned away from Lee and hollered at his men. "Weapons, ammo, ordnance and food go in the trucks. Leave the bodies where they are."

Around the compound, Menendez's crew began to gather up the stacks of weapons they'd liberated, while others searched the compound's buildings for anything else that might be of use to them.

Menendez turned back to Lee. "So you want to go stand in front of the bunker. Make sure Breckenridge sees you. If he's still there."

"That bunker's our ticket," Lee pointed out. "This raid will give us some guns and ammo. Maybe some food. But what's sitting in that bunker will keep us operating out here for a lot longer. And it's our best bet at figuring out what's going on with the bunkers—and with Tex."

Lee realized that Menendez bore an edge of suspicion in his gaze.

He understood the questions that must be rolling around in the sergeant's head.

"We're on the same team here," Lee assured him. "We both want to figure out what's happened to Tex. And we both want to rip *Nuevas Fronteras* to shreds. I think we'll be more effective together. But I guess that's up to you."

"But you're going to go to that bunker regardless," Menendez reasoned.

Lee nodded. "Yes, I am. But not tonight. Tonight, we need to see what kind of goodies we pulled in. Re-up on ammo and weapons."

"You got another place we can go? One that's not so close to La Casa?"

"Yeah," Lee answered. "We got OP Elbert."

Menendez pulled his head back. "Those cannibal fucks?"

Lee gave Menendez a significant look. "Well. Let's just say they're not doing much cannibalizing lately."

Menendez considered this and then shrugged. "Tex wanted them gone anyways. Guess I should thank you for saving me the trouble."

It was strange to Lee to consider what a month had done to him.

Strange and uncomfortable.

He remembered being at one of Tex's hideouts, and speaking secretively to Abe and Julia. About how they weren't so sure of Tex's motivations. How they didn't like how he was planning to wipe out OP Elbert simply because they were a liability.

But…

Times change.

People change with them.

Abe shifted his weight. Rested both hands on the buttstock of his hanging rifle. "Lee."

Lee had been tensing for it.

Dreading it.

Knowing it was coming.

The tension came out of him in an unforeseen blast of irritation. "Dammit, Abe. We're this fucking close, and you wanna bail out now?"

Abe seemed taken aback by the unexpected heat of Lee's response. But then his expression darkened, and his eyes flashed like thunderheads. "First off, getting some fuel back to the UES isn't *bailing out*, Lee. That's the whole reason we came down here in the first place." Abe took a step toward Lee, and thrust his hands out wide. "And whaddaya mean 'this close?' Close to what? To knocking on the door of that bunker and seeing who answers? Of *maybe* finding Tex? Of *maybe* being able to run your vendetta against Mateo Ibarra for a little while longer? But for how long, Lee? How long are you gonna keep doing this?"

Lee faced his friend—and sometimes his strongest opponent—and he didn't look away. His hands clenched into fists at his side, and he thought about just doing it—shit, they'd been heading for a fight for quite a while now…

But then he just bit his bottom lip until he thought it would bleed. And that was good. That was what he needed right now.

He needed a little more pain.

He needed to be reminded.

Abe stood, arms still outstretched, the question hanging between them.

Lee released his clenched fists. Then nodded towards the tankers. "Take them and go, then."

"I can only take one, Lee."

"Then do it."

Abe's hands flopped to his side.

They watched each other for another moment, both of them knowing what the other needed, what they wanted, and neither willing to give it to the other. They each held it hostage—Lee would never admit that Abe was right, would never let him leave on good terms, and Abe wouldn't stay, wouldn't let go of the original mission.

Lee was the first to look away. He was the first to cut the cord that bound them together.

Because he had other places to be. Other things to do.

He had his own mission to complete.

"Go on, then," Lee said.

And said nothing else.

And neither did Abe.

What could either say?

They both knew that they weren't going to give up what they wanted. So what was the point in saying anything else at all? To restart the argument all over again, so that it could wind up in the same spot?

Could they have wished each other good luck? Could they have told each other to stay safe out on those dangerous roads?

Maybe. But they didn't.

Abe dipped his head, turned, and walked away, towards his own mission.

Lee watched him go for a few steps, and then turned and walked towards his own.

***

As darkness descended on Checkpoint Scarecrow, the Hunter-Killer squads started to get antsy.

Sam stood in the turret of their Humvee. Pickell had been in the thing for several hours straight, scanning the perimeter of their checkpoint. Billings had ordered Sam to swap out with Pickell so he could grab some food and water.

The other squad's vehicles were arranged, as before, in a large circle, their gunners situated behind their various machine guns, facing out into the gathering darkness, and slowly getting more and more worried about sitting around after dusk.

It was one thing to run night ops, which was a shaky thing anyways. But at least during night ops they moved. They hunted. They did their job.

No one wanted to just sit around, waiting for the primals to sniff them out.

If they were going to be sitting still, they wanted to be sitting still behind the high voltage wires of the Butler Safe Zone.

At the back end of the Humvee, Billings and the other squad leaders were assembled. The fastback was popped open. Sam couldn't see Loudermouth's unconscious body from the turret, but he knew the severely injured man had been laying there for hours.

Sam kept his attention out on the perimeter, but that didn't mean he was deaf. The gathered team leaders at the backend of the Humvee kept their voices down, but Sam heard them anyways.

"The hell'd you give him?" Paige growled. "He's been out for four hours now."

Squad 10—The Reapers—had the only real medic deployed with them today. He was a quiet old soul of only thirty years by the name of Poggs. He didn't rise Paige's bait, but answered calmly. "I gave him a fentanyl lollipop. He needed it."

"We needed to debrief him," Paige returned.

"He was barely hanging on," Poggs replied. "I'm surprised he had the energy to yell at us. That probably took everything he had left. Both shoulders are dislocated. Same with his hips. I'm concerned about a fractured pelvis. And his BP isn't where it should be." Poggs paused. "Better that he live to give you a full debrief than die because we didn't administer proper care."

"I would've liked to make that call before you stuck the fentanyl in his mouth."

"All due respect, but my priority is to administer care."

Billings's voice interjected. "Is he gonna make it, then?"

"Probably," Poggs answered. "But that 'probably' turns into a 'maybe' if we stay out here."

"It's stupid to sit here in the dark," one of the other squad leaders put in. "We either need to get moving back into Augusta and waste some primals, or head back to Butler."

"I'm not going back into Augusta until we debrief Loudermouth," Billings said.

"Okay," Paige grouched. "You take Loudermouth back to Butler, and we'll get some CKs in your absence."

"CKs and incentives aside," Billings responded, his voice betraying his irritation. "That's a stupid idea, Paige."

"Why? Because you're spooked?"

"No, because Loudermouth is alive," Billings shot back. "Doesn't that strike you as a bit odd? That the primals deliberately broke his legs and arms—incapacitated him, but didn't kill him?"

"If they were trying to use him as bait for a trap, they didn't spring it very well," Paige said. "To me, it looked like they ran."

"Right. Which is another thing I don't like. When have you ever seen them run?"

"None of what you're saying tells me that we're in any more danger than we normally are."

"Yeah, well, I'm glad you're so sure of yourself, Paige, but in my mind, when weird shit starts happening, that's a good time to step back and re-evaluate your strategy."

"Fine. Call it into first sergeant, then. Let him make the call. But I can tell you right now, he wanted Augusta cleared five hours ago, and here we sit, having made zero progress on that front. So you tell me what you think Hamrick is gonna say."

"Hamrick's a hardass, but he's not stupid," Billings said.

"Alright," Paige invited. "Go ahead, then."

Sam's gaze strayed from the perimeter just enough to perceive Billings stalk around to the front passenger's door. He gave Sam a blistering glance, and Sam shot his eyes back up to where they were supposed to be.

"Quit eavesdropping, Ryder," Billings gruffed as he slumped into his seat.

Sam heard Billings snatch up the radio handset and switch to the command channel. "Squad Four to Alfred Actual."

One of the TOC operators answered. It sounded like the same woman as earlier.

"Alfred to Squad Four, standby for Actual."

Billings waited. Sam heard him tapping out an irritable rhythm on the dashboard.

Jones and Chris sauntered over, their rifles slung, NVGs propped up on their helmets.

"What's the word, sarge?" Jones asked, leaning on the front fender. "These NVGs are giving me a wild headache. Heard Poggs has some fentanyl. Think he'll give me some if I suck his dick?"

"Not now, Jones," Billings grunted.

"Ooh. Sorry." Jones held up a hand in surrender. "Didn't realize we were in Serioustown."

Sam braced himself, knowing that he would be in the crosshairs.

Jones lounged up against the front of the Humvee and his gaze drifted up to Sam. "Ryder. Honeybuns. You got a purdy mouth on ya. Think you can get some fentanyl for me?"

Well, that didn't take long. Sam smirked, but kept his eyes out on the perimeter. "You know, Poggs is literally ten feet that way," he said, jerking his head to the rear of the Humvee.

"Is he?" Jones leaned out, craning his neck to see around the open fastback. "Shit. Shut my mouth, then."

The radio inside popped, and First Sergeant Hamrick's voice came over. "Alfred Actual here. Who is this and what do you have?"

"Sergeant Billings with Squad Four, sir," Billings replied.

"Did Loudermouth wake his ass up yet?"

"No, sir. He's still under sedation. Poggs recommends moving him back to Butler. Based on what I saw in Augusta, it's my recommendation that the entire Hunter-Killer group pull back to Augusta and wait to hear from Loudermouth."

"That's not possible, sergeant. We need Augusta cleared."

"I understand that, sir. I want to clear Augusta, too. But there's some wonky shit going on with these primals. I think Loudermouth is going to be able to fill us in on some details that might help us target them with less risk to the squads. I wouldn't be telling you this if my hackles weren't way up, first sern't. I want to clear Augusta and get back to Bragg as much as everybody else does. But there's something going on here."

The radio remained silent for a long moment.

Jones and Chris sat very still, listening.

Sam, despite his orders not to, couldn't help but eavesdrop. The radio speaker was right underneath him.

"What's Sergeant Paige say about it?" Hamrick finally asked.

Billings cursed under his breath before transmitting back. "Sergeant Paige believes that my squad should escort Loudermouth back to Butler, and the rest of the Hunter-Killers should proceed with a night op."

Sam cringed, waiting for Hamrick's response.

"Copy that, Billings. Paige will take charge of the Hunter-Killers and proceed with night ops. Your squad will return Loudermouth back to Butler, immediately. How copy?"

Billings swore. Then transmitted: "Solid copy, first sern't. We'll be oscar-mike in five. Out."

Billings slapped the receiver back into its cradle. "Jones, go get Pickell. You heard the man. We're heading back."

True to his word, they were on the road five minutes later.

Poggs huddled in the back with Loudermouth's unconscious body.

On the squad comms, Paige organized the remaining teams with a distinct note of triumph in his voice. The Wardogs, Lead Farmers, Reapers, Highlanders, and Alphas were heading back into Augusta to continue the hunt. Squad Four was escorting the wounded back to Butler.

Jones was uncharacteristically quiet.

Having relinquished the turret to Pickell again, Sam sat in his usual seat, behind Chris as he drove them along the dark roads. He looked over to Jones and couldn't tell if the other man was pissed that they weren't going in with the others, or if he sided with Billings's assessment.

Sam happened to agree with Billings—when the primals started doing strange things, it was best to take a step back and figure out what was going on. But that didn't stop him, and probably everyone else, including Billings, from feeling like the outsiders.

The other squads were heading into the fray.

And Squad Four felt like they were tucking their tails and running.

Perhaps sensing this general mood, Poggs spoke up from the back. “Billings.”

“Yeah?”

“You made the right call.”

“Hmph.”

“And I’m not just saying this as a medic. I’m saying this as a fellow warrior. We always go into the unknown. But this is some next level shit. Paige made a bad call.”

Billings didn’t respond.

“Just do me a favor,” Poggs continued.

“What’s that, Doc?”

“Don’t take it on yourself.”

Billings turned around and looked at Poggs through the dark interior of the Humvee.

Poggs nodded to him. “Discretion is the better part of valor. You advised the prudent course of action, and you were ignored. No matter what happens tonight, they made their choice.”

“You saying you think something bad is going to happen?” Billings asked, his voice quiet.

Poggs shrugged. “I’m saying that if it does, remember that it’s not your fault.”

Billings gave the medic a slight nod and then turned back around.

The rest of the trip rolled by in silence.

Even the squad comms were quiet, before they passed out of range.

Like standing in the calm eye of a hurricane.

***

Captain Maclean Marlin was pretty sure that he was going to rip Benjamin's head from his shoulders.

His squad trailed behind him as he erupted out of the stairwell and onto the top floor of the call center that they'd been camped at for the last few days. They were pissed too, but also a little hesitant—was Marlin going to do something rash?

The industrial metal door slamming off of its stopper caused Lieutenant Wibberley and all of his squad to poke their heads up above their little fortress of cubicle walls, fingers tingling, and hands unconsciously moving towards their weapons.

"Where is that faggot?" Marlin snapped.

Being a good lieutenant, Wibberley saw a possible poor decision on the horizon, and skirted out of their encampment to intercept Marlin before he got to the door to the office where they'd staged the kid hours ago.

"Whoa, whoa," Wibberley pumped his hands. "What happened?"

"I'munna fuckin' kill him."

Wibberley made a rapid decision, and scooted between Marlin and the office door, placing a hand on his chest—firm enough to get through his superior's cloud of anger, but hopefully not disrespectful…

Marlin pulled up short, and looked at the hand on his chest, then up to his second in command with a look like he might want a go at him too.

"Can you just tell me what happened before we create an international incident here?"

The term *international incident* seemed to remind Marlin of what they were doing.

They were a political envoy.

This was a foreign country.

This was not the wastelands of the Canadian tundra, where mistakes could be simply left for the wildlife to pick clean and if you forced yourself to forget about it, then you erased it from reality.

They'd been in those places before. The whole team had.

But this wasn't one of them.

Here, their actions had deep and far-reaching consequences.

Marlin took a breath and it hissed out of clenched teeth, like cold water cooling hot metal. The captain lowered his voice, as his squad gathered around him, only a few paces off the door beyond which the kid Benjamin was sequestered.

Marlin jabbed a finger at the door. "The kid's mom is dead."

Wibberley blinked a few times, trying to process how exactly that was the kid's fault.

Marlin clarified a moment later: "She's been dead for weeks, Wibberley." His anger turned into a sneer of disgust. "We found the buildings that he told us about, where he and his mother had been hiding out—or abandoned, or whatever…" Marlin rubbed his jawline. "We could smell it the second we stepped in, but we kept searching…hoping it wasn't the case. But we found her. In a room. An office. Bloated and rotting. Piles of shit all over the floor."

Marlin's Adam's apple bobbed like he was struggling with a memory of gagging.

"Okay," Wibberley soothed. "So the kid's mom was dead. That's fucked up."

"Damn right it's fucked up. He knew she was dead and sent us in there anyways, putting our lives on the line for a corpse."

"The kid's a little wonky in the head," Wibberley said, almost whispering now, aware that the kid in question could probably hear them through the door. "He just spent weeks, stuck in a room with his dead mom. I mean…is it surprising that he's a little special now?"

A shadow of pity glided across Marlin's expression. He seemed to grit his teeth against it, like he hated the feeling.

Wibberley pressed on. "We don't really know how important this kid is to the social structure of this United Eastern States thing. Maybe not important at all. Probably not. But you go in there and beat the shit out of him…I dunno. I personally don't really want to show up on their doorstep with a flag of truce, saying we're a diplomatic envoy, oh, and by the way, here's this chap we recovered from Fort Bragg, please ignore the bruises."

The argument hung there in the air between them, as though teetering on a narrow fulcrum…

Marlin made a growling noise and looked away.

Wibberley let out a quiet breath of tension.

He knew that the bad decision had passed them by.

Knowing this, his duty as second in command was completed, and he gave his superior a nod, as though he had the utmost confidence that his captain would make the right decision.

Cooled, and also aware that the kid inside the room had likely heard the voices outside of his door—if not every word, then at least the basic gist—Marlin stepped up to the door, and pressed it open, but then he simply stood in the doorway and didn't go in.

The kid named Benjamin sat in his chair. He didn't look at Marlin as the door opened. His head was turned, his eyes fixed on the wall. Red rimmed. Wet streaks down his cheeks. But otherwise no blubbering. No sniffing. No hitching of breaths.

No sign of emotion at all, outside of the tears.

Marlin immediately felt even worse.

Wibberley was correct.

Could you fault the kid for being a little crazy? He'd probably tried very hard to keep his mother alive. And when he'd died, what else did he have to keep him going in the darkness?

Just a grim fantasy that things would be okay.

That he wasn't all alone in there.

That he wasn't facing death all by himself.

Marlin drew in a big breath through his nose. "Benjamin. You know that your mother is dead. You knew that already. Didn't you?"

Benjamin continued to stare at the wall.

Marlin felt a little bothered, but just as he was about to repeat his question, Benjamin nodded, once.

"How'd she die?" Marlin asked, his tone flat.

This one took even longer for Benjamin to answer, but now Marlin saw the struggle. It rippled subtly behind the young man's features, like dark things just beneath the surface of a still lake.

"I don't know," Benjamin whispered.

Like hell you don't know, Marlin thought.

But he said nothing.

Something was going on. There was more to this story than Benjamin was telling them. Which then called into question everything else that he'd told them. How much of it was delusional? Exactly how insane was this kid?

"Listen," Marlin said.

Benjamin gave no response.

"Look at me when I'm talking to you."

Benjamin dragged his eyes to Marlin's.

Marlin lowered his chin. Arched his eyebrows. "We got a lot of kilometers between us and this Butler Safe Zone. You give us bad intel again—you put me and my team in danger again—I'll kill you and leave you on the side of the road and never mention that we found you."

Again, Benjamin didn't react much. Just stared at Marlin.

"You understand?" Marlin demanded, irritation making a sudden comeback.

Benjamin nodded.

Marlin held his gaze for another moment, trying to impress upon Benjamin how serious he was about that threat. But as he pulled himself out of the doorway and closed the door behind him, he thought that he understood the look on Benjamin's face.

Benjamin was thinking that being killed and left on the side of the road was perhaps his best option.

NINETEEN

DECISIONS

CAPTAIN TERRENCE "TEX" LEHY knew how to be alone. He'd been alone before.

That's what he kept telling himself as he sat in a chair, facing a glowing computer screen in the dark.

This is no different than all the other times you were sequestered to your home bunker.

But it *was* different. Because all those other times, back before the world had gone to shit, he'd just been Captain Lehy, a Coordinator for Project Hometown. One man, living a quiet life out in the middle of the Texas countryside. And when the Washington Worry Warts saw something they thought might be a threat to the survival of the nation, down he went into his bunker, to wait for the all-clear.

In all those other times, including the last time, when the all-clear never came, and the Washington Worry Warts had finally been right about something, he'd just been one man, following orders.

But then he'd become Tex. He'd become the leader of a guerilla movement, aimed at keeping Texas out of the hands of people that had no business calling themselves Americans. He hadn't been a man following orders since then.

For four years, he'd been the man *giving* the orders.

His troops, his guys, his boys…they were like his children, in a way. And like his best friends in other ways. And he'd been surrounded by them. He'd eaten with them, bled with them, suffered with them.

They'd become his family.

And he'd grown accustomed to being surrounded by them.

And now they were gone.

So yes, he knew how to be alone. And yes, he'd been alone before.

But this *was* different.

Now he thought about them, almost nonstop. What had happened with them? Were any of them still alive? Had they all died in the trap that Cornerstone and Greeley had laid for them at the Comanche Creek Power Plant?

Were any of them in on it?

And had he done the right thing by taking his bunkers offline?

That was the one that haunted him the most.

That was the question that kept him lying awake at night.

When he'd crawled out of the lake after that night when Captain John Bellamy had betrayed him, and attack helicopters from Greeley had raked his men with devastating fire, and Cornerstone mercenaries had finished them all off, Tex had hit the road, and not looked back.

It had taken him a week, but he'd made it to his northernmost bunker, Bunker #3, right on the edge of where Texas and New Mexico and

Oklahoma's borders converged. He'd been nearly dead—dehydrated and half-starved and hounded by primals down to his last bullet—but he'd made it.

And then he'd shut himself in.

And the first thing he'd done, after sticking an IV line in his arm to get some fluids back into him, was to go to the bunker's control room, boot up the computers, log into the Texas mainframe, and reset the security systems at all his bunkers back to their default.

Which meant that no one except Tex could get access to them.

This was how all Project Hometown bunkers had been originally designed. So that only the Coordinator in charge of them could get access. And that Coordinator had to have his GPS device in his possession, and had to pass through a daunting battery of alphanumeric passwords and biometric security scans, just to get into the elevator that would take them down into the bunker.

Over the course of the next two weeks, Tex had nursed himself back to full strength, and spent a lot of time trying to reason out who might still be alive, and who, if anybody, he could trust.

It was a short list, made shorter by the fact that most people on it were dead.

Menendez was on that list. But he was probably dead.

Tzetzelewska—Cheech—*would* have been on the list, if Tex hadn't watched his body fly into pieces after a strafing run from the gunships at the power plant.

Lee and Abe?

Tex didn't even know where to begin with them.

Maybe they were dead.

Maybe they'd been in on it the whole time.

It certainly didn't seem like they'd been in on it, and if they had, they sure as shit risked their lives to pull it off—those choppers and the Cornerstone operatives had shot at them just as much as everyone else.

But Tex had no way of getting in contact with them even if he wanted to.

All things considered, there was only one name on the list that he trusted, and who he still could get in contact with, from the safety of his bunker.

And Tex was staring at the most recent message from him.

Tex had reached out to Captain Tully from New Mexico the day before.

Tully had his back up against the wall. Greeley had been gunning for him hard, and he'd been putting out his own fires and trying to stay alive and free from a Greeley takeover for more than a year. He probably didn't have much to offer Tex, but Tex was out of options.

Tex had sent the message, bunker to bunker. He hadn't expected Tully to respond, perhaps for weeks, as he wasn't sure when the other man would make it to a bunker and see the message waiting.

But, twenty-four hours later, Tully had responded.

It was not what Tex wanted to hear, but at least it was something.

Cornerstone has my back against the wall, the message read. **I'm not sure how much help I can be to you, brother. I might need to bug-out to Texas. If you want to meet, tell me a place and time, and I'll be there.**

Tex looked at a laminated map of northern Texas, propped up against a console to the left of the computer screen with the message displayed on it. He leaned forward, his eyes narrowed.

He felt exposed. Unsecured. Like his hand was being forced.

The web camera on the top of his monitor seemed to stare at him. To watch him.

It wasn't plugged in. Tex was paranoid about things like that.

It was supposed to be used for communications between Coordinators—so that they could video chat, if necessary.

Perhaps that would be a good idea now…?

No. He couldn't keep covering his ass.

He couldn't sit in this bunker forever.

He had to do *something*.

He'd made his list. He'd reasoned it out.

Best not to second-guess himself now.

He selected a tiny waystation of a town, close to the New Mexico border. It would be accessible to him. He could make it there within several hours and set up an overwatch. Paranoia, perhaps, but he wanted to watch Tully arrive before he exposed himself.

He needed to give himself enough time.

Decision made, and determined not to agonize over it any longer, he typed his reply:

Pine Station. The TX DOT facility. Noon, tomorrow.

***

The Butler Safe Zone did not have a full medical center like Fort Bragg.

What they had was a wing of the Taylor County High School, with a slapdash collection of medical machinery that they'd confiscated from nearby urgent cares and family practices that lay beyond the safety of the high voltage wires.

It was here that Squad Four brought Loudermouth's body, arriving shortly before midnight.

Displaced from Fort Bragg, Doc Trent was not the lead physician at the "Butler Hospital," as it was called. But he was the one on call that night, and he met them at one of the side entrances to that wing of the high school, with a stretcher, a nurse, and bags under his eyes.

Chris pulled the Humvee up close to the doors, and the whole team filed out. Sam went to the rear and opened the fastback, releasing Poggs from his cramped position in the back with Loudermouth's body.

Doc Trent and the nurse with him rolled the stretcher around to the back, mumbling curses in his usual ornery way. "What the hell happened to this guy?"

Sam helped Poggs hoist Loudermouth's limp form out of the back and onto the stretcher. Loudermouth let out a groan that might've been half-formed words.

Poggs ignored Trent for a moment, and spoke to Billings. "Looks like the fentanyl might be wearing off. You should get Master Sergeant Gilliard and First Sergeant Hamrick down here, ASAP." Then, to the doctor, who was already probing Loudermouth's body with a pair of gloved hands, he said, "This is the team leader that got taken by the primals earlier this morning. Superficial bite mark to the right trapezius. Both shoulders are dislocated, and both hip joints are broken. Pelvis didn't crackle when I moved it, but I'm still concerned about a fracture. His blood pressure is low, but it stabilized some. He's had two bags of LR and half a fentanyl lozenge about five hours ago."

Trent nodded along as Poggs and the nurse began to wheel the stretcher towards the doors. "Anything for the bite?"

"Cleaned it out as best I could. I don't have antibiotics in my kit."

Sam followed them, his eyes on Loudermouth's form.

A hand on his shoulder pulled him back.

He turned and found Jones smirking at him. "What, are you a doctor now, Ryder? Let 'em work." Jones looked over Sam's shoulder, his expression turning lustful. "That nurse, though. Amiright?"

Billings stood up from the front passenger's seat of the Humvee where he'd used the command radio to call in to Hamrick. He closed the Humvee door, then nodded towards the retreating stretcher. "Come on, Jones. We're going in there. Hamrick and Gilliard will be here in a bit, but if Loudermouth wakes up, I want to hear what he has to say."

Jones shrugged, releasing his grip on Sam's shoulder. "Never mind then. Come on, Ryder."

The squad hustled up, making it to the doors before they swung closed, and shuffling through.

The stretcher moved down a hall to the right, Doc Trent's voice murmuring back at them over the squeaking of their boots on the floor tiles. "Let's get him in the X-Ray before he wakes up."

They didn't have that much time.

Loudermouth suddenly thrashed, his head whipping around, but his dislocated limbs only flopping. The first bit came out of his throat in a guttural scream, but then it clarified.

"Ryder! Ryder!" Loudermouth slurred, but it was at the top of his lungs, and there was no denying who he was asking for. "Ryder!"

"Calm down, buddy," Poggs tried. "I got you."

Loudermouth screamed louder. "Ryder! RYDER!"

Doc Trent kept the stretcher moving, but whirled around, his eyes exasperated. "Any of you Ryder?" he called out over Loudermouth's screaming.

Billings shoved Sam forward. "Go on, private."

Trent peddled his hands at Sam, impatient. "Calm him down!"

Sam scrambled forward, unsure why Loudermouth would be calling out for him. Maybe because he was still half out of his mind on fentanyl. Maybe because Sam's had been the face that he'd seemed to fixate on as he'd been pulled to safety.

He went to the side of the moving stretcher, striding fast to keep pace with it. He almost grabbed Loudermouth's limp hand but thought it might hurt him, so he put his hand on the man's heaving chest instead.

"It's alright," Sam said, not knowing what else to say. "I'm here."

Loudermouth immediately quieted.

The nurse prepared an injection.

They turned a corner and stopped at a door with a hand-written plaque that said X-RAY.

Loudermouth's eyes struggled to focus on Sam's face. He looked drunk. Sweat had broken out all over his face, which Sam supposed was a good thing—at least he wasn't dehydrated anymore.

"Ryder," Loudermouth said, nearly whispering now. "Don't let them go in there."

Sam nodded. "Okay."

"Tell them. You have to tell them." Loudermouth's head rose up off the stretcher, the cords of his neck straining. "There's thousands. It's a colony. And they saved me. They saved me for the babies. And they have a brain."

Sam's brow was creased into a confused frown, but he kept nodding.

The nurse stuck the needle into Loudermouth's IV line and delivered the whole payload.

"I saw it," Loudermouth rasped. "I saw her. She's not like the others. Tell them." His eyes crossed. His words became soupy. "Tell 'em…'ell 'em there's…thousands…"

His head dropped back, eyes half-lidded, unseeing. His mouth hung open, moving with breathy syllables that made no sense.

"He's out," the nurse announced. "Let's go."

"We got it, gentlemen," Doc Trent said over his shoulder as the nurse shoved through the door to the X-Ray room.

Poggs stood off to the side, recognizing when he was no longer needed.

Sam stood next to him, and the stretcher bearing Loudermouth slipped through the door, and it swung shut, leaving Poggs and Squad Four standing in the hallway, looking a little dazed.

"The hell was that about?" Jones said.

Sam found Billings's concerned gaze. "I don't know. But you need to tell Hamrick to pull the squads out of there."

Billings shook his head. "I already told Hamrick. He didn't listen. Maybe *you* should try."

Sam looked aghast. "Hamrick hates my guts."

"What about Gilliard?" Billings said. "Doesn't he know you?"

"Yeah, he knows me. But I'm still just a half-boot private."

"Well, Loudermouth's not. And you're the one he gave the message to."

"Speak of the devil," Jones murmured, looking down the hall.

Sam and Billings followed his gaze. First Sergeant Hamrick approached, wearing his UCPs, and Master Sergeant Gilliard strode beside him, wearing khakis and a t-shirt.

Carl and Hamrick stopped, facing the squad, with the door to the X-Ray room between them. Carl raised an eyebrow at Billings. "What's going on?"

"Master sern't," Billings nodded. "Just got Loudermouth into the X-Ray. They had to sedate him again. But he said some things when he was conscious just now." Billings gestured to Sam. "He spoke to Private Ryder."

Carl's cold, gray gaze settled on Sam. "Alright. Ryder. What'd Loudermouth have to say?"

Sam shifted his weight. "Sir, I couldn't make a lot of sense of it. He was only partially conscious, I think—"

"Master sergeant didn't ask you what you thought," Hamrick growled. "Less editorializing. Just tell us what he said."

Carl cast an annoyed sidelong glance at Hamrick and raised a finger, which was sufficient to command silence. “Go ahead, Ryder.”

Sam swallowed. “Yes, sir. He said not to let them go in. He said there were thousands. Something about saving him for babies. And that they had a brain.”

Hamrick let out a disgruntled little chuff, but Carl’s face remained impassive.

Except for one tiny twitch of an eyebrow.

“Who was he talking about?” Carl asked.

“I understood him to be talking about the squads when he said don’t let them go in. And I think he was talking about the primals when he said there were thousands. I don’t know what he meant about the babies or the brain.”

“He was drugged,” Hamrick commented. “Rambling.”

The corner of Carl’s mouth made a downward twitch, but he didn’t respond to Hamrick. Instead, he looked at Billings. “Sergeant, have your men stand down and get some rest. But I want you and Ryder in the TOC with me. Now.”

TWENTY

QRF

THEY DIDN'T HAVE FAR TO GO.

The TOC had been erected in the high school gymnasium.

Billings and Sam walked behind Hamrick and Carl.

Sam found Billings's eyes, questioning whether he was now going to be in the permanent shit-house with Hamrick. Billings gave him a small nod, as though to reassure him that he'd done the right thing.

Ahead of them, Hamrick kept throwing barbed looks at Carl, but Carl walked, staring straight ahead, not oblivious to the looks, but not caring either.

"If we pull the plug on Augusta, we're going to have to clear a completely new route," Hamrick was saying in low tones. "It'll take weeks to establish a new route. And we might even have to move the comms relays. And whatever route we find might not be any safer."

Carl answered, his voice almost bored. "Half of the squads are deployed into Augusta right now. If we have to find another route, I'd prefer to do it at full strength, and not sacrifice half of our guys to stubborn stupidity."

Hamrick clamped his mouth shut.

Carl waved a hand. "Billings. Ryder."

Sam and Billings quickened their pace to Carl's side.

"Tell me about Loudermouth and his injuries."

Billings fielded the question, much to Sam's relief. He explained, mostly verbatim, what he'd heard from Poggs.

"Tell me what you think of that," Carl commanded.

Billings blinked a few times and didn't look over to Hamrick, who was glaring now. "Sir, I think the primals deliberately incapacitated him. I think they were saving him—and maybe others, I'm not sure—to feed their young. That's what I think he meant when he mentioned the 'babies.'"

Carl didn't respond.

"We're already aware that they're procreating," Hamrick griped. "This isn't anything new. Certainly nothing to justify an inordinate amount of concern."

Carl ignored him yet again. "Your initial reports this morning were of the primal pack being about a hundred in numbers. Loudermouth quotes a thousand. Was he out of his mind, or do you think he saw something you didn't?"

"I can't say, sir," Billings admitted. "I prefer to err on the side of caution, and assume he saw something I didn't."

"If his estimation is close, then Augusta could be housing a colony comparable to the one that took over Fort Bragg," Carl reasoned. "Up until a month ago, we didn't even know the primals operated in groups that large. What do you think about his comment about the brain?"

"I don't know," Billings answered again. "It would be pure conjecture on my part."

"Yes. I'm asking you for your pure conjecture."

They rounded a corner and the gymnasium doors lay ahead of them.

Carl stopped there and looked at Billings, waiting.

Billings took a breath and plowed forward. "Sir, those primals that took over Fort Bragg—they weren't like the hordes from before. The hordes were…disorganized. More like herds, with a herd mentality. Where one decided to go, they all followed. The primals that took over Bragg were different. They worked together, but they didn't follow each other. There was some sort of coordination happening."

Hamrick made another dissatisfied noise, but chose to say nothing this time.

Carl regarded Billings for another moment. Then finally nodded. "Those observations are consistent with the facts. That doesn't mean they're true. Just consistent."

"Yes, sir."

Carl turned and grabbed the gymnasium door, pulling it open. The others followed him inside.

The interior of the gymnasium was dark. There were plenty of overhead lights, but they were switched off to accommodate visibility of a bank of monitors that stood to one side of the room.

This was Sam's first time in the TOC—there weren't a whole lot of reasons for half-boot privates on a kill squad to go to the TOC. He had expected it to be much shabbier. The bank of monitors impressed him, even though it didn't look like they showed much. Maps, mostly. Basically an electronic sand table.

Still, Sam felt relieved. Like maybe their lives were in better hands than he'd originally thought.

He followed the others around a few rows of tables at which there were multiple computer stations. Only two techs were working, both in what Sam recognized as US Air Force uniforms. One was a male, stationed on the far end. The other was a female, and that's where Carl was heading.

Sam wondered if this was the one that Jones thought sounded "hot."

She was a petite, dark-skinned woman with her hair pulled up into a tight bun. Sam didn't think she was particularly attractive, but then, he doubted Jones would care.

Carl took a position over her shoulder, looking at her screen, and then up at the bank of monitors. Four of the monitors shared the same image, and Sam recognized it as the one on her screen. It was a map of Augusta, on which were displayed small truck icons, labeled with the squads they corresponded to.

"When did you have contact last?" Carl asked her.

She consulted a notepad to the right of her keyboard and mouse. "Twenty-three thirty."

"About a half hour ago," Carl observed. "Call up Sergeant Paige, please."

Sam and Billings exchanged a glance.

Sam felt the mood tense. He wasn't sure whether this was shared by anybody but him and Billings. Carl seemed mostly at ease. Hamrick seemed eager to prove them wrong, and thereby prove himself right.

Maybe Sam was just worried.

The tech—Staff Sergeant Lopez, according to her nametape and stripes—took up the handset of a SINCGARS radio, and held it to her ear, and transmitted. "Alpha Actual, Alpha Actual, this is Alfred."

"Speaker, please," Carl said.

Lopez flipped a switch on the radio console.

They waited.

Sam's gut continued to tighten with each passing second.

"Yeah, this is Alpha Actual, go ahead with it, Alfred."

He sounded busy…but otherwise okay.

"Got Alfred Actual and Master Sergeant Gilliard on the line," Lopez said. "Standby." She handed the receiver to Carl.

"Sergeant Paige, this is Master Sergeant Gilliard," Carl transmitted. "Sitrep, please."

"Roger that, master sern't," Paige came back after a pause. "Got a small group of primals playing hide and go seek with us. We've been pursuing them into center city. Last sighting was about fifteen minutes ago, around one of the towers. Reporting two CK's for Alpha Squad. Looking to see if we can't flush the rest of them out. Over."

Carl contemplated the bank of monitors. Alpha Squad's icon sat close to the downtown area of Augusta. "Copy two CK's for your squad. Paige, can you advise the maximum number of primals you've sighted?"

"Uh, yes, sir. Highest number we've spotted is about eight in this particular pack we've been tailing. Minus the two we took out. Over."

Hamrick sniffed and cast a derisive look in Billings's direction.

Billings kept his eyes glued to Lopez's screen.

Sam wasn't sure whether to feel relieved for the squads still engaged in Augusta, or worried for himself and Billings for sticking their necks out like this.

Carl keyed the radio again. "Any sign of the larger group of a hundred or so reported by Squad Four earlier this morning?"

"No, sir," Paige answered, sounding vindicated. "No sign of that many primals."

"Copy. Standby." Carl lowered the receiver, and didn't look at anyone in particular, but seemed to offer up the next question to anybody: "Any reason we can think of that the primals would be on the retreat?"

Hamrick cleared his throat. "Because we went after them hard." He gave a begrudging glance towards Billings again. "Sergeant Billings pulled the big red handle, and everybody went in hot. The primals aren't dumb. They're smart enough to know a fight they can't win. So they backed off."

A slight frown crossed over Carl's brow. "Sergeant Billings, what brought you in contact with the place where you recovered Loudermouth?"

"Sir, we caught sight of a single primal," Billings answered, his voice wooden. "It was the only one we'd seen since Loudermouth's squad got taken out. We pursued it. Last sighting was around the building where we recovered Loudermouth—part of the Augusta Technical College. Then we heard Loudermouth calling out, recovered him, and pulled back to reassess."

"And did you come into contact with any primals during that time?"

"No, sir."

Carl nodded, and let out a slight sigh through his nose, as though resigning himself to something. He brought the radio up again. "Gilliard to Paige, you're cleared to proceed until oh-three-hundred hours, and then I would like your troops to bring it back home and swap out with the other squads." He hesitated, with the PTT still engaged. "Be advised, we had a brief conversation with Loudermouth concerning the possibility of a large group of primals numbering in the thousands. This is unconfirmed. Just keep your head on a swivel."

"Wilco, master sern't. Over."

"Nothing further. Out." Carl handed the receiver back to Lopez.

He turned to Billings and Sam. "You guys did the right thing by Loudermouth. I'm glad you were able to retrieve him and get him back to safety. Get some sleep. You'll be on duty at oh-six-hundred to push out past Augusta with the rest of the squads."

For a brief second, Billings's mouth opened, like he had something else to say. But then he thought better of it, and gave a curt nod. "Roger 'at, master sern't. Thank you."

Billings about-faced and headed out of the gymnasium, Sam on his heels.

They hit the corridor, and started heading for the nearest exit to the school.

Behind them, Sam heard the gymnasium door latch shut. He cast a glance over his shoulder to ensure they were alone in the hall.

"So what do we do now?"

Billings chuffed. "What do you mean, 'what do we do'?"

"What about everything Loudermouth said?" Sam insisted.

Billings shook his head. "Loudermouth was high as fuck, Ryder. Just let it go. We got our orders. That's all you need to worry about."

***

A large brick building one street north of the high school had been converted to a combination motor pool and barracks for the Hunter-Killer squads. Butler didn't have much else to offer with everyone crammed in together, so the squads made do with what they had and slept on cots if they were lucky, and blankets if they weren't.

Most of the vehicles were stationed on one end of the warehouse, closest to the multiple bay doors. On the opposite side of the vast, open building, the squads had all claimed their individual spaces. Tents, sheets, and walls made of pallets delineated the territories of individual squads.

Sam and Billings navigated the dark building by the use of the weaponlights on their rifles. Squad Four was in a nice, cozy corner, so they had the luxury of two brick walls. A series of pallets and some camo netting completed their home.

All was quiet in the warehouse. All the other squads were getting their shut-eye, and Sam and

Billings padded into Squad Four's "Underworld," as Jones had dubbed it.

Chris snored softly on a bare, twin mattress, a poncho liner pulled up to his chin.

Pickell slept silently in a hammock he'd made out of a reclaimed parachute, strung between two metal support pillars.

Jones had a cot, and he stirred when Sam and Billings ducked into the Underworld. He sat up and flicked on his headlamp's red light.

"What's the word, Sarge?" he whispered.

Sam and Billings had already doffed their armor before entering the warehouse, so that they wouldn't wake everyone with the sounds of ripping Velcro fasteners. Billings laid his gear at the side of his own cot, while Sam settled onto his pile of blankets and cardboard—kind of like a homeless man, he thought—and started shucking off his boots.

"Word is," Billings whispered back. "We're pushing past Augusta, starting at oh-six-hundred. So go back to sleep."

"Huh," Jones murmured. "Well, that was anti-climactic."

Sam thought about a shower, and how nice that would be. If he woke up at oh-five-thirty, he might be able to squirrel down to the high school and get one in. But then they'd be out in the field again. It almost seemed like a waste.

Of course, he could sleep in an actual bed and take a real shower in a real bathroom if he went to Angela's house. She still insisted on referring to it as "home," as though that title applied to both of them.

But Sam had changed. He'd become Private Ryder.

He wasn't the same boy that needed to be taken in.

And he had his squad now.

Thinking about going back to being just *Sam*, and *Angela's kid*, made him feel listless, like going back in time to a period in your life when you were powerless, and having to live through it again.

No, he wouldn't be going back to Angela's house. Not for showers or nice beds.

He settled into his bed, leaving the covers off for now. His skin felt tacky with dried sweat. He'd just have to ignore it.

"Hey, Ryder," Jones breathed out into the darkness.

As Sam's eyes adjusted to the dark, he began to make out the pattern of the camo netting overhead. "What, Jonesy?"

"Was she hot?"

Sam smiled, in spite of himself.

Some things you could always depend on.

Annoying though he might be, Jones was one of them.

"Yeah, man," Sam said, because he knew that's what Jones wanted to hear. Maybe it would give him sweet dreams. "She was hot."

"I fucking knew it."

"Night, Jonesy."

"Night, Ryder."

Sam closed his eyes and drifted for a time, his thoughts dispersing into a dozen different directions, but none of them strong enough to keep him awake. Exhaustion folded over him, as reliable as Jones, and he fell into it.

***

A horrendous rumble and clatter seized Sam from sleep, and ripped him into the world.

He didn't even sit up. The second his eyes came open, his heart immediately dropped into high gear and he rolled. He grabbed his rifle and then hit the concrete floor on his knees.

Someone's attacking, he thought.

And then, *No, it's a freight train.*

And finally, as the others around him came awake with less urgency—which told him it wasn't anything to fear—he was able to realize that it was the bay doors of the warehouse opening.

Jones husked out an early-morning laugh. "Jesus, Ryder. What were *you* dreaming about?"

There were shouts. But they weren't panicked. Just commanding.

Billings squinted, though the interior of the warehouse was still dark.

No light was coming in through the open bay doors.

"What time is it?" Billings murmured, rolling into a sitting position.

Chris checked the glowing face of his watch—one of the few timepieces that anybody had. "Oh-two-forty-five."

Cognizant again of his rifle in his hands, Sam lowered the muzzle and looked at Billings. "The other teams aren't pulling back until oh-three-hundred."

Billings stood up. "Something happened."

A figure suddenly appeared between the two pallets that created the doorway of Squad Four's Underworld. "Yo, Billings!"

"What happened?"

"Teams got hit. I don't have the deets. They called for QRF. We gotta roll. Five mikes."

Billings didn't waste time, and neither did his team. He spun away from the door and said, "Strap up! We're rollin' in five!" But everyone was already moving.

Jones yanked his UCP pants on. "Who has QRF?"

"Five and Seven," Billings answered, using their squad numbers.

Sam slipped his armor back over his head. It wasn't even dry yet from wearing it earlier. And he thought, *Can you even call it a Quick Reaction Force when it's two hours out?*

The sound of two vehicles roaring to life filled the warehouse. A horn blared. The engines revved and the vehicles sped out of the warehouse. That would be Squads Five and Seven.

Billings stamped his feet into his boots. "If five other squads couldn't hack it, two more ain't gonna make a difference," he growled.

And Sam knew that Billings was thinking the same thing he was: *Thousands.*

By the time they got to where Chris had parked their Humvee the night before, nearly every squad was suited up and tumbling into their vehicles. Under the sound of squad mates calling to each other to make sure they had everything they needed, Sam heard the command channel crackling and murmuring.

Since Squad Four's Humvee had been the last one in that night, they were positioned close to the door. The second that Chris sat in the seat, Billings pointed forward, switching on their own radio.

"Head for the gates. We'll get a sitrep on the way out."

Sam had barely closed his door before they were moving forward.

They cleared the bay doors, and Pickell started climbing for the turret.

"Stay down here, Pickell," Billings ordered. "Until we get a briefing."

Pickell crouched in the narrow space between Sam and Jones.

The Butler Safe Zone was quiet and dark around them. The Hunter-Killers were the only ones moving, forming a line of vehicles rolling steadily towards the gates.

The command channel sounded again, one of the QRF reporting in. "Command, command, this is Stackers on QRF, leaving the gate. Can you advise what's going on?"

"Alfred to Stackers," said a male voice this time. There was a slight pause in his voice, and Sam heard someone else speaking in the background. "Alright. Squads Four, Five, Seven, Eight, Nine, and Eleven. Switch to secondary command channel."

They were keeping the main channel open for the squads that were in Augusta, and apparently engaged.

Billings reached forward and switched to the secondary command channel.

The squads reported in, one by one. Billings called them in last, as they approached the gate. The sentries stood by, waving them through.

First Sergeant Hamrick's voice came over the secondary channel. He sounded tired and pissed. "Alfred Actual to all responding squads, get your asses to Augusta ASAP. Standby on this channel for briefing."

They roared through the gate, and out into the night-blackened world, the other squads nosing up close behind them.

Billings sat silent in his seat, shaking his head slowly.

Hamrick came back on the line. "Responding squads, your buddies in Augusta hit a major snag in the downtown area. They are currently pulling out of the city. Squad One issued a request for QRF about seven minutes ago. You are to head for Checkpoint Joker and go no further. Your job is to assist in their extraction, not to get directly involved. You are *not* to enter into Augusta, or go near the beltway. Engaged squads are reporting large numbers of primals active in the downtown area. Sound off if you copy."

The squads sounded off again, indicating they understood.

Sam's eyes stayed locked onto Billings, wondering if he was going to say anything.

"Squad Four copies," Billings reported, and then ended the transmission. He was still shaking his head.

It was one of the other team leaders that asked the question.

"Stackers to Alfred Actual. Any idea on actual numbers, sir?"

There was a long pause over the airwaves, and Sam could imagine Hamrick standing there, gritting his teeth.

"No solid numbers, Squad Seven," Hamrick growled. "Reports are that it's several times larger than the hundred that was reported yesterday morning."

"Oh, you sonofabitch," Billings spat at the radio console. "You mean *thousands*! You self-righteous, vindictive piece of shit! *Thousands*!"

"Whoa," Jones mumbled, casting a glance at Sam. "I take it this has to do with your wonderful conversation with our fearless leader last night."

Sam only nodded in response.

"Enough of this bullshit." Billings twisted in his seat, looking at his squad in the back. He didn't shout, but his voice was forceful. "Cards on the table, gents. Loudermouth came to for all of thirty seconds yesterday before the sawbones took him. He said that he'd seen thousands. We reported this to Hamrick. He ignored us." Billings's eyes skewered each of them in turn. "I don't mind dying, but I'm not gonna do it because that prick is an idiot. I'll stand in front of a firing squad before I comply with some shit I know is wrong. Hopefully that won't happen today, but if it does, I'm giving you all fair warning, I might refuse an order."

Pickell shifted in his crouched position. "All due respect, Sarge. You sound like a hammer lookin' for a nail."

Billings frowned at him, his face lit only by the glow of the headlights ahead of them. "I'm not *looking* to refuse an order, Pickell. You all know me better than that. I'm just giving you fair warning, if you don't like what I do, you're welcome to hitch a ride on someone else's wagon when the time comes. I won't hold it against you."

Maybe it was because Sam had been there with Billings when they'd told Hamrick what Loudermouth said. But he surprised himself by being the first in the squad to speak up. "I'm with you, Sarge."

"Yup," Jones said, uncharacteristically serious. "I know you won't lead us wrong."

Chris and Pickell only nodded.

That seemed to be good enough for Billings. He turned back around.

"All squads," Hamrick's voice issued from the speaker again. "Switch back to main command channel and standby."

As soon as the radio was switched back, another squad leader's voice came over the line, tense but controlled: "...passing Checkpoint Scarecrow now, enroute to Checkpoint Joker. No visual over the course of the last mile or so. I think we lost them."

"Roger that, Reaper Actual. Proceed to Checkpoint Joker and standby." The TOC operator paused on the line. "All responding squads, hold your traffic unless it's an emergency. We're going to continue to attempt contact with Squad One." The transmission went out, and then came back a moment later, the operator speaking slowly and deliberately. "Any member of Squad One, Alpha Squad, this is command. Please respond. Over."

Everyone in Billings's Humvee was silent, listening for a response.

The line remained empty.

Devoid of life.

Billings shook his head again. "We told them. We fucking *told* them."

***

Carl was back in the TOC again.

He hadn't slept. Knew he wouldn't sleep now.

His face felt drawn and lifeless. He sorely wished that they had some source of caffeine, but that was a luxury from another time.

Lieutenant Derrick, who had been one of Fort Bragg's Watch Commanders, stood to his side. He was reprising his role, but now here in Butler instead. Watch Command was responsible for the guarding of the Safe Zone, and typically wasn't present in the TOC where the Hunter-Killer operations were controlled, but this was something of an *all hands on deck* situation.

"Sir," Derrick said in an undertone. "You want me to send a runner to wake President Houston?"

Carl considered it for a moment, then shook his head. "No, not yet." He knew which way she would start to swing decisions. He preferred not to have her muddying the waters yet. "But I do want you to call in Major Brinly. We might need his Marines."

Lieutenant Derrick nodded. "Yes, sir. I'll send a runner immediately."

Carl crossed his arms over his chest, and set his right fist against his mouth.

Hamrick, standing over their on-duty TOC operator, turned and looked at him.

They said nothing, but they didn't need to. Their eyes spoke volumes to each other.

They'd made a mistake.

That much was clear.

How big of a mistake?

Well, that remained to be seen.

TWENTY-ONE

THOUSANDS

IT WAS ROUGHLY a hundred and fifty miles to Checkpoint Joker from the Butler Safe Zone.

Two hours and some change, at the Humvee's top speed of 70 mph.

An agonizing two hours, marked every ten minutes, by command transmitting into the dead silence: "Any member of Squad One, Alpha Squad, this is command. Please respond. Over."

"We're getting close," Billings called out. "Pickell, get on the fifty."

Pickell clambered up into the turret.

Again, command tried to hail Alpha Squad. And again, they got no response.

At least, not for a long few minutes.

And then, as Sam turned away from the radio, knowing that Paige and his team weren't going to respond, like they hadn't responded every other time, the radio crackled.

It was just an open line. It lasted for maybe three seconds.

Billings leaned forward.

Everyone in the Humvee—except Pickell, who couldn't hear from the turret—refocused on the radio.

"Did you hear that?" Jones murmured, nearly hanging over Billings's shoulder.

"Yeah, I heard it."

"Was that command or Squad One?" Jones demanded.

"I don't know, Jones," Billings snapped. "I heard what you heard."

The radio opened again.

"Command to the last station transmitting, we did not copy. Please re-transmit. Over."

Silence again.

It drew out for nearly a minute, the TOC operator and whoever was hanging over their head trying to give whoever it was that had transmitted ample time to respond. Then the operator tried again.

"Command to last transmitting station, if you cannot advise verbally, click comms twice to acknowledge."

This time the response was almost immediate.

But it wasn't two clicks.

The channel opened again. A low hiss. An open line.

And then a low voice, barely more than a whisper.

It made a noise that might've been a word, or might've been a groan.

A slurred consonant, followed by a protracted exhale.

And then the transmission ended.

"What was that?" Jones said. "What did they say?"

"It sounded like 'no,'" Chris said, from the driver's seat.

"Everyone shut up," Billings snapped, holding up a hand.

"Command to last calling station, please repeat. We did not copy. Squad One, is that you?"

But whoever it was didn't repeat themselves.

Through the darkness ahead of them, Sam caught sight of a glimmering collection of vehicle running lights, drawing closer.

"Checkpoint Joker," Chris announced, as they approached it.

Checkpoint Joker was the furthest and most southerly checkpoint from Augusta. It was an old towing company with an attached impound lot. Again, selected for its relative defensibility, though if Sam were to take a guess, the eight-foot-high barbed wire fences weren't going to stop a thousand primals.

Probably not even a hundred of them.

In amongst a collection of old, impounded vehicles, the technicals, Humvees, and MATVs of the Hunter-Killer squads gathered, their headlights off to prevent blinding themselves, but their running lights on.

Squad Two—Snake Eyes—had taken up security at the main gate of the impound lot, their vehicle positioned right in the middle of the gate so that any incoming vehicle had to slow significantly and carefully sidle around the narrow space they'd left to either side.

Their gunner tracked the incoming vehicles for a moment, but then lifted the barrel when he recognized them. Two other members of the squad stood out front of the vehicle, waving in the last of the QRF, followed by Billings's Humvee.

The second that Chris rolled them to a halt, Billings grabbed the radio receiver and made a very brief transmission, obviously not wanting to step on anything else that might be radioed in from whoever that was trying to speak only moments ago.

"Command, command, go to secondary."

Billings didn't wait for a response. He switched the radio over.

"Alfred on secondary. Go ahead last calling station."

"Alfred, this is Squad Four Actual," Billings' eyes scanned around and behind them through the Humvee windows, apparently taking a mental count of all the squads. "Responding teams have all arrived here at Checkpoint Joker. We're standing by for orders. Over."

A long pause ensued over the radio.

A rap on Billings's window drew his attention. He dropped the reinforced glass.

Sergeant Roble from Squad Eight—Wardogs—stood outside, looking antsy. "Did you hear that last transmission? Was that Paige?"

Billings shook his head. "I have no clue who that was. Could've been nothing."

Roble made a "Pshuh" noise that one might have expected more from a petulant teenager than a soldier in full battle rattle. "It wasn't *nothing*, Billings. That was someone saying something."

"It sounded like 'no'," Chris repeated.

"That's what I thought, too," Roble agreed.

Sam had heard something else, but he kept that to himself for now.

"Sergeant Billings," Hamrick came back on the line, all business. "That last transmission had to've come from Squad One's vehicle. Last known location of their vehicle was in center city. If we've got live soldiers out there, we need to at least make an attempt at contact. I want you to slip in as close as you can get, and just see if you can get eyes on that vehicle and report what you see. Over."

Billings stared at the radio. "I can't tell whether this is punishment for making him look bad, or his way of apologizing." But he keyed the radio. "Wilco, first sern't. Proceed towards Augusta and see if we can't get eyes on Squad One's MATV."

Another voice came over the comms this time. Master Sergeant Gilliard's. "Sergeant Billings, take two other squads with you. And remember this is recon only. If you can get eyes on without getting yourself hemmed up, then great, but use your good judgement and pull back if you need to. We're not going to lose any more squads tonight."

Sam felt a slight easing in the tension of his guts. Hearing the command from Gilliard took a bit of the sting out of it. This wasn't punishment—Gilliard trusted them not to make a stupid, hazardous decision and put more people in jeopardy.

"Roger that, master sern't," Billings responded, then looked to Roble.

Roble nodded without hesitation.

Billings transmitted again: "Squad Eight, Wardogs, will come with…"

"Andy'll come too," Roble asserted. "Put the Metalmouths on there."

"…As well as Squad Five, Metalmouths. Over."

Hamrick's voice again: "Command copies. Get it done, Sergeant Billings. Out."

***

In the strange twilight of dreams that existed between waning sedation and consciousness, Loudermouth thought that she was there, standing over him again.

He felt terror, making his heart thrash.

But he also felt a low, pulsing warmth, in the bottom of himself.

Everything was indistinct.

The details were shadowed by fear and drugs, but he knew in that moment what he'd known then: She was not like the others. She was not deformed, not terrible. But she was also not entirely human.

He saw every curve of her naked flesh. Arms, corded like an athlete's—but not long and ape-like. Hands that were long-fingered and callused, but not clawed. Not like the others. Breasts, full and young. Thighs, powerfully muscled, but sleek, a dark thatch of hair between them. A face that was not inhuman, shrouded by lengths of dark, dreadlocked hair, with eyes peering out, as cold and violent as a lioness.

Strange and terrifying, and yet powerfully feminine.

Fear and hatred, and a very real, very conscious desire to either flee or to try to kill her, and yet he was powerless to do either. And as she crawled toward him with a liquid sort of movement, and drew herself over him, and mounted him, despite it all, some base part of himself rose to her, hard and hot.

She smelled like a wild animal. Her skin hot, like a fire burned beneath it. He felt her heat pressing down against him and despite the agony in his broken hips, despite his logical mind screaming and rebelling, he felt himself pressing back.

Hands as hard as iron gripped his face.

He met her terrible eyes, and he hated them and wanted to shoot them out of her skull, and somehow, in a swirl of something deeper than all of that, he wanted them.

She growled a single word from a mouth not entirely human, and not entirely primal.

"Go!"

***

Loudermouth reeled back into reality with a yelp.

For a second, he thought that she was still there.

He tried to lurch away, but he was immobilized.

"Easy," a soft voice said.

Not the same voice. Not the growl.

Loudermouth's wide eyes, still seeing half of his dream mixed with reality, blinked a few times until the horrible fiction of his imagination slipped away, like rain off a windshield.

A woman in scrubs looked down at him. "Sergeant Loudermouth," she said. "You're okay. You're in the Butler Safe Zone. You're safe."

Relatively safe, his mind shot out, almost as a reflex.

His eyes surged down towards his body. He saw that his hips were in something of a cast, irons pins going through them like a torture device. His arms weren't in casts, but they lay, limp and throbbing ominously at his side.

He tried to move. Managed to curl his hands into fists, and make his feet wiggle.

"Don't move too much," the lady in the scrubs told him. "We've put your shoulders back in their sockets, and pinned your hips back together, but the more you move, the less you'll heal. So try to stay still as much as you can."

Still staring at his casted lower body, Loudermouth's mind began to run, began to shake off the dregs of the drugs they must've given him. He began to parse through the real and the fantastical. What he had stored in his memories, and how they'd been mixed into a mess by the dream.

Some of that had happened.

Some of it hadn't.

He couldn't recall anything sexual about the moment that he'd seen her. But his recollection of her, he felt, was accurate. And even now, the vestiges of the dream had tainted it with that bestial eroticism. He felt the otherworldly burn, low in himself, and was disgusted with it.

He'd been too scared when he'd seen her in real life for any of the shit in his dream to have really happened.

But he'd dreamed that it had.

And that disturbed him.

Christ, I'm fucked in the head.

But there was more to it than that. And he knew it. And he left it there, and made an unconscious promise to himself that it would remain there, buried.

He dragged his eyes back to the nurse, the real world taking hold of his thoughts again. "Have they pulled out of Augusta?" he croaked. His throat was dry and barren. "Where is everybody?"

The nurse only shook her head. "I don't know about that stuff, Honey. I'm just a nurse."

If he could've reached out and seized her, he would've. But all he could do was make his tone forceful.

"Nurse, I'm not fucking around. You need to get me someone in charge. First Sergeant Hamrick, or Master Sergeant Gilliard. Someone."

The nurse seemed on the cusp of saying something along the lines of "No, you need to rest," but after a moment she appeared to relent.

"I'll get Doctor Trent, okay?"

And before he could argue with her, she'd hustled out of the room.

***

The sky blanched gray to the east.

Sam could see the individual trees now, as their Humvee approached Augusta. They'd passed Checkpoint Scarecrow a minute ago, and the road ahead of them rose up, and Sam knew that this was the bridge over the I-520 loop.

Billings shifted about in the front seat. "Guys, I'm going to do something unusual."

His team listened. No one spoke.

"Chris, go ahead and pull us to a stop. Right here."

Their Humvee rolled to a halt, the brakes squeaking. Behind them, the rumble of the two other squads' vehicles shifted to an idle as they stopped behind them.

Billings keyed the squad comms on his rig. "Billings to Roble and Andy, keep your men in the vehicles. But I'm going to dismount. Clear the sides of this bridge and make sure there are no surprises. How copy?"

Roble answered up, some hesitation in his voice. “Sure, Billings. We copy.”

Billings pushed his door open. “Pickell, stay sharp on that fiddy. Jones and Ryder, you’re with me.”

Sam unlatched his door and slid out into the world. His feet tingled in his boots as they supported his weight after so long cramped in the back of the vehicle. The cool morning air surrounded him, still and silent.

Not even the birds had woken up yet.

He stepped to the front of the Humvee, where Billings and Jones stood.

Billings indicated the sides of the bridge with a knife hand. “Sam, you take the left, Jones you take the right. The second you see anything moving, you call it out and get back in the truck.”

“Hua,” Jones murmured, his usual spirits subdued.

Sam simply nodded his acknowledgement.

Then he moved to the side of the bridge.

Jones moved to the opposite side.

Billings started walking.

The vehicles behind them eased forward.

Sam’s pulse was hard, but not particularly fast. He sidled up to the concrete barrier to the left side of the bridge. He held his breath and peered over.

He almost expected a face to be staring up at him from below, all fury and gnashing teeth.

But below him, it was too dark to see.

He forced his feet to keep moving.

He angled his rifle up and over, thumbing his weaponlight on.

The beam blazed down below him.

Just brush, at first. The leaves of it reflecting the light back at him. The shadows created by the weaponlight shifted ominously, but there was nothing in them. Only shadows.

Sam continued to move forward, sweeping his light back and forth.

A hissing noise sounded, very close by.

Sam's heart shot into his throat, and he almost called out, until he realized it was just his rig, brushing up against the concrete barriers.

Shit. Calm down, Sam.

They moved onwards and upwards. The bridge had a slight grade to it. The top seemed like a horizon line, beyond which Sam saw the tips of buildings in the downtown area, charcoal gray against a navy sky.

He approached the top, his attention now split between looking over the side, and continuously checking the horizon line as it seemed to gradually sink before him, revealing more and more of the city.

What would he see from the top of the overpass?

Thousands of primals, waiting for them?

Back over the side. Another sweep of his weaponlight.

About twenty-five feet below them, the beam played weakly over a collection of defunct vehicles, some of them standing askew in the middle of the lanes of I-520, most of them shoved off to the side. The remnants of a traffic jam from long ago. People trying to flee the city as everything went to shit.

They seemed so ancient where they stood, rusting and moldering, in lanes sometimes half overtaken by the encroachment of scrub brush. Every one of these scenes felt like finding archaeological relics of a civilization that time forgot.

A civilization that was dead.

A low whistle caught Sam's attention.

His eyes went to Billings, and saw that his sergeant stood at the apex of the overpass now, his fist raised over his head, indicating a halt.

The vehicles stopped moving forward.

Sam and Jones hustled forward, so that they also stood at the top of the slight grade.

The city of Augusta, Georgia, laid out in front of them. Sam could see the rest of the overpass, descending down into the dimness. His eyes scanned through the halflight, looking for any sign of movement.

Sam and Jones converged on Billings.

Billings had a pair of large field binoculars that he'd rummaged from the back of the Humvee. He held them at chest height, his rifle hanging on its sling. He pivoted in place, seeming to orient himself.

"Alpha Squad should be straight in that city center," he mused aloud.

Appearing to have settled on the appropriate direction to begin searching, Billings raised the binoculars to his eyes.

"Just keep watch," Billings said, as he scanned across the urban terrain laid out in front of him.

Sam and Jones both directed their gazes down and outwards.

Shadows, and charcoal blocks. That's what the lightless city looked like to Sam.

After a moment, Billings made a discomfited noise, but kept he glass up to his eyes. "Too many buildings. I can barely see the streets. Let alone

Alpha's MATV." Finally, he lowered the binoculars. "We're never going to see them from here."

Sam didn't like that. "You want to move us in closer?"

Billings let out a slow breath through his nose. "That seems like a horrible idea."

Sam nodded. "Yeah, it does, Sarge."

"Gilliard wanted us on point because he knew we weren't going to do something stupid," Billings reasoned, almost like he was trying to assuage his own guilt for not pressing on. "Something stupid like waltzing right back into the spot where we just lost one of our squads."

Sam couldn't agree more. And frankly, he felt no guilt about it. He felt that he and Billings had been reasonably circumspect, and that Alpha Squad had chosen to ignore the writing on the wall. Now Alpha Squad appeared to have paid the price for their bravado. That wasn't Sam's fault. He wasn't going to take that on himself.

But then again, he was just a half-boot private.

Billings was a sergeant. He tended to take responsibility for things.

"No," Billings finally asserted, fully lowering the binoculars. "This is dumb. We came to see if we could put eyes on. There's no way we're going to put eyes on from here. And I'm not committing us to going in there. We gotta call it—"

"Movement," Jones said, his voice taut.

Sam felt sparks through his limbs. He jerked his rifle up into his shoulder pocket.

He was about to ask where, but then saw it himself.

Shit!

Straight ahead of them, no more than a quarter mile.

Right where the overpass reconnected with the city and seemed to sink into the darkness, a shape had detached from the shadows, and was moving towards them.

Sam put his cheek to his stock and sighted through his optic.

"Hold fire," Billings rasped. Then, over the squad comms, "Guys, we got movement down at the base of the bridge, I want everyone ready to reverse the hell out of here. Standby."

His heart now truly throttling up, Sam forced himself to dip his rifle so that he could see clearly over the top of the optic.

The shape came to a stop.

A malformed jumble of limbs.

Not just one figure, Sam realized. It was one figure, clutching another, almost like a body shield.

A high, lilting moan reached their ears.

"Oh shit," Sam whispered. "Sarge, that's Paige!"

Billings snapped the binos back to his eyes, but Sam saw enough, even with his unaided eye. As his focus honed in through the dimness, Sam saw the rough outline of Paige—his gear, his fatigues, the shock of bright blond hair standing out.

Arms and legs, hanging limp.

He was not moving on his own power.

He was being carried. By a primal.

Sam dropped.

The primal was directly behind Paige.

Sam knew he couldn't take a shot that precise from a standing position.

He flattened his body out on the cool concrete, resting his rifle on its mag and sighting through his optic at the dim collection of shapes, roughly four hundred yards away from them now.

It was still going to be a tough shot.

"I think I can take him," Sam muttered, his cheek weld muffling his words. "You want me to take him, Sarge?"

"Negative!" Billings hissed. "Just hold on!"

The two figures halted.

Another moan. Paige was definitely still alive. And immobilized. Just like Loudermouth had been.

The red dot of Sam's optic wavered. He took a deep breath and forced himself to let it out slowly. Despite his ratcheting pulse, he forced the reticle to stop jiggling about. He saw the gray shape of the primal. He saw its head.

He needed to hold over. Put the dot over the top of the primal's head.

The primal partially released Paige's body, and the soldier slumped to the ground onto his knees. The primal held him erect with one hand.

But now the primal's entire upper torso was visible.

"I can take him out," Sam said again.

And maybe Billings was about to give him the order to do it.

But the primal reached a hand around, gripped Paige under the chin, and with one yank, ripped Paige head from his body.

Sam fired. The gunshot split the morning air, and drowned out something that Billings had shouted. Sam couldn't tell what it was. He watched the primal jerk, even as it held Paige's head aloft.

He fired again, and the primal jerked again.

But didn't go down.

It threw the head at them.

It released Paige's body, and the corpse slumped to the ground, as the detached head struck the concrete and rolled a few feet.

Sam fired again.

Struck again.

"Ryder! Let's move!" Billings shouted.

His perception suddenly widening out of the tiny world seen through his optic, Sam became aware that Jones and Billings were beating feet for the Humvee.

The primal tilted its head back and let out a howl.

The first three rounds had struck the creature in the chest, even though Sam had held eighteen inches high.

He adjusted so the dot was a little higher. Maybe a full two feet above the primal. And squeezed one last round.

The primal's head snapped back, and it collapsed.

But the howl didn't end.

The howl continued on, growing louder.

Coming from a multitude of throats.

Hundreds.

Thousands.

"Ryder! Move your ass!"

Sam thrust himself off the concrete, gulping air, and he ran.

TWENTY-TWO

THE CODE

LEE SLID BETWEEN TREES, his feet rolling on the outsides, soft across the forest floor.

To his right, a second column snaked through the woods, about fifteen yards from him.

Just far enough that their shapes were lost in the blue cast of dawn. The quiet susurration of their boots in the leaves barely audible.

They'd left their vehicles a good ways south. The rumble of trucks could carry for a long distance, and they wanted to make sure that, if there was anybody unfriendly around the bunker, they wouldn't see Lee and Menendez's crew coming.

Up ahead of them, the point man held up a fist and sank to his knees.

Lee followed suit.

The comms in Lee's ear hissed, and the point man's voice came through as a whisper. "Captain. Sergeant. Up here."

Lee glanced over to the right, where he saw the shadow of Menendez's shape rise up and move up the slight incline they were positioned on. Lee slipped out of his position and followed suit, converging with Menendez at the top, where the point man was crouched.

"Whatcha got?" Menendez whispered.

The point man was one of the younger soldiers. Smallish, and lean—though everybody was lean these days. He tapped his ear and pointed further ahead through the woods. "Just heard something. Sounded like voices."

Lee frowned, and inclined his ear in that direction. He wasn't surprised that he hadn't heard it. After years of gunbattles, many of them in tight, enclosed spaces, his hearing wasn't what it once had been.

The point man, being as young as he was, hadn't had the time to destroy his eardrums to the extent that Lee had. His hearing was still sharp.

Squatting on his haunches at the top of the small ridge, Lee thought he heard what the point man had detected. A low mumble of voices, carrying through the woods.

Menendez looked to Lee. "We're within several hundred yards of the bunker."

Lee nodded. "Someone's outside of it."

Another voice reached them, and this time it was all too clear.

The words were not audible, but it was definitely a raised voice. Some urgency to it.

Lee shifted his weight. "Keep rolling," he said. "But we don't know who that is, so take us in nice and slow. Let's keep the element of surprise."

The point man nodded once, then rose up from his knees and crept off through the woods.

Menendez and Lee waited until he'd got about twenty yards ahead of them—just visible through the trees—and then they started moving. Menendez made a motion to the others behind them, and the whisper of lightly disturbed leaves continued.

Ahead of them the land dipped, and then flattened out.

The last time Lee had been here, he'd gone in and out by vehicle, taking the dirt road to and from. But he thought he recalled how the terrain had been, and he remembered it as being on a plateau of sorts.

As they moved through the woods, the occasional lilt of voices became clearer.

At one point, the slamming of a car door reverberated through the woods.

Someone let out a long string of curses.

Lee's pulse began to accelerate. The hard, steady beat that he knew so well. Unconsciously, he began to force his breathing into a steady pattern—sucking in a breath, then blowing it out through pursed lips.

Maybe it was Breckenridge, or one of his men. Maybe they were dealing with something on the topside of the bunker.

The point man came to a stop again. Lee could see enough now that he could tell the point man was close to the edge of a clearing, though he couldn't see much beyond that. The point man didn't transmit this time. He went prone, then rolled onto his side and made a quick motion with his hands.

Lee and Menendez approached again, going low, taking the last few yards to the point man on their hands and knees, and then sliding into place on their bellies, the three of them shoulder to shoulder.

The point man put two fingers to his eyes, then pointed straight ahead. His words were just an exhale of breath: "That's not us."

Lee peered through the pale dawn light.

About ten yards ahead of them, the trees cleared out. There was some brush at the tree line that obscured parts of the clearing beyond, but Lee was able to make out the basics.

There were three technicals and one van parked in the clearing.

Across from the vehicles stood the entrance to the bunker, disguised, as many bunkers were, as another bit of ubiquitous utilities—this one a shack that sat at the base of what was apparently a small cell tower.

There were men gathered around the vehicles. About a dozen of them.

And the point man was right.

They weren't Tex's men.

Every one of them was armed, a conglomeration of various rifles. The technicals were equipped with what Lee identified as M240s, and the gunners gripped their machine guns, addressing them to the entrance of the bunker.

They looked like they were waiting for something.

One of the men, who was again uttering a string of curses, paced back and forth, his eyes locked on the bunker entrance.

"*Nuevas Fronteras*?" Menendez whispered in Lee's ear.

Lee stared at the dozen armed men, feeling his heart thudding against the forest floor. He nodded once. His mind shot off into several directions, grasping questions and hurling possible answers.

Were they trying to take the bunker? And if they were, why weren't the bunker defenses chewing them to shreds? Lee had activated his bunker defenses before—automatic turrets that every bunker was equipped with. They had succeeded in ripping apart an entire horde of infected that had surrounded the bunker. They should've been able to make quick work of a dozen men.

"Whaddaya wanna do?" Menendez asked.

Lee licked his dry lips with a dry tongue, but before he could answer, a hiss of hydraulics reached their ears.

Lee's eyes shot over to the bunker entrance.

The doors slid open.

They issued a single figure.

Not Breckenridge.

Not any of Tex's men.

The figure jogged up to the man that had been pacing and cursing. He had armor plates on his chest and an AK in his hands. He jabbed a finger back behind him. "They got us pinned down right at the entrance!"

The man's voice felt overly-loud in the stillness.

The pacing man stopped pacing, and cursed again, and it wasn't until this moment that Lee realized it was an amalgamation of Spanish and English curses. And when the man spoke, it was with a thick accent.

"The rest of you—go." He swiped an arm at them, as though scooping them towards the bunker. "Use the grenades. Blow them the fuck out of there."

"That'll wreck the supplies," one of the men said, clearly a native English speaker.

The man in charge whirled on him. "I don' give a fuck about the supplies right now! Mateo wants the bunker, he's gonna get the fuckin' bunker! We can't get the fuckin' bunker until you kill them all! No more questions. Get it done."

The dozen men standing out in the open made for the bunker door.

The man in charge led them.

"Breckenridge is down there," Menendez strained out. "But how are these guys getting in?"

The man in charge stopped at the bunker entrance. He accessed a panel in the side of the door, and rapidly tapped in a code.

Lee half-expected the bunker defenses to come alive as they were programmed to do—to respond to a wrong code with lethal force.

But they didn't.

The doors slid open again, and the dozen men piled into the large freight elevator that would take them down to the bunker. The doors slid shut behind them.

The man in charge remained topside.

"They've got the codes," Lee whispered, as he watched the man stalk away from the bunker entrance. "How did they get the codes?"

"We gotta stop them," Menendez urged. "We can't let them wipe Breck out!"

Lee's eyes shot over to the technicals. The gunners had remained behind. Three machine guns still trained on the door. He blinked rapidly, trying to compute everything, but hardly any of it came together in any sensible fashion.

Compartmentalize. What do you know?

Nuevas Fronteras had access to the bunkers. How that happened didn't matter—it only mattered that it was true. There were four men. Three machine gun turrets, and one man standing alone, although armed with an M4.

That man had the code to get in.

"We need to take the lead guy alive," Lee said.

How the hell were they going to accomplish that?

Menendez stared at him, the same question in his eyes.

Lee hissed softly through his teeth. Then he keyed his comms. "Everyone, target the gunners in the turrets. Do not shoot the man in the white t-shirt that's standing outside. Me and Menendez will handle him. Open fire when you see us charge him."

"We're gonna charge him?" Menendez gaped.

"You got a better idea?"

Menendez didn't respond.

Lee stared at their target.

He was pacing again. Only twenty yards away, but twenty yards was a lot of distance to be running at someone. The man would have ample time to respond. But they didn't have a choice. He was the one with the code. And time was running out for whoever was holding out inside that bunker. Every second Lee wasted up here, grenades were going to get thrown, and men were going to die.

"We gotta do this," Lee said, more to himself than anything. He keyed the comms again. "Everyone, let me know when you're in position and ready."

There was a slight pause.

Off to the right, Lee heard a rustle in the leaves, and his heart squirmed into his throat, fearing the man in charge might hear them. But he just kept pacing and murmuring to himself.

"Squad's ready," one of Menendez's men responded with a whisper. "Targets acquired. It's on you."

No choice.

They had to do this.

Lee rose up off his belly, trying to keep low, but get his feet under him.

Beside him, Menendez did the same.

"Go right, I'll go left," Lee breathed out. "If you gotta shoot him, take him in the pelvis."

Lee forced himself to wait.

The man was pacing again. Occasionally turning his back on them. That would give them invaluable seconds.

This is a bad idea.

But his other thoughts were like fire burning through him: *How many are even left alive down there?*

How long do they have?

Not long.

The man in charge turned away from them. His head tilted back, staring at the sky, letting loose something in Spanish that might've been a prayer, or another string of invectives.

Now.

Lee thrust himself up.

The dry leaves beneath him slipped under his feet. He almost went down. Caught himself on a tree, then used it to sling himself forward. A branch cracked. A low-hanging limb ripped across his face.

Lee's eyes never left the man in charge.

Out of his peripheral, he saw Menendez, pulling ahead, and angling out, putting a little distance between Lee and him so that the man would not be able to take them both so easy.

The woods rushed.

The man jerked, looked over his shoulder.

Rifle reports bellowed out of the tree line, and one long string of automatic fire from one of Menendez's SAW gunners, raking the bullets across the vehicles.

The man in charge flinched at the thunderous noise, eyes going wide, his grip seizing down on the rifle in his hands.

Out of the corner of Lee's perception, he saw the nearest turret gunner begin to swing his M240 in Lee's direction, and then he flailed about and crumpled, puffs of red mist erupting from him, giving his corpse a brief, crimson aura.

Only ten yards, and Lee was at a full sprint.

The man in charge finally met Lee's gaze.

His eyes jagged left, catching sight of Menendez too.

A brief moment of indecision—exactly what Lee had hoped for—he couldn't decide which to fire on first.

Five yards.

The man made a decision.

Raised his rifle. The muzzle like a black, unblinking eye, staring right back at Lee.

Lee raised his rifle, his finger going to the trigger.

An automatic burst came from his left, ripping through the man's midsection and knocking him off balance.

Lee speared him, rifle-first. The muzzle of his weapon gouged right under the man's chin, and a fraction of a second later, Lee's entire body slammed into him. They flew three feet through the air and crashed into the side of one of the technicals.

For brief moment, it was all dust and whirling limbs and squirting blood.

Lee gasped, his diaphragm shocked by the impact, but his mind ferociously intent on his task. He raked the butt of his rifle across the man's jaw, scattering teeth. He reached for the man's rifle, but a flurry of dust flew over it and Menendez came sliding in, seizing the rifle before Lee could and flinging it away from the man.

Lee coughed, forced a breath into his lungs, then posted up on the man, his legs cinching tight around them man's waist, ready for a fight.

The man's eyes rolled around, dazed. His hands scrambled about, and for a second Lee thought they were trying to fight him, but then he became aware of the warm wetness he felt against his thighs.

The man tried to clutch his wounds.

Lee reared back, and raised his rifle up to his eyes, giving the technicals a quick scan.

All three gunners were down.

"Get him up," Menendez growled.

The man beneath Lee got his voice back. No more words, English or Spanish. Just a high, panicked whine.

Lee stood up on trembling legs. Menendez snatched the man's right arm, and Lee took his left. They hauled the wounded man up, and Lee's eyes shot down to where he saw the dark spread of blood soaking through the man's white shirt and pants.

"Get up!" Lee growled, his voice barely returned to him.

The man's head lolled, his mouth open and gaping at Lee and Menendez as they stood him up. But his legs weren't supporting any of his weight. They flopped around uselessly beneath him. Either shock, or one of Menendez's rounds had shattered the pelvis.

Lee and Menendez traded an urgent look, and they both knew.

They had only moments before this man bled out.

Behind them, Menendez's squad sprinted out of the woods. They called commands to each other that came through Lee's scarified ear drums like he was hearing them from under water.

Lee pushed the man towards the bunker door. "The code," he rasped as the man's feet dragged through the dirt and threatened to trip Lee and Menendez. "You're gonna type in the fucking code, or I'm going to open your guts."

Menendez's squad rapidly cleared the technicals for anyone that was left alive, but no one was.

Lee and Menendez reached the bunker, their captive moaning between them. They thrust him up against the wall where the control panel sat. Lee posted his left hand up against the man, pinning him to the wall, then placed the muzzle of his rifle against the base of the man's skull.

"The code!" he shouted in the man's ear. "Type in the code!"

"Ah," the man said. "Ah."

Menendez slammed an elbow into the man's back. "Do it!"

The man's eyes didn't appear to be able to focus on the panel. They kept squirrelling around, like he was drunk. His brows furrowed. He raised a blood-covered hand up to the panel. It shook, scattering drops of red down the wall.

Menendez reached around and seized the man's wrist to steady it, then placed it against the number pad. "*El codigo, puto!*"

Lee stared hard at the man's fingers as they traced blood across the control panel and left red fingerprints where he touched the keypad.

One. Five. Three. Nine. Eight. Zero.

Lee seized the mental image, and repeated the numbers manically in his head.

A hydraulic hiss.

"Cover!" Menendez shouted to his men, who were close behind.

The doors to the freight elevator slid open.

Two of Menendez's squad took up positions to either side, rifles trained on the interior of the elevator. Only stainless steel gleamed back at them. It was empty.

"We're good," Lee said, then wrenched the dying man back off the wall and let him collapse in the dirt. For a bare second, Lee considered leaving him to die.

Mercy, or perhaps expediency, won out.

He put a bullet through the man's temple.

He whirled around, and found Menendez looking at him.

Menendez nodded. Lee nodded back.

One-five-three-nine-eight-zero.

Lee put his back to the control panel. Menendez's squad gathered outside the doors, rifles ready, eyes intent.

"The rear of the elevator will open," Lee called out. "We'll have an open lane on the back and side of whoever is down there, but we're gonna be crammed into one spot. Hug the walls. Go high and low. Hit 'em hard, and be careful for friendly fire."

A round of nods.

Menendez's squad piled into the elevator, Lee and Menendez entering last.

The doors slid closed behind them.

Nine men, crammed into a tight space.

It was as far from an ideal assault as you could get.

Four of them against the left wall, Lee and four others against the right.

"Going down," Lee called, and hit the button. There were no floors or levels in these bunkers. The elevator only had two positions—up top, or down below. And they were going down below.

The elevator jerked under their feet. Began to descend.

The men nearest the rear of the elevator that would open into the bunker went down to one knee. Their buddies crowded close behind them, their thighs pressed against the kneeling men's backs. The others found tiny slices of angles and put rifles there. As many guns pointed at the threat as possible.

"Don't stop shooting," Menendez commanded. "We take them out first, and then we worry about the wounded."

And every single one of them knew there would be wounded.

Some of them were going to die.

Maybe all of us.

Their one advantage was that the cartel men below them didn't know they were coming.

That would last for one second. Maybe two.

It would only take one brave asshole with a grenade to kill every last man in the elevator.

The elevator slowed.

Stopped.

The doors slid open.

TWENTY-THREE

THE BUNKER

MOST OF THE TIME, when Lee was in the middle of fighting, things went very fast, and it was over before he could really think about it.

This felt as though he were slogging through time while suspended in tar.

Four men in front of him, their bodies angling out, each one a little further than the last, so that Lee stood nearly in the center of the elevator—right in the fatal funnel—just to get his rifle safely past the shoulders of the man in front of him.

His body fought him. Fear clashed with determination. Wanting to kill. Abhorring the thought of a bullet finding his flesh. His vision tried to shrink, but he breathed it back open again.

The doors slid open.

The sound of gunfire crashed in at them like water breaking a dam.

Through banks of gunsmoke, the figures of men were just dark shapes—wraiths slipping through fog. The shapes hugged walls and flattened themselves behind their dead friends. Weapons flashed and spewed smoke and lead.

All of this in a split second, viewed through the window of his optic.

A red dot in the center, seeking a life to end.

No one had even noticed the elevator door opening.

Lee put the red dot on the side of a man's temple and removed the front of his head with a squeeze of his finger.

All nine guns in the elevator roared, and Lee's hearing dimmed to a hum.

The man in front of Lee leaned out, and Lee leaned with him—his support hand gripping the soldier's shoulder.

They both shot the next man. A wisp of a shape that stopped moving after that.

One of the cartel men brought his weapon to bear on the elevator. Lead projectiles clattered over the stainless steel innards. Bee stings peppered Lee's face and neck. He flinched involuntarily against them.

Three rifles pounded that one man into oblivion.

The soldier at the lead of their stack crumpled.

The man directly in front of Lee jerked, a round ricocheting off his armored side. Lee felt it strike his own armor like a hit to the chest with a ball-peen hammer.

"You're good! Stay up!" Lee shouted.

Menendez's stack inched forward. The lead man crouched, and leaned out, taking a slim angle to fire at a target Lee couldn't see. Lee searched desperately for something moving to put a bullet into, but all the shapes directly in front of the elevator were down.

Someone let out a muffled shout.

Lee realized what they'd said only when the small black object rolled into the door of the elevator.

Lee started toward the grenade, his eyes wide, his throat stinging as it sucked in burnt propellant. One of the guys in his stack slid out, like a soccer player slide-tackling an opponent, and booted the grenade out.

Everyone in the elevator pulled back, as one. Heads went down. Arms covered faces.

Thunder smashed the air.

Lee felt the sharp spike in air pressure like a blow to his nose and ears.

When he opened his eyes, his vision swirled and danced with stars.

The man who'd booted the grenade was crawling back inside, one of his legs mangled, the boot hanging from the end of his ankle, barely attached.

Lee leapt out of his stack, going low underneath everyone else's line of fire. He snatched the shoulder straps of the wounded soldier's armor and hauled backward in one great heave of movement, pulling the man out of the doorway, and sending both their bodies toppling into the back of the elevator.

Menendez yelled. Lee couldn't understand it. But a glance showed Menendez waving his hand in front of his face, palm out.

Cease fire

The soldier in Lee's grip writhed, clutching at Lee out of pure reflex, and then bending at the waist, reaching for his wounded leg.

Lee rolled the man over, then straddled him with one leg. He pressed the man's torso to the ground, shouting, "You're okay! You're okay!" even though he knew the man wasn't. Wide blue eyes stared up at him in pain and panic.

The man's hands gripped Lee by the wrists. Lee wrenched himself free.

His shaky vision scoured across the wounded man's armor. A dirt-covered black Combat-Application Tourniquet, strapped to the webbing above the man's spare magazines. Lee ripped it free and snapped it open.

He spared a glance over his shoulder. Muddled sounds began to make it past his damaged ear drums. The two stacks of men hugged the walls of the elevator now, and Menendez was in the center, leaning towards the open doors and shouting something into the smoky ruins of the bunker.

A distant clatter of gunshots answered and Menendez flinched back.

Menendez whipped around to Lee, his eyes wild, and he spoke. Lee stared at his lips, and discerned the gist of what Menendez was trying to communicate.

They think we're cartel.

There was nothing Lee could do about that.

He grabbed the soldier's wounded leg and pulled the open tourniquet up over his flopping boot, shouting at Menendez as he did, "Keep calling to them!"

Menendez went down to one knee. He was far enough into the elevator that whoever was still shooting at them from down the main hall of the bunker wouldn't be able to get an angle on him—yet. He cupped his hands over his mouth and began bellowing: "Friendly! Friendly! Friendly!"

Some of the soldiers in the elevator began to take up the chant with him.

Lee blinked, felt something trickling down his face. He dragged his cheek across his shoulder, felt a painful rasp, and when he glanced at his shoulder saw a smear of red from where the bullet fragments had chewed him up.

It wasn't the first time that'd happened. Lee's face was pockmarked with old spalling scars.

He pulled the tourniquet up below the man's knee, and pulled it tight, then began to wrench at the windlass. The soldier below him recovered himself and grabbed onto Lee's shirt sleeve with both of his hands and groaned.

The fire from down the hall tapered off.

Menendez gulped smoky air and continued his shouting, his voice cracking and going hoarse.

One of those calls must have finally fallen upon a pair of ears capable of hearing them. The gunfire came to an abrupt halt.

Menendez made the call twice more, and then wilted.

Lee put one more crank on the windlass and then strapped it down. He ripped his arm out of the wounded soldier's grip, gave him two strong pats to the chest, and stood up.

There were two other downed soldiers in the elevators, their buddies hovering over them and working on their wounds. Lee took one look at their dead eyes staring at nothing and knew it was pointless. He kept it to himself.

He stepped up behind Menendez.

The sergeant had his rifle hanging from its strap, and both hands protruding out from cover, showing his palms to the men down the hall, waving them back and forth.

Lee edged around him, gaining a sliver of view down the main hall of the bunker. Numerous doors led off from the main hall, and through the choking pall of gunsmoke, he saw men crowded in these doorways, weapons still addressed down the hall towards the elevator.

Lee cupped his own hands over his mouth. "Sergeant Menendez! Captain Harden! Hold your fire!" His throat felt raw and phlegmy. He coughed when he was done shouting, then looked down at Menendez. "I'm gonna step out. You ready?"

Menendez nodded.

Lee put his hands out first, like Menendez had done, and then stepped out of the elevator, and into full view of the men down the hall.

His body was locked, his jaw clenched, waiting for some scared private down the hall to put a bullet in him. He was fully prepared to jump back into the elevator at the first sound of gunfire.

There were some murmurs from the other end of the hall that might've been full voices—it was hard for Lee's ears to understand anything but a shout.

But gradually, one of the figures stepped out, and stood in the center of the hallway, dipping their head to see under the skein of gunsmoke that still drifted around the ceiling.

It was Breckenridge.

The man's eyebrows arched. "That really you, Captain Harden?"

Lee held his hands up—something of a shrug. "Yeah, it's me, Breck. Hold your fire, I got Menendez and—"

A bark tore Lee's concentration in half.

At the other end of the hall, Breckenridge reacted to it as well. He straightened from peering under the fog of smoke, and stepped aside.

There was a clatter of claws across the concrete floor of the bunker.

A small, brown and tan shape emerged from around a huddle of soldiers.

Lee didn't move. He stayed locked in that same position, with his hands held up at his side, and he stared without expression. The figure didn't run to him. It only hobbled. One of its rear legs was held up off the ground. The lupine face regarded the soldiers around it, until it slipped passed them, and then its golden eyes locked onto Lee, and it quickened its pace.

The tail even gave a tiny wag.

Lee felt a shudder work through him, and realized for the first time how goddamned cold it was down here, compared to the heat of the outside that he'd grown so accustomed to. His teeth gave a tiny chatter inside his head. He clamped them down.

He watched the dog approach. Its body language showed guilt, but also pleasure—just to be in the presence of someone that it knew.

Deuce had never been a fan of strangers.

Breckenridge followed the dog down the hall.

Deuce stopped, right at Lee's feet, and he thought he saw something like terminal exhaustion in it. Or perhaps Lee was projecting that feeling.

Have you ever run, just as far and as fast as you could possibly go? And when you stop, you think that maybe you could've kept on going for a little longer, but the second your feet stop pounding the ground, you can't pick them up again.

Inertia seizes you. Your momentum is lost.

Your body in motion has ground to a halt, and it will now take ten times the effort simply to lift a foot, than it would have to go on without stopping.

That is what Lee felt in that moment.

He felt himself grinding to a halt.

All of this manic momentum, driven by a fuel sourced entirely from the blackness of his hatred, pumped up and refined by grief and loss—it all ran out suddenly, like a fuel tank that doesn't have a gauge, and you don't know you're running dry until you stop dead in your tracks.

He found it hard to take a breath. His armor felt suddenly huge, the weight of it on his chest insurmountable. He felt like he might not be able to continue to stand, but then, he couldn't possibly lower himself to the ground.

He forced air into his lungs.

Swayed on his feet.

Deuce put his head between Lee's knees, and didn't move. His low-hung tail gave another, tiny wag. Blood oozed out of a hole in his right, rear thigh.

Lee gradually became more aware of people moving now. People calling out. People shouting. There were wounded down there. Wounded soldiers to care for. And here Lee stood, staring at a dog, briefly unable to move.

His father's voice in his head: *"You just ran until you could barely even move anymore, and then I'd have to carry you back, crying, because you'd run the skin right off the balls of your feet."*

But now he'd run himself empty, and there wasn't anyone to carry him.

He would have to carry himself.

Focus. Compartmentalize.

Don't get dragged down. You still have work to do.

Breckenridge stopped in front of Lee. He pointed to Deuce. "He got caught in the crossfire."

Lee nodded stiffly.

Between his knees, Deuce let out a barely-audible whimper.

"Breckenridge, that you?" A voice called out from behind Lee.

It was Menendez, emerging from the elevator.

Breck's face split into a shaky grin. "Holy shit, Menendez! I didn't think I'd…"

The rest of it faded into a blur of noise and movement.

Lee looked down at Deuce. The dog's wounded leg trembled, and deep inside of Lee, something twisted, and maybe it fractured. Lee was too numb to tell. Only reason asserted itself right then.

Do the wounded need my help?

Around him, Menendez and his squad bustled down the hall, like Lee was a stone in a fast moving river. They rushed to help their own wounded, and Breck's wounded down the hall.

Someone called "Got a live one!" behind Lee, and then a security shot shook the air of the hallway. "Nevermind!"

No one seemed to care or notice.

Everyone was busy.

The wounded were being cared for.

Except for one.

Lee stooped, and put his arms around Deuce's chest, and under his rump, being careful not to grab his wounded leg, and he hefted the dog up.

Deuce grumbled, but didn't resist. He had never been a very affectionate dog—Deuce was much too concerned with business, with smelling out primals, and with alerting his team, to worry about such inanities as human affection.

Deuce was a working dog, through and through.

Just like Lee.

But as Lee carried the dog down the hallway, Deuce craned his head back and stuck his muzzle in the crook of Lee's sweating neck. Lee felt the cold, wet nose. And he felt Deuce inhaling him, as though remembering for the first time how much comfort he had taken in the past from this human.

Lee spoke for the first time, and it was only a whisper: "I got you, buddy."

Lee trudged across a few dead men. His eyes went down to their eyes, and saw the dim half-lidded gaze, and knew they were gone, and he continued on.

He kept passing doorways, and in those doorways, he would look into the room to see if there was a place to put Deuce, but the armory was filled with wounded men on crates of ammunition and on the stainless work table, and the storage room had two other wounded laying on boxes of freeze dried food, their blood marring the cardboard.

At the rear of the bunker stood a small common area with a single shower stall and several cots. Lee wasn't sure whose cot it was that he was about to use, but he swept a blanket off so it wouldn't get bloody, and then he knelt and laid Deuce on the cot, so that his wounded leg was facing up.

Deuce tried to bend to lick the wound, but Lee pushed his muzzle out of the way. "No. Stay." He touched the leg, and saw that the bullet appeared to have gone in the back of Deuce's thigh at an angle, and exited on the other side of what would be Deuce's hamstring.

It must've happened at the outset of the firefight, because the wound was already clotting. The blood that came out of it looked dark.

Around Lee, the post-combat chaos swirled.

And yet he stayed kneeling next to the cot, eyes on the dog.

He probed Deuce's leg bones, to see if anything seemed broken. No way to be sure without an X-ray, but nothing crackled or crunched and Deuce didn't cry out or give a pain reaction.

Lee had very little on his person. He wished that he was still well-equipped enough to be carrying tourniquets and combat gauze or an IFAK, but it had been a while since he'd gone into a gunfight with anything more than the weapon in his hands.

If he'd had the gauze, he'd have used it on Deuce's wound.

Instead, he used the old t-shirt that he wore, because that was what he had.

He set his rifle on the floor next to him and used his teeth to rip through a section at the bottom of the shirt, tore it free, all the way around.

Lee balled up a section of the shirt, placed this against the wound, and then wrapped the leg as tightly as he could manage. It wasn't ideal, but it would have to do for the moment.

Lee pushed back from the cot, looking around, wondering if there was anything else that he could do. There was a liter-bottle of water, half-full, at the base of the cot. Lee took this. Uncapped it. Cupped his hand under the mouth of the bottle, and poured water into his palm, holding it next to Deuce's muzzle.

Deuce leaned into Lee's hand, and lapped at the water. His tongue was dry and raspy against Lee's skin.

"There you go, buddy," Lee said. "Get some fluids in you."

Lee felt himself shake again. This time not from the cold.

He bit down against it.

Hissed through his clenched teeth. "You stupid mutt. Don't you run off like that. Don't you do that shit to me." Quieter: "I told you to stay. I told you. On the hill. I said 'stay.' Do you not understand what that means? None of this would've happened if you hadn't run off!"

Lee stopped talking when he realized he wasn't entirely sure what he was talking about.

Or perhaps simply didn't want to look too closely at it.

It'd been a while since he'd bothered to look inwards.

In a way, it had been nice to be free of that.

Deuce finished taking water just before the bottle was empty.

Lee recapped the bottle and then thrust himself up onto his feet.

He became aware of a harsh ringing in his ears. He cringed against it.

A voice behind him. He jerked, and whirled around.

Menendez stood behind him. "You alright?"

Lee stared for a moment like he didn't recognize the man, but then nodded. "Yeah. Tinnitus. I'm fine."

Menendez's eyes jagged down to the dog on the bed, but he said nothing about it. His face was serious. He threw a thumb over his shoulder. "You need to come with me, Cap. To the control room."

Even the control room had not been spared from the tide of wounded, though the few men inside this room did not appear badly injured. They were whole enough that when Lee walked into the room, Breckenridge nodded to the wounded men and their buddies helped them stand and shuffle out.

Menendez closed the door behind them.

It was only the three of them in the room now.

Breck slumped against the workstation. "What happened? How the hell did the cartel get in here?" he looked right at Lee. "How could they have done that?"

Lee frowned and brought a hand up, sliding it down his face. His skin was greasy. His palm smelled of dirt and gunsmoke. He pushed through that sudden exhaustion that had overcome him out of the blue. Tried to get the ball rolling again.

You don't have time to be slow. You don't have time to be tired.

You need to figure out how the cartel got an access code.

He blinked a few times, and found Breckenridge and Menendez both watching him.

"You sure you're alright?" Breck asked, his gaze narrowing.

"Fine," Lee grunted. "Just…trying to get my thoughts in order."

"We've been down here the whole time," Breck continued, as though he thought maybe filling in some blanks might help. "About a week after y'all's strike on the power plant, your dog showed up, and we went out and got him. But that was the last time we were able to get in and out." Breck looked significantly at Lee. "We got shut out of the system. Couldn't get access to shit inside this command room, because the code that Tex originally gave us wouldn't work. We were afraid to go topside after that because we figured we wouldn't be able to get back in."

Lee nodded. "You were right. If the code to the mainframe had changed, then the code to get in would have changed with it."

Menendez perked up. "Well, you got the code to get in, right? You got it from that cartel motherfucker. Does that mean you can get back into the mainframe?"

Lee nodded, and started towards the main computer terminal, then stopped. He drew back, frowning.

"What's wrong?" Breck demanded, looking at the computer briefly, as though it had done something to scare Lee away.

"I'm just..." He bit his lip, trying to force clarity on himself. "There's only one way the security codes would have changed in the first place—and that's if Tex gave the command to put the security settings back to their default. The default being that Tex would need to actually be present, with his GPS device, to get access to any bunker."

"Right," Menendez said, trying to see where Lee was going with this. "We talked about that being likely. Tex was running blind, probably didn't know who to trust, and didn't want to leave the bunkers open to whoever might've betrayed him."

Lee nodded, but waved Menendez down. "Yeah, I know. But what I'm getting at is...there's only one way the security systems can change, to default, or *from* default."

Breck looked at the ceiling, halfway there mentally. "And that's if Tex makes the change."

Lee nodded. "Because the changes require the Coordinator in charge—they require a whole shitload of biometric scans and codes only the Coordinator knows."

"So, again, we're back to the original question," Breck said, bringing his gaze down. "How'd the cartel have the code to get in?"

"Exactly," Lee said. "And there's only one answer: Tex gave it to them."

Menendez immediately rebelled. He shook his head and waved his hands. "No. Hell no. Tex wouldn't do that."

Lee stood very still, looking at the monitors of the computer stations.

Breck blew a perturbed breath through his lips. "I gotta agree with Menendez here. Tex would never."

"I didn't say that he betrayed us," Lee murmured.

"What?" Menendez looked like he was about to start taking personal offense.

Lee rounded on him, a tiny flash of irritation restarting the engine in him that had stalled out. "What if he was *forced* to make the change? Did you think about that possibility? I'm not saying he dimed you out like a coward. But what if they got him locked up somewhere, hanging from his toenails?"

"He wouldn't," Menendez asserted, but it was hollow.

Lee looked at him like he'd revealed a belief in some childlike fantasy. "He would, under the right combination of time and pressure. Trust me, Menendez. Everyone breaks if you torture them long enough. Or if you have the right pressure point."

There was a great, hollow silence that suddenly filled up the room like a noxious gas.

Lee saw Breck and Menendez both turning the concept over in their minds.

And he saw when they realized that it *had* to be the truth, because there wasn't another way. The only way the security systems would ever change was if Tex held his thumbs to the readers, his eyes to the scanners, and inputted the proper codes that only he knew.

They weren't willing to admit that Tex would have done it outright—Lee didn't believe that either.

Which meant the only other logical conclusion was that Tex had been coerced into it.

"But how?" Breck groaned, managing to voice the very thing they were all thinking.

"Could be anything," Lee spat, the spark inside of him beginning to smoke again. Flare. Burn. "Could be torture. Could be that they're holding something over him."

"Easy way to get an answer." Menendez pointed to the computer that Lee had decided not to unlock. "Send a message. See who answers up. See what intel they give."

Lee grimaced. "I'm afraid we're going to give more intel than we get."

"What are they gonna learn that they don't already know?" Breck pointed out. "That we're down here? Shit, man. I'm pretty sure they'll figure that out when they realize that the squad they sent here to route us out is all dead."

Lee had to admit that he was right.

In fact…

"Shit." Lee snatched out and smacked the small web-camera that sat on top of the monitor, sending its lens pointing backwards at the wall.

"Could they see us through that thing?" Breck gaped.

"Maybe—"

The computer chimed.

The black screen blinked, came to life.

On the screen, a main window, requesting authentication in order to get access to the computer. Behind that prompt, another window, slightly smaller.

(1) Message Received

All three men stared at it.

Lee didn't want to do it. But it suddenly felt like it was out of his hands now. He *had* to do it.

He leaned forward. Poised his fingers over the keyboard. Looked at the little cursor, sitting in the blank white box that requested the passcode to get access to the system.

He typed it in.

Hit enter.

The password request disappeared.

The message automatically populated the screen.

It was marked as coming from Tex, but that was only because it was originating from one of Tex's bunkers. Lee had no doubt that he wasn't speaking to Tex in that moment—and if it was Tex typing the message, then he was only doing it under duress.

Too late, Lee. I already saw you there.

Lee's finger's twitched over the top of the keyboard. His eyes coursed over the message several times, trying to think of how he wanted to play this, what exactly he wanted to say, or *should* say. Hell, maybe he should say nothing at all. Maybe they should all just grab as much as they could from the bunker and get gone before—

By the way, this is Mr. Daniels, CEO of Cornerstone Military Applications. Before you get pissed and shut me down, I should tell you it's really in your best interest to stay with me online and talk things out. Life or death, you might say.

Menendez thrust a knife hand at the computer. "Who the hell is this?"

Lee grit his teeth. "Exactly who he says. He's the one in control of Greeley—more or less."

He's the one with all the mercenaries. He's the one that sent them down here to kill you. He's the one that set the trap at the power plant.

He's the one that killed Julia.

Lee swore hotly at nothing and everything.

He shouldn't have let Abe take the stupid tanker and drive back to Georgia. Abe knew this Mr. Daniels—had worked with him during his time in Greeley before defecting to North Carolina. He could've provided invaluable insights into what type of man that Lee faced right now.

As it stood, Lee would have nothing to go on but his gut.

Goddammit, Abe! The one time I need you…

Lee took a breath through his nose and quelled the urge to bash in a response out of pure emotion. For the last month, he'd been the wolf. He'd been the one calling the shots. He'd been the one putting others in terrible dilemmas.

Now, for no other reason than a deep and abiding suspicion in his gut, he felt that he'd been outmaneuvered. Like finding yourself suddenly on a rickety platform that might crumble if you moved too aggressively.

No.

Best to be reserved.

Play it cautiously.

He typed his response: **This is Harden. Say what you're going to say.**

He clicked send. And then waited.

The response took a long time coming.

Long enough that Lee began to wonder—was this some sort of trap? Was this Mr. Daniels just stalling, while ground troops moved in to surround the bunker? But then, that would create something of a stalemate, wouldn't it? He, inside the impregnable bunker, with enough supplies to hold out indefinitely. Cornerstone or *Nuevas Fronteras*, stuck topside, in the heat, with the primals.

No, there has to be something else happening here.

The computer let out its low chime.

The response had arrived.

Getting right to the point: Tex is agreeing to work with me in exchange for the lives of a certain civilian population in New Mexico. I would suggest that you do the same. Last night, my Cornerstone operatives were able to pacify the settlement called Triple Rocker Ranch. There are still approximately 100 civilians present. They are alive and well. We were able to take the settlement with minimal resistance.

That was it.

Lee stared at the message, re-reading it, because he thought there must've been a point to it that he'd missed. Clearly, Mr. Daniels intended to manipulate Lee into cooperation with him, but he hadn't said exactly how that was going to go down…

A second message followed.

You have until 2000 hrs (that's roughly sunset) to turn yourself in to my men at Triple Rocker Ranch. If you don't show, I kill everyone, including Tex. If you try to fight, I kill everyone. If you try to trick me, I kill everyone. You get the point. And if you're wondering if I really will, just remember: Tex believes me, and that's why he's cooperating. See you at 2000 hrs. Best, Mr. Daniels

TWENTY-FOUR

DOMINOES

DANIELS WAITED PATIENTLY to see if there was going to be any response.

It didn't seem like there was.

He pushed himself back from the workstation and took a look around his environs, giving a small smirk of appreciation for the typical overkill of the United States government that had constructed this bunker.

Project Hometown had been quite the basket to put their eggs into.

The weak point had been the operatives. Hard to say what people will do when the world around them comes crashing down. But even so, it had been marginally successful—more than half of the Project Hometown Coordinators had come over to Greeley.

Unfortunately, it only took a few to screw things up, as Lehy and Harden had proved.

Not for long, though.

Daniels stood up from the lone chair that occupied the bunker's control room. One of his operatives stood behind him, waiting for orders.

"Stay here," Daniels told him. "Monitor the messages in case they contact back, but I don't think they will. You've got the satphone. If anything happens, contact me immediately."

"Understood, sir," the operative said.

Daniels left the control room. The doors to the elevator were almost right across the hall. Daniels called the elevator and then rode it topside. He couldn't help but bounce on the balls of his feet as he waited. Part of it was nervous energy, and part of it was satisfaction.

Daniels was not a chess player, but he imagined that this must be what it felt like when you executed a winning strategy, and things fell into place perfectly.

He'd used Mosquero to get to Tully. Then he'd used Tully to lure Tex out of his bunker. Once they had him strung up, it was just a matter of finding the right buttons to push, which, in this case, was small populations of helpless civilians (Mosquero again).

Jesus, but the Coordinators were a bunch of Captain Americas.

Did they really think they could save everyone?

Maybe Lee Harden would be different. Daniels would have to wait and see. The usage of a civilian populace had been so successful getting Tully and Tex to cooperate, he'd figured, *Hell, why not try it again?* Sure, it wasn't very original. But then again, if a plan's not broke, don't fix it.

One by one, the dominoes were falling.

Tully, then Tex, and soon Lee Harden.

And after that?

Mateo Ibarra.

Let the stupid wetback think that Daniels was crawling at his feet for oil.

Daniels had plans of his own.

In one masterfully executed stroke, Daniels was solving several problems at once.

And he couldn't wait to see the look on Lineberger's face when President Briggs handed him an official officer's commission—at or above Lineberger's own rank, of course.

That would almost be reward enough.

The elevator stopped, and the doors slid open.

Two of his operatives waited for him outside. Two black Tahoes sat with their engines running.

The two operatives fell into step with him as he strode towards the rear Tahoe.

"Any trouble with him?" Daniels asked.

"No, sir. He's quiet."

Daniels nodded. "We're heading to Triple Rocker Ranch. Get on the horn with our units on the ground there and tell them we're enroute. Get a status update on the civilians. Make sure everything is calm and settled. Wouldn't want anyone getting uppity and fucking our plans up, huh?"

The two operatives acknowledged. One opened the rear door of the SUV for him. Daniels climbed in, and then the two operatives jogged off and got into the lead Tahoe. The two black SUVs immediately started moving again, heading south for Triple Rocker Ranch.

Daniels twisted and looked into the rear of the SUV, at the form that was hogtied, gagged, and hooded in the back. "Tex, I know that you must be horrendously uncomfortable. We're on our way right now, and when we get to where we're going, we'll get you a little more comfortable, alright?"

He didn't expect an answer.

Tex wasn't able to answer with the gag in his mouth.

Daniels regretted having to transport him in this manner, but he was under no illusions as to how dangerous Tex was, and he wasn't going to take any chances. Once they got to Triple Rocker Ranch, he needed to put Tex on display. Lee would be watching. And Daniels needed to prove that he held the cards that he claimed he did.

Daniels turned forward again, and looked out the window at the dusty Texas landscape as it flew by. In the distance, a cluster of shapes lounged in the shade beneath a copse of trees and watched the two SUVs roll by.

It was kind of like a safari out here.

Daniels began to whistle a tune.

***

"You can't do this," Menendez said, following Lee into the armory.

Lee brushed past another soldier who was working on a wounded man lying on a crate of grenades. He went all the way to the back of the room, where the gun racks were held. There weren't many left. But Lee wasn't here for them.

He stopped and turned to Menendez. "I'm not doing anything." Then he stooped down and grabbed a large container, pulling the lid off and revealing a collection of pre-loaded magazines. He grabbed two of them.

"Then why are you grabbing fresh gear?" Menendez demanded.

"Because I'm going to go have a look."

"At Triprock?"

"Yes."

Menendez shook his head. "The fuck you need mags for then? You gonna storm the goddamned castle and rescue everyone by yourself? Shit, I knew you was crazy but this is off the charts."

Lee smiled, but it was a bleak thing. "These are just to get me there. I need to put eyes on. Okay? I need to see if this Cornerstone fuck has what he says he has."

"He's trying to lure you into a trap."

"Maybe. I'll see about that too."

"He's just trying to get you out in the open, and then he's gonna take you down, Lee. Don't fall for this bullshit."

"I'm not falling for anything."

Menendez gritted his teeth, and made a growling noise. He turned as though he was going to leave Lee alone, and then spun back around. "What do you think's gonna happen when you get there? When you scope it out? Huh?"

"I'm gonna see if he's got what he says he's got," Lee reiterated.

"Yeah." Menendez nodded, putting his hands on his hips. "You're gonna see exactly what he wants you to see. You're gonna see a bunch of sad little civilians, lined up. Waiting for someone to come save them. And then what, Lee? You just gonna walk away from that?"

"If I need to."

"If that was true, you wouldn't even be going."

Lee held both magazines in one hand, and he began tapping them on his thigh, staring at Menendez.

"He wants you to look at their faces. He knows that if you do that, he's got you."

All the sudden, Lee wanted to hurt Menendez. He couldn't say why, only that it felt like a reflex. And it was only the pure lack of logic to it that held Lee back, but his hand flashed out and hit Menendez in the chest—not hard, but enough to push him back.

Menendez seemed surprised for a second, and then his eyes blazed, and he looked like he might come back at Lee and start swinging. Lee stuck out his chin, inviting it.

"And what do you want me to do then?" Lee demanded.

The soldiers on the other end of the room watched them, and Lee saw they were trying to figure whether this was something they should intervene in, or leave alone.

Menendez's expression softened. "Don't go. Stay with us. Fuck them. Fuck Daniels and his plan, and fuck the civilians."

"And what about Tex?" Lee grated. "Fuck him, too?"

"You know as well as I do that Tex doesn't want you to give into this shit."

Lee pushed a breath through his clenched teeth. He said nothing, because he knew that Menendez was right. Tex would want Lee to ignore this.

"You can do more good with us," Menendez pressed on. "Triprock was already lost—you said so yourself! You and Abe left them, and told them to get out, and they didn't listen, and that's on them, not you."

But there was a difference, and Lee knew it. You could tell someone to stay out of danger, and maybe you could wash your hands of it at that point. But if the person was in danger, and it was in your power to stop it, what kind of a person were you if you still turned your back on them?

This isn't who you are, the raging part of Lee argued. *You left all of that savior-complex bullshit behind you. It died with Julia.*

But then why did he feel sick to his stomach at the prospect of turning his back on Triprock?

And why did the idea of going hold so much allure?

Menendez could sense that he had Lee questioning himself, and he pressed his advantage. "Stay with us. Keep fighting."

Lee felt the tension suddenly dissipate out of his shoulders.

His mouth opened and he let out a short sigh.

He brought his hand up to Menendez's shoulder. "Take care of my dog, will you?"

Then he pushed past the man, and headed towards the door. The other soldiers in the room looked down at the men they were supposed to be helping, as though they were deaf and hadn't overheard anything.

At the door, Menendez called after him.

"You want to die, don't you?"

Lee stopped in the doorway. His heart thudding like a burglar caught in the act. And then, without responding, he pushed through and out into the hall.

A quick glance to his right showed Breckenridge, standing in the hall outside of the control room, watching him. Lee turned his back on him, and kept walking. All the way down. To the common area. To the cot where Deuce lay.

A soldier with a bandage around his head and a bloody patch showing through where his ear should've been, sat next to Deuce. To Lee's surprise, Deuce let the soldier pet him. Deuce had always been so skittish around strangers.

But…

Deuce was a survivor.

And he'd been in this bunker with these men for weeks.

Lee didn't know how much dogs thought, how much they reasoned. But he thought that perhaps Deuce hadn't expected Lee to ever come back. Perhaps he'd figured it would be best to find a new human.

And for a moment, standing there and watching the two of them, Lee wanted to lie down on that cot, and close his eyes, with the familiar scent of the dog's fur in his nose, and go to sleep, and maybe wake up someplace else entirely. Someplace where no one else was.

Some place with a lot of green grass and a sun that warmed you, but never baked the life out of you.

Some place that didn't exist.

Lee stepped up to the cot, and the soldier looked up. He straightened and looked self-conscious.

"Captain Harden," the soldier blurted. "Is…is this your dog?"

Lee bent down, then settled his knees on the ground.

Deuce looked up at him, his ears perked. He leaned towards Lee and licked at his face a few times, brushing his chin with warmth.

Lee put his scarred hands up, sinking his dirty fingers into the dog's fur on either side of his head, scratching behind his ears. And Lee felt himself slipping away. Like this reality was just a shoreline that a riptide might pull him away from.

"No," Lee eventually said. "He's never been anybody's dog."

"He seemed pretty happy to see you," the soldier pointed out.

Lee kept scratching behind the dog's ears. A sensation that had roots spreading down to the parts of Lee where he never bothered to go anymore. "Yeah." He looked at the soldier. "He seems to like you, too."

The soldier smiled. "I've been feeding him. I like dogs. My family always had a bunch of dogs. You know. Back before."

Right.

Back before.

Lee removed his fingers from Deuce's fur. Retracted his hands.

Deuce watched him, his golden eyes taking in Lee's face in that oddly perceptive way. Like he knew what Lee was doing, even though Lee wasn't sure of it himself.

He grabbed his rifle, and pressed himself up onto one knee, the rifle butt braced on the ground. He nodded to the soldier. "I'm gonna go. You keep taking care of him while I'm gone. Okay?"

"Don't you want him to go with you?"

Lee shook his head. "No. And he needs to heal. Look after that wound. See if you can't get some clean bandages for him. And make sure it doesn't get infected. What's your name, by the way?"

"Pearson, sir. Julian Pearson."

"Alright, Julian." Lee stood up. "You take care of him."

"Will do, captain."

Lee turned and left. He thought he might've heard Deuce whine, but it was hard to say over the murmur of conversation in the room.

Lee stopped at the control room.

Breckenridge and Menendez were both inside. Their quiet but heated conversation came to an abrupt halt, and they looked at him expectantly.

"Any teepios topside?" Lee asked.

Breckenridge blinked a few times, then turned his attention to the monitors that showed the various views of the outside world around the bunker entrance. From Lee's vantage point off to the side, the pictures weren't all that clear, but he saw the shapes of the two technicals, and the bodies around them.

Nothing moved.

Breckenridge looked back. "All's quiet. From what I can see."

Lee nodded. "I'm taking one of the technicals."

"You don't have to do this."

Lee ignored him. "Menendez, you remember the code?"

"One-five-three-nine-eight-zero," Menendez recited. "We've already used it to get the bunker defenses back."

Lee nodded. "Keep a look out for Abe, too. When he comes back."

Menendez's face looked scrunched and unhappy. "Right."

Lee considered things as he looked at them. “If there’s a way out, I’ll come back.”

Breckenridge looked uncomfortable. Menendez only nodded.

Lee rode the elevator topside. The doors opened and he stepped back out into the hot Texas morning. The air was heavy and scalding, and yet, as Lee walked to the technical, he found it easier to breathe than he had in the bunker.

TWENTY-FIVE

CHAIN OF COMMAND

SAM TRUDGED THROUGH A SOUP of his own weariness, and his uniform clung to him, dirty and sweaty and used up.

His socks felt like slimy coatings inside of his boots. His mouth tasted dusty, and for the first time, he felt like drinking some of the horrible brew that the soldiers concocted.

They'd released him from his After Action Report only moments ago, at eleven in the morning.

He walked out of the interrogation room of the Sheriff's Office, and gave it a look over his shoulder that was both exhausted and disdainful. He didn't care for the fact that this was a room where they used to interrogate criminals, but he supposed they used what they had around here.

He left the Sheriff's Office and walked a few blocks down to the high school.

But his mind would not release him.

His mind pulled him ever onwards through his desire to go back to Squad Four's Underworld and get some sleep.

He walked through the halls of the former high school until he reached the place where they had erected their temporary hospital, and there he found one of the nurses.

Sam stood in front of the teacher's desk that had been wheeled out into the middle of a hallway to serve as a receiving area. The nurse sat there behind it, staring up at him with bright curiosity and helpfulness, and he thought that he could spend the rest of the day just hanging around with her.

"Sir?" she said.

"What?" Sam drew in a breath, as though waking.

"I said, is there something I can help you with?"

"Yeah. I need to speak to Sergeant Loudermouth."

"He's resting right now. He had a long night."

Sam actually laughed.

The nurse's smile waxed somewhat confused.

Sam waved it off. "Nevermind. What about Doc Trent? Is he still in?"

"Not normally, but as it so happens, he's been locked up in his office all morning and hasn't left." She frowned. "But he asked not to be disturbed. And he's not technically on duty. Doctor Hughes is, though. Would you like to speak with him?"

Sam leaned on the desk, for no other reason than he was tired. He shook his head. "No. I'd like to speak to Doc Trent."

"Maybe I can leave a message?"

Sam sighed. "Look. Ma'am. I don't want to be a dick. But I need to talk to Doc Trent. Now, you can either show me where Doc Trent is, or I can just go around opening all the doors until I find him. And, no offense, but there's probably not much you can do about that."

The nurse bristled, and her pleasant expression fully soured.

Sam's fleeting fantasy of spending the day relaxing in the glory of her presence fled him. But he was not to be deterred. Partially because he was too tired for bullshit, and partially because he was too keyed up from what he had witnessed. He meant what he said.

"Well," the nurse said, standing up. "Come with me. But if Doctor Trent gets mad, I'm going to blame it on you."

Sam followed her, thinking, *If Doc Trent gets mad, that will be the least of my worries.*

She led him down the hall a ways, to a portion of the school that looked like it had formerly been the domain of the faculty. She pushed into one glass-walled main office, and then stopped at a door on the other side.

Sam looked around, wondering if this was the principal's office.

Interesting.

Back when things like schools had existed, and Sam had been in one, he'd never been to the principal's office. He'd never been to detention. He'd never gotten a bad grade. He was roundly unpopular. The less enlightened of his peers would harass him verbally about being from the Middle East. The more enlightened ones just ignored him and considered themselves merciful for doing so.

The thought of things like that made him want to laugh again. The ridiculousness of the things that had once been his entire world.

Now, standing in dirty, scraped up fatigues with the smell of gunsmoke clinging to his skin, and violence curdling in his heart, he could barely even recognize that former iteration of himself.

He'd once had excellent college prospects.

Now he had bodies.

Not that having bodies on you made you a badass. Simply that it was a horribly poignant dividing line between what he once was and what he was now.

The nurse knocked on the door. "Doctor Trent, there's a…soldier here to see you."

Sam dragged his attention back to the door, and to the pretty young woman knocking on it. For a brief moment, he thought about asking her to hang out with him. But then he remembered that she was probably ten years his senior, and what on earth were they going to do together?

Besides, despite his best efforts to not be a dick, he'd kind of been a dick.

The door flew open, and Doc Trent drew himself up as though loading a rebuke, but then looked at Sam, and frowned as recognition came to his eyes.

"Oh. Angela's kid. Right?"

Sam didn't have the energy to be defensive. "Sure."

"Uh, Sam, is it?"

"Yeah. Can I talk with you?"

Doc Trent mumbled something unintelligible, but then moved out of the doorway and held the door open, bobbing his head as an invitation for Sam to step in.

Sam tried to smile at the nurse, but she avoided his gaze.

Oh well.

Sam stepped into the office and closed the door behind him as Doc Trent retreated a few hasty steps to stand by his desk, as though this was a source of power and comfort to him. From what little Sam knew of Doc Trent, that was probably accurate.

"What can I do for you, uh, Sam?"

"Did you have a chance to speak to Sergeant Loudermouth?"

Doc Trent made a face that looked like Sam had just brought a bucket of sewage in the office with him. But then, there was something else there. Something that lit up the man's eyes. Something like good, old-fashioned scientific curiosity.

"Yes," Doc Trent said. "Yes, I did."

Sam nodded. "Sir, I've just been back from Augusta. And…there is something happening with the primals. Something that I don't think the higher-ups are aware of, or maybe they just don't want to admit it. But I hadn't had a chance to speak to Loudermouth. Or you. And I'd like to know what you think."

Doc Trent shuffled sideways, like a hesitant crab, and then settled himself into his seat. "Yes. Well. Loudermouth had a lot of…very interesting things to say. Can you, perhaps, go into a little detail as to what you saw?"

As Doc Trent spoke, Sam's eyes roved across his desktop, and he noticed a worn out notebook sitting open in the center of it, and when his eyes landed on it—pages of cramped, tiny writing—Doc Trent hastily shut it.

Sam raised his eyes to Doc Trent's. "Is that Jacob's notebook?"

Doc Trent leaned back. "It is."

"Are you finding any answers in it?"

"Perhaps." Doc Trent leaned forward, and slid the notebook off to the side. "What was it that you saw in Augusta, Sam?"

Sam's legs felt like logs. He saw that there was a chair pushed off to the side of the room, not positioned in front of the desk. He grabbed this without invitation and dragged it over so that it was facing Doc Trent, and then he sat himself down in it.

Interesting how exhaustion could make you bolder.

Leaning back in the chair, Sam recounted everything that had happened, for the second time that day. The first time had been during the After Action Review. He wasn't sure whether what he was saying to Doc Trent was supposed to be kept secret, but he thought that if it was, then that was dumb. This was information that needed to be figured out. Not horded until it bit them in the ass.

When he finished, he noticed that Doc Trent had interlaced his fingers together on the desktop, and that the knuckles were white.

After a moment of silence, Doc Trent seemed to recover himself. "So, you say you heard a voice. Over the radio."

"Yes."

"And you think it spoke English."

"Yes. That's what I think." Sam leaned forward. "What do you think about that, Doc?"

Doc Trent considered this. "Is there any way it could have been one of the team members on the radio?"

Sam shrugged his shoulders. "Maybe. But it didn't sound like them."

Doc Trent nodded. "Let me ask you, Sam. If I tell you something, maybe even a few somethings, is it going to get back to Angela?"

Sam raised his eyebrows. "Well, frankly, sir, if it's important information…then yes."

Doc Trent nodded again. "Good. Someone in this God-forsaken shit heap needs to start paying attention. Now, listen…"

***

Sam went back to The Underworld.

His gear was still scattered his bed from when he'd shucked it off and followed the rest of them out for their individual interviews about what had happened.

A few of the large industrial lights were on, but not all of them, as several squads were trying to get some sleep.

Jones and Pickell and Chris were all racked out. But Billings remained awake, and his eyes shot to Sam as he stepped under the camouflage netting that made their roof.

Billings sat up. "Where'd you run off to, Ryder?"

He kept his voice down, but Sam could tell he was irritated, probably at having to stay up and wait for Sam, like a parent for their wayward teenager.

Sam squatted on the edge of Billings's cot. "I went to talk to Doc Trent after my AAR."

Billings tilted his head. "And?"

"Have you heard what command might be doing with Augusta?"

Billings made a face. “You know they don’t talk to me.”

Sam waited.

“But I have heard that they’re mobilizing a portion of the Marines.”

“To assault Augusta?” Sam balked.

“That’s what it sounds like. What’d Doc Trent say? Has he talked to Loudermouth?”

Sam nodded. “I think…well, it’s not what I think. It’s what Loudermouth says. And what Doc Trent believes. He was studying Jacob’s notebook. He says he thinks that what happened in Fayetteville and Fort Bragg, that’s what happened to Augusta. That’s why all these primals are congregating in one place.”

Sam registered that Jones had come awake and sat up in his bed, frowning at them with squinty eyes. But he said nothing, and seemed inclined to listen.

“Loudermouth says he was being kept alive as food. That the building he was in was a sort of nursery. A…breeding ground, I guess.”

Billings shook his head. “We didn’t see any other primals besides that one that led us there.”

“Loudermouth claims they were there,” Sam said. “He claims they hightailed it when they saw us coming.”

“That doesn’t sound like something primals would do.”

Sam’s hands came together, the fingers wrestling with each other. “Doc Trent says they’re evolving. He says they’ve been evolving. And he says he thinks that these large colonies aren’t really colonies at all, that they’re big, temporary breeding grounds. He says it makes sense. That there’s *precedent* in the natural world for this type of behavior."

"Shit." Billings rubbed his face. "So, what about the transmission? What about the voice we heard?"

Sam's hands stopped wrestling. He clenched them together. "Yeah, that's the other thing. Loudermouth claimed he saw something. Doc Trent says he called it a 'brain.' It was a female primal that was…different. More human. But still primal." Sam's eyes went up to Billings. "And Loudermouth says that she spoke to him."

Billings puffed out a disbelieving breath, but then sat there, silent.

There was more that Sam knew now. Some of it was what Doc Trent had told him. And some of it was his own thoughts. All of it was theoretical. But they were theories that somehow seemed right. They made sense. And they were consistent with everything that Sam had seen.

"These breeding grounds," Sam said, his voice little more than a whisper. "They're breeding with these more human-like females, these 'brains.' The strongest males, to the smartest females. And I think these females are…controlling them, somehow. And they're protecting their breeding grounds."

Jones rustled in his bed. "Is that why they yanked Paige's head off?" he whispered. "To warn us off?"

Sam nodded. "They're smart. And they're getting smarter. And if all of this is true, then I think we know what we'll find when we get back to Fort Bragg. Shit, I'm not even sure that we should go back."

"So we should just let 'em breed?" Jones hissed. "Fuck that, man. We need to nuke their asses."

"We can't," Billings said, his voice flat. "All we got's ground pounders. All we got is infantry in trucks. And you see how that's working out for us."

"I don't know what the answer is," Sam said. "I just know that command isn't taking Loudermouth or Doc Trent seriously. And I think…I think that's going to kill us all."

Billings nodded, then reached across to Sam and poked him in the shoulder. "Fuck chain of command, Ryder. You need to speak to Angela."

***

Sam knocked on the door of the tiny white house, and waited.

He heard a thunder of footsteps, and then a small face peered out of the mottled glass sidelight to the right of the door. A halo of frizzy curls. Bright blue eyes. A sudden, big smile.

The door flew open.

"Sam!" Abby squealed, then grabbed him about the midsection.

He put an awkward hand around the smaller girl's shoulders and gave her a squeeze.

She pulled her head back, her nose wrinkled. "You stink, Sam."

Sam smiled, though it didn't reach his eyes. The sudden burst of affection had taken him back. He hadn't even been thinking of the little girl who had become his kind-of-adoptive-sister.

"Hey, Abby," Sam murmured. "Why aren't you in school?"

Abby rolled her eyes with great drama. "It's Sunday, you big dummy."

Sam raised his eyebrows. "Oh."

Was it really? Days of the week tended to blend together. Weekends didn't mean much anymore. Unless you were a school kid, apparently.

"Why don't you live with us anymore?" Abby said, twisting around and fidgeting, but keeping her eyes locked on Sam's face.

Sam found himself searching for appropriate answers.

Because he didn't want to be seen as Angela's son?

Because he didn't want to be reminded of every way that he was different?

Because he found this fake family life stifling?

Sheepishly, he turned and pointed in the general direction of the warehouse where all the Hunter-Killer squads were housed. "I'm just right over there. But sometimes I have to get up really late at night, or really early in the morning, and you wouldn't want to hear me tromping around at all hours, would you?"

Abby was absently swinging her arms back and forth. She managed a shrug, somewhere in there. "I wouldn't care. I miss you."

Sam blinked a few times.

What the hell do you say to that?

"I, uh, miss you too." He frowned. Cleared his throat. "Listen, Abby, is…your mom here?"

If Abby noted the oddness of Sam calling Angela "your mom," she decided not to say anything about it. More likely she hadn't even noticed.

She bounced one time. “Yeahsure. Mom! Sam’s here!”

“Hey, Sam!” Angela’s voice called out. “In the kitchen. You want some lunch?”

Sam felt something hot and uncomfortable settling onto his neck. He pushed through the doorway, and closed it behind him.

TWENTY-SIX

VISITORS

THE GUARD AT THE FRONT GATE of the Butler Safe Zone heard the engine before he saw it.

He was in the shade, leaning up against one of the four posts that kept the corrugated metal roof over his head—great for the aforementioned shade, as well as not getting piss-soaked every time it rained.

His buddy on duty sat in a rusted metal folding chair, slumped against the M249 that rested on the sandbag walls of the guard post, pointing at the front gates.

Beyond the gates, the highway stretched for a good distance, straight as an arrow.

The guard squinted into the distance and perked up. "Hey, we got any more trucks coming in?"

His buddy stirred himself from God-knew what sort of fantasyland kept him entertained for eight hours of holding a machine gun. "What? No. I don't think so. Last of the Hunter-Killers came in two hours ago. I think."

The guard pushed himself off the post. "Well, there's a vehicle coming."

"I can call up command and ask for confirmation," his buddy said. "Maybe there's a late comer."

"Yeah, go ahead and get 'em on the horn." The guard leaned over the sandbag wall, propping his elbows on it for stability and bringing his field glass up to his eyes.

Behind him, he heard his buddy picking up the old trench-phone and calling it in.

At a distant point in the highway, where the heat from the blacktop shimmered the air, the guard watched two Humvees materialize out of the watery light. The shapes were distinct enough that he ID'd them before they were fully visible.

"Got visual on two Humvees," the guard told his buddy, and his buddy relayed to command over the trench phone. "Moving pretty slow, but approaching the front gate. What do they want us to do?"

"...approaching the front gate," his buddy finished up. "Please advise."

They waited.

The guard kept watching.

His buddy kept listening.

His buddy nodded. "Roger that." He held the trench phone down. "Command says we don't have any trucks out in the field right now."

The guard noticed something else through his glass. Someone had stuck their arm out the passenger's side of the lead Humvee, waving what looked like a white T-shirt. "Hey. Tell command they're waving a white flag."

"Command, they're waving a white flag." A long pause. "No. They're still approaching. Yes, they appear to be armed. Both trucks have turrets."

“Hold on,” the guard said, frowning through his glass.

“Stand by,” his buddy told command.

Still frowning, the guard lowered his field glasses. “Tell command they’re flying a Canadian flag.”

***

Sam had excused himself from any top-level dealings. Angela had been close to insisting he be present when she called her commanders and leaders together for an impromptu powwow, but Sam couldn’t imagine standing there under the withering gaze of Gilliard and Hamrick, after going behind their backs to talk to Angela about the primals.

So, he opted to make himself scarce.

Sam turned a blind corner of a building, and started to cross over the main drag of the Butler Safe Zone, angling east to head towards the Underground, and possibly some much-needed sleep.

It was a testament to how exhausted he was that he hadn’t cleared that corner.

Checking corners had become something of a habit, even inside the Safe Zone.

Sam cast a glance over his shoulder.

And then he paused there, with one foot in the road, and one foot on the sidewalk.

People were gathering in front of the building he’d just rounded, looking down the street towards the front gates. And when he followed their gazes down that long, straight stretch of road, he saw a few more clusters of rubberneckers, and then a big traffic jam of soldiers in various uniforms.

They all looked tense about something, but Sam couldn't really tell what it was. A lot of heads dipped towards each other, quiet conversations taking place, knife-hands pointing in different directions.

His eyes fixed on the scene at the front gates, Sam turned and stepped forward until he stood at the back of the small group of people that were watching. A quiet murmur tumbled between them as theories were passed back and forth of what could possibly be happening at the front gates.

Obviously it wasn't primals, because the troops weren't shooting and didn't seem *that* worried.

But it definitely wasn't something friendly, or they would've been a lot more relaxed, and probably wouldn't need those two guntruck Humvees that framed the road, their turrets pointing outwards beyond the gates.

"What's going on?" Sam asked in an undertone to the person directly ahead of him.

All he caught—because he was focused on the gate—was that she was short and had brown hair.

She turned to him, speaking as she did: "Not sure. Somebody showed up at the—"

Sam looked down, wondering why she'd cut herself off, and found himself staring at Charlie.

If any of the other people around them had not been so focused on what was happening at the front gates, they might've noted the very odd interchange between a boy and a girl.

The two of them, staring at each other in what appeared to be stark terror, their mouths partially opened like words had blocked up their throats.

For a moment, paralyzed.

Sam snapped out of it first. “Right. I’m sure I’ll hear about it later,” he said. Then, letting his desire to be rid of her overcome his curiosity, he turned away…

But not before glancing upwards one more time.

Not before seeing the gates, sliding open.

Not before seeing a group of people striding into the Butler Safe Zone.

They looked like soldiers.

Except for one of them.

One of them was Benjamin Sullivan.

What the hell?

Charlie must’ve seen the look of puzzlement on his face. She followed his gaze, and she saw what he saw, and she recognized Benjamin Sullivan too.

Benjamin Sullivan who had drugged and then raped some girl in the Fort Bragg Safe Zone.

Benjamin Sullivan, whose mother had been manipulated by Elsie Foster, the leader of the Lincolnists, to try to poison Abby Houston with infected tissue from a primal.

Benjamin Sullivan, who had been left behind during the evacuation of Fort Bragg.

Flushed, Charlie shot a look over her shoulder at Sam, and he recognized in it that she was just as surprised as he was—and just as concerned.

Because Benjamin knew about Charlie.

And if Charlie’s secret came out, Sam’s would too.

Sam swallowed and clenched his jaw.

Then he turned away and marched towards the Underground.

***

Angela stood, not behind her desk, but in front of it, and the few feet between her and Carl Gilliard was empty. Her hands were planted on her hips, and her lower jaw jutted like a challenge.

"Let's be clear on one thing, master sergeant," Angela said. "You should have pulled me in when this was going on."

Carl arched an eyebrow. "This was a military matter—"

"You should have pulled me in," Angela cut him off, raising her voice.

Off to the side, Doc Trent stood with his balding head bowed, his hands clasped together at his crotch, attempting, apparently, to meld into the wall like a chameleon.

Carl evaluated Angela, and he didn't see a whole lot of give.

Not a lot of room to maneuver.

The pinched eyes, and the tight lips told him what he needed to know.

So he nodded, and became very formal. "My apologies, Madam President. I—"

Angela swiped a hand through the air. "Cut the bullshit, Carl. Let's just get it all out of the way right now, okay? Every time you say 'Madam President,' it's like you're telling a joke. I'm gonna call you Carl, and you're gonna call me Angela, got it?"

Carl didn't respond.

Angela didn't need him to.

"You may not like the fact that I'm in charge, and guess what? Neither do I. But that is the cards that we've been dealt. I am the one in charge. I am also the one that is keeping approximately a thousand pissed off civilians from dragging you to some half-assed witch-hunt court martial for what you've been doing. So we may not like each other much, Carl, but we need each other. That's just the way this is. And moving forward, you're going to tell me when things like this are happening, whether or not you wanna be bothered. You don't get to play it like that. That's not how this is going to work. It *can't* work like that."

She stopped short of making an implicit threat.

She felt that was the wisest course of action.

Carl had been straining at the leash of her command for a long time now. Enough was enough. After discovering what had happened to the Hunter-Killer squads the previous night—and the fact that she hadn't been told what was happening—she was livid.

But threatening Carl was pointless.

Carl was a smart man. He knew the consequences. He knew how the world worked. If Angela wanted to be a strong leader, she needed to simply let nature take its course. Strong leaders didn't have to make threats. It was simply understood.

Carl bent his head in fractional obedience. "Fine. Angela."

Angela held his stare. Those ice-cold eyes of his. But she was not cowed.

She raised a hand and pointed to Doc Trent. "Go ahead, Doc."

"Oh. Right." Doc Trent straightened up. "Ahh…so, the primals."

Carl dragged his gaze off of Angela, and directed it at the doctor.

Angela did the same, though she was already aware of what he was going to say. She'd heard it first from Sam, and then from Doc Trent himself, and then she'd dragged the doctor into her office, and sent for Carl.

"Based upon Sergeant Loudermouth's eyewitness account, as well as certain behavioral traits that we've observed in the primals, and how they've been evolving, I've come to certain conclusions that I think bear pretty substantial implications for—"

"Tell him about the breeding grounds," Angela interrupted.

Doc Trent blinked, flustered and trying to find his train of thought again. "Yes. Right. The breeding grounds." He reached up and adjusted his glasses. Seemed to settle himself. Straightened his back. Squared his shoulders. "I've developed a theory that I believe to be consistent with the behavior that we've observed in the primals—in particular, this relatively new phenomenon of the primals gathering in large numbers. A behavior they haven't exhibited until recently."

Carl and Angela continued to stare at him.

Doc Trent's eyes went back and forth between them, and it seemed like he was realizing for the first time who he was talking to, and that this was not a group of people that really cared about how he'd come to his conclusions—at least not yet. They just cared about the conclusions themselves.

He swallowed.

"They're gathering in large numbers to breed. That's what happened to Fayetteville and Fort Bragg. And that's what we stumbled on in Augusta. They're breeding grounds. All these different packs are coming together, in order to mate their strongest with their smartest. Sergeant Loudermouth observed female primals that he described as being near-human in appearance, that showed clear intelligence markers far beyond what we've seen so far—"

"Like what?" Carl demanded.

"Like speaking."

"Speaking?"

Doc Trent nodded. "The female—the near-human one—she spoke to Sergeant Loudermouth."

"What did she say?"

"She said 'Go.'"

"That's one word."

"Yes, sir."

"That could've been a grunt."

Doc Trent nodded. "It could've been. However, you were in the TOC last night, weren't you?"

Carl gave Angela a sidelong glance. "Yes, I was."

"And you heard the voice over the radio, didn't you?"

Carl frowned. "How did you know that?"

Doc Trent waved it off. "Don't worry how I knew it. That wasn't one of your men. And it clearly said a word, didn't it?"

"Well, I'm not completely sure—"

"It said 'Go,' just like the female that spoke to Loudermouth." Doc Trent seemed oddly confident now. He nodded at them, as though it wasn't a question of the accuracy of his interpretation, but merely a question of when these two laypeople were going to understand what he was trying to explain. "The strongest leaders of the strongest packs, mating with the most intelligent, and human-like females.

And given their rapid gestation. Not only is the population going to continue to skyrocket if we don't do anything about them, but they're going to continue to get stronger and smarter. It's a breeding program, basically. The primals are breeding themselves to have the best possible chance of survival. And also, I believe these smarter females are…controlling things somehow. Using rudimentary strategy. As your squads have witnessed, recently."

Through the glass front of the office, Angela's eyes strayed to a young man in uniform, hurrying towards the door.

He stopped, made brief eye contact with her, and then knocked gently on the door.

Angela waved him in, wondering what the hell this knew emergency was going to be.

The young soldier—wearing corporal's stripes—pushed open the door and then stood there. "Madam President. Master Sergeant. First Sergeant Hamrick sent me. We have visitors currently being detained at the front gate."

By the look in the corporal's eyes, Angela could tell that there was something more to it than just "visitors."

She waited.

The corporal looked at her. "They claim to be an envoy from Canada, ma'am."

TWENTY-SEVEN

THE LAST HOUR

YOU WANT TO DIE, DON'T YOU?

Lee squinted out across the bright, dry landscape to the settlement a mile from him.

The sun baked his back.

I want you to tell me that you don't have a death wish.

A slow throbbing had begun at the base of his neck and was now reaching its fingers up to the back of his head.

You can't save everyone.

But did you even try?

Worst of all, his heart would not stop beating so rapidly.

It seemed that it would begin to slow, and then some other thought would enter his brain, some new way of looking at the situation he now found himself in, and then his heart would start to rocket again.

You'd run until you couldn't run anymore. And we never did find out where you were trying to get to. Hell, I don't think you ever reached it.

Daniels had not been bluffing.

Cornerstone held Triprock.

What he hadn't mentioned, was that *Nuevas Fronteras* was also there. Between the two forces, which mostly kept separate from each other, Lee had been taking a count. Many of the Cornerstone men wore identical uniforms, which made them harder to separately identify. But as it stood, there were no less than forty armed hostiles in Triprock.

The bulk of these were cartel foot soldiers. They meandered about in small packs of men, strutting about the compound like they owned it and always had. And Lee wondered if any of them remembered him from last time. He wondered if they remembered him taking them down and making them run for their lives.

They certainly didn't act like it.

The Cornerstone operatives were more reserved, but no less confident.

Except for a few roving patrols around the perimeter of the ranch, the majority of the mercenaries stuck to the main house. The house where Lee had captured Joaquin Leyva.

Lee's brain felt split and scattered and muddied. His thoughts were divided against themselves, and he could not make them reconcile. He wanted desperately to do something, but no matter what angle he addressed this problem from, there didn't seem to be a solution.

And Menendez had been right.

The second that Lee had seen the civilians, he'd known in his gut that he couldn't walk away from this.

And Lee felt positive that Mr. Daniels had meant what he'd said—that he would kill everyone if Lee didn't submit himself by sundown.

It had felt somewhat academic before he sat in the dirt and looked through a scope and saw the civilians. Saw Sally. And Eric. And Catalina.

Now it was very real.

They would all be dead by sundown.

Unless Lee did something.

To submit seemed wrong. But the fight looked impossible.

Even if Lee had the time to go back to the bunker and organize Menendez and Breckenridge, and form a plan of attack, they'd still be outnumbered two-to-one against a fixed objective.

And they wouldn't even have the element of surprise.

Cornerstone and *Nuevas Fronteras* were waiting for something like that. They were ready for it.

Lee swore under his breath, and spoke to an imaginary Abe. "I shouldn't've let you take that tanker back."

What he didn't say, what he barely admitted to himself, was that he needed Abe to tell him what to do. To place his vote in one column or the other, and thereby push Lee's deadlocked brain into a decision.

Either go and give yourself up to save the civilians.

Or leave, and never look back.

But as long as he was wishing for people he could not have…

He closed his eyes against the sun.

I wish you hadn't gone. I wish we'd never left Fort Bragg. I wish we'd found a way to stay together.

I wish, I wish, I wish.

He opened his eyes again.

Stark, true reality.

You could not wish for things. They simply were, or were not. The only things that happened were the things that you made happen, and you could only work with what you'd been given.

Menendez's parting words to him continued to echo around in his skull.

You want to die, don't you?

But Menendez had only been half-right on that count.

I thought I'd be dead by now.

Lee would accept death…if it meant something.

If his life bought the lives of a settlement's worth of civilians, that would mean something. He had no problem laying his life down for others. He'd been doing that very thing, more or less, his entire adult life.

But he could not simply submit himself if there was another way.

He would welcome death, but he wouldn't kneel to it.

If there was a way, an opportunity, to keep fighting, he would always take that path.

But it seemed that path was no longer available to him.

And when you had no paths available, when you were out of options, then all you could do was play for time. All you could do was wait. Be patient. And keep watch.

And that's what Lee did.

He lay on that dusty ridge, shrouded by clumps of grasses, and shaded by a copse of shinnery oak. And he watched. And he waited. For anything. Any path other than the one laid out before him.

Time went by, sometimes creeping, and sometimes disappearing in a flash. At times, the minutes stretched endlessly. And at other times he would glance at the progress of the sun and feel another jolt of his heart as he realized how close it had fallen towards the horizon.

He gave himself every last minute that he could.

For the situation to change.

For another option to present itself.

For the cloud of thoughts to suddenly clear, and an obvious idea that he had overlooked to smack him in the face…

But none of that happened.

He watched the sky turn from bright, hazy blue, to deeper and deeper shades. And when the sun was close to touching the horizon, Lee knew that his time was up.

And then Lee made a decision.

If there wasn't another way, then he would walk his own damn self into death's gates. And he'd do it willingly, not kicking and screaming for one more day.

It was a small distinction, but a distinction nonetheless.

Whatever was going to come, would come.

Lee would go willingly.

Keeping his eyes open, until death itself closed them for good.

***

It was an odd sensation for Daniels to know that, somewhere out there, Lee Harden was watching him.

He stood in the dark of the main ranch house in Triprock.

He'd ordered everyone to remain lights-out. He knew damn well the type of people he was dealing with. If he gave even the slightest shred of opportunity to Lee or his cronies, they would take it and hand Daniels his ass.

So the inside of the ranch house remained dark, because Daniels didn't want to backlight himself to any snipers in the distance.

He stood back from the windows a good ways. He looked out the front. There was the deck, and on the deck, Tex stood, with his arms tied to the rafters of the overhanging porch roof. He was still gagged, but they'd removed the blindfold so that anyone watching them from the low ridges in the distance would see that they did indeed have Captain Terrence Lehy captive, and that he was alive.

Daniels wondered if Lee was going to do the smart but cold-hearted thing and walk away.

Or if he was going to do the honorable but stupid thing, and show up, as instructed.

Or if he might do the ballsy but foolhardy thing, and try to attack them.

Who are you, Lee?

What kind of man are you?

He got his answer only seconds later.

A shout reached Daniels's ears. It sounded distant—probably one of his sniper/spotter teams in the wreckage of the main barn, which provided the best field of view, but appeared to have been partially blown up.

Daniels straightened, and reached up, touching the earpiece of his comms in the self-conscious way that men do when they're not accustomed to things sticking in their ears.

A second later, a calm voice spoke on the radio. "We have contact. One male. East, southeast, about a mile out. Standby for confirmation on ID."

Daniels drummed his fingers on the sides of his pants. He wore armor, and a sidearm. He thought about the rifle that he'd chosen not to carry, and wondered for the hundredth time if this was the beginning of a counter-trap set by Lee Harden.

It would be interesting to see how this played out.

The front door of the ranch house opened and Griesi stepped in. "Sir, you want the birds to come in now?"

Daniels flinched with irritation. "No, I don't want the goddamned birds right now. If I wanted the birds I would have told you to bring them in. Keep them staged in the distance. Harden could have men with RPGs waiting to fire on them if they show up. Let's wait and see."

Griesi dipped his head, then slipped back through the door.

"Overwatch to Mr. Daniels," the radio murmured in Daniels's ear. "We have a positive ID. It's definitely Lee Harden. He's approaching the compound. He appears to be unarmed."

Daniels tried to resist micromanaging his men—they were all tier one operators. But his anxiety was so strong right now, at the very edge of success, that he couldn't help himself. "Roger that. Make sure everyone's watching their lanes. Keep three-sixty coverage. Has anybody spotted anything—anything at all—in any other direction?"

A slow, steady litany of responses filtered back through his earpiece. And was Daniels mistaken or did they sound a tad longsuffering, like they were humoring a worried mother?

Well, fuck all those cock-swinging commandos.

Someone had to do the worrying around here.

The last of the responses came in.

No one had seen anything, in any other direction.

Could it really be? Was Lee Harden *actually* turning himself in?

Daniels rested his hand on the butt of his pistol. Shook his head.

Nope. He wouldn't relax. Not until he had Lee Harden hogtied and in the air on a fast-moving helo. Actually, he wouldn't really relax until he had Lee back in Greeley, in a small, dark cell that was impossible to escape from.

Maybe he wouldn't even relax then.

Maybe he wouldn't really relax until he watched Lee's body slump over after a firing squad had done their work and executed the most notorious traitor the country had known in the last century.

But before any of that could happen, before he could get Lee Harden to face justice in Greeley, he had one more stop to make.

He had one more loose end to tie up before this package was truly gift-wrapped.

***

Tex stared out from the porch of the main ranch house, and he groaned low in his belly, and thought, *Don't do it, you stupid sonofabitch! Don't give up!*

Dead ahead of him, there was open space, interrupted only by low cattle fencing. From his perspective on the raised porch, Tex had a clear view all the way out to where the lone figure strode toward Triprock.

To Tex's left stood the other ranch houses. To his right, the big barn, from which the sniper team had first spotted Lee coming towards them.

Was it Lee?

Tex couldn't tell. But the men around him seemed fairly sure of it.

This has to be part of a plan, Tex told himself. *He's got something up his sleeve. He always does.*

But the closer that the figure in the distance drew, the more Tex began to fear that there wasn't anything else.

And could Tex really blame him?

He wanted to. But he couldn't.

Even he, Terrence "Tex" Lehy, probably one of the most pragmatic and militaristic members of Project Hometown…yes, even he had given in.

It's one thing to be pragmatic about the civilian population.

It's another thing entirely to have their lives in your hands.

In the end, Tex wasn't as hard-hearted as he'd thought. He couldn't do it. He couldn't just let those people all get slaughtered. No matter the cold, horrible logic of the arguments that ran through his head—*He might kill them anyways!* and *You'll save more lives by not giving in!* and *Letting Greeley have access to your bunkers will be worse for everyone in the long run!*

None of it mattered in the end.

Because all of that was theoretical.

What was real were the people staring down the barrels of Daniels's hired guns.

And now Lee had been given the same choice. And he'd made the same decision that Tex had.

Which meant that they were fucked.

Daniels held all the cards.

Tex and Lee had nothing.

In the distance, beyond the cattle fences, the figure of Lee Harden was now within about a hundred yards of the edge of Triprock. No crazy plan had become apparent. No contingent of heretofore unseen forces had sprung out of the dust.

It was just one, lonely figure, striding towards them.

A team of soldiers that Tex couldn't see shouted at Lee over a bullhorn. They must've been behind the big barn. The snipers in the hayloft stayed glued to their rifles and their scopes, ready to splatter Lee's brains into the Texas dust if anything started to go sideways.

And even if it did, at this point, they would still win.

They would still have killed Lee Harden.

The small figure of Lee halted, and complied with their directions.

He raised his hands above his head.

He turned to reveal his back.

There was a roar of two engines, and the technicals that bore the Cornerstone welcome party tore out across the dry plain, leaving clouds of dust behind them that obscured whatever happened next.

It was over.

***

"Target's secured," Daniels's earpiece buzzed. "Positive ID. We're bringing him back."

"Roger," Daniels murmured, keeping his words brief, so as not to betray the shake in his voice. He kept fidgeting, so as not to show the tremor in his limbs.

He marched to the front door and pulled it open.

Griesi turned and looked at him.

Daniels nodded. "Bring in the birds."

He stepped out of the ranch house. Into the open. He looked over at Tex. "Secure him. Get him ready for transport." Then he stepped off the porch and stood in the center of the compound.

A figure approached.

One of Mateo Ibarra's lieutenants.

He was not as casual as many of the others. He had a military bearing, and he wore dark jungle fatigues that had faded with sun and constant use. He had been, Daniels believed, a man of some importance in the Panamanian army. He held an FN-FAL rifle in his grip, and eyed Daniels with a look of perennial suspicion.

Daniels licked his lips. "Where would Mr. Ibarra like us to meet him?"

The lieutenant tilted his head to one side. "You will be transporting with helicopter, no?"

Daniels nodded.

"Then I will come with you." It was not a question. Almost a command. "When we are in the air, I will give you the location."

Daniels smiled in what he hoped was a comfortable fashion. "Of course. Not a problem."

And it wasn't. Daniels had already prepared for this.

Two of Daniels's technicals roared through the front gates of the ranch and came to a stop right in front of the main ranch house. It wasn't until their engines downshifted into an idle that Daniels became aware of the distant background thump of the approaching helicopters.

Two gunships—the same two Apaches, in fact, that had executed the trap at the power plant a month before.

And also the Blackhawk. For transportation.

Out of the lead technical, two Cornerstone operatives emerged, dragging a hogtied and hooded figure. They stopped in front of Daniels, holding the body upright.

Daniels reached forward and grabbed the rough, black fabric of the hood. He pulled it up.

Lee Harden looked up at him, a rag tied into his mouth to gag him. His eyes looked black in the gloom, and Daniels was struck by the expression in them—or, more correctly, the lack of expression.

They looked like spider's eyes.

Daniels suppressed a shudder that he wasn't sure whether was born of excitement or something much darker.

It was him. Without a doubt.

Lee Harden. Bound and gagged and on his knees.

Daniels almost grabbed his pistol and ended it right there, just to make goddamned sure. It may have been, he thought, the smartest thing to do. But there was a problem with men like Lee Harden. There was a problem with people who became mythical.

You couldn't just kill them. You had to kill the myth as well.

There was a reason they used to do public executions.

If Daniels executed Lee Harden right here, then his legend would live on.

And that was not something they could afford.

Daniels pulled the hood back over Lee's face, not wanting to look at those dark eyes anymore. "Good," he said.

The sound of the approaching helicopters grew louder.

"Secure them in the Blackhawk," Daniels said. "Secure them *well.*"

TWENTY-EIGHT

THE PATH

PLASTIC ZIP-CUFFS.

The double-looped kind, with a locking mechanism in the center.

These were around Lee's wrists, fastened tight so that already his fingers began to tingle from lack of blood flow. His hands secured behind his back. And they were around his ankles, too.

He couldn't run. He couldn't fight.

They'd hogtied him at first—lashing the zip-cuffs of his wrists to the zip-cuffs of his ankles. But they'd released him from that to put him in the Blackhawk. Then they'd secured him to one of the jumpseats. Lee wasn't sure what they'd used to strap him there, but they'd done it tight.

Strapped to a chair. Wrists locked behind his back. Ankles immobilized. Black bag over his head so that he couldn't see anything. Rag in his mouth so that he couldn't speak.

With him in this position, the helicopter rumbled towards a destination that Lee didn't know. It could have been north. It could have been south. Part of him believed he was heading north to Greeley, but there had been a man who was clearly not Cornerstone standing right beside Daniels when the hood had come off for that brief moment on the ground.

That man had been cartel.

And the fact that a *Nuevas Fronteras* man was in the helicopter with them, made Lee believe that maybe they were heading south.

Lee considered his options, and saw that there were none.

All he could do was continue to sit and wait.

In a way, his world had become very simple. There were no more decisions to make—he'd made them already. Now he was on a track, like being strapped into a rollercoaster. Either death was going to reach him first, or an opportunity was.

And he thought he knew which one it would be.

Maybe this is best.

Had he saved the people of Triprock?

Well, that was difficult to say. It would be nice to believe that he had. He decided that he would not think any more about it. It was a waste of mental effort. He would choose to believe that he had saved them.

He had, at least, tried.

He pictured Sally and Eric and Catalina. Pictured them safe.

He would hold onto that picture, when he was staring at his own death.

Or at endless torture.

He had no delusions that he would be spared that, if Daniels turned him over to Mateo Ibarra.

But that was also wasted mental effort.

If the knives came out, or the vats of acid, or the branding irons, or whatever else Mateo Ibarra might come up with…well, then, Lee would deal with it when it came. It did him no favors to think about it now. And he felt that if he let his fear of it grow, then it would unman him in the end.

If he was going to die, he would do it clear-eyed.

He would not let them see pain. He would not let them see fear. He would not let them see grief.

All they would see would be hate.

He'd burn with it until he was ashes.

And so he closed his eyes, though it made little difference inside the hood. And he let the helicopter bear him towards wherever his final destination was. And he breathed slow and deep, and he focused on that, and nothing else. He existed only in that moment, in a space between thoughts, between emotions, between memories.

It didn't take long.

Lee felt the sudden deceleration. And then a drop in altitude.

Were they there already?

His stomach gave a lurch that had nothing to do with the dropping altitude.

He tried not to think about how close he was to the end.

Eyes open. Head clear.

He opened his eyes to the black fabric. And he waited.

He breathed in through the nose. Held it. Breathed out.

To his right, someone opened the main doors of the Blackhawk. Sound and wind came roaring in. The smell of exhaust managed to make it in past the hood. Lee felt the fabric flapping against his face. Spit had pooled where the gag didn't allow him to close his mouth, and now spilled over onto his chin. The flapping fabric smeared it around.

Their descent slowed. Then the bump of the landing gear hitting the dirt.

Immediately the roar of the Blackhawk's engines deflated, powering down.

Beneath it all, Lee heard the very faint sounds of people yelling to each other, but again, he couldn't make sense of anything they said.

Eyes open. Head clear.

Someone grabbed him. He felt metal nudge him in the temple, and he knew that it was the muzzle of a rifle.

"Do what I say," a voice shouted over the exterior noise. "Or I'll blow your fucking head off."

Lee didn't respond. It struck him as an idiotic thing to say. He was going to his death anyways. This was not a matter of obedience. If they wanted him to comply, they'd have to remove any other option.

Which, to their credit, it seemed like they were doing.

Whatever they'd used to strap him to the jump seat came loose, and then was pulled away.

They hauled him off the jumpseat. Two operatives, one on either side of him. With the zip-cuffs on his ankles, he couldn't walk, so they jammed their hands under his armpits and carried him out.

The noise and the buffeting wind grew louder.

There was a step down.

He was on the ground now.

He heard the rotors whooshing overhead, slowing down. They didn't push him out from under them, though. They put him on his knees, a pace or two away from the body of the helicopter.

Whatever it was that they intended, they planned to do it close to the Blackhawk.

His two escorts didn't leave him, but there was some additional movement from behind him.

Something jostled into him, on his left.

It felt like someone else kneeling beside him.

Experimentally, Lee gave the shape a little nudge with his shoulder.

It nudged him back.

Then a hard rap struck the back of Lee's head.

"Cut that shit out," the voice commanded.

But Lee thought, *That's Tex. He's here, right beside me.*

Did Daniels really intend to turn them over to the cartel?

It seemed to be shaping up that way.

Lee could think of a lot of reasons why Daniels would do that.

He could also think of a lot of reasons why Daniels wouldn't.

The Blackhawk's rotors had slowed to the point that Lee could hear the individual blades as they passed overhead. The engine whine was not as oppressive, and Lee could hear some other details now.

The sound of vehicle doors, opening and closing, somewhere ahead of Lee.

Then there was nothing for a while.

Lee stared at black fabric. Off to his right, he perceived a muted glow that he suspected was the sunset. He wasn't sure if that information was useable or not, but that meant he was facing south.

A steady wind blew at him now. Not the downdraft of rotors. A real wind. And it smelled of the ocean. And something else…

Not exhaust, though it had a ghost of that same petrochemical scent.

This scent was more sulfurous.

That's crude oil.

A new voice reached Lee's ears. One he hadn't heard before. Very faintly accented.

"You bring the most wonderful gifts, Mr. Daniels. I hope you won't think it too forward of me that I'd like to look at their faces. We must all be sure of where we stand, no?"

Daniels's voice came next, tension masked by a casual façade: "Of course. Business is business."

And then the hood was gone.

Air.

You couldn't call it fresh, with the scent of crude oil and tide pools. But it was unadulterated by Lee's own exhales, and so it seemed fresh. The scents of the outside world hit him stronger now.

He blinked. Took in his surroundings.

The sky was a dusky gray. In the west, a hellish orange smear.

Rotor blades passed lazily overhead.

They were on a paved road, cracked and potholed. Lee stared straight down it, to where it led to a large structure that appeared to be constructed of concrete blocks and pipes that ranged in diameter from small to truly massive.

Oil refinery.

A cloud of steam poured from the top of the structure in a steady geyser.

A working *oil refinery.*

Between him and the refinery, two technicals, and a very nice Mercedes SUV. Many armed men that wore no uniform. One in faded jungle fatigues—the cartel man that had been at Triprock and then in the helicopter with Lee.

And one other man, standing front and center, wearing loose, white clothing.

He had shoulder-length black hair, and smiling, friendly eyes.

Near to Lee, Mr. Daniels stood, straight-backed, facing the man in white.

To Lee's left, Tex knelt. Also bound. Also gagged.

Lee managed a brief glimpse over his shoulder, which garnered him another rap on the side of the head with a rifle butt, but not before he saw four Cornerstone operatives—two guarding Lee, and two guarding Tex—and a gunner, manning an M240 in the door of the Blackhawk.

Lee faced forward again, his left temple stinging from the blow.

The man in white walked forward. The wind billowed his clothing about his chest and legs. His hair curled around his smiling face. He wore black cowboy boots with silver tips. They seemed very well-maintained.

He stopped, about ten yards from Lee, and he stared at him.

Lee stared back.

"So," the man said, easier to hear now that the helicopter had quieted. "*Nadie y Ninguno*. The infamous Lee Harden and Terrence Lehy." The man smiled ruefully and shook his finger at them. "You've caused me a lot of heartache."

Lee didn't bother to correct him. He kept looking into his eyes. The man's words flowed around him, and seemed inconsequential.

This was Mateo Ibarra. The one who had drowned Tomlin in oil. The one who had sent men to kill Lee—and almost succeeded. The one who had helped lay the trap that had claimed the life of the one person in the world that Lee loved.

Lee showed none of the fear. None of the grief.

His eyes only showed hate.

A frown crossed over Mateo's smiling face, like a wisp of a cloud on a sunny day.

He looked up at Mr. Daniels. Raised his eyebrows, as though waiting for something. His hands rose a few inches from his side and then fell back. A gesture that said, *So, what are we waiting for?*

Mr. Daniels shifted his feet. The dusty concrete crunched beneath the soles of his boots. "Señor Ibarra, these aren't exactly gifts."

Mateo's expression didn't really change. It just grew stiffer. Like a skein of ice hardening over water. "Oh? Your communications with me made it sound as though you wished to solve the problems between us. As though you were in dire need of the fuel that I could provide you."

"You know," Mr. Daniels said. "You once told me that I needed to clean up my house. You said yours was already clean. But…then you started having problems."

"Problems that *you* created," Mateo said, a little too quickly.

Mr. Daniels smiled. "I've cleaned up my house. And now I've cleaned up yours. Consider that the gift. As for Tex and Harden, I'm going to need something in exchange for them."

Mateo's hands left his side, clasped each other in front of him. "I see. How much fuel do you want?"

Mr. Daniels nodded towards the refinery in the background. "How much fuel does that refinery produce?"

One corner of Mateo's mouth twitched up. "A lot."

Mr. Daniels shrugged. "That's what I want, Señor Ibarra. I want whatever that refinery produces."

Mateo chuckled. "You want all the fuel that this refinery produces?"

"No. I want the refinery."

"The entire refinery? Please." Mateo's eyes scoffed. "My desire to have these two men is strong, but not that strong. I am, first and foremost, a businessman. The pleasure of revenge comes a bit further down on my list of priorities. I'm afraid that if you seek a deal, then we don't have one. But if you'd like to give me a gift, you'll find me a very generous ally."

"They also come with Captain Lehy's GPS unit," Mr. Daniels said, like a man laying down his winning hand, card by card. "And access to all the bunkers across Texas."

This caused Mateo to hesitate, but only for a second. He shook his head. "Bunkers that are half-depleted. Even if they were full, it would still not be worth it. You forget, I have the entirety of Central and South America behind my back. It is not hard for me to find weapons and ordnance."

As Mateo spoke, Lee became aware of a distant, staccato chopping.

Lee glanced at Mr. Daniels, and though he could only see the side of his face, he thought he saw that the Cornerstone CEO had heard them too.

"You misunderstand me," Mr. Daniels said. "I'm here to claim that refinery as the rightful property of the United States government, on whose sovereign soil your presence is only *just* tolerated, due to our apparent mutual interest. Tex and Harden and the bunkers…they aren't really a payment, you see. Think of them more like…a severance package."

Mateo's smile broadened. "I'm surprised at you, Mr. Daniels. You speak very reckless for a man with only five armed men around him."

The sound of helicopter rotors had become more evident now.

Impossible to ignore.

Mr. Daniels inclined his head, as though just hearing them. Then he turned and looked to the skies behind them. When he turned back around, he had a smirk on his face. He waggled a finger in the air, as though gesturing to the growing sound itself. "Five men, yes. And two Apache gunships."

For the first time, Mateo looked unsure of himself.

It was quickly obscured by a flash of rage.

"You are going down a bad path, my friend," Mateo said. "I'd advise you to take a moment and reconsider your stance. I'm not the man you want to double-cross."

"There's no double-cross," Mr. Daniels said, as though Mateo were being melodramatic. "We're simply negotiating. And, as you said, we must all be sure of where we stand. I'm simply showing you where I stand. And where you stand." Mr. Daniels's voice hardened, no longer accommodating. "Which would, ideally, be about five miles south of this refinery, along with every man that's in there right now."

The sound of the gunships had stopped growing louder.

They're hovering, Lee realized. *Just within range.*

Mateo's eyes had narrowed to slits. "What a very American thing to do. What is the phrase? Gunboat diplomacy, no?"

Mr. Daniels shrugged. "More like gun*ship* diplomacy."

"You will throw away our entire alliance for this one refinery?"

"There is no alliance, Señor Ibarra. There's only the facts. I have two gunships, and two platoons of men on the way, and I want that refinery. If you remove all of your men from the refinery and agree to move peacefully five miles south, then you can leave with the Texas bunkers, and your revenge on these two men here. If you don't…well, then, that is your choice too. And it will probably be the last one you make."

Mateo's teeth flashed behind his short beard. "And what's to stop me from killing you now and taking what's mine?"

"I suppose nothing," Mr. Daniels admitted. "Except that you won't really have a chance to enjoy much after that. Have you ever seen what those gunships can do? Oh. Yes. Of course you have. You saw the bodies at the power plant." Mr. Daniels chuckled. "They're frighteningly good at their job. Absolute killing machines."

Mateo drew himself up and snorted. He held out his hand. "Fine. The GPS. And Tex and Harden.

Turn them over. I will remove my men from the refinery."

"So you can hide in the refinery and give us one last spiteful battle?" Mr. Daniels shook his head. "That would end up destroying too much of the structure. Don't be ridiculous. You'll remove your men first, and when they are completely out of the refinery, then I will release the GPS and the prisoners to you, and you can go off to whatever shithole bandit hideaway you crawled out of and do whatever it is pieces of shit like you do."

Mateo's men tensed behind him. Grips shifted on rifles. Their eyes darted to the Cornerstone men across from them, and then to the gunships in the background. Tongues flashed across lips. Calculations were made. The results were not favorable. No one dared to raise their rifle past a low ready, and yet everyone felt like they might be shooting at each other at any moment.

"You mean to trick me into leaving and then keep them for yourself," Mateo hissed through clenched teeth.

Again, Mr. Daniels answered with a casual shrug. "You never can tell, can you? But the question is, what other option do you have?"

The two men stared at each other in stony silence.

Their soldiers only moved their eyes, looking for any twitch that might set off the shooting.

Lee knelt on the pavement, bound and gagged, and completely unable to defend himself. And yet his heart was steady. His breathing deep and even.

Eyes open. Mind clear.

When it happened, it happened all at once.

TWENTY-NINE

BURN

THE FIRST THING LEE KNEW was that the shots hadn't come from Mateo's men.

His eyes were fixed on those cartel men, and none of them had even raised their weapon.

And yet, Lee perceived a sudden flurry of *zzzip-THWACK* sounds, so close together an untrained ear might've thought they were all one noise.

He felt warm spray on the back of his neck.

And bodies falling.

He saw two more things in that micro-second: Expressions of shock on Mateo and his men; and Mr. Daniels leaping backwards for the cover of the helicopter.

Then the bodies of the two men guarding Lee toppled onto him, and flattened him to the ground, and the door gunner in the Blackhawk opened up.

Then the air was saturated with gunfire and lead.

***

Abe Darabie jacked another .338 Lapua Magnum round into the rifle, and let out the breath that had been burning in his chest. His muscles were still on fire from the run up to his shooting position.

A twelve-hundred yard shot, with his heart pounding in his chest—difficult even for him.

Beside him, the three snipers from Brinly's Marine detachment had already settled back into their scopes for follow-on shots. They'd only just had time to deploy their rifles and coordinate their targets before they'd taken the shot.

If they'd received the GPS location ten seconds later than they had, Abe wasn't sure that Lee would still be alive.

You don't know if he's alive now!

Abe blinked sweat out of his eyes and seized down on his breath again. The scope of the rifle was still centered on the Blackhawk, but now he couldn't see Lee—the Cornerstone operator whose ticket Abe had just punched had fallen on top of his friend.

And now the whole scene had devolved into chaos.

The muzzle of the Blackhawk's M240 spouted a yellow starburst and a steady stream of smoke, raking 7.62mm projectiles over the two cartel technicals while the *Nuevas Fronteras* soldiers fired back, tearing the sidewall of the Blackhawk to shreds, even as the Cornerstone leader—Mr. Daniels, Abe recognized—scrambled around the nose of the helicopter and dove for cover on the other side.

Rounds smashed through the cockpit, and Abe saw the windows abruptly painted red.

Abe shifted, trying to target the cartel, but they had beat a hasty retreat as they fired haphazardly at the Blackhawk. The two technicals had slammed it into reverse, and the men had hightailed it, and the last of them—a man in white—went sprinting back towards the refinery, and then slipped out of sight beyond a copse of trees that obstructed Abe's view.

Those trees might've saved Abe's life.

He was already aware of the two Apache gunships that hovered about a mile north of the meeting between Cornerstone and *Nuevas Fronteras*, but they surged back into the forefront of Abe's mind as they let loose with their cannons, targeting the fleeing cartel.

"Check fire!" Abe snapped, pulling his own finger away from his rifle's trigger. "Don't give those birds anything to shoot at!"

Their hide was deep in some brush, directly east of the Blackhawk. They'd been lucky that their first barrage hadn't drawn the Apache pilots' attention. There was no need for them to push their luck now.

Abe rolled onto his side, looking at the lead Marine, a gunnery sergeant. "Get on the horn with Brinly and tell him we need all hands at the refinery, *right-fucking-now*!" Abe grabbed the satellite phone from where it lay in the dirt just to the right of his rifle—the antenna already extended, and the line to Breckenridge and Menendez already open.

He snatched it up and placed it to his ear. "The location you pulled from Tex's GPS is spot on! I got positive ID on Mateo Ibarra and Daniels from Cornerstone! Get everyone you can and haul ass!"

***

Lee had to give the door gunner his due: He didn't go down without a fight.

Half-buried under the corpses of two Cornerstone operatives, their blood and brain matter trickling down his face and neck, Lee watched the gunner stand behind his M240 and let it eat, only a few tiny breaks in fire keeping it from its full cyclic potential.

The first flurry of responding rounds from the cartel tore up the side of the helicopter, and the gunner took three of them, punching holes in his gray flight suit and jerking his body around.

He didn't go down. His eyes didn't even seem to register the fact that he'd been shot. He just re-centered the muzzle of his machinegun and kept firing.

The sound of the gun, just a few yards from Lee's head, felt like being punched in the forehead at the rate of nearly 600 times a minute.

Two more rounds hit the gunner.

The muzzle dipped towards Lee, still firing.

Lee shrunk into the bodies that covered him as bullets screamed by his head.

The gunner righted himself and ripped the muzzle back up.

Lee couldn't even see the gunner's face anymore behind the smoke coming off the overheating barrel.

One more round came in from the fleeing cartel, and that was the one that it took.

The gunner's head snapped back and his body slumped.

The machinegun went silent.

In the absence of that roar, Lee could hear other things now.

The Apaches were firing. He heard the reports, and felt the impacts through the dirt that he lay on.

He heard the roar of the technicals' engines.

The screaming of men—both wounded, and those trying very hard not to be.

And he heard Mr. Daniels, shouting to his men that were no longer alive.

Eyes open. Mind clear.

If there was a way out, Lee was going to take it.

And his way out came to him in a sudden flash, and in the shape of a smoke-billowing, almost-red-hot machinegun barrel.

But it wouldn't stay hot for long.

Lee thrashed his body. That was the best that he could do. He was on his side, buried under two grown men. It felt like he couldn't get enough movement with their weight bearing down on him. His motions were stunted. He screamed through his gag, stars sparkling in his vision.

Then one of the bodies slumped off of Lee's back, and he had more wiggle room.

He kicked the other one, catching the body in the fabric of its pants and managing to press it off of him. He kicked it again to clear it from his intended path.

Gasping for breath, he looked up at the machinegun barrel.

Still smoking. But it was losing that dangerous near-glow.

The sounds that came out of him as he moved were involuntary. They were snorts, and growls, and yelps, all muffled by the cloth in his mouth. He didn't even know he was making them. His only worry in the world was trying to get his body across two yards of dirt, without the use of his arms or legs.

A bizarre memory crashed through his brain.

Defensive Tactics, from God-knew how many years ago.

A defensive, oh-shit movement that the instructors called “shrimping.” A weird, thrashing, hip-bucking movement across the ground, that made every single trainee wonder, *When am I going to use this?*

But Lee was using it right then.

Anything it took.

Each thrash only gave him a few feet. But that was all he needed.

He became aware of Mr. Daniels, who had drawn the pistol on his hip, and was now firing it in a rapid discharge of *pop-pop-pop*, around the front of the Blackhawk.

As he *shrimped*, Lee saw the man’s boots, from under the belly of the helicopter.

And then Lee was there.

The deck of the bird was right above his head.

He sat up with a grunt. He couldn’t get his feet under him—not with his ankles secured together. So he used his head. He craned his neck, and hooked his jaw over the lip of the helicopter’s deck. He cried out as metal cut hard into his ear and he writhed his entire bodyweight up by the use of the side of his face.

Then he rolled. Smashing his face into the deck. His nose cracked, as he used it to prop his upper body up.

It didn’t matter. He had his feet under him.

He turned his back on the smoking machinegun barrel.

He bit down on the gag in his mouth, and then thrust his plastic zip-cuffed wrists against the scorching hot barrel. The pain didn’t wait to greet him. It slammed into him, all the way up his arm and into his spine like he'd touched one of the high voltage wires around a Safe Zone.

He screamed.

And knew instantly that Mr. Daniels had heard him.

He strained at his bindings, pulling at the plastic as it melted and bubbled, right along with his flesh. He felt the slightest give, a gooshy sort of elasticity—

And then his wrists snapped apart.

The zip-cuff still hung from his left arm, but his right was free.

Mr. Daniels edged into view on the other side of the Blackhawk's open door. His eyes were wide and scared. His pistol was locked back on an empty magazine. His gaze hit the dead gunner.

And then he saw Lee.

"Motherfuck—" Mr. Daniels dove for a spare magazine on his belt.

Lee slapped the barrel of the M240, sending it spinning around on its mount. He seized the grip as it swung around.

Mr. Daniels mashed the magazine into his pistol's magwell, his eyes focused not on Lee now, but on the muzzle of the M240.

Lee fired.

Five 7.62mm projectiles spat out, smashing Mr. Daniels's body from hip to shoulder. He flew backwards into the dirt, the pistol tumbling out of his hands, still with its slide locked back.

A muffled scream from somewhere to Lee's right.

His eyes snapped over. Saw Tex, trying to thrash towards Lee.

Lee tried to call out, but all that issued from his throat was a crackling moan. He ripped the gag out of his mouth.

The two Apache gunships thundered over his head in a sudden calamity of noise and rotor wash. Lee squinted against the flying dust, looking up at them.

They hadn't seen what had happened to Mr. Daniels at the Blackhawk. They were pursuing the cartel's technicals, which were almost back to the refinery now, trying to get to the concrete structure that would give them some cover.

Tex screamed wordlessly again, pulling Lee's attention back.

"Hang on!" he managed to articulate this time.

Lee still had no use of his legs.

His eyes tore across the Blackhawk's cabin, searching for something, anything. They landed on the dead door gunner, but he didn't have anything on him. Then Lee spun and looked at the two dead operatives.

True to form, they both had knives.

Lee went down to his knees and pulled himself through the dirt to the closest body. He snatched the knife out of its sheath, then rolled onto his back, bringing his legs up. He stabbed the knife at the thinnest point of plastic he could perceive, which was the band going across his right ankle. His boots saved him from gouging his own flesh out.

He sawed at it, gasping out curses.

The plastic broke.

Same as his wrists, the zip-cuff remained dangling from one ankle, but he had the use of his feet back. He rolled again, thrust himself upwards, and then scrambled towards Tex.

He stopped. Looked south.

Tex screamed at him again.

The Apache gunships worked in a hovering circle, trying to get angles on one of the remaining technicals. The other technical sat in a smoking heap, halfway between the Blackhawk and the refinery.

Those gunships wouldn't be distracted for long.

And something else…

Something that burned through Lee like a sudden grassfire after a lightning strike.

He had no way of knowing if these were the same Apache pilots that had attacked them at the power plant. But it didn't matter. They bore those sins. They were guilty by association.

Staring at the two hovering forms, he knew without having to even think about it, that he was going to do something that might end up killing him. But he'd already decided it. His eyes were savage, his teeth bared. He snarled as he turned away from Tex.

He clambered onto the deck of the Blackhawk, shoving the door gunner's body out of his way and spinning the still-hot M240 around to face the gunships. That barrel had definitely been overheated, but Lee had neither the time nor the inclination to locate a replacement and swap it out.

The five rounds that he'd pumped into Mr. Daniels had been the last in the chain. Lee knew that, because if there had been any more, he would have put them into Mr. Daniels.

Two more green cans filled with linked M61 armor-piercing ammunition sat secured to the deck to Lee's right. He ripped the clasps from one of the ammo cans and hauled it up into place, swapping it out with the empty can fixed to the side of the machinegun.

Tex had gone silent, seeing what Lee was doing.

Lee's hands worked fast, his eyes focused on his task, while he saw, in his peripheral, the two gunships, still making their slow circle around the refinery, searching for targets. Still distracted.

He jabbed the first round of the chain into the feed tray, then slapped the cover assembly down over it. Racked the cocking handle.

He settled into it, his feet braced wide, his cheek mashed down onto the buttstock.

Iron sights. A ghost ring and a tree.

It was not easy to take down a helicopter with small arms fire.

But it also wasn't impossible.

Lee put the sights on the first Apache, which was broadside to him. He aimed for the nose, gave his sight picture a lead, and some elevation, and then pulled the trigger.

Five round burst.

The moment the sights settled and became clear again, he gave another five round burst.

And another. And another.

He watched the hits on the gunship's body. Ripping through the control modules under the cockpit, across the main body where all the heavy machinery lay, and then into the tail boom, shredding fiberglass and aluminum, and wrecking the helicopter's innards.

The spall burst out as the rounds struck, like gouts of dust. The last burst of rounds from Lee clattered across the Apache's tail rotor, and Lee saw bits of black go spinning off into the air.

The Apache wobbled violently. A noise reached Lee's ears, like mechanical things tearing themselves apart.

The Apache began to spin, at first gaining altitude as it did. For a few seconds, it looked like the pilot might be able to stabilize it, and the helicopter pointed it's nose towards the sunset, the pilots clearly intending to get the hell out of there…

Then something came loose. Something slammed wrong on the bird's interior. The noise of it was like the sound of cars colliding. And immediately, black smoke began to gutter from the engine housing, as the Apache tried hard to head west, but rapidly dropped altitude, and began to spin out of control.

Lee didn't wait to see it crash—maybe it would, maybe it wouldn't, but it was damn sure out of the fight.

He gulped air, and shifted his point of aim.

The other Apache was already turning on him.

Lee fired wildly, trying to get rounds out, even as the Apache began to move laterally to its threat, rather than sticking to its previous hover. Its main gun came around, now half turned, now three quarters, and now facing Lee.

Lee released the M240 and dove out the back of the Blackhawk. He hit the dirt in a tumble of limbs, rolling across Mr. Daniels's corpse, as the center of the Blackhawk flew to pieces in a barrage of fire from the Apache's main cannon.

There was a distant crash, and Lee knew the first Apache had gone down.

He rolled, and caught a glimpse of the sky through the open doors of the Blackhawk, and he saw the second Apache, roaring towards him.

Lee's rounds had been ineffective.

And now it was just him and a gunship.

The Apache roared overhead, the wind beating at Lee's face.

Lee got up and scrambled across the front of the Blackhawk's nose, to where Tex lay on the other side. The body of the Blackhawk was hardly any cover from the Apache's guns, but it was better than being out in the open.

Lee skidded to a stop beside Tex, whose eyes were wide—and enraged.

Lee glanced skyward, and saw the Apache tilting, banking hard to the right, coming around for another pass.

Probably the only one it would need.

Lee pulled the gag out of Tex's mouth, then hooked his hands into Tex's armpits and pulled him closer towards the semi-cover of the Blackhawk's cockpit.

"What the fuck are you doing?" Tex yelled, his words mushy after so long with a gag in his mouth.

"Tryna get out of here alive!" Lee snapped, as his back hit the body of the Blackhawk.

"You don't shoot a fucking M240 at a fucking Apache!"

"Didn't have another choice!"

The clatter of Apache rotors, approaching.

The pilot, searching for his targets.

Would probably end up chewing the Blackhawk to shreds to be safe.

Lee held onto Tex, who was still cursing at him.

That was okay. Lee understood.

He sucked in air thick with dust and spent propellant and the acrid chemical scent of explosive 20mm rounds. It stung in his throat, and dried his tongue. He looked up into the darkening sky. Looked at the refinery, with its cloud of steam crowning it.

His eyes flicked to the left, and he saw the Apache coming around, catching them now in its visuals, and bringing its main gun to bear.

Lee couldn't outrun this.

He did the only thing that came to his mind in that moment.

He pushed Tex to the ground, and flattened his body over him.

His body wouldn't stop one of the rounds. But it might save Tex from shrapnel.

Tex's eyes glared up at Lee, disbelieving.

"It's okay." Lee said. "I'm okay."

There was a sound like the air being rent.

And then that distinctive clatter.

Of mechanical things gone wrong.

Lee dared a glance over his shoulder.

Saw the remaining Apache dipping sideways, spewing black smoke, pounded by a barrage of incoming tracer rounds from the east. It spun, its nose going skyward, its main gun spitting out at nothing.

Lee looked to the east, tracking multiple lines of concentrated tracer fire back to their sources, and found the silhouettes of four military vehicles about a quarter of a mile distant, sitting stationary to give their gunners a stable platform.

Lee's jangled brain was so shocked by the simple prospect of not being in a million pieces that it took him a moment to connect the dots.

Whoever the hell that was, they must've been the ones that took out the Cornerstone guards.

He had no idea who it was, but in that moment, the old adage was true: The enemy of my enemy is my friend. And those were his best friends at that moment.

The Apache hit the ground and tumbled in a clatter of disintegrating rotors and dirt and metal components flying out like debris from an asteroid strike. It rolled into the center of the paved road that led to the refinery, and stopped in a wash of dust and smoke.

"Get me up!" Tex yelled.

Lee snapped back to the present.

He was still alive.

He was still in the fight.

He'd found a path.

THIRTY

SAVAGES

LEE WRENCHED HIMSELF off of Tex. Went to the nearest Cornerstone body—he had no idea where he'd dropped the other knife, but they all had one on their kit. He batted around the dead man's rig until he found it, then returned to Tex, and cut him free.

In the distance, Lee became aware of the rumble of approaching engines.

"Who the hell is that?" Tex demanded as he stumbled to his feet.

"No clue," Lee said, working the blade through the zip-cuffs still attached to his own wrist and ankle. "But friendly or not, I'd like to be armed when they get here."

Lee and Tex turned to the dead bodies of the Cornerstone operatives.

The Apache that had fired on Lee and chewed up the side of the Blackhawk had also taken out two of the corpses, scattering them into pieces and rendering their kit useless—their armor was mangled and torn, their weapons looking untrustworthy.

But the other two—the ones that had been on Tex—were unmarred.

Except for the bullet holes in their heads.

Lee and Tex rushed to these two bodies, each taking one.

Lee stripped the rifle and sling from the body. A SCAR-16. Lee was familiar enough with the platform to use it. He checked the magazine and the chamber. The previous owner hadn't even had a chance to fire a round—the rifle was fully loaded.

Lee set the rifle next to him, casting a glance over his shoulder and seeing that the vehicles were close now—only a few hundred yards away. Two Humvees and two MATVs.

He ripped the Velcro cummerbund from the dead man's armor, then grabbed it by the shoulder straps and pulled it free, trailing comm wires.

A piece of dirt to Lee's left exploded.

His first thought was that the approaching vehicles had fired on him. But then the rifle report splashed over him, and he snapped his head towards the refinery, and saw in the shadows of the structure, a white shape, spewing puffs of gunsmoke, and sending more lead his way.

Mateo.

"Cover!" Tex yelled, but Lee was already moving. The dead operative's arm caught up in the plate carrier for a moment, forcing Lee to drag the whole body, but with a violent jerk, the arm flopped loose and Lee dove for cover around the front of the Blackhawk.

He skidded through the dirt, resisting the urge to hug the side of the helicopter, but instead thrust himself away from it to improve his angling.

Tex was right on his ass, but he turned the front of the helicopter too sharp, and his legs went out from under him, sliding in the layer of gravel that had accumulated on the top of the battered pavement.

Lee swore, dropped the plate carrier from his left hand, then reached out for Tex.

Tex lurched up to get his feet under him. He reached for Lee.

Then toppled sideways in a spray of blood.

Lee yelled. Maybe his name. Maybe another curse. All he could tell was that his throat felt scraped raw.

Tex was still alive.

The left half of his face was missing.

His mouth worked. Hand still reaching for Lee.

Lee grabbed him by the wrist and hauled backwards, pulling the body across the gravel-strewn pavement, into cover. A flurry of bullet impacts chased at Tex's feet.

The approaching vehicles slewed to a stop, kicking up yellow clouds, their gunners swinging their turrets around and firing heavy bursts of .50 caliber fire towards the refinery.

Lee grabbed Tex by the head, trying not to stick his fingers where the flesh had been torn. Half of Tex's upper teeth were missing. His mouth was filling up with blood. He tried to speak and then coughed, splattering Lee's face with it.

Lee blinked it away, then tilted Tex's head to the side, letting the blood fall out of his mouth so he could breathe. Tex pulled in a shuddering lungful, then tried to speak again, but he couldn't make words. All that came out was "Guh. Guh."

He had enough of his mouth left that he should've been able to say something.

Maybe it was just the shock.

But Lee thought something much worse: *Something went into his brain.*

Bullet fragment. Bone fragment. It didn't matter.

Lee's eyes searched the bleeding tatters of Tex's opened face, trying to think if there was anything that he could do. He found himself saying, "Hang on, Tex! Hang on!" But he didn't know what he was telling Tex to hang on for.

His mind ran in the same, tight loop.

Through all of his medical training for combat trauma.

But even the best medic couldn't do anything about a shot to the head.

Brain swelling. Maybe I can give him an ice pack to keep the brain from swelling too much.

He lifted his head and saw figures running towards him, sprinting in that hunched manner that every man takes when there's incoming fire.

Desert digital uniforms.

Marines.

And then someone, behind the Marines, who wore a t-shirt under a tan plate carrier, and a set of worse-for-wear combat pants.

"Lee!" Abe shouted at him.

"I need an ice pack," Lee called.

The three Marines came sliding into cover, one of them taking a firing position through the Blackhawk's open doors, the other going low and shooting under the belly of the craft.

They were receiving plenty of incoming fire. More than just Mateo would be able to hand out.

How many cartel are inside that refinery?

"Ice pack!" he said again—repeating the only thing he could come up with.

The third Marine came down on his knees right there at Tex's side, trailed by Abe.

"Lee!" Abe yelled at him, grabbing him by the back of the neck and forcing eye contact.

"What?" Lee snapped.

"He's dead! We gotta move!"

Lee looked down.

Tex's eyes looked, for just an instant, like they were staring at Lee.

But when Lee moved his head, he saw that they didn't track.

They were half-lidded.

Already going dry.

A speck of debris clung to the pupil of one, and Tex didn't blink it away.

Lee still held the man's bleeding head up off the ground. He set it down.

And, for a few beats, he seemed to hang there, suspended in a nebula created of dust and gunsmoke. He existed in a vacuum, and he heard nothing outside of himself. Just the beating of his own heart. The scrape of the air through his dried-out throat.

The cartel was shooting, and the Marines were shooting back.

People were shouting.

Another battle.

Another gunfight.

Another dead friend.

Something passed close over Lee's head, and he ducked, but his eyes never came off of Tex, and that little speck of dust on his cornea, and how dried out he suddenly looked, so barren.

He never even had a chance to fight.

And that, maybe above all else, was the worst thing of all.

That someone like Tex, who'd spent his entire life fighting, could go out like this, with his wrists raw from being bound, and no weapon in his hands.

I'll fight for you, Lee thought to yet another friend that he no longer had.

Because that's what Lee did.

That's what he always did.

He fought for others.

I'll kill them all.

Something blazed a hot path, right across the back of his neck.

Any closer, and he'd have a severed spinal column.

It was a slap in the face that brought him back to himself.

He reached behind him, grabbed the SCAR-16 and the chest rig that he'd dropped. He pulled them towards him, doing his best to stay low.

His breathing came in quicker now.

Purposeful.

Charging himself with oxygen.

He pulled the armor over his head, set to strapping it about himself. "Mateo Ibarra," he said to Abe, his voice a thick growl. "He's in the refinery."

"Lee," Abe countered. "We should—"

Lee's hands rocketed up from the plate carrier and grabbed Abe by the collar of his own armor. He was done with arguments. Done with talking. There was nothing inside of him now but a supernova of all the bad things that had been coalescing—not just since Julia's death, but for years…

For every time Lee'd been backed in the corner. For every time Lee had been punished for being civil, and reviled for being a killer. For every time he'd ever tried with everything in his being to keep his friends from dying, only to fail, time and time again…

For all of that, he was going to kill everyone.

And no one would stand in Lee's way.

Not even Abe.

"We should finish what we started!" Lee snarled.

Abe's eyes searched Lee's, and found only hate.

There could be no turning back now.

Now there was only forward.

Now there was only vengeance.

It didn't matter the forces that were arrayed against them, it didn't matter the odds. They'd been through worse. In a thousand different ways, they'd been through a thousand hells, and they were still here.

They were the only ones left.

And they would have what they came for.

Abe nodded. "Let's go, then."

Lee snatched the SCAR-16 off the ground.

Another Marine ran to them. This one Lee recognized.

"Captain Harden!" Brinly called out to him as he ducked incoming fire and knelt down where Lee and Abe were. "Angela—"

The mention of the name sent an electric jolt through Lee that bore with it a myriad of feelings he had no intention of handling in that moment. He cut Brinly off. "Have your gunners concentrate fire on the front of the refinery. Whichever truck is up-armored, have them start rolling towards the main structure, and me and Abe will be on their ass."

Brinly blinked a few times, and for a second seemed about to object, but then it was as though he recognized that Lee—and Abe as well—were going to do this no matter what. And he simply nodded.

"You got it, boys." He keyed his comms and relayed the orders. After a moment, he leaned out of cover for a quick peek, then grabbed Lee by the shoulder, forcing him to look where he was looking. He pointed to one of the MATVs. "That's your up-armored truck. The one with the Punisher skull painted on the back. You copy?"

Lee dipped his head in acknowledgement. "Abe! Let's move!"

As they darted out of cover, Lee heard Brinly shout at the other Marines taking cover behind the Blackhawk: "Get on my ass! We're goin' with 'em!"

Pavement flew under Lee's feet.

Disassembled bodies to his right. The shredded structure of the helicopter.

A Humvee roared across his path, close enough for Lee to taste the exhaust, it's M2 gunner pumping bursts of .50 caliber fire at the refinery. The trucks spread out, creating separate bases of fire, and trying to keep moving.

The MATV with the Punisher skull was dead ahead, angling its front towards the refinery, its armored turret chattering away.

A few places in the refinery—dark windows surrounded by concrete walls—had sprouted muzzle flashes. The road burst in tiny pockmarks to Lee's right and left, and a few rounds moaned right over the top of his head, forcing him to duck even lower as he sprinted.

He reached the back of the MATV and sucked pure diesel exhaust. He coughed, turned his head towards the marginally-cleaner air to his left and cleared his lungs. Abe crashed into the back of the MATV and then slapped the rear doors.

Only a second after that, Brinly and the three Marines that had taken cover behind the Blackhawk stacked up tightly around Lee.

The MATV had already started to roll forward after Abe pounded on the door, but Brinly still transmitted to the squad leader inside: "You got troops right on your tailpipe! Don't outrun us!"

The MATV didn't outrun them, but it didn't dawdle either.

The driver jumped it up to a pace that forced Lee and Abe to run behind it to maintain cover.

The Marines ran alongside them, and, as the refinery began to tower over them—and shave away some of the valuable protective angles of their cover—they began to scrunch in, ankles pummeling each other, nearly shoulder to shoulder.

A rattling of incoming projectiles across metal grew to a sudden crescendo, terminated by someone crying out.

Shit, Lee thought. *Gunner's down.*

Not a second later, he heard the turret cease firing and Brinly shouted, "Gunner's down!"

The incoming fire intensified, the MATV still edging closer and closer to the main structure of the refinery—now at about fifty yards.

Something nipped one of the Marines that was on the outer edge of their scrum of bodies. He swore and then shouted, "I'm fine! Keep moving!"

Lee just kept running, and trying to control his breathing. His entire world was the sound of bullets pinging off metal, and the tan ass-end of the truck filling his vision.

The MATV suddenly lurched to a stop, and Lee and Abe slammed into the back of it, and the Marines mushed into them like a six car pileup on the interstate.

The backend of the MATV's troop carrier cracked open. The Marine on the inside stuck his face in the gap and shouted. "We're sitting under a big-ass pipe! You got a little bit of cover, and then open ground for fifteen yards to the side of the main building, you copy?"

Lee looked at the Marine. "Can you see an entrance and is it open or does it look barricaded?"

The Marine nodded and knife-handed at an angle to the right. "Double steel doors to the right-hand side of the main building. Looks like the main entrance. They're closed. Don't know if they're barricaded."

Brinly shouldered up to the door. "We need to get Lee and Abe into that building. Bunder, when we run for the door, I want you to edge out from the cover of that pipe overhead and let your gunner chew the fuck out of the windows. The rest of us, cover high and to the sides. When we're set, Bunder, you're gonna use the MATV to ram those double doors open."

Bunder—the Marine in the door—nodded with a hasty "Aye, sir."

Brinly turned to Lee and Abe. "Y'all got grenades?"

Lee had already taken stock of his stolen rig and he shook his head.

Brinly turned back to Bunder and held out a hand. "Grenades. All the grenades you got."

Bunder turned to the other Marines in the box with him. "You heard the major! All the 'nades you got!"

A stream of little baseball-sized metal balls came flowing out of the back of the MATV, passed hand-over-hand from Bunder to Brinly, and then to Lee and Abe.

Brinly gave Lee a knowing nod. "There ain't nobody in that building that needs to live. Frag and clear everything."

Lee stuffed his pockets and any other spare space that could hold a grenade. "Roger that."

"On you, boys," Brinly said.

"Cover!" Lee called out. "Moving!"

Abe peeled the corner, Lee right behind him.

The grenades in his pockets slammed around, pummeling his thighs as he sprinted with only enough distance between him and Abe for their feet not to trip each other up.

The MATV lurched forward, and whoever had taken the turret opened up again.

The cover of the giant pipe that ran overhead disappeared in an instant.

Lee ran through open space. Not even breathing. He had twenty more yards to go to the front doors. He bore down, pushing every ounce of himself through his legs, slamming pavement.

The windows above them sparkled like camera flashes in an arena.

The ground around them burst in a dozen places.

Something snapped through Lee's flesh, high in his right trapezius, and then, immediately after, a blow to his midsection that nearly stopped him in his tracks.

Ten yards.

Make it there.

Do it because Tex can't.

He pressed forward again, trying to recover his momentum, hoping he wasn't about to feel the pain of a gut wound.

Ahead of him, dust and spall erupted off of Abe's chest and his body twisted, mid-run…

Then they slammed into the concrete wall of the main structure.

Lee gasped for air, as Marines hit the wall to his left, stacking up.

You're there.

Good.

Kill them all.

"Abe! You alright?" Lee shouted.

Abe put his back to the wall, coughed hard, and smacked his chest, like he was trying to clear it of stubborn phlegm. "Good!"

Only then did Lee look down at his own midsection.

The plate carrier was torn up. One of the magazines sat in splinters, the internal spring and some bent-up rounds spilling out like odd mechanical guts. He stuffed his hand under the armor and felt his belly. It was wet with sweat, but there were no holes in it.

He ripped the destroyed magazine out and threw it off to the side.

The MATV's turret spat a steady stream at the windows over their heads. The Marines around them had rifles high and low, covering their stack.

Lee looked at the windshield of the MATV, and nodded to a driver he couldn't see. The engine roared. The big tan truck jumped, the front end rearing up like an enraged bull.

"Standby!" Lee yelled to the others in the stack.

The MATV struck the double doors with an enormous crash that Lee felt through his entire skeletal structure. The doors simply disappeared, somewhere into the building. Cinderblock wall went in with them.

"Ready!" Abe called out. He had his rifle slung to his chest, and now held a grenade in his right hand, his left hand clutching the ring-pull.

The MATV rumbled, shifting gears into reverse. From inside the breached structure, Lee heard the crackle of rifle fire and the *ping* of it striking the front end of the truck.

Lee let his rifle hang and snatched out a grenade.

Kill them all.

The MATV cleared the breach.

Lee and Abe, eyes locked on each other's movements and unconsciously synchronizing themselves, yanked the pins, and then chucked the grenades through the breach.

"Frag out!" they shouted, then turned away from the hole in the wall and shielded their unhelmeted heads with their arms.

The building shook at their backs, the explosions jarring the air in their chests. A gout of dust and smoke came spewing out of the breach, and a clatter of debris tumbled after it.

Kill them...

Lee felt a hard hand on his shoulder, and one of the Marines shouted, "Move!"

Lee scooped his rifle up and shouldered it as he spun and faced the breach. His movements carried the unconscious surety of the infinitely practiced.

Abe hit the entry first.

Lee hesitated a half step to let him go, then let his feet slip right in behind Abe, the muzzle of his rifle following as close behind Abe's head as possible. The two of them flowed seamlessly through.

Abe broke left.

Lee pivoted his shoulder off of Abe's, breaking right.

Smoke.

High explosives.

Shapes moving.

Three shattering reports, directly behind Lee, shaking the room, and Lee didn't flinch, didn't look around.

Kill…

Dead ahead, a man appeared through the smoke, stumbling upright. Lee didn't wait to identify the threat. They were inside this building. They were all a threat. He thumbed the safety off and squeezed the trigger a microsecond after, three rapid blasts that sent the shape of a man reeling off into the wall.

More movement. To the left.

Lee breathed out through pursed lips, snapping to the left with both eyes open, even as the brass casings from his first three rounds were still falling. His eyes met his target's, and through the thinning smoke, saw the terror in them, and then the reticle of his optic fell into place on that man's hairline, and Lee squeezed out four rounds. Two of them splashed his brains out the back of his head.

All of it in the span of time it took Lee to go one step in, and one step over.

His feet stopped, knowing his position subconsciously. His rifle kept tracking left, until his eyes saw the backs of two Marines, plunging directly into the room. He whipped the rifle back around. Assessed his first target.

The eyes were still moving, Lee thought.

He put a round between them.

Then back to the second target. He couldn't see the eyes, but the man lay spread eagle, and did not move. One of the passing Marines gave the body a security round, and Lee figured that was enough.

Only then did he dip the muzzle of his rifle and look back to the left side of the room…

He heard movement, to his right—behind his back.

He spun, bringing his rifle back up.

The body hit him hard.

He caught no sight of who it was, or where the hell he'd come from, but he saw the man's teeth bared in effort and savagery, and his eyes, wild with fear and the desire to kill Lee. Almost manic.

He slammed into Lee, and at the same time, grabbed a hold of the muzzle of Lee's rifle, just as Lee snapped the safety off and fired a round that smashed harmlessly into the concrete floor.

The man drove into Lee, crushing him back against the wall.

Lee grunted and growled with animal effort. He tried to extricate his hands, but the man pinning him was a flurry of movements—batting his wrists every time he started to move, and pummeling his face with rapid strikes…

Lee bore it for a moment.

Thinking, *You're not the one that gets to end me.*

Lee released his grip on his rifle—it was uselessly pinned against his side now anyways—and brought his arms up to cover his face from the blows, each impact jarring his brain.

Then he twisted hard. Slammed one elbow into the side of the man's face, and bought himself a fraction of a second.

He grabbed the man's shoulders, clinching him, but unable to see anything past the stars in his eyes, simply operating on pure instinct, fueled by hate, sparked by the thought that this man didn't get to be the one to stop him.

Lee rammed his knee into the man's groin.

The air came out of him in a wheeze.

The body folded.

Lee drove him back with a yell that didn't sound like him at all.

The man toppled in front of Lee, and Lee went down on top of him, and his hands were there, and his rifle was there, but his hands were closer, and the man's face was there, right in front of Lee, his eyes scrunched in shock and debilitating pain, and Lee hated those eyes, and he wanted to crush them…

He rammed his thumbs into the corners of the man's eyes.

Felt warmth. Felt wetness.

The man screamed and gnashed his teeth.

It wasn't enough to simply gouge a man's eyes out—Lee knew that. He wasn't trying to blind the man. He was trying to kill him.

So he circled his thumbs. He coiled them around the slippery cord of the man's optic nerve, and then he pulled them out, taking bits of brain with them, and sending the man into convulsions from which he would never recover.

Lee dropped the pieces of flesh.

He staggered to his feet, his breathing ragged.

He swiped his palms off on his pant legs and brought his rifle up again, checking the magazine and action to ensure that his tussle hadn't caused a misfeed. His hands felt clumsy as he did this. He frowned, having to focus hard to get the movements right.

You're good.

Keep moving.

He brought his eyes up. Brought himself back into the present.

Around him, chaos swirled. Marines still poured through the room, checking nooks and crannies. Abe stood directly to Lee's side, looking like he'd been heading to Lee's aid.

They stared at each other.

They traded a nod.

"You good?"

"I'm good."

Back to business.

The two of them moved while the Marines called out to each other. They moved instinctively towards an industrial metal staircase that appeared to lead to a second floor, and a catwalk that accessed several large pieces of equipment.

Lee covered high as they approached the stairs, checking the catwalk and the equipment. Abe focused on the door.

Lee took the stairs first, shouting over his shoulder, "Going up!"

The call was echoed around the room, and the Marines began to fall in behind Abe.

Lee had to turn as he ascended the stairs, going up sideways. The catwalk was clear. No bodies hiding around the equipment.

He reached the top. An industrial door with a narrow, reinforced window on the handle-side. Lee moved to the hinge-side of the door, taking a quick look through the window as he did. Beyond looked like a walkway, lined by windows. No hostiles.

Abe took the latch side of the door, positioning himself close, but with enough room to let the door swing. He held his rifle in his right hand, a grenade in his left, the pin already pulled. Not exactly what they taught you in training, but sometimes you have to make things up as you go.

Abe nodded.

Lee ripped the door open.

Abe stepped to the side, clearing a good portion of the left side of the walkway beyond, then tossed the grenade to the right.

BOOM!

And then they were moving again.

Abe going right this time.

Lee going left.

The walkway was empty. What looked like a hundred yards of steel-grated flooring, heading to separate wings of the refinery on either end.

Marines came through the door. There were more of them than before. Perhaps the ones from the carrier box of the MATV.

Brinly came through last.

Lee's eyes caught movement, dead ahead through the bank of windows right across from him.

He leapt forward, looking down towards the ground.

Below the windowed walkway, a single technical spun its tires, the driver just now stomping on the gas.

In an instant, Lee saw the gunner, wheeling what looked like an M249 around in their direction—

—and a white shirt, in the front passenger's seat—

—A flash of long, black hair—

"Cover!" Lee shouted, spinning and grabbing Brinly as he did, because he was the closest man to Lee's reach, and pushing him back away from the windows, and down.

The windows shattered.

The rattle of the M249 ripped the air.

Lee and Brinly hit the deck, and all Lee could think was *He's getting away! Mateo is getting away!*

THIRTY-ONE

HELLFIRE

LEE SAW THE ROUNDS punching through the glass and the edges of the steel-grated floor.

Lee dove off of Brinly, crabbing madly across the floor using one knee and one hand, angling around the incoming fire as the vehicle sending it retreated.

"Don't let that technical get away!" Lee screamed.

He came up on one knee, leaning out from the catwalk, nothing to break his fall to the ground below—the glass completely obliterated. He shouldered his rifle, put the optic on the fleeing technical and started firing as fast as he could keep the reticle on target.

A tire went out.

The technical lurched, but kept going.

He heard Brinly yelling something, but he couldn't tell what the man said.

Lee raised his point of aim, still firing.

The gunner twitched and crumpled behind his M249.

Lee didn't stop. Wasn't going to stop. Couldn't stop.

He's getting away!

Lee's thoughts were almost in a panic.

He was not a man that was prone to panic. But the thought of Mateo Ibarra getting away, when Lee was so close to him—had been so damn close—was too much.

A groan eked out of Lee's chest as he fired, as though he was straining physically to put the rounds on target, he wanted them to strike the man down so bad…

A stream of orange tracer fire came, seemingly out of nowhere, and plowed into the front end of the technical. The front tires exploded in a shower of rubber and dust. The vehicle fishtailed, then angled left, while the tracer fire tracked it, pounding the engine compartment to scrap metal.

The technical struck a concrete pylon.

Lee was already thrusting himself to his feet. "Cease fire!" he yelled at Brinly, his voice cracking, not giving a shit about his contradictory commands. "Cease fire! Tell them to stop shooting!"

Before anyone could stop him, or ask him where the hell he was going and why the hell he didn't want the Marines shooting at the technical anymore, Lee had already plunged through the door, and was flying down the staircase, his feet hitting each tread so fast Lee thought he might lose control and face plant.

He'd already lost control.

Don't be dead! Lee willed. *Don't you fucking dare!*

He hit the bottom. Leapt over a dead body.

He knew his rifle was almost empty. He dropped the magazine, not bothering to retain it—he was in too much of a rush—and he ripped a fresh magazine from his pouch and slammed it home.

The breached double doors clattered against the ground as Lee pounded over them, skidding through the scree of concrete rubble outside. The MATV that had rammed the door had now backed up about twenty yards, in order to get a line of sight on the fleeing technical.

The gunner's M2 pointed that way, but didn't fire.

Lee charged around the corner of the main structure.

He kept thinking, *Cease fire! Don't shoot him! Don't kill him!*

But he was beyond words now. He was beyond the reach of any human touch. He had delved into savagery. He was primal.

As he rounded the corner of the refinery's main structure, the technical came into view. Smashed into a support pylon—one of the many that held up a superstructure of massive pipelines. The technical issued thick gouts of gray smoke from its crumpled engine compartment. The airbags had gone off. The gunner was slumped behind his weapon, chewed to pieces by incoming fire. All that Lee could see of the driver was a mess of gore on the windshield.

But the passenger…

The white shirt.

The long black hair.

Slumped over against the deflating air bag. Beginning to stir.

Lee raised his rifle as he ran, but he didn't slow, and he didn't take the shot.

His eyes went low—under the carriage of the ruined truck.

A steady trickle of fluid. Vapors causing the air beneath the truck to ripple and roil as though they were a heat mirage.

A tiny tongue of flame flicked out from under the hood, sucking at oxygen.

Somewhere far behind him, perhaps from another world, Lee heard someone call his name. But he was not that anymore. He was Nobody.

His pounding feet began to slacken, his pace less rushed.

No one was shooting. Mateo Ibarra was still alive, and he raised his head, and moved his arms, and maybe said something, but Lee could not hear him, because the passenger's window was closed and had somehow not been shot to pieces.

Gray smoke began to fill the truck's cab.

Mateo's movements went from bleary to urgent, in a snap.

The flames from under the hood grew more dominant.

Lee slowed to a jog, and then a walk.

He could hear Mateo now. He could hear him speaking in Spanish. He did not understand all the words, but he heard that many of them were directed at God. But Mateo did not know what Lee knew. That whoever pulled the strings of the universe had allowed Lee to live, and the only reason that Lee was alive was to kill.

Lee had struck a deal.

And Mateo was a part of that deal.

And so Mateo might not know it, but his prayers fell on deaf ears.

Lee stopped, about three paces away from the vehicle.

Mateo had found the door latch and was yanking at it, but the cab had crumpled when it hit the pylon, and the door was stuck. Smoke filled the space inside, and Mateo began to gag and choke. He pounded at the glass, and his eyes fell on Lee, only paces away.

Lee stared at him, and in his eyes was nothing, and Mateo saw it.

Mateo Ibarra. His eyes wide, streaked with tears born of choking air. A gash in his forehead, dribbling blood down the side of his face. His black hair stuck to it. His teeth flashed as he screamed at Lee—perhaps to curse him, perhaps to beg mercy.

Lee stepped forward and raised the rifle in his hands.

Mateo stared at the muzzle.

Lee slammed the barrel into the corner of the window, shattering it.

Smoke billowed out.

Mateo thrust his head out and gulped clean air, gasping and coughing.

Smoke inhalation could make someone pass out.

Lee wanted Mateo to be conscious for a little while longer.

Mateo got control of his lungs and blinked at Lee. Then he reached out a hand. "Pull me out!" he demanded.

Lee gave no response. He stepped back.

Under the car, a terrible orange glow suddenly brightened. Lee heard it, like the sigh of a great beast unleashed. And he stepped back further.

When the car went up, it was not dramatic. The gas tank didn't explode. It simply flared, and the flames grew bright and hot, and angry.

Mateo began to thrash. He tried to pull himself out of the window, but he was stuck somehow. Probably his legs. Pinned under the dashboard.

"Get me out of here you sonofabitch!" Mateo screamed, tearing at his legs like a coyote trying to free itself from a trap.

Lee squinted against the heat pouring from the truck. Even several paces away, it made his skin feel puckered and tight.

Mateo gnashed at the air. His eyes wild. "Is this what you want?" his voice shook with an attempt to be calm through what must have been terrible pain. "You want to see me burn alive, you sonofabitch? You want to watch? You want to listen to me scream?"

And then he screamed.

At first, he screamed in defiance.

But then the expression of his face changed. All worldly matters ceased to exist, and there was only the desire to escape the all-encompassing agony that swirled around his feet, growing up his body, engulfing the cab.

His face, and his screams, became desperate.

High pitched.

Mateo Ibarra shrieked.

And in another life, another time, Lee might've had mercy. But the very man that wanted his mercy so bad at that moment, was the same man that had surgically removed that part of Lee's soul when he'd taken everything from him.

And so Lee watched, and he felt nothing.

He watched it like a tired man watches a sunset, knowing night and rest will follow soon.

The heat was almost too much to bear, but Lee did. He bore witness, and he didn't look away.

Mateo found words. They were filled with invocations and invectives, and in the end, they begged. They begged for death. They begged for a bullet.

Lee did not know if Mateo could see him through the melting skin that was sloughing off his face, but he flipped the safety on his rifle, and he let it hang. He did not raise his hands, but he simply held them at his sides, and he turned his palms out towards Mateo, as though he were bathing, either in the heat, or the screams.

Somewhere in there, a gulp of air seared Mateo's throat shut, and he screamed no more.

Blackened nubs of fingers gripped the sizzling sheet metal of the door, but the muscles that made those arms and fingers operate had been cooked away. Mateo's body thrust itself back into its chair in a final spasm. And for a moment, the only thing left on Mateo's body that still moved was his jaw, the flesh bubbling off of it, splitting, oozing, and the fat catching fire, but the jaw still working, like he was biting at the air.

And then that stopped too.

Lee stood there for a while longer.

Until the flames danced in his eyes.

Until all that was left was blackened bones.

And then Lee finally stepped back, to stand at the edge of the firelight, where the heat would not singe him, while the darkness gathered at his back, and he heard the calls of Marines, one to the other, like coyotes in the night, and the rumble of their trucks, and sometimes their headlights would splash over Lee, but the glow of the fire was brighter.

Lee felt that he'd been burned away too. That certain tethers had been immolated, and that what was left behind was something raw and pink—something that had lain under the surface of hard-bought calluses.

He thought back to another fire, another glowing circle.

It was the last night they would all be alive and in one place together.

Lee, Julia, Abe, Nate, and Tomlin, in a circle.

They'd all left that fire. And they'd never again been whole.

And between that fire, and this one, something had happened to them all. And the thing that had happened to them was a man, whose bones were now charring to ash. And without him, it was almost as though the past months had been burned away too—that the timeline they'd sat on had disintegrated, and if Lee looked to his right or his left, he would see their faces again, smiling at him over the fire, laughing around a jar of moonshine.

He did not look. But if he had, he would have seen one of them.

He would have seen Abe.

Not *No One*. Not *Nadie.*

Abe Darabie. Who stared, not at the fire, but at Lee.

The darkness had long-since deepened to black when they both turned away from the faltering fire that still smoked and guttered in the shell of a vehicle with nothing inside of it at all, and the only clue that there might've once been something being an oily pile of ash that gusts of wind coming in off the coast would stir and scatter.

The Marine trucks had positioned themselves around the refinery. More Marines had shown up, these ones in troop carriers. Brinly had command. He had control. Occasional bursts of gunfire told that the Marines were still clearing the refinery.

Lee and Abe walked without words, down the cracked and potted pavement, towards the ruined Blackhawk.

They passed, to the right, the wreckage of one of the Apache helicopters. The one that had taken the crossfire from several M2's at once.

The cockpit hadn't held together on impact. The pilots lay in several pieces.

They continued on.

In the distance, to their left, Lee saw the glimmer of low flames. He could just make out the shape of the helicopter lying in the dirt, like a felled beast, about two hundred yards away. That would be the one that he engaged with the M240.

He wondered if either of the pilots had made it out.

Probably not.

And even if they did, there was a lot of unfriendly territory between them and Greeley Colorado.

If they'd survived at all, they'd had about the same chance of survival that Lee had allowed others.

The same chance they'd given Julia.

Lastly they arrived at the damaged Blackhawk, and they stood on either side of the body of Mr. Daniels, where it lay, spread eagle in the dirt, facing the sky with eyes like dusty marbles. In the harsh glow of Abe's weaponlight, Mr. Daniels's skin was stark white.

They looked at him for a while.

"That's all of them, I think," Abe said. He glanced up at Lee.

Lee nodded. Didn't say what he was thinking.

For now.

A flicker of lights came from where the long, flat road disappeared into the distant tree line. The noise of approaching engines became evident.

Lee raised his rifle, suddenly exhausted. "Daniels said he had Cornerstone on the way."

The headlights flickered.

Abe stared at them. "Hang on."

The lights flashed. The high beams strobing a couple times.

"Hold your fire," Abe grunted. "That's Breck and Menendez."

Lee slowly let the muzzle of the SCAR-16 sink back towards the ground. "How are they here?" he looked crosswise at Abe. "How are *you* here?"

Abe's thick, black beard twitched, and it might've been a grim smile under there. "You're welcome, by the way. For taking out the two guards."

"Oh. Thanks."

Abe took a breath, as the headlights continued to approach. "I met Brinly's convoy when I was almost back to Butler. They'd just been deployed to see what was going on. I started trying to get in contact with you to let you know I was coming back with some Marines. Eventually I got into contact with Menendez and Breckenridge. They told me what you'd done. They told me what the message from Mr. Daniels said. On a hunch, I had them access the location of Tex's GPS device from their bunker control room. Sure enough, it was at Triprock. We tried to make it there. Almost did, but then the location moved to here. Man…" Abe shook his head. "We had to haul ass, Lee. Almost didn't make it."

"Well. You did."

"Yeah. We made it."

Lee nodded and sighed. "We made it."

He could see the vehicles now. It was Menendez's ratty squad, and the technical that Lee'd left behind outside the bunker. In it was stuffed every man that wasn't too banged up to fire a rifle, and a few that looked to be right on the edge.

One in particular, Lee noticed. In the bed of the truck that came to a halt last in the convoy. A soldier with white bandages around his head—bloody where an ear should have been. And a dog that looked more like a coyote, standing beside him, looking at Lee with his ears perked.

Deuce leapt out of the back of the truck before it stopped moving. He hit the ground running, like a tan bolt of lightning. All Lee could do was lean back, until his knees touched the deck of the Blackhawk behind him, and then he sat, feeling the ashes of something old and used up fly away from him.

Deuce took a running jump and scrabbled across the metal deck of the Blackhawk, and then planted himself against Lee's chest, and Lee put his arm around the dog. Deuce gave him one solid lick across the side of his neck—a rare display of affection—and then sat, very close to Lee, and looked out at the bodies, as though he were curious how they got there.

Lee held onto him. He held on.

He didn't say a word as Breckenridge and Menendez both trotted up and saw who it was that lay at the nose of the Blackhawk, half his face gone.

They looked up at Lee, like they didn't believe it could really be Tex lying there on the ground. Or maybe they couldn't believe it was Tex, and not Lee.

Eventually, they picked him up, as though they couldn't bear to see him lying there with the bodies of his enemies. Menendez, Breckenridge, and a few of their soldiers—all men that had served together and worked under Tex—they bore him up, and took him to the back of their truck, and they laid him there with a solemn silence that made it easy to picture him ensconced in a flag-draped coffin.

A voice reached Lee's ears. It was Brinly's, and he was talking to somebody.

Talking *at* them.

Or…

Lee turned and looked.

Through the wreckage of the Blackhawk, he saw Brinly stalking towards them with two of his Marines in tow, all of them backlit by the dwindling vehicle fire, and the headlights of the MATVs and Humvees splashing across the refinery structures. But Brinly wasn't speaking to his Marines.

He had his hand up to his head. A satphone to his ear.

"…secured the refinery. Yes. That's correct…That, I'm not sure about, but whatever we can pump out of this place, you can be sure we'll be sending back your way. And based on preliminary reports, I think it might be a good amount."

Brinly's eyes flicked to Lee's, a small communication taking place in that look, and then he angled around the front of the bird, and stopped in front of Lee. Still listening.

Then, "Yes, Madam President. Actually, I'm looking at him right now. And he is in one piece.

Shockingly enough." Another long pause. A faint twist in the thin line of his lips. "Of course. Standby."

Then he held the phone out to Lee.

"For you, Captain Harden."

Lee took the phone. Carefully. Like it was made of glass instead of hardened polymers.

He wondered where the fear had gone. He should be hoping for another interruption in the satellite connection. He should be hoping for…anything. Anything that would end, or even postpone, speaking to the person on the other end of the line.

But he didn't feel that.

He glanced up at Brinly, still holding the satphone out in front of him, and he said, "Daniels mentioned Cornerstone troops on their way here. He didn't specify when. We should get in. Batten down the hatches…"

Lee felt a hand on his shoulder.

Abe gave him a nod. "I'll handle it."

And then there was nothing else to say or do.

It was just Lee, and his dog, and a phone in his hand, connected to a person who, on the other side of the country, was somehow still indelibly etched in a part of Lee that he'd long pushed under. But perhaps the layers of himself that had grown over that part of him in the intervening years…

Well, perhaps those were the layers that had burned up with Mateo Ibarra.

He put the phone to his ear.

Heard a breath on the other end.

Closed his eyes.

"I'm here, Angela."

THIRTY-TWO

RUN

AFTER NEARLY TWENTY MINUTES, Angela pulled the satphone away from her ear.

All around her, the streets of the Butler Safe Zone were dark, save for the few street lamps allowed to burn at strategic places. In the distance, the windows of several residences glowed.

Her ear was hot. The satphone was warm—the battery almost drained now. She would have to plug it in to recharge.

Not all those twenty minutes had been spent speaking to Lee. She'd also spoken to Major Brinly, and Abe Darabie, and a man introduced as Sergeant Menendez, and another introduced as Breckenridge.

Things were moving. Things were coming together.

For the first time in a very, very long time, Angela felt a long-forgotten sensation, that might have been a line to a single buoy of hope, wrapped around her ever-sinking stomach, pulling her back up.

And for the first time in a long time, she'd heard Lee's voice.

Not just a voice that came out of a man named Lee.

But she'd heard *Lee*. The voice of the man she'd known when it was just her, and her daughter, and an orphaned kid named Sam, and a ragtag group of survivors living in a place they called Camp Ryder.

For the first time in a long time, when she'd spoken to Lee, she'd recognized who she was speaking to.

She turned around and faced the Sheriff's Department building. Inside, the lights were on. Inside, there were people moving about, soldiers bustling, officers huddling. Carl Gilliard. Hamrick. Doc Trent. Even Ed himself.

And, inside one of the interrogation rooms, a man with a Canadian flag patch on his shoulder, who had introduced himself as Captain Maclean Marlin, and told her he was here to "appraise the benefits of an alliance with the United Eastern States."

Well. She thought that Captain Marlin might want to know that UES forces had just taken control of a fully operational crude oil refinery on the Gulf of Mexico.

She walked towards the doors of the Sheriff's Office, an unfamiliar sensation spreading across her face.

It was a smile.

It was a possibility.

***

Lee looked out at the black waters of the Gulf of Mexico.

Behind him, the refinery chugged out its product, but Lee couldn't smell it now, with his face in the wind. All he smelled was salt. And tidewaters changing.

Beside him, Deuce sat. He was still, for once in his life.

You'd run until you couldn't run anymore. And we never did find out where you were trying to get to. Hell, I don't think you ever reached it.

Lee wasn't sure what it was that he'd been running for. It was hard to keep track, when so many things that he'd found had been taken from him.

The people he knew.

Good friends.

Lovers.

Julia.

Maybe even himself.

He looked south, to where the beach stretched out towards Mexico, and then north, towards a country torn in two, and he couldn't tell the difference. In this place, there was only the constant force of the waves, and all other things knelt to it, and it was the only thing that ever lasted.

The long sands stretched out to either side, and they didn't look much different.

But they felt different.

So he turned himself toward home, and he ran, and Deuce ran with him.

He ran until he couldn't run anymore. And maybe he didn't reach what he was heading for, but this time he knew what it was.

He knew what he was running for.

FOR UPDATES ON THE LEE HARDEN SERIES, MAKE SURE TO FOLLOW D.J. MOLLES AT FACEBOOK.COM/DJMOLLES AND SIGN UP FOR HIS FREE NEWSLETTER AT http://eepurl.com/c3kfJD (If you're typing that into a browser, make sure to capitalize the J and D)

READ ON FOR A PREVIEW OF D.J. MOLLES' NEW NOVEL

BREAKING GODS

BREAKING GODS

VIII And the gods perceived a great
wickedness in humanity, and that
every inclination of the thoughts of
the human heart was only evil all the
time, IX and that they would never be
satisfied, and that they wished to
swallow all the stars. X The gods saw
what the human beings were building,
and all that they had become, and all
that they intended to become, XI and
the gods said to themselves, “Come,
let us go down to them and destroy
everything they have built so that they
will not swallow all the stars.”

Translated from the *Ortus Deorum*

2nd Song, 3rd Stanza

Chapter 0
BEGINNINGS

He sits in prison and his sentence is death.

He does not know who he is, or what he is capable of.

And yet, destiny hurtles towards him whether he knows it or not.

Before we see who this condemned man is, let us look back to who he *was*, just a few days before. Let us go back to a battlefield, and a scavenging crew, and a series of events that will place this young man on a path from which he can never come back. A path to discovering who—and what—he really is.

If, of course, he manages to survive that long.

Chapter 1
SCAVENGERS

The Truth and The Light were murdering each other in droves.

Perry and his outfit waited on a dusty escarpment to pick over their dead.

It was the month of the Giver of Death. At night, the Deadmoon waned, and the days were short. The battle had begun later than usual today, and already the sun leaned westward. If it ran long, the crew might have to scavenge after dark. Boss Hauten did not like to scavenge after dark, and so he stood off to the side, fidgeting impatiently as he waited for the slaughter to be over.

Perry sat away from the ledge, his back against a comfortable rock. Around him, the rest of the outfit waited, holding quiet conversations and occasionally laughing at a joke. At twenty years old, Perry had already been on the crew for three years. That made him a middleman, with only a few others having more seniority than him.

First, there was Jax. He was a crotchety, white-bearded old fart that had been on Boss Hauten's crew since time immemorial. He held the job of "chief primer," and he guarded it jealously because it was easy work and he was ancient.

Second, there was Tiller.

Tiller was an ass, and he got along with nobody. Least of all Perry.

Lastly, there was Stuber.

While the rest of them waited, backed away from the edge of the cliff, hoping not to catch a stray round, Stuber stood at the edge in his battered armor and looked down at the battle that splayed out in the valley below. He watched the violence, always with an element of yearning, like a captured animal pines for the ferocity of the wilds.

The clasps on the back of his spaulders still had a bit of Stuber's old *sagum* cape.

The cloth was now sun-faded. Almost pink.

But it had once been a bright red.

Red for The Truth.

Staring at the ex-legionnaire's back, Perry felt a mix of unpleasant things rising up in his throat like gorge. Fear. Hatred. Loathing.

All things best kept hidden. It wouldn't do for anybody to guess Perry's past.

Stuber turned like he felt Perry's gaze on him. Those predatory eyes of his stared out from the rocky promontory of his face. A broad grin split the dark growth of his short beard.

"Shortstack," he beckoned with one massive hand. "Come watch."

Perry shook his shaggy, brown head. "Nah. I'm good."

Stuber's face darkened. "Come watch. Don't be bleeding vagina."

Perry grunted irritably, but rose up from his comfortable rock. It was probably the best seat on this ridge, and he was being forced to give it up. He dusted the back of his pants off and took a few steps forward, hunching his head down as he did, thinking about stray rounds from the battle below.

"You remember what happened to Hinks?" Perry griped, remembering how the poor girl's head had just seemed to cave in, like an invisible hammer had struck it.

"Hinks was an unlucky bitch," Stuber said dismissively. "She'd barely come back from the ants the day before." He snapped his fingers impatiently. "Come on. You're going to miss the best part."

Perry glanced behind him. Back to his comfy rock.

Tiller had already slid into place there. He crossed his booted feet and stretched himself with a great, dramatic sigh of pleasure. Then he smiled at Perry and mimed jacking off, completed by flinging an imaginary substance at Perry.

Perry's fingers twitched, and his brain tried to dip into the place where it always went when conflict was imminent—a place of flowing, red momentum that existed deep in Perry's brain—but the second that his body tensed to react to Tiller, a huge, callused hand grabbed Perry by the back of the neck and pulled him up to the edge of the cliff.

Stuber's hands were like iron wrapped in sandpaper.

"Look," Stuber commanded.

"I've seen it before."

"You've never seen *this* before."

"I have. Many times."

"Every battle is different."

"They look the same to me."

"That's because you're a peon. Here it comes."

Down below them, three or four miles away, the two armies prepared to converge. Blue on one side. Red on the other. Their *sagum* capes brilliant in the afternoon sun. Smoke coiled and wreathed them. Flak burst like black blooms in the sky above them. Mortars launched with a constant thumping rhythm and were shot out of the sky by the autoturrets. Gales of tracer fire scoured back and forth, lancing the crowds of men. Every once in a while a mortar shell would get through and a hole would appear in one battleline or another. Stuber didn't seem to care which side it was—when the bodies blew apart, he laughed.

The two armies were within a hundred yards of each other now. Their front lines were shielded phalanxes that inched towards each other, gaining ground stride by stride while bursts of bullets clattered back and forth, searching for a chink in the wall of shields. A body would fall, and the fire would concentrate on that hole, trying to kill more of the men behind it, but in seconds another shield would appear to plug up the hole, the dead soldiers trampled under their comrades' feet.

The two armies had closed the gap.

"Foreplay," Stuber said. "If the battlefield were a whore's bed, this is the part when you finally get to stick your dick in."

Below them, the gunfire intensified.

The mortars silenced, the two sides too close now for the shelling to continue. The autoturrets turned their focus on the front lines. Hammered shields. Created holes.

The space between red and blue was filled with bright muzzle flashes and glowing tracers and billowing smoke. It crescendoed, madly, and then, all at once, there was a break. A release.

The two sides crushed into each other.

"Haha!" Stuber thrust his hips. "Yes!"

Perry thought of the dead, crushed underfoot in the melee, in the stabbing, in the contact shots that would blow them open from the big .458 rounds. He thought about the way the mud would be a slick red-brown as he sloshed through it later, the dusty world watered by thousands of gallons of blood, but it would never be enough to bring the earth back to life.

At the rear of the two armies, further back than even the autoturrets, two armored command modules hovered on their turbines above blocks of troops waiting in reserve. On the deck of the modules stood the paladins.

Demigods.

They wore the colors of their side. Watching. Commanding.

Perry had never seen one of them die.

***

"Dogs and ants and spiders!" Hauten yelled at them.

Their buggy trundled its way down the rocky slope towards the valley below. A warm wind blew crosswise down the valley, buffeting in Perry's ears and making him squint against flying dust.

He could see the redness below. The floor of the valley had become a butcher's house. Bodies strewn about. Both The Light and The Truth left their dead where they'd fallen.

How many dead in six hours' worth of fighting?

Perry guesstimated that there were about a thousand bodies below.

Each body containing five liters of blood.

Draining.

Five thousand liters of blood in that valley.

"Dogs and ants and spiders!" Hauten bellowed over the wind and the rumble of the buggy's tires, and the struggling whine of the electric drive.

The buggy teetered at a steep angle that made Perry's insides feel watery and he clutched the roll bar nearest him.

"Keep your eyes peeled!" Hauten continued. "Watch what you grab! Watch where you put your feet! Don't die, because I can't afford to bury you!"

"What does he mean?"

Perry, still clinging to the rollbar as the buggy now listed to the right on what felt like a forty-five degree slope, looked over his tense shoulder at the girl riding next to him. Her name was Teran. She was new to the outfit. She'd come on with them at their last stop in Junction City. She claimed to have experience. Perry had discovered that that was a lie.

Perry doubted that Hauten had been fooled. Probably he kept her on because he thought he had a chance to fuck her. She was what they called "outfit pretty." Which was to say, in a town amongst other women, you wouldn't look twice. But in an outfit full of guys…yeah, you would.

"The crows come first, but they won't do anything," Perry answered, his voice wobbling with the shaking of the buggy. "Then the dogs. They smell the blood. They're mean, but they won't attack you unless you're alone. Then the ants come up from underground. Don't step on their hills—they'll tear you up. Almost lost a girl a few months back because of that."

Poor old Hinks.

"What about the spiders?"

"The spiders sometimes make nests in the shell casings. They jump out and catch the flies. But they'll catch a finger too."

Teran blinked a few times, facing forward. "Aren't we supposed to collect the shell casings?"

"Yes."

She processed this with a frown, and then seemed to hunker down. Her lips flattened into a grimly-determined line. The wind whipped a bit of her sandy hair into her eyes. She pulled it back and tucked it behind her ear, where it promptly came loose again.

The buggy lifted itself over a rock, and then started to tip.

Stuber, who rode on the backend of the vehicle slid to the left side and leaned out as a counterbalance.

Perry clenched down hard, knowing that if the buggy started to tumble, he'd be meat by the bottom. They all would be. Except for Stuber, who'd simply hop off the back.

Why did Hauten have to drive like such an idiot? There were a million other routes off the damn ridge, but of course, he had to take this one, because it was the shortest, and he was in a rush to make a profit.

All four tires touched the ground again.

Perry let the air out of his chest slowly.

A moment later, the ground began to level out.

"Why are you doing this anyways?" Perry asked her.

He half-expected a sharp response from Teran. Most women that he'd seen come onto the outfit knew that they were the outsiders and that Hauten was probably trying to fuck them. Hauten rarely hired a female that wasn't outfit pretty. They were always a bit defensive, and Perry couldn't blame them. That didn't make them very pleasant to be around, but then again, there weren't too many people on the outfit that were.

But Teran just shrugged. "All the places to make an honest living in Junction City were full up. So I figured I'd get on an outfit. This happened to be the outfit."

"You gonna ditch us when you find a steady town job?"

It was loud enough with the wind and the tires rumbling, and other peoples' shouted conversations that Perry wasn't concerned about being overheard. He didn't really think Hauten would care anyway. Turnover on the outfit was high amongst greenhorns, and nothing to balk at.

"Depends on how much Hauten pays," she replied.

"You ever goin' back to Junction City?"

This time she did look at him. "I dunno, Perry. You ever going back to what you did before?"

Perry stared at her. He didn't care for the way she said it. Like she knew about Perry's past. But that was impossible. No one knew. He'd never told anyone.

He quickly changed the subject. "When we get to the bottom, stay with me. Do what I tell you and watch where you put your feet and your hands."

The smell of blood was palpable now.

Perry could taste it on his tongue.

It was more humid down here in the valley than it had been on the ridge.

Despite it being the Deadmoon, out here where the earth had been scorched, the sun shone hot, no matter the time of year. And when it baked a pond made up of five thousand liters of blood, then it turned the valley into something of a steam room.

"Dogs and ants and spiders!" Hauten reminded them one last time, and then began to slow the buggy. As it rolled to a halt amid a cloud of dust, he looked back at them from the controls. "Work quick and we won't have to mess with any of that shit, yeah? Alright. Get to work."

Perry slid out of his seat and over the horizontal bar of metal. The black paint on it was hot to the touch. Flaking off. Rusty underneath. He went to the back, and Teran followed.

"Jax! Tiller!" Hauten called out, exiting his driver's seat. "Get some guns."

At the back of the buggy, Stuber had dropped to the ground. His Roq-11 .458 rifle was strapped to his back at the moment. He pulled a long, battered, black case out to the edge of the buggy's cargo bed. He undid the locks and lifted the cover.

Inside were two shotguns nestled next to each other, and a large, silver pistol.

The Mercy Pistol. Stuber left that where it was, but he grabbed the two shotguns in each of his meaty paws and turned, just as Jax and Tiller trotted up.

Tiller made it a point to shoulder past Perry.

Stuber shoved the shotguns in their hands. Jax ran his sunken, blue eyes over his, charged a round into the chamber, and then shoved his arm through the braided sling. He turned and walked off.

Tiller had the shotgun in both hands and he tried to pull it, but Stuber held on.

Tiller stared up at the ex-legionnaire, confused.

Stuber held the shotgun in his right hand. With his left, he jabbed in index finger like a dart into

Tiller's chest. Tiller let out an offended yelp and glared.

"Don't be an asshole," Stuber growled.

"I won't," Tiller grunted indignantly. He jerked hard and Stuber let him have the shotgun.

Tiller checked his action, just like Jax had, although the movements were not as sure. Tiller did most of what he did in an attempt to look as experienced as Jax.

When Tiller was satisfied that he had a loaded shotgun, he gave a baleful look over his shoulder at Stuber, and then marched off. He made another attempt to shoulder Perry, but Perry saw it coming and slid out of the way.

"'Scuse me," Tiller said anyways. Kept walking.

Perry felt that flowing river deep inside of him.

The blur of red.

As much as Perry enjoyed watching Stuber mess with Tiller, it only meant that Tiller was going to be more pissy than usual today.

"Come on," Hauten hollered, reaching the back of the buggy. "Buckets. Work quick. Quick, quick, quick. Lezgo lezgo lezgo."

There was a stack of buckets. They hadn't made it down to the valley in their original, stowed position. Perry grabbed two from the jumbled pile and gave one to Teran. He started towards the battlefield.

"We're here for the brass. Don't try to loot the bodies: some of the legionairres booby-trap themselves before they die. Besides that, we've got a delicate understanding with several other scavenging outfits—they let us have the brass, we let them have the armor, or the tech, or whatever their flavor of scrap is. All you gotta do is pick up brass. If it's severely dented, leave it. If you can see a spider web inside it, leave it—those things are poisonous. Don't try to move anything that already has an ant mound on it. If you notice anybody that's still alive, don't touch them, don't move them, and don't talk to them. Just call for Stuber."

The very first body they reached was still alive.

A man with half his face blown off.

His chestplate rose and fell with hitching breaths. His massive shield lay still attached to his left arm, dented and dinged, the edges chipped from thousands of projectiles that had skimmed by him.

But one had found him. And one was all you needed.

His blue *sagum* identified him as a legionnaire of The Light.

The dying legionnaire reached a hand towards them. He tried to speak, but couldn't.

Perry first eyed the man's right hand to see if he was still armed. Both sides left the bodies, but they were careful to retrieve the weapons. Funny how they did that.

Perry saw no weapons. He turned his head to project his voice back over his shoulder, but he kept his eye on the dying soldier in front of him.

"Stuber!"

The soldier knew what was next. Whatever he wanted, he forgot about it, and his outstretched arm fell to his side. He sat there with his chestplate heaving, his one good eye still looking straight at Perry.

Perry heard the sound of retching behind him.

He glanced over his shoulder, and saw Teran, doubled over with a thick rope of yellowy stomach juices issuing from her mouth and nose.

He turned back to the dying legionnaire.

The man's one remaining eye was a pleasant hazel color. The eye was nice and round. Thick lashes. He might've been a popular man with the ladies, Perry thought, though with half his face missing, it was difficult to tell if he was handsome. Maybe he just had nice eyes.

Stuber came over. Perry gestured to the dying soldier.

Stuber knelt before the man, as he would so many times that day. He put his hand on the soldier's forehead and he said the words that Perry didn't even need to hear, he knew them so well by now.

"In the eyes of the gods, it matters not the color of your banner, but the courage of your heart. Under the watchful gaze of Nur, the Eighth Son, all warriors are brothers. As your brother, I bear witness to Halan, the Eldest Son, that you have fought your fight. Be at peace. Accept this mercy, and go to The After."

The dying man closed his eyes as Stuber put the large, silver pistol against his head and gave him mercy.

And, as he always did, Perry watched, and thought, *That could have been me.*

And that made him think of the Tall Man.

END OF PREVIEW

ABOUT THE AUTHOR

D.J. Molles is the New York Times bestselling author of *The Remaining* series. He is also the author of *Wolves*, a 2016 winner in the Horror category for the Foreword INDIES Book Awards. His other works include the *Grower's War* series, and the Audible original, *Johnny*. When he's not writing, he's taking care of his property in North Carolina, and training to be at least half as hard to kill as Lee Harden. He also enjoys playing his guitar, his violin, drawing, painting, and lots of other artsy fartsy stuff

You can follow and contact him at:
Facebook.com/DJMolles
And sign up for his free, monthly newsletter at:
http://eepurl.com/c3kfJD
(If you're typing that into a browser, make sure to capitalize the J and D)

Made in the USA
Coppell, TX
13 January 2020